6/13
12/13

 W9-CCK-764

DATE DUE

GAYLORD   #3523PI   Printed in USA

The Avalon Ladies Scrapbooking Society

Center Point
Large Print

Also by Darien Gee and available from
Center Point Large Print:

Friendship Bread

**This Large Print Book carries the
Seal of Approval of N.A.V.H.**

The Avalon Ladies Scrapbooking Society

Darien Gee

CENTER POINT LARGE PRINT
THORNDIKE, MAINE

This Center Point Large Print edition
is published in the year 2013 by arrangement with
Ballantine Books, an imprint of The Random House
Publishing Group, a division of Random House, Inc.

Copyright © 2013 by Gee & Co., LLC.

All rights reserved.

The Avalon Ladies Scrapbooking Society is a work of
fiction. Names, characters, places, and incidents are the
products of the author's imagination or are used
fictitiously. Any resemblance to actual events, locales,
or persons, living or dead, is entirely coincidental.

The text of this Large Print edition is unabridged.
In other aspects, this book may vary
from the original edition.
Printed in the United States of America
on permanent paper.
Set in 16-point Times New Roman type.

ISBN: 978-1-61173-734-9

Library of Congress Cataloging-in-Publication Data

Gee, Darien.
The Avalon Ladies Scrapbooking Society / Darien Gee.
pages ; cm.
ISBN 978-1-61173-734-9 (library binding : alk. paper)
1. Scrapbooking—Fiction. 2. Female friendship—Fiction.
  3. Large type books. I. Title.
PS3611.I5834A94 2013b
813'.6—dc23
                                              2013001260

3095038

F
GEE

For Mary Embry,
with love

Acknowledgments

Many people helped shape the book you are holding in your hands. I offer a full and grateful heart to: Libby McGuire, Linda Marrow, Jane von Mehren, Gina Wachtel, Sharon Propson, Penelope Haynes, Dana Isaacson, Junessa Viloria, and Angela Pica, plus the hard-working editorial, production, marketing, public relations, and sales teams at Ballantine Books. My agent, Dorian Karchmar, at William Morris Endeavor not only helps craft my books but also my career. Thanks to Simone Blaser, Tracy Fisher, Raffaella De Angelis, Laura Bonner, Annemarie Blumenhagen, and Covey Crolius along with their respective co-agents from around the world.

I have great appreciation for my foreign editors and publishers: Patrick Gallagher, Annette Barlow, Kate Hyde, and Kate Butler at Allen and Unwin in Australia; Pedro Almeida at Leya in Brazil; Laetitia Amar at Michel Lafon in France; Laura Casonato at Edizioni Piemme in Italy; Juliette Van Wersch at A.W. Bruna in the Netherlands; Nicola Bartels at Blanvalet in Germany; Lynn Chen and Patrick Jia at China Times in Taiwan; Katarzyna Rudzka at Proszynski in Poland; and the team at Beyaz Belina in Turkey. Also thanks to Orli Moscowitz at Random House Audio.

To my husband, Darrin, and our three children: Maya, Eric, and Luke. Thank you for your support, love, and humor. Remember that everything begins with our relationship with ourselves. Never stop learning and growing, and keep seeking new experiences. Happiness and joy are your trump cards; make them your priority.

Always joining me and my pages of possibilities are Nancy Sue Martin and Patricia Wood, friends who ask the hard questions, make themselves available at odd hours, and love the work of writing and life as much as I do. Susan Buetow helped me keep the Friendship Bread Kitchen (www.friendshipbreadkitchen.com) open for those who love books with a slice of Amish Friendship Bread on the side.

Thank you all.

The past is our very being.

—DAVID BEN-GURION

We do not remember days,
we remember moments.

—CESARE PAVESE

The Avalon Ladies Scrapbooking Society

Chapter One

The goat was Connie's idea.

"I'm not so sure about this," Madeline Davis says, frowning. At seventy-five she's trying to make her life simpler, not the other way around. Then again, running a tea salon isn't what most people her age are doing these days. Madeline's days are busy, yes, but she goes to sleep each night happily content, her heart full. And for the past year she's had Connie Colls, her tea salon manager, an unexpected godsend with black spiky hair who has also become her friend and housemate.

Now Connie is tearfully looking at her and Madeline feels herself wavering. Connie has never asked for anything before and seeing this young woman about to cry is more than Madeline can bear.

"Well . . ." she says reluctantly. "Maybe for a couple of days until you can find a more suitable home." She watches as the goat sniffs its way around the garden, then starts chewing on a patch of orange nasturtiums.

"Oh!" Connie wipes her eyes and hurries toward the goat. She waves her hands over the flowers in an attempt to shoo the goat away, but the animal ignores her.

Lord, Madeline knows how this is going to go.

She watches as Connie tugs unsuccessfully on the goat's makeshift collar, a frayed rope with a tail that has been chewed through. Well, the good news is that the goat belongs to someone. They just have to find out who.

"I'm going inside," she tells Connie, who's trying to drag the goat into the shade of a walnut tree.

"Thank you, Madeline," Connie says, forcing a bright smile. "She won't be any trouble at all, I promise."

"Hmm. Well, I think she's eating my Double Delights."

Connie turns, stricken. *"No! No roses! Bad goat!"*

Madeline just shakes her head and walks through the back door of the house into the kitchen.

The morning light streams in behind her, a generous sliver of sunshine falling onto the farmer's table that rests in the middle of the kitchen. Fresh loaves of Amish Friendship Bread, scones, and muffins are cooling on wire racks. Two arugula-and-bacon quiches are in the oven. Her kitchen is fragrant and inviting, and Madeline knows that her customers find these smells a reassuring comfort. They come to Madeline's Tea Salon for that very reason—the promise of good food and an encouraging smile. A kind word and possibly a joke or two, depending on her mood.

If they're lucky they may get more, like an impromptu performance by Hannah Wang, the young cellist who used to play with the New York Philharmonic and who now resides in Avalon. There's Bettie Shelton, too, with her mobile scrapbooking business. She comes in under the pretense of ordering a pot of Darjeeling tea while she indiscreetly sets up her wares at an adjoining table. On the days Bettie is here even the least crafty Avalonian or unsuspecting tourist is sure to leave with a packet of patterned paper and random embellishments. Madeline remembers what happened last month when a group of men had lunch at the salon, hunched over a table as they ate, speaking in low whispers. It was clear by their body language that they didn't want to be disturbed. Bettie, however, had marched up to them undaunted. Less than a minute later the men found their table littered with colorful ribbons and glittery sequins. Two men bought scrapbooking starter kits, dazed looks on their faces as they handed their money to Bettie. As quickly as she had arrived, Bettie was gone, leaving everyone to wonder what happened while Madeline cleared her table with a chuckle.

The small brass bell over the front door tinkles. A pair of women walk in, smile at Madeline, and choose a table by the window. Madeline knows it's only a matter of time before the tea salon will be bustling with people and laughter.

She selects several tins of the chamomile and rooibos tea blend from the large antique armoire that graces the dining room. She's not sure what came first—discovering so many wonderful finds at garage sales and antiques stores and then pondering what to put in them, or knowing that she wanted to sell her own tea blends and looking for an artful way to display them. It was a small thing to help pass the time in those early months when business was slow, but now it's taken on a life of its own. Connie wants them to open an online store but that's more than Madeline is willing to take on right now. At the moment this balance feels just right, however hectic it may be.

In the kitchen, Connie is at the sink, scrubbing her hands. "Serena took off into the neighbor's yard but she's back now," she says, a look of apologetic guilt on her face when Madeline walks in. "She, uh, kind of ate a few heads of lettuce from their garden."

Madeline raises an eyebrow. "Kind of?"

Connie fakes a cough. "Well, she ate them, but then she threw them back up." Connie wipes her hands on a dishtowel, avoiding eye contact. "I'll call the vet later to see if there's anything special we should be feeding her. Maybe Serena has a delicate stomach."

Goodness. Madeline isn't sure what's more concerning, that Connie has named the goat or that the goat has found its way into Walter

Lassiter's vegetable garden. His wife, Dolores, doesn't mind the steady traffic of the tea salon but Walter is always looking for something to complain about. Madeline has a feeling that a stray goat may push him over the edge.

"I'm sure Serena's stomach is fine," she says, handing Connie the tea. "Do you mind wrapping these? Dora Ponce is putting together a gift basket for the Rotary Club auction and I told her we'd make a donation."

"Sure." Connie drapes an apron over her head. "I'll use that pretty paper I picked up at the farmer's market last week. Ruth Pavord is selling her whole stock—she's going to start making birdhouses instead." Connie is about to say more when there's a holler from the dining room. It's followed by the unmistakable sound of porcelain breaking.

"Help!" they hear one of the women shout. "There's a wild beast in here!" Connie hurries to the dining room. There's a stern reprimand and then another exclamation accompanied by the sound of more good china crashing to the floor.

To outsiders Avalon may look like a non-descript river town, but Madeline knows better. She reaches for the broom and dustpan with a happy sigh, then heads to the dining room.

Isabel grasps the hammer and pounds the FOR SALE sign into her front lawn. The earth is hard and unyielding, dry from too much Illinois heat, another long hot August that shows no sign of relief. Maybe she should have watered the lawn first. Maybe she should have hired that redheaded kid from down the street. Maybe she should have called a real estate agent to list her house properly instead of trying to do it on her own, like so many things these days.

But Isabel doesn't want to wait for people to call her back, to check their schedules, to haggle a fee. To find the garden hose, wherever that is.

Bang bang bang. The sign shakes and shivers.

Last night, when she was the last person wandering the dusky streets after a seven o'clock showing of *The Man from M.A.R.S.*, Isabel had stopped at the hardware store to pick up some laundry detergent. There they were, right by the entrance, on clearance. Fifteen cans of paint stacked in a pyramid, pointing to the sky.

Isabel thought about her house, of the stove and kitchen table, of the fridge and nubby dishtowels. The living room furniture, the bedroom set, the chipped cherrywood table in the hallway. She thought of her tired walls, the ceilings, the doors. There was a time when she dreamed they'd live in that house forever, have children in it, grow old in it. But Isabel had to let that dream go. So what's she still doing in Avalon?

"I'll take them all," she'd told the cashier, handing him a hundred-dollar bill. "And some of those brushes, too."

She declined a drop cloth, spackle, turpentine. Too many things to remember. *Just the paint,* she'd said. And then she saw it. A sign, bent at the corners, leaning forlornly against the bags of organic lawn fertilizer.

FOR SALE BY OWNER.

She bought that, too.

Isabel steps back to survey her work. The sign is crooked, but it's clearly visible from the street. She knows her neighbors will be curious, maybe even nervous that she's selling. Avalon is the sort of place where most people come to settle down, where families spend whole lifetimes. Isabel herself married into this small town, Bill having been born and raised here. Buried here, too, almost four years now.

There's a flutter of curtains from the house next door. It's her neighbor Bettie Shelton, the town fussbudget. Isabel knows Bettie had a hand in spreading the news about Bill's departure and then his death two months later, a wrong turn down a one-way street. Casseroles had sprouted on her porch like mushrooms.

"Isabel Kidd!" she hears Bettie holler from inside her house. Bettie's silvery-blue hair is still in curlers. She struggles to open the window, then settles on rapping the glass, the look on her face indignant. "What the heck do you think you're doing?"

Isabel gives the sign a tap with the hammer.

"Isabel? Do you hear me?"

Isabel pretends to pick at a speck of dust on the sign.

"ISABEL!"

Exasperated, Isabel scowls. "Of course I hear you! Who doesn't hear you?" Catty-corner from her house, Isabel sees Peggy Lively emerge from her house, dressed in her fuzzy pink bathrobe. "You hear her, don't you, Peggy?"

Peggy stares at Isabel and the hammer for a moment before glancing down the empty street. Then she grabs the morning paper from her walk and hurries back inside, slamming the door shut behind her. Isabel hears the lock sliding into place.

Isabel shoots Bettie an annoyed look and then gives the sign one last pound for good measure. She heads back into the house, knowing that Bettie's prying eyes are watching her retreat.

In her living room, the paint cans are laid out like a labyrinth, waiting. Isabel hesitates, tentative, suddenly unsure. Putting up the FOR SALE sign was easy, knowing it could be pulled up at any time, no harm done, a whim put to bed. But this is different. Once done, it can't be undone.

She reaches for the can closest to her, uses a screwdriver to crack the lid open. She gazes at the placid pool of paint. *Whisper White.* She gives it a stir, the smell tickling her nose.

Her first stroke on the wall is uneven, streaking, her second stroke no better. But still the paint glistens, beckoning, a stark contrast to the tired gray hue that's been there for years. Isabel dips the brush again and swirls it until the bristles are heavy with paint, then lifts and tries again. This time there's a thick swath of white, smooth and complete. She follows with another stroke, bolder this time.

It goes faster than she thinks, and soon the entire wall is done. It's a blank stare looking back at her, giving away nothing. Isabel leans closer, looking for a hint of the past, but sees nothing other than her own shadow as the tip of her nose bumps against the damp wall. *Ouch.* And then Isabel remembers other white walls.

There, that wasn't so bad, was it?

No, doctor, it wasn't.

Of course he had asked her when she was in a morphine-induced haze, easy and agreeable, happy to talk to anyone and everyone. Bill had been by her side, stunned and sad, knowing that this was it, their last chance. They weren't going to try anymore. It didn't matter, he would try to assure her when she lay in bed, night after night, her pillow damp with tears. It was enough, just the two of them. He'd hold her fingertips to his lips and kiss each one gently. A promise.

It would be a few more years before Bill would leave, that promise forgotten. They had said it wouldn't change them, but it had, and whatever it was they lost they couldn't get back. Isabel wasn't happy but she wasn't unhappy, either. It was tolerable. She still loved Bill and she knew he loved her, and yet a whole chasm spanned between them, pushing them further and further apart with each day that passed. If she had to she could live out her life this way, in polite deference to each other, a peaceful coexistence in the same space, the same life. It wasn't ideal but it was enough for Isabel. Not, apparently, for Bill.

What is it with dentists and their dental assistants? It's an embarrassing cliché that Isabel has to live with. My husband left me for his dental assistant, a woman ten years younger than me. At the time Isabel had thought it couldn't get any worse, that nothing could usurp this abandonment, but she was wrong.

She hadn't been prepared for the baby announcement, had cracked the seal of the envelope without thinking. She thought it was a belated sympathy card, a few months late. She pulled out the stiff card and saw a chubby cherub of a baby with Bill's unmistakable bright blue eyes and Dumbo ears.

So now, at the ripe old age of thirty-eight, Isabel Kidd is alone. No husband, no children. An unsatisfying job as a customer service representative for a corrugated paper company in Rockford, about forty-five minutes away. Some money from Bill's pension. His share of the dental practice went to his partner, Randall Strombauer, a man Isabel never cared for. He's the one who hired the assistant with an eye, Isabel suspects, of having her all to himself. Randall was the single guy while Bill was safely ensconced in a marriage of twelve years. An open playing field with Randall as the only player. But, of course, things have a way of not working out as planned.

The remaining walls in the living room look shabby and lifeless, dull neighbors to the freshly painted wall. That's how it goes sometimes. She could keep it as an accent wall, but she feels for the others. They deserve a fresh start as well. After all, they were all innocent bystanders.

This time she'll do it differently—no need to slap one stroke on after the other. After all, this is her house, her walls. She can do whatever she wants with it.

Isabel dips her brush and begins again.

Yvonne Tate checks the address one last time before shoving the scrap of paper into her pocket. The house in front of her is a modest bungalow with a white picket fence, sycamore trees lining the street. She opens the gate and goes up the walk, noticing the postage-stamp lawn and garden. Flower boxes filled with geraniums and impatiens in a summer burst of colors line the windows, butterflies dancing in the garden. It's a sweet home.

Yvonne presses the doorbell and waits. She hears voices inside, a man and a woman arguing. A second later the door opens.

"May I help you?" The woman is in her late twenties, young and pretty. Her husband stands behind her, about the same age.

"I'm Yvonne Tate. Tate Plumbing. You called about an emergency?"

The couple stares at her. The wife looks past Yvonne for another person, presumably the "real" plumber, while the husband gawks at Yvonne, his mouth slightly open in surprise.

"It's just me," Yvonne tells them good-naturedly. She knows she doesn't look the part. She's slender and athletic, her blond hair pulled back in a ponytail. She has the requisite T-shirt, jeans, and work boots, along with her toolbox, but even with these accoutrements and no makeup she is still often mistaken for a model. "We spoke on the phone an hour ago?" she reminds the woman. Yvonne pulls out the piece of paper. "Megan and Billy Newman, right?"

Megan Newman stares at her. "Yes, but I thought you were the receptionist."

"I am the receptionist. I'm also the bookkeeper, sales director, and of course, plumber. I'm a one-woman show." Yvonne glances at her watch.

"Now, why don't you show me the problem?"

Megan doesn't look convinced but her husband is quick to step aside and invite Yvonne in, earning him a glare from his wife.

"How long have you been doing this?" Megan asks, a skeptical look on her face.

"Ten years, though I've only been in Avalon about six months. I'm licensed in three states and have a flawless track record." Yvonne takes in the honey-colored hardwood floors, the gingham curtains, the slipcovered couch and loveseat. Fresh flowers in glass vases are dotted throughout the house, wedding pictures everywhere. "So what's the problem again?" she asks.

Megan and Billy exchange a look. "It's probably easier if we show you," Billy says.

Yvonne follows them into the master bathroom. Once in the bathroom, she lets out a small giggle but quickly composes herself. "Oh," she says. "I see."

Pots and pans are stacked in the bathtub.

"It's temporary until we figure out what happened in the kitchen," Megan says hurriedly. "We'll show you that later. This is the problem in here."

The bathroom sink is new, with two antique faucets, one labeled HOT and one labeled COLD. Megan turns the knob on the left for the cold water, but water shoots out from the faucet on the right, and vice versa.

25

"I thought I installed it right," Billy says, scratching his head. "But obviously it's a bit messed up."

Yvonne points to the piping below the sink. "You'll also want to install some shut-off valves."

"I was going to do that next," Billy says, unconvincingly.

"I told him we should hire professionals for the plumbing and electrical projects, but no, he had to do it himself." Megan shoots her husband a look. "And that's not all. Come on." She motions Yvonne to follow her.

In the kitchen Megan opens the doors beneath the sink, revealing a maze of bizarre piping, including a cut-up milk jug attached to the P-trap with zip ties and duct tape. "The kitchen sink leaks so bad that we can't use it at all," Megan says. "Billy rigged up this contraption to catch the water but there's so much we don't even bother. It was supposed to be a temporary thing but we're coming up on three weeks. I can't take it anymore!"

"It's not so bad . . ." Billy begins.

"We're doing our dishes in the bathtub, Billy!"

Well, that explains that. "These are pretty easy fixes," Yvonne assures her. She turns to Billy. "Why didn't you put a bucket underneath, by the way?"

Billy opens his mouth to respond then scratches

his head. "Yeah, that does make better sense," he says sheepishly.

Yvonne grins. "I should be able to take care of everything today," she tells them. She quotes them a price and Megan nods enthusiastically.

"Yes," she says. "Please start right away."

"I thought it would be more expensive," Billy says, surprised. "The other company we called quoted us almost double."

Yvonne shrugs. She doesn't worry about the competition, has always had an attitude that there's enough business for everyone. "I'll give you an itemized invoice of the work when I'm done, too."

Megan is humming happily as she goes to the fridge and pulls out a carafe of iced tea. She pours each of them a glass, then nods to the backyard. "I'll be outside." She gives her husband a pointed look before leaving.

Yvonne opens her toolbox. Billy shoves his hands into his pockets, shifting his weight from side to side.

"She's mad at me," he says. "I guess I'm a dope for trying to do our own plumbing."

"You're not," Yvonne tells him. "It's great that you tried, Billy." Yvonne is used to coming to the rescue after disastrous DIY plumbing projects—this is nothing. She's all for people learning how to take care of their homes and perform simple home maintenance tasks, but you have to do your homework, have to put in a little more time beyond watching a three-minute YouTube video on how to seal your tub. "I'm sure you would have figured it out eventually," she says kindly.

He smiles, grateful, then casts a longing look toward Megan who's leaning back on a lawn chair, her hands shading the sun from her eyes.

"Go join your wife," Yvonne encourages. "She's just ready to have your house in working order. You've been married about a year?"

Billy looks at her in surprise. "Eleven months," he says. "How'd you know?"

Yvonne gives a nonchalant shrug as she digs through her tools for a crescent wrench. Yvonne doesn't tell him what else she thinks, that Megan is clearly nesting. And slightly hormonal. She's seen it in clients before. She's not sure that Billy knows yet, or maybe not even Megan, but Yvonne would bet her bottom dollar that Megan is pregnant.

"She just wants to make your home nice," Yvonne tells him. "Go sit with her."

Billy grins and then lopes outside after his wife. Yvonne smiles.

Her job isn't dull, that's for sure. She's seen everything in this business—men who try to sweet talk her or aggressively haggle or even intimidate her to get a lower fee. She's been asked out more times than she cares to remember, once by a woman even. She's heard every joke in the book about plumber's crack and whether or not she wears a thong. She's used to it, but it doesn't happen often. Most of her clients are nice, decent people, surprised to find a young woman in this line of work, but supportive nonetheless. It's one reason why she loves what she does.

Her job also reminds her that things are not always as they seem, that her life is her own, always has been and always will be. Still, it wasn't until ten years ago that Yvonne understood that she needed to step up and own it.

It came at a price. On the days where she's feeling lonely or homesick, she battles temptation to pick up the phone, to get on a plane, to look up information she'd be better off not knowing. As difficult as it can be sometimes, Yvonne knows she has to stay the course. It's too painful otherwise.

She looks outside and sees Billy sitting in the chair next to his wife, talking to her. Megan laughs at something he says, and Billy leans over to give his wife a kiss.

It's tender and sweet, but Yvonne has to look away. She swallows the lump in her throat and gets back to work.

Chapter Two

"Here you go." The bartender hefts a plastic bag full of bottle caps onto the bar. There's the sound of metal cascading into a lazy pile as the bag almost tips over, the top unsealed. "Whoa!"

"I got it," Ava says, catching the bag in time. The bag is nice and heavy in her hand, and already a couple of bottle caps catch her eye—a navy blue one with a yellow starburst and a red one with white block lettering across the top. Quite a few are bent but that's okay—she wants to practice a few new techniques and they'll do perfectly.

"Great reflexes," the bartender says, grinning. His name is Colin. He unties the apron from around his waist and tosses it into a pile with the dirty towels.

"It's parenthood," Ava says, giving the bag a shake, delighting in the weight of it. There's easily two hundred caps, maybe more. "I've caught many a falling sippy cup in my time."

"In your time?" Colin does a quick appraisal of her and Ava laughs, knowing she looks like a kid herself these days, careless and frayed around the edges. "How old is your son again?" Colin has two boys of his own, in high school.

"Four, going on twenty." Ava reaches for her wallet. "And I'm twenty-eight going on fifty."

"I hear that." Colin instantly reddens. "I mean, not that you look like you're going on fifty, because you're obviously not. You don't even look twenty-eight . . ." He grimaces and shakes his head. "Sorry, that came out wrong. I just mean that I know what it's like to have your hands full."

"It's okay. I know." Ava smiles. "Well, thanks for this. How much do I owe you?"

Colin holds up his hands. "This one's on the house. It's my last day."

"Your last day?"

"Got laid off. A bunch of us did. Restaurant's 'renovating.'" Colin gestures to the booths and tables around them, empty even though it's only an hour past lunchtime. "They're going bare bones until business picks up. But I found a new job at the Avalon Grill starting tomorrow, so I'll be all right."

"The Avalon Grill?"

"Yeah. I'll check with my manager, but I'm sure it won't be a problem to put aside some bottle caps for you if you don't mind driving over to pick them up. It's about an extra fifteen minutes from Barrett."

"Yeah, I know." Ava remembers a pear-and-blue-cheese salad that she used to have for lunch all the time and her stomach rumbles, hungry. "I used to work in Avalon."

Colin writes something on a piece of paper, then slides it across the bar toward Ava. "Here's my number. Call me in a couple of weeks and I'll let you know what I have. Or, you know, call me anytime." His eyes hold hers for a second longer than usual, then he glances away, embarrassed.

Ava doesn't quite remember Colin's marital situation but knows he's either divorced or separated, both of which are already far too complicated for Ava. He's a nice guy and she appreciates his help these past couple of years, putting aside used bottle caps for her and charging no more than a cup of coffee for them, but she can't see beyond that right now, doesn't want anything beyond that right now.

"Thanks," she says. "But I don't want to put you out."

"It's no problem—" he begins, but Ava shakes her head, her guard back up. Awkwardly she slips the piece of paper into her purse and offers her hand. "Well, good luck, Colin."

She can tell he wants to say more, but he doesn't. Instead he takes her hand and gives it a shake, his cheeks still pink. "You too, Ava."

In her car, Ava lets out a long breath. She gives the bag a poke, sad that she won't be seeing Colin again, weary at the thought of having to find another source in Barrett for her bottle caps. She knows Colin takes special care not to bend them more than necessary, has seen him use a soft cloth over the bottle opener, careful not to scratch the cap. He makes it look easy and effortless and most customers don't even notice that he's taking this extra step, but Ava knows.

She feels herself blinking back tears. She was foolish to let herself get attached, even in this small way. But Colin is one of the only people she can talk to and he's a decent person, which counts for a lot.

Still, she should know better.

Ava starts her Jeep. The engine reluctantly kicks over, a sign that there's trouble up ahead, or at least something that will need attention. A new fuel pump, the starter, a weak battery, who knows.

"Please," she whispers under her breath. The engine revs and Ava feels a spark of hope that things will be all right.

Then the Jeep sputters and dies altogether.

Frances Latham gazes at the small black-and-white photograph in her hand. The mop of black hair, the chubby cheeks, the searching dark eyes staring back at her.

"Beautiful," Frances breathes.

The package came yesterday. Reed, her husband, knew it was coming because people started posting on the boards that their referrals had arrived. Pictures were posted with virtual cheers from everyone in the group with the same log-in date from the time their adoption application was accepted by the Chinese government.

But there was envy, too, and anxiety for those who were still waiting. Frances had been ecstatic and then crashed, crying, her emotions bouncing all over the place. Why hadn't they received their referral? What if something was wrong? Reed assured her that everything was fine, but how did he know? How did any of them know? They finally called the agency and the agency confirmed that yes, people were getting their referrals, and the Lathams should receive theirs by the end of the week.

And then Jamie Linde arrived in his UPS truck, a package in hand. Frances could tell by the look on his face that he knew what it was. He didn't seem at all surprised by the hug or the tears, and even offered to take a picture of her holding up the heavy, flat envelope. Frances got Noah, her five-year-old, to take the picture because she wanted Jamie in it. She had the picture printed the next day and wrote on the back, "Me with our stork, Jamie Linde."

Reed came home immediately and they opened the envelope together. When they saw the picture clipped to the stack of documents, Reed's eyes got wet and Frances gasped. "She's beautiful! Look at her, Reed!" He nodded and wiped his eyes.

There is still more waiting ahead, but now they know. They know that this little girl is the one that will make their family complete.

Frances closes her eyes, feels the hot tears of joy and relief coming again. They've already made copies of the picture so Reed can take one to work and each of the older boys wanted one as well. Frances taped copies on the fridge, the bathroom mirrors, the home office, the car. She sent framed copies to her parents and to Reed's mother.

But this one, the original, the one that came from China and taken by someone who had looked this little girl in the eyes, this is the picture Frances holds in her hands.

Mei Ling. Our daughter.

Frances and Reed pored over every detail, put stickies on the pages to send to the agency to get translated, made notes in their notebook of questions and things that needed clarifying. But the bottom line is that they are one step closer to bringing her home.

The phone rings and Frances jumps to answer it. "Hello?" Her voice is breathless.

"Hi, sweetheart." It's Reed, and Frances smiles. He sounds tired, but happy. "How's your day going?"

"Good. Wonderful. Perfect. Do you have to ask?"

Reed laughs, a low baritone that reminds her of Reed's father. Frances wishes that he was alive, that he could meet this little girl, his soon-to-be granddaughter. "I guess not. I'm calling to see if you want to take the boys out for dinner. Give you a night off."

"I already have a marinara sauce simmering on the stove," she says. "With meatballs. It's spaghetti night, remember? Tuesday?" Frances is gazing dreamily at Mei Ling's picture and then it hits her. "Wait. You're going to be traveling again, aren't you? Where? When?"

"Arizona. One week. I leave the day after tomorrow."

"Reed . . ."

"Fran, I know. But there's no way around it. And the way I see it, the more I do now, the easier it'll be when I have to put in my vacation days when we go to China to pick up Mei Ling."

Frances tucks Mei Ling's picture back into a wax-paper envelope. "I wish I knew when that was going to be."

"I know. Me too."

The timeline is sketchy at best, but now that they've been matched with Mei Ling, it could be anywhere from six months to a year before a travel date is set. They have to be ready either way, and even though there are a few more hoops to jump through, the worst is over.

"So dinner in or out?" Reed asks. "I have to go in a minute—one more meeting and then I can head home."

"Let's go out," Frances says. She can refrigerate the sauce for another day. At least there

36

won't be any dishes to worry about tonight.

"Did the agency say anything about the medical records yet?"

"No. I sent them an email this morning but I haven't heard back. I didn't want to call and hound them any more than I already have." Frances turns the heat off on the stove.

"I'll call them before I leave the office," Reed says. "See you soon."

"Bye."

Noah struts into the kitchen. That's his thing these days—he likes to walk in and command a room. Reed says Noah is a lot like his uncle, Reed's younger brother, Jason. Too smart for his own good, Reed often says, and always the center of attention. But Jason must be doing something right, because he's living in an expensive apartment in Los Angeles, an entertainment lawyer to the stars.

"Mom, Brady won't let me play with the airplane. *My* airplane, the one I got for Christmas." Noah folds his arms across his chest and looks cross.

Frances puts away the dry packages of spaghetti. "Can you give him something else to play with? What about his fire truck?" She starts clearing the table, readying it for breakfast instead.

"He hates that fire truck. He wants my airplane, but it's mine. I'm going to hit him."

"Noah." Frances frowns. "We do *not* hit in this family. Got it?"

Noah isn't fazed. "Then I'll lock him in the closet."

Frances is glad there's nobody here to witness this, especially any of the caseworkers who did the home study for the adoption.

"Noah, you're a big boy. Find something else to play with."

Noah huffs, "Mom!" but turns and stomps back to his room. Frances listens for a yell from Brady, but it doesn't come. In a few minutes they have to go pick up Nick from a friend's house, so they'll have to stop playing anyway.

When the spaghetti sauce is transferred to a container to cool and everything else is washed and put away, Frances grabs her keys and calls to the boys. "Time to get Nick. Everybody in the car!"

When there's no answer, Frances walks down to the boys' room. At some point they'll outgrow this house but for now, Frances likes how cozy it is. All three boys share a room and she likes knowing that at night, they're all tucked in and together. She's an only child and she always longed for a sibling, always wished she had a brother or a sister to share a room with, to grow up with. Maybe that's why Mei Ling feels so right, so perfect for their family. The boys have one another just like Reed has Jason, but Frances knows that having a little girl is going to change everything for them, and for the better.

Reed teases her that it's all about the fluffy pink dresses and frilly hairbows, but they both know it's much more than that. It's about the softness that comes with having a girl in the home. For Frances, this sweet angel is her long-held wish, her secret hope from the day she married Reed. She always knew she'd have a daughter, and it always surprised her whenever she found out she was having a boy. She wouldn't trade her sons for anything, of course, but always there was the waiting, the expectation. Now it can be put to rest. The daughter she has been waiting for is finally coming.

Frances turns into the boys' room and gasps. Noah and Brady are standing around the remains of a toy airplane, which Noah is proceeding to smash to bits with a plastic baseball bat. Brady is laughing as pieces fly everywhere.

"Noah Tyler Latham! You stop that right now!" Frances hurries forward as Noah takes another swing at the airplane.

"Can't, Mom," Noah says. "Airplane crash."

"Airplane crash!" Brady repeats, delighted. He's three. He claps as a plastic shard flies across the room. "Boom!"

"Boom!" Noah roars, and brings the bat down as Frances tries to grab it. He nails her in the foot and she tumbles toward the beds. "Oh! Sorry, Mom."

Frances catches herself, then gives her foot a shake. It stings, but she knows nothing is broken.

"I thought you liked this airplane," she says grabbing the bat as Noah readies for another swing.

"Nah," Noah says with a shrug. "We're over it. Right, Brady?"

Brady beams. "Right!" He scoops up an armful of parts and tosses them in the air before Frances can stop him.

"Stop! Boys, get in the car *now*." She pushes them toward the door. "And then you're cleaning this up when we get home." She gives Noah a firm look.

"It was Brady's idea," Noah starts to protest. "Make him do it."

"Brady is three." Frances points toward the garage. "GO."

Noah trudges out the door with Brady on his heels. Frances stares at the destruction in their wake. She loves her sons, but this supposedly typical-boy behavior is too much. She sees Mei Ling's picture in a frame on the boys' dresser, and feels herself soften once again. Already Frances feels back in balance, no longer outnumbered by all the testosterone in the house.

"You and me," she says, rubbing her foot. She touches the frame gently. "Tea parties and dress-up. We'll show these boys how it's done."

Chapter Three

Connie checks the kitchen clock, then quickly unties her apron and washes her hands. She has a few minutes before their day officially starts and she's done as much as she can for now.

She hurries upstairs, then quietly opens the door to her bedroom and slips inside. Before Madeline bought the tea salon, it had been a B&B so Connie's room is more of a suite than a room, with a small sitting area and a nicely appointed private bath. It's included in her pay, which is more than she received at the laundromat where she was an attendant for almost five years. There's a tiny window alcove where Connie curls up every morning to write in her journal. Sometimes she'll go out on the small balcony and sit in one of the wrought iron chairs and gaze at the backyard where they've renovated the gardens and added outdoor seating.

But now she kneels on the floor by her bed and lifts the bed skirt. She reaches underneath until her fingers curl around a handle. She pulls out a suitcase, old and battered. She presses buttons on either side of the handle and the latches pop free.

Inside is the familiar musty smell of mothballs and time. It's mostly empty since Connie has moved her clothes into the armoire and antique dresser, her belongings having found a place in this space Connie gets to call her own. All of her belongings, that is, except this. A plastic folder that's cracked along the seam and held together with a thick rubber band. Connie pulls off the elastic, snapping herself in the process. Her wrist is stinging as she opens the folder and pulls out a series of photographs.

Connie at four, Connie at eight. Connie at the state fair with blue cotton candy stuck in her hair. Connie selling Girl Scout cookies. Connie with her father at the swimming pool, water streaming down her face as she grins atop her father's shoulders. She was ten there. A year later he would die of a heart attack, slumped over his desk at home, the ink from his fountain pen smeared across a sheet of paper.

There is only one picture left. Connie at thirteen. She's at a petting zoo, flanked on one side by a small herd of Boer goats, and on the other, her mother.

Connie touches the photo, runs her fingertips along the goats, the outline of her mother's face. Connie looks for a hint, for a sign of whatever her mother must have been thinking. In the picture her hands are on Connie's shoulders. They're both wearing Bermuda shorts and sandals, sleeveless shirts, broad sun visors, a smile for the camera. Connie had no idea what was going to happen next, a mere few days after their return home. She found the empty bottles of sleeping pills first. An accidental overdose, they said.

Connie was put with one foster family after the next. None of the families she stayed with were all that terrible, but they weren't that wonderful, either. The first family ignored her mostly, and Connie probably would have stayed there if they hadn't been arrested for lottery mail fraud. The husband in the next family was a chain smoker and Connie would feign lying on the floor, her hands around her neck, pretending to choke. "Get this damn girl out of here!" he'd bellow to his wife. Connie didn't last there long. The next family had other children who treated Connie like dirt but Connie didn't care anymore. They didn't know her, didn't have any idea what was going on inside of her. When she made honor roll for the school year, they left her alone, dubbing her as both weird and geeky, someone not worth their time at all.

By the time she was sixteen Connie figured out that if she could prove to the judge that she was one-hundred-percent self-supporting, she could be legally emancipated before the age of eighteen. She found a part-time job, a cheap place to stay above the Pizza Shack. She was able to juggle school easily enough, and when her foster family announced that they were moving, the judge looked at all her paperwork, at the thick file showing her foster-care history, the glowing recommendations from her teachers, the absence of any living relatives. A swipe of a pen and she was free.

Connie puts the pictures back into the folder, stretches the rubber band around it once again. She hasn't shown these pictures to anyone, not even Madeline. She might one day, but for now it feels safest like this, a small dose that reminds her of who she is and what she had. Once upon a time, she was part of a family. And once upon a time, she was loved.

"Connie!" Madeline calls up the stairs. Connie quickly begins putting everything away. "Connie, we have more goat drama!"

Connie slides the suitcase under the bed and blows out her breath. Serena was eating her way through Madeline's garden so Connie put up a makeshift fence. Serena has been bleating her protest ever since, making life unbearable for everyone within earshot.

Madeline is anxious for her to find Serena's owners, but Connie can't bring herself to do it. As good as Madeline is to her and as much as they talk, Madeline has a whole other life and set of friends, family. Connie has herself, Madeline, and now, Serena. She just wants a little more time with her, that's all. Besides, there must have been a reason Serena chewed through that rope, right? And who knows what her previous owners were like? Connie can't send Serena back home without doing a little research first and knowing she'll be okay.

There's a knock on the door. "Are you in there?"

"I'm here." Connie opens the door, brushes a lock of hair from her face.

"Serena's found her way into Walter Lassiter's garden again," Madeline informs her. "And I believe he has the water hose out."

"Oh!" Connie hurries past her and clambers down the stairs. "I was planning on reinforcing the fence tonight. I'll do it now."

"We have those quiches that need to go in the oven soon," Madeline reminds her.

"Quiches! Right!" Connie hollers over her shoulder, almost tripping. "I'm on it!"

She emerges from the back door in time to see Walter aiming the hose at Serena. "That'll show you to get into my petunias!" he hollers. A spray of water hits Serena's back and she startles, then dodges unsuccessfully as Walter sprays her again. Connie watches, horrified, unsure of what to do. Madeline has come up behind her.

And then Connie sees it, a gleam in Serena's eye.

"Serena, no!" Connie shouts, but it's too late.

Serena has her head down and she's charging Walter Lassiter. Walter drops the hose and runs for the house. "Dolores! Help!" He's almost to their back door when Serena bumps into his butt, pushing him off balance enough to fall into the lilac bushes by his house.

"Oh dear," Madeline murmurs, her hand covering her mouth, stifling a laugh. "This isn't good."

Serena is trotting back toward them, smugly satisfied, and heads toward the fenced area of the property. She nudges the gate open and slips inside.

Walter Lassiter is upright now, brushing the dirt off his pants. "I'm calling animal control!" he yells at them before storming into the house. Dolores is standing on the steps with a helpless look on her face. She lifts her shoulders in an apologetic shrug.

Connie looks at Serena, who's back in her pen and munching on grass, oblivious. Connie clears her throat. "I think I'll put those quiches in now," she says. Madeline just nods her assent, and the two women go inside.

Max waves the paper in front of Ava's face, tugs on the frayed hem of her skirt. "Mommy, look."

"Hold on, Max." Ava squeezes one more lemon into the water, then gives the solution a stir, the bottle caps tapping gently against one another. She'll soak them overnight to remove any rust, then take a soft toothbrush and work the groove of each cap with soapy water, making sure to remove any remaining debris. She'll finish with a layer of clear lacquer and then, once they're dry, she'll be able to start working on them.

He tugs again. "I drew free people. You, me, and Daddy."

"Three," Ava corrects automatically as she throws away the discarded lemons. "Th-th-th. *Three.*"

"Free," Max repeats solemnly. "F-f-f. *Free.*"

Ava sighs. She hopes it's baby talk that Max will grow out of some day, that a speech impediment won't be one more thing he has to deal with.

She wipes her hands and turns to her son. "Okay, let me see."

Max beams and holds up his picture. Sure enough, there are three figures. No distinguishable body parts, just round blobs with dots for eyes and a nose, a squiggly mouth, varying in size from small to big.

"Wow, Max, that's wonderful." Ava kisses the top of his head, sweaty from a full day at preschool. It's the second week and she still hasn't gotten into a routine with bath and bedtime, two things she'd been casual about in the past, but she doesn't want him tired in the morning. Or hungry, which means she needs to do some meal planning, too.

The tuition was a stretch, but she couldn't do it anymore, the 24/7 with no breaks, no backup. The school offered financial aid, which helped, but still it's a big bite out of their budget, right after rent. Max cried every morning last week (as did Ava, the minute she was out of sight of the school) but now he's either resolved to being there or likes it. Last week she'd been stunned with the sheer quiet of their small house and didn't quite know what to do, her long to-do list evaporating into thin air as she sat and sat, her mind a blissful blank. But this week she's back on track. She's been doing legal transcription work at home and while the pay is good, the work is inconsistent and there aren't any benefits. She can't go back to doing what she used to do and her jewelry will hopefully supplement their income, but Ava knows it won't be much. No, she needs to find a full-time job now that Max is in school.

"Okay, into the tub for you," she says, sticking the picture on the fridge with a magnet. Max's chest puffs out proudly and Ava is overwhelmed with love for her son. His eyes look large behind the thick glasses, a bright beautiful blue that reminds her of someone else she loves, too, and the heartache begins.

Max races off, struggling to take his shirt off, his skinny little legs carrying him as fast as they can. Ava prays he doesn't run into a wall. He doesn't.

"Bubbles?" he begs as he steps out of his pants.

"Not tonight—" she begins, because the bubble

bath is reserved for special occasions and not regular school nights, at least that's what she tells him. The real reason is because it's expensive. Max has mild eczema and can't use the cheap stuff on the grocery store shelves.

She touches the picture on the fridge. Maybe Max said it right the first time.

Free. Ava wants to be free, wants the same for Max.

"Mommy?"

"Okay," she says. "Bubbles it is!" She rushes up after him, giving his naked torso a tickle as Max bursts into peals of delighted laughter.

Isabel lays on her back in the middle of the living room floor, staring up at the ceiling. The smell of fresh paint has yet to fade but Isabel doesn't mind—on the contrary, it reminds her that things are no longer the same. Her walls are so pristine that she's reluctant to put anything back on them. Calendars, pictures, paintings, it doesn't matter. She likes how spare everything feels. If anything, she should take more out. The furniture, the end tables, the floor lamps. Strip it all bare. Start from scratch.

Isabel laces her fingers together, rests them on her chest. For once her mind isn't with Bill or that homewrecker, but with the freshly painted walls, the past slowly being replaced by the present. What should she do next? Tackle the exterior?

Wash the screened windows? So many choices. Isabel notices how pale her skin looks against her white blouse and the white cotton cuffs of her shorts, the only clean things in her closet. She hasn't had a tan in years.

Plain vanilla, she thinks. That's what Bill used to call her. He meant it affectionately because she was so fair, so even-keeled, so go-with-the-flow, but Isabel always felt struck by the comment, as if he were saying that she was boring. Colorless. When he left her for Ava that was the first thing to cross Isabel's mind. Ava, with her brightly colored dresses, her painted toenails. Ava, full of color, while Isabel was the sort of woman who blended in with the walls.

She hears the sound of someone walking up the steps to the porch. Then a crack, a splintering of wood. Isabel sits up, her ear trained to the door. There's muttering, then a knock.

"Isabel? I know you're in there. Open up."

Bettie Shelton. No surprise there. It's either her or the Jehovah's Witnesses as the rest of the neighborhood has taken to leaving Isabel alone.

"Isabel? I'll have you know I practically put my foot through a rotted board on your stairs. I could have fallen straight through! I'm not going to sue, but you're going to have to find somebody to fix that thing."

Yeah, that would have been Bill. The weekend he left her he was going through his list of honey-do's—cleaning the gutters, power washing the windows. He was in the middle of mowing the lawn when he stopped. Just stopped. Isabel was in the kitchen, scrubbing out the oven, when he appeared in the doorway and told her he was leaving.

He seemed genuinely full of regret. He loved Isabel, but he loved Ava, too, and she was pregnant. He looked so sorrowful that Isabel almost felt sorry for him. *Almost.* He packed his things fast, as if he knew exactly what he was going to take and what he was going to leave behind. He left the lawn mower by the maple tree and it was a week before Bettie Shelton eventually rolled it into the garage.

The house is in sorry shape and Isabel knows this—she's let a lot of things go. It's not only the money but the time, the brain power needed to figure out what to fix and what to replace. She just doesn't have it. She's managed the past four years with things being the way they are, so what's a couple more?

Maybe the house will sell. She hasn't had any calls yet, not even a nibble, but she only needs one buyer, right? Maybe she'll downgrade to a condo somewhere. Clean and simple, no gutters to worry about, no rotting porches. Maybe she'll leave Avalon altogether and start over someplace new. It's a thought. There's nothing tying her down here, after all.

"Isabel?" There's a rap on her window. "I can see you lying on the floor. Are you going to answer the door or what?"

Isabel holds her breath, doesn't move.

"Isabel?"

Isabel wills Bettie to magically disappear.

"Isabel, I know where your spare key is." Bettie Shelton's head peeks through the side window.

Damn it all. Isabel sits up and glares at the door. "It's open!"

The doorknob turns and Bettie steps in. She's wearing a house dress and flip-flops, her silvery-blue hair fuzzy from the heat. She frowns when she sees Isabel sitting on the floor, then looks around. "You painted?"

Isabel manages a nod. She's never been particularly friendly with Bettie, who's a bit too scrappy for someone as plain vanilla as Isabel.

"Huh, you painted your walls white. All of them." Her eyes bug out when Isabel stands up. "And you *match*."

"I'm redecorating," Isabel says, hoping that will get Bettie off her back. "Getting the place ready for the new owners."

Bettie gives her a hard look. "Did you sell it?"

Isabel squirms. "Not yet, but I will."

"Well, you'd better fix that busted step," Bettie declares. "I could have killed myself, I'll have you know."

No such luck, Isabel wants to say, but instead

she asks, "Is there something you need? Eggs? Flour? You know where everything is. Have at it." Isabel waves in the general direction of her kitchen. Last year when the town was baking Amish Friendship Bread, Bettie was coming in unannounced, borrowing ingredients at will. Isabel didn't notice at first, too mired in her own problems, until she found her flour container suddenly empty, the small jar of vanilla upended, grains of sugar crystals dotting the floor. Her supply of gallon-sized Ziploc bags was disappearing at an alarming rate. It wasn't until Bettie complained that Isabel was out of cinnamon that she finally figured it out.

Bettie surveys the living room critically. "I wanted to invite you to join our next meeting. Second Thursday of the month. No previous experience necessary."

Isabel reluctantly stands up. "Previous experience for what?"

"Scrapbooking." Bettie straightens up to her full height, 4'11". "I'm president and founder of the Avalon Ladies Scrapbooking Society, in case you didn't know."

Isabel does know, as does half the town—Bettie won't let them forget it. Their street is clogged with cars whenever there's a meeting. "Thanks, but I have plans."

"What plans? You don't have any plans. You never leave this house, Isabel Kidd. I've been watching you." Bettie points two fingers to her eyes then points them at Isabel. "You don't go anywhere."

"Untrue. I go to work and last week I bought paint." Isabel studies the rug on the floor. God, how old is it? She and Bill had bought it together—it was one of the first purchases they made when they got married. There's history in this rug, history Isabel doesn't care to remember. She starts to push a couch against the wall, almost running over Bettie's toes.

Bettie frowns, her eyes narrowing suspiciously at Isabel. "I am even willing to waive the membership fee for the first month. It's normally fifteen dollars and includes a starter pack for the monthly theme. But, under no circumstances are you to tell anyone that I am doing such a thing. It would look like nepotism." She jumps out of the way as Isabel drags a coffee table across the floor.

"Like I said, I have plans." The furniture out of the way, Isabel crouches and tries to roll up the rug. It's long and wide, too heavy and unwieldy for one person. Isabel starts from the middle, the sides, the corners—none of it matters. The rug is stubborn and lies limp in her arms, unwilling to move.

Bettie is watching her. "Would you like some help?" she asks.

No, Isabel most definitely does not want help from Bettie. The thought of being indebted to this

54

woman in any way is more than Isabel can bear.

"No," Isabel huffs, lifting an end and attempting to fold it over. "I got it." The rug rebels, heavy with dirt and memories. Isabel falls back in defeat.

"Oh, this is ridiculous." Bettie marches over and stands next to Isabel. "You roll from there, I'll roll from here. You just need to gain momentum, that's all. Let's go. One, two, three!"

Together they push and roll the rug until it's no more than a fat cylinder of fabric at the end of the living room. They stand up and Isabel looks at the lustrous hardwood floor that's been covered all these years. She suddenly feels buoyant, encouraged. She's going to call Goodwill to come and get the rug. She casts a look around. Maybe she'll give them the couch, too. Maybe she'll give them everything.

"Next meeting is tomorrow night, at my house, from six to nine. Bring your own refreshments and a pair of good scissors, if you have them." Bettie bats the dust away from her face. "Come five minutes early. If you don't like it, you don't have to come to another meeting. I'm all about one-hundred-percent customer satisfaction, and that includes Society members, too. See you at six!" And before Isabel can protest or argue, Bettie turns and walks out the door.

Enid Griffin, 56
Travel Agent, Avalon Travel

Enid Griffin peers into the pot of Gerbera daisies and wrinkles her nose. The brown streaks on the once-red petals are a dead giveaway.

"I knew it," she huffs, pulling herself upright. She's formidable, almost six feet, and full-figured to boot. At fifty-six she's a fair blonde with only a hint of gray, her hair perfectly coiffed and sprayed into place. "Thrips!"

She marches around to her desk, which was custom-made to accommodate her large frame. She sits down, indignant, and starts rapidly typing on her keyboard.

"I know you said Napa Valley but I am telling you, wine country is overrated," she says to the young couple sitting across from her. "You want your honeymoon to be memorable, don't you?"

"Well, yes . . ."

"And these days, with divorce rates so high, I think you can't NOT afford to invest in your marriage. New experiences, new adventures!"

The young couple looks skeptical. "All of our friends who went to California said it was wonderful, and that Napa was so romantic . . ." the girl begins.

Enid dismisses this with a wave of her hand.

"California has an allure, but I'm looking at you two and thinking . . ." Her eyes twinkle as her voice drops into a low, conspiratorial whisper. *"Texas."*

"Texas?"

"Texas! Here we are. South Padre Island." Enid turns her computer screen toward them. "Turtle hatchlings! Palm trees! Orange groves! Wonderful fishing, too—some of the restaurants will even cook your catch. Plus you're close to Mexico so you could cross over for a little day trip. You'll save money and bring home lots of memories. Your own, not some cookie cutter memory downloaded from a website. I mean, do you two even drink wine?"

The young woman says uncertainly, "Well, I drink Chardonnay sometimes . . ." as her fiancé says, "I'm more of a Budweiser kind of guy."

They turn to stare at each other, surprised. "You said you wanted to go to Napa Valley," the young woman accuses her fiancé.

"I said I *would* go," he clarifies. "But I mean, yeah, if a bottle of wine costs the same as a six pack . . ."

"More," Enid says.

"Yeah, if it costs more and doesn't even taste as good . . ."

The young woman's voice is shrill. "That's why we're going! So we can learn to appreciate these things!"

"Why? What's the point? I'm not going to be buying the stuff when we come back. We can't even afford it now."

"Maybe we will!"

"Massages," Enid interjects. "With the money you'll save you'll be able to do lots of fun things. Dance clubs, windsurfing, kiteboarding, parasailing. You kids are young, you should be doing fun things together. You have the rest of your lives to be gargling fermented grape juice." She sends a document to the printer and readies a travel folder for them. They aren't going to make a decision today—she knew that when they first walked in. In fact, Enid is willing to wager that this will be the first of many decisions they won't be able to agree on. "Is there any wiggle room in your budget?" she asks.

The woman says, "Yes," as the young man says, "No."

Enid's right hand hovers over her drawer. She knows what this young couple needs, and it's not wine country or heading to the gulf coast. Still, she was planning on saving it for herself, for her own trip later this year. She finally decided to bite the bullet and take that cruise to Greece, something she always wanted to do but hasn't, because she was waiting. Waiting, perhaps, for someone to come along that would be a good companion, a husband even, but that hasn't happened. There are plenty of nice men in Avalon but none of them are Enid's type, and she's not getting any younger. When Bettie Shelton showed her the selection of new page kits, Enid decided, this is it. She marched back to her office and booked her ticket, and for the first time in her thirty years of being a travel agent she made up a travel folder for herself.

But as she watches this young couple tripping their way to the altar, she thinks, *God bless 'em.* She also thinks, *Good luck.* She knows she missed this part, this supposed happily ever after, but watching it unfold in front of her, it doesn't always look so happy. In fact, it looks like a lot of stress and anxiety and argument and tears. The people who come to her are supposed to be going on vacation, but to see how worked up they get, you'd think you were dragging them to the dentist for a root canal. Enid thinks of Mac and Judy Mullins, regular customers of hers. They saved all their money to travel when Mac retired, but when that time came, it turned out he didn't have any interest in leaving his Barcalounger. Each trip requires hours of cajoling on both her and Judy's part and, boy, is it exhausting. Mac always ends up acquiescing in the end, but it's never without a fight. Why, Enid often wonders, do people sometimes want to make things harder than they need to be?

"Look," Enid says, sliding open her drawer. She pulls out a thick cellophane packet and pushes it toward them. "Here. An early wedding present."

The couple stops arguing long enough to look at the cellophane packet with a frown. "What is it?" the young woman asks, her nose wrinkled as if in disgust.

"It's a scrapbooking kit. A starter kit, actually, but you can get more pages and doodads from Bettie Shelton if you want to do a whole album." She taps a label affixed to the corner of the packet with Bettie's contact information in large, bold letters. "When you're older, even a year from now, this will be the place you'll go to relive the moment."

"We have digital cameras on our phones," the girl says smartly. "With video." She glances at her fiancé as if to say, *Can you believe this?*

Enid is undaunted. "Pictures are only one part of it," she tells them. "And these days people take hundreds of pictures and none of them get printed or put into a photo album. This is different— when you scrapbook, you're evoking the memory of the feeling and the experience by the colors you choose. The little mementos you paste to the page." Enid breaks the seal of the packet and spreads the contents onto the table. "You take your favorite pictures, you look at all of this, and you think, what fits? What goes together? Not just aesthetically, but emotionally. Scrapbook pages capture all of it. For example—how did the two of you meet?"

The couple grins shyly and Enid sees both of them soften. She thinks, *Yes. This is what it's about, isn't it?*

"Bowling alley," the young man says. "Her ball jumped the gutter into my lane."

"It was heavier than I thought," his fiancée protests in her defense, but she's finally relaxed, happy. She reaches for his hand and beams at him.

"Wonderful! So look . . ." Enid shuffles through the loose alphabet letters and quickly spells out at the top of the page, YOU BOWLED ME OVER. "You pick up a coaster or something with the name of the bowling alley and stick it on here, along with some of your earliest pictures."

"I still have that scorecard somewhere," he says. "I bowled a two-fifty that day."

"Perfect!" Enid exclaims.

The girl chooses a thin black border and slides it to the top of the page. "We could even make the whole page look like a scorecard," she says. "What about this?" She rearranges Enid's letters and adds a few others to read SPARES AND STRIKES. "If you get a spare or strike, it's still a perfect ten," she explains.

"Ah," Enid says with an approving nod. She watches them as they pick through random die cuts and trims, reminiscing about that day and talking about the amateur league they're both in. Then the lightbulb goes off.

"Say," she says. "What do you think about a

bowling honeymoon? Playing different bowling alleys? Choose some that might be close to other points of interest, with a nice B&B nearby? Do you have any interest in that?"

The couple looks at her blankly, then a slow smile spreads across both of their faces. They gaze at each other and then at Enid, all aglow.

"Yes," they say in unison, their bodies leaning toward each other. "We do."

Chapter Four

"I'm afraid I'm going to have to keep the water off until tomorrow." Yvonne clicks off her flashlight and steps back from the large puddle of water pooling on the floor.

Her client furrows her brow. "Tomorrow? But that's not possible!"

Yvonne points to the pipes underneath the sink. "All that piping needs to be replaced—the leaks won't stop until that's done. If you put off addressing the problem, it'll only get worse."

"But tonight is the night of my scrapbooking meeting. I'm expecting quite a crowd, you see, and I've already set everything up." Yvonne's client waves to the dining room where tables and chairs have been laid out, as if for a bridge or poker match. There are stacks of colored paper and other glittery sorts of things on every table, gel pens and scissors with odd edges. A paper cutter and laminator are on the buffet, along with some other bizarre contraptions Yvonne doesn't recognize.

"Well, it's up to you, of course, but if it were me I wouldn't wait. I'd do it right away but I won't be able to get everything until tomorrow. The best we can do is keep the water off for now and move your party elsewhere."

"Elsewhere? I'm expecting people in an hour!"

Yvonne gives a sympathetic shrug. "Sorry. It's either that or have your house under a foot of water by morning, Mrs. Shelton."

Her client huffs. "It's *Ms.* Shelton, but don't call me that, it makes me feel old. Call me Bettie." She purses her lips, thinking.

Yvonne starts to put her things away. There's nothing she can do right now, and it'll be up to her client to make the call. Avalon is filled with these lovely old bungalow-style homes but Yvonne's seen the same problem in three other houses and expects it'll be an ongoing issue for many Avalon homeowners. The houses have so much history but the plumbing and electrical are dated, and most people don't bother to fix anything until it's a problem or already too late.

Bettie reaches for the phone and dials a number. She covers the mouthpiece as it rings. "What do I owe you?"

"Nothing. I haven't done anything yet."

"What? Nonsense," Bettie scoffs. "Surely you have some sort of service fee."

"Yes, but this was quick and on my way home. Besides, I can't do anything today so don't worry about it for now." In fact, Yvonne has yet to charge anyone in Avalon for a service call. She knows many people are having a hard time but she's doing okay. She can afford to give a little as long as she's paid for the actual work.

Bettie puts a finger to her lips, shushing

Yvonne. "Connie? It's Bettie." She smiles sweetly into the phone. Yvonne is about to leave but Bettie motions for her to wait so she leans against the counter.

The smile quickly fades from Bettie's face, replaced by one of irritation. "BETTIE SHELTON. I know you know it's me, Connie Colls, so don't pretend you don't recognize my voice . . . I do so sound the same on the phone . . . Yes, I most certainly do—oh, forget it. Is Madeline there? . . . Well, where is she? . . . Two hours? . . . Well, I suppose I could talk with you. I wanted to let you know that I thought it would be a lovely thing if we held the meeting of the Society at the tea salon tonight. Give you a little business, though of course I expect some sort of group discount . . . What do you mean you have a book club group tonight? . . . Well, what about the dining room . . . What? A rehearsal dinner? For who? Oh, that's right. I suspect she's pregnant, don't you? . . . No, I am not gossiping, I am merely stating an observation . . . fine. Goodbye." Bettie hangs up the phone and stares at it indignantly, her hands on her hips. "That Connie Colls thinks she runs the place! Madeline would be shocked if she knew how she treated me. She almost ruined a sale the last time I was there."

"Do you have an old towel?" Yvonne asks. "We should wipe this water up. I don't want you to slip."

"Now this is what I'm talking about!" Bettie declares as she heads toward the hallway closet. "Such good manners. It's appalling how rude people are these days, Yvette, wouldn't you agree? I wish more young people were like you!" She hands Yvonne a faded beach towel, beaming.

"It's Yvonne," Yvonne says with a smile. "And I'm not *that* young."

"Twenty-two?" Bettie guesses.

Twenty-two. Yvonne wishes. Then again, twenty-two was her worst year, the year when everything fell apart, when it was clear she was as lost as lost could be. Things are better now that she's had the time to put it all behind her, to start anew. "More like thirty-two."

"Thirty-two? Really?" Bettie looks impressed, as if Yvonne has done something quite remarkable.

Yvonne quickly mops up the water. "Where should I put this?" she asks when she's done, holding up the sopping towel, but Bettie is on the phone again.

"Isabel?" Bettie calls loudly into the phone. "Isabel, are you there? Pick up the phone." Bettie taps her foot impatiently, waits a few seconds longer. Eventually she hangs up, a grim look on her face. "Well, I suppose that's how it's going to go. What's your name again, dear?"

"Yvonne."

"Right." Bettie squinches her eyes, thinking

hard. "Yvonne, Yvonne, Yvonne. Got it. So Yvonne, would you mind helping me a few minutes more? I think you're right—it's best we move the meeting to another location. My neighbor next door has a nice open space—she's redecorating—and her living room will be perfect. It shouldn't take too long to move everything over."

It's the end of the day and Yvonne was only planning on going home and watching a little TV, grabbing a little something to eat. She can spare a few more minutes.

"Sure," she says.

Except that it's not a few more minutes. A half an hour later she's still bringing things into the house next door—the tables and chairs, all the scrapbooking supplies, the generous hors d'oeuvres Bettie has prepared. Yvonne's starving now, unable to keep her eyes off the cauliflower crostinis, the deviled eggs with scallions and dill, the stuffed artichoke hearts.

"There," Bettie finally says, satisfied. She looks around the room, nodding her head in approval. "Scrappetizers are the key to any successful scrapbooking event, Yvonne. It's a little-known fact, but crafters always work better on a full stomach. That's certainly true for me, at least. Now where did I put those serving spoons?"

Yvonne collapses into a folding chair. She's a whiz with the wrench, can unscrew even the tightest of bolts, can lie in uncomfortable positions for long periods of time while working in the underbelly of a house or building. But this home-entertaining stuff? It's exhausting. The multitasking, the timing, the attention to detail and overall presentation. She thinks of her mother, then pushes the thought away.

Bettie's already put a sign up on her door instructing the members to come next door, and soon women are drifting in, delighted by the unexpected change of venue. More covered dishes and plates arrive, Yvonne can't bring herself to get up from the chair, unaware of how truly exhausted she was until now. And hungry.

"Yvonne, you must stay," Bettie insists as she introduces Earlene Bauer. "Earlene is the dispensing optician at the Avalon All Eyes Vision Center. Fixed me up nice and proper with my bifocals though I only need them when I'm reading."

"And driving," Earlene reminds her. "I've seen you driving without them."

"Oh, I always drive with them, Earlene," Bettie assures her earnestly.

Earlene gives her a knowing look. "Bettie . . ."

"It's Missy Parks!" Bettie exclaims, turning away from them. "Missy, come meet Yvonne. She's my fabulous in-house technician!"

"Oh, how lovely," Missy says, walking over. Her face is lit up with interest. "Now what exactly is an in-house technician?"

That's what Yvonne was wondering as well.

"I'm a plumber," she says, holding out her hand. She doesn't believe in mincing words, in recategorizing what she does to make it more palatable for other people. Day-to-day living depends on good plumbing, and Yvonne knows this even if they don't. Still, Earlene and Missy suddenly shrink back, glancing at Yvonne's hands, which they assume have been swishing around the inside of a toilet bowl. It's one of the biggest fallacies out there—that plumbers only work on toilets or leaky sinks. In fact, Yvonne's made most of her money working with heat and air-conditioning fittings as well as the piping for new construction projects and housing developments.

"Gosh, I completely forgot! I'm just getting over a cold." Missy safely tucks her hands behind her back. "I wouldn't want you to get all germy."

"A cold in August?" Bettie frowns.

"Are those the new theme packs?" Missy asks, stepping over to one of the tables. "So nice to meet you!" she calls to Yvonne over her shoulder.

Bettie pats Yvonne on the arm. "They're not all as open-minded as me, I'm afraid," she says with a shake of her head.

"Bettie, I've brought friendship bread," a lady says, holding up a four-layer cake that makes Yvonne's mouth water. "Hazelnut Cappuccino Royale! I have to admit I was a bit liberal with the instant coffee mix, but it turned out wonderful, don't you think?"

"It's divine, Lorna. Go ahead and place it right over there. Well, we may as well start eating. We have a lot to do tonight." Bettie claps her hands for attention. "Ladies! Fill your plates and take a seat. The program will begin soon!" She loops her arm through Yvonne's and steers her toward the food. Yvonne can't wait to dig in.

"Bettie, is there any ice?" someone calls out.

"In the freezer, Claribel," Bettie replies. "Second shelf."

"Bettie, where's the bathroom?" someone else asks.

"There's one in the hallway, first door to the left. There's also one in the master bedroom, but it may be best to—"

"WHAT THE HELL IS GOING ON IN HERE?!"

The women stop talking and turn to see a woman in her late thirties standing in the doorway, a bag of groceries in hand.

"Isabel!" Bettie hurries forward, unwittingly dragging Yvonne along with her. "You made it!"

"To my own house? What's going on?"

"Society meeting, dear. Monthly get-together of the Avalon Ladies Scrapbooking Society. I know I told you!"

"Yes, but you didn't tell me you were going to have it *here*." Isabel glares at Bettie.

Yvonne tries to disentangle herself from Bettie's grip but Bettie's holding on, steadfast.

"There was a last-minute crisis, wasn't there, Yvonne? Yvonne is my in-house technician—"

"Plumber," Yvonne corrects.

"—and she wisely suggested I move the party elsewhere as my house is in no condition to entertain. Isn't that right, Yvonne?"

Isabel turns to Yvonne, her hazel eyes flashing. Yvonne squirms. "Well, yes, but—"

"And since I helped *you* move *your* furniture around the other day, I thought you'd be happy to extend the same courtesy to me, a fellow neighbor in need." Bettie blinks innocently.

"You could have at least called . . . Wait, how did you even get in here?" A look of consternation crosses Isabel's face. *"I am hiding my key in a new place, Bettie!"*

"For the record, I did call, as Yvonne will attest, but there was no answer," Bettie says smugly.

"Because I was at work!"

"Well, I don't have your work number, now do I? You should give it to me for next time."

"Never." Isabel is gritting her teeth and Yvonne notices that there's a gallon of mint chip ice cream on top of all the groceries in her shopping bag. Yvonne's stomach gives a growl.

"Goodness, poor Yvonne is starving. You go put your groceries away, Isabel dear, and you can join us. We have plenty of food."

Isabel is struggling to keep her composure as the other women look on. "I was looking forward to a quiet dinner," she says under her breath. "So if you could please tell everyone to leave—"

Bettie reaches into Isabel's bag and plucks out a TV dinner. "Really, Isabel," she says with a *tsk*. She tosses it back in Isabel's bag. "I'm going to fix you up a plate. You can sit with Yvonne. She's new to the Society, too." Bettie gasps. "You can be scrapbooking sisters!"

Ew. Yvonne cringes. By the look on Isabel's face, she doesn't care much for it, either.

"I should be going," Yvonne says. As hungry as she is, she's had enough drama for one day. She just wants to go home.

Isabel finally looks triumphant. "Thank you," she says smugly. "Now if everyone else could—"

"Girls," Bettie says. Her voice is suddenly serious. "I think you would both do well to sit. We're late as it is and the food's getting cold." The women hovering around them stop talking and raise their eyebrows. A second later, they've scattered to different parts of the room.

Isabel and Yvonne are about to protest again but Bettie says again, much more sternly and loudly, "SIT."

Both women sit.

Bettie takes the grocery bag from Isabel and heads to the kitchen. "Lorna," she calls, her voice sweet again. "Can you get the girls some food, chop-chop? Make sure they get some of that lovely purple cabbage slaw. And Sue Pendergast's tomato salad. Sue, you have got to give me that recipe. I always put in too much balsamic vinegar and it turns the whole dish!"

The two young women watch as Society members descend upon the buffet, commenting on the different dishes, pouring cups of iced tea, then depositing two paper plates in front of them laden with food.

"I don't believe this," Isabel is muttering. Her fists are clenched.

Yvonne wants to be sympathetic but really, what's the big deal? Obviously Bettie and Isabel are chummy enough because Bettie seems to know her way around Isabel's house. Either way, it's not her business. She picks up her fork, not interested in debating this particular topic with Isabel, with anyone. "Well, cheers," she says, holding up her paper cup of iced tea.

Isabel turns and looks at her, then reluctantly picks up her own cup, knocking it halfheartedly against Yvonne's. Yvonne quickly downs her iced tea and starts in on the food. "Wow, this is really good," she says with a happy sigh. Everything tastes fresh and delicious. "I haven't had a home-cooked meal in a long time."

Yvonne is so engrossed in her food that she doesn't notice Isabel slowly unfurling her fists and reaching for a fork. And then, like her tablemate, Isabel begins to eat.

Chapter Five

"Attention! Attention! The August meeting of the Avalon Ladies Scrapbooking Society is now in order." Bettie holds a wooden mallet decorated with sequins and fabric scraps. She bangs it several times on a block of wood painted hot pink and decoupaged with printed tissue paper.

A hush sweeps the room. All eyes are trained on Bettie as plates of food are quickly finished and disposed of. The women move swiftly to their chairs, their faces all business.

Bettie peers at her notes over her reading glasses. "I'm pleased to welcome new members Emily Spiller, Thelma Talley, and Trudy Hughes. Many thanks to Bev Smitts for sharing her album, 'The Great Outdoors,' where she scrapbooked about husband Roosevelt's hunting trip last fall. And Georgia Wellington's album, 'A Day at the Zoo,' gave us lots of wonderful ideas on how to incorporate found objects into our pages—I thought the peacock feather was a particularly nice touch. Edie's feature of last month's meeting in the 'Out and About' section of the *Avalon Gazette* was well received, thank you, Edie. Based on an eighty-three percent response from Society members we saw a rise in the use of distressed ink, a decline in the use of patterned brads. Now on to the Treasurer's report . . ."

Isabel takes a bite out of the remaining cracker on her plate. Several heads turn around and frown.

Annoyed, Isabel puts down the cracker and mutters, "Well, I'm done. Think I'll go home now." She gives the women in front of her a pointed look. "Oh wait. I *am* home."

Yvonne stifles a laugh.

". . . And finally, I'd like to thank Isabel Kidd for opening up her home to us tonight. Isabel, stand up so we can give you a round of applause!" Bettie gestures for Isabel to stand up.

"Pass," Isabel says flatly, a disinterested look on her face.

"Oh, come on," Yvonne says, grinning. "It won't kill you." A few women seated around them nod in agreement.

Isabel gives Yvonne an incredulous look but reluctantly stands up. The women clap heartily and Isabel sits back down. Yvonne gives her a pat on the back and Isabel smiles sheepishly.

"Okay, we have a lot to do today and I know I promised that we'd get to the new fall lay-outs." Bettie peers out at the group. "Anyone? Anyone?"

There's an excited buzz as hands immediately shoot up.

"Didn't you say we'd be working with chipboard? I've been waiting to make one of those coaster albums for the grandkids. And have you seen the new Pebbles Chips? They're adorable!"

"I'm hoping we'll be making page pockets and incorporating family mementos. I want to scrapbook my sister's baby shower before she delivers."

"The Jenni Bowlin alpha letters in oranges and browns would be perfect. Oh, and the new Prima flowers . . ."

Isabel exchanges a bewildered look with Yvonne.

"It's Greek to me," Yvonne says. "But I have to admit, I'm curious. I overheard someone saying they paid over two hundred dollars for a cricket. Is that for real?"

"A Cricut, a die-cut machine," someone whispers from behind them. "You can cut anything with it. Paper . . ."

"Fabric . . ."

"Vinyl . . ."

"Felt . . ."

"Yes, we get it, thank you," Isabel says.

"Bettie hosts swarms twice a year," the woman continues. "It's like a crop, when we all get together to scrapbook, except a swarm is when we share our Cricut machines and cartridges with scrappers who don't have them. You can cut any shape or pattern, letters, and in every size . . ."

Isabel closes her eyes and pretends this is all a bad dream while Yvonne listens with interest.

Claribel Apple, a neighbor from down the street, digs through her bag and hands something to them. "I made this card at the last swarm. I'm giving it to my husband for our anniversary next month."

"If you don't end up keeping it for yourself," her friend chuckles.

"I know!" Claribel exclaims. "I love it so much I don't know if I can give it away. You know he'll just stuff it in his sock drawer."

Yvonne nudges Isabel and nods at the card. "Hey, this isn't so bad. Look."

Reluctantly Isabel looks over. The card's a bit sappy (*"In your arms is my favorite place to be . . ."*) but she has to admit it looks all right, like an expensive card you'd buy in one of those stationery stores in the city. "Nice," she mutters.

Yvonne hands it back to the woman and turns back toward Bettie, her eyes glowing with renewed interest.

"Those were all good guesses but we're going to have even more fun," Bettie is saying. She pauses for effect and her eyes grow wide, the women in the room leaning forward in nervous anticipation. "We're stitching our layouts this month!"

There's a delighted gasp and another round of applause.

Isabel claps her hands over her ears and looks at Yvonne. "I'm going crazy."

"Now, I have six-page layout packages here for those of you who want to take a shortcut," Bettie is saying as she walks around the room. "It includes borders, tags, paper, some adorable brads and rub-ons, cutouts, and of course suggestions for how to lay everything out and then stitch it up by hand or machine. Otherwise you're welcome to use your own papers and ideas. The kit is free to Society members and $9.99 for guests." She stops in front of Isabel and Yvonne and hands them each a pack, then places a finger over her lips in a secretive smile. "We have extra tools at our Scrap Station over there . . ."

Isabel glances over. "My dining room table, you mean?"

". . . and don't forget to swing by the swap table. Members bring supplies they no longer need or want and swap them for something that might work better. Most of the time people are glad to get rid of stuff so help yourself if you see something you like." Bettie turns and hollers, "Okay, ladies. We have two hours left. Let's get scrappin'!"

The women begin to assemble themselves around makeshift tables. Rolling file boxes and organizers are opened and items immediately placed on the table—cutting boards, pens and markers, adhesives, plastic containers of embellishments, stacks of paper, loose photos.

"Are we cropping or scrapping?" Yvonne whispers. "I'm confused."

"Maybe we're crapping," Isabel suggests, but no one bites. She looks at the packet in her hand. "Oh, scrap! I don't have any pictures." She snaps her fingers, feigning disappointment.

"You live here." Yvonne helps open a portable camping table and sets it up in front of them. "I'm sure you have something. Don't you have a big box of unsorted photos somewhere? Everyone does."

Isabel does have a box like that but it went into the attic when Bill left, along with all the photo albums and framed prints. When he died, Isabel could only bear to be up there long enough to find a good photo for the memorial. She hasn't looked at the boxes since then and doesn't intend to anytime soon. Instead she says, "I just painted so I moved a bunch of stuff around. I can't remember where I put anything."

"You can always put the layout together and add your photos at another time," Lorna says as she walks by. "That's what most of us do anyway. You can't get it all done in one evening, after all. What would be the fun in that?"

There's a chortle of laughter as Lorna walks on.

"It took me a whole weekend to scrapbook the trip Jazz and I took to the San Diego boardwalk last year," Cyndi Bloom remembers.

"I love San Diego!" Yvonne exclaims. "How long were you there for?"

Cyndi is looking through an assortment of edged scissors. "Three days."

"Wait," Isabel says. "It took you the same amount of time to scrapbook a trip you went on?" Isabel can think of lots of things she can do in a weekend, and scrapbooking isn't one of them.

Cyndi thinks about it. "You're right, it took me longer. I spent two days power-planning my pages before I started. But I don't really count that because I usually watch TV at the same time."

Isabel shakes her head, incredulous, and looks to Yvonne for confirmation about how nuts this whole scrapbooking thing is. But Yvonne is already hard at work, strategizing with one of the ladies about whether she should cut a mat for a photo and, if so, whether it should be vertical or horizontal.

"I can't decide," Yvonne says, more to herself than anyone else. "I think most of my pictures are horizontal, though." She looks up at Isabel and begs, "Come on, don't make me do this by myself. It's fun!"

A smart retort is on the tip of Isabel's tongue when she sees her neighbor across the room bend down to pick up a piece of paper that's fallen to the ground. Despite her age Bettie is quick on her feet, but for a second Isabel sees something else, a look of confusion crossing her face, a sudden intake of breath as she glances around the room, her brow furrowed. No one else is paying attention as Bettie is frozen for a moment, lost, the piece of paper still in her hand.

And then she's back, striding across the room at a clip, tossing the paper into the trash, giving suggestions and helping people rearrange different scrapbooking elements on their pages.

"Isabel?" Yvonne is looking at her. "Come on. You game?"

"What?" Isabel looks back at Yvonne, probably the only other person in the room that she has any interest in talking to and who seems to be fine talking to her. Isabel sneaks one more look at Bettie but she's laughing now, holding up a paper flower and pointing to one of the petals, demonstrating some kind of technique with a needle and thread. Maybe she was imagining it, but Isabel can't be sure. Either way, Isabel has no place to go until this whole thing is over and done with. Resigned, she breaks the seal on the cellophane packet and spreads the contents on the table in front of her.

Max is asleep in Ava's bed. Ava tries not to make a habit of it, knows that the parenting books say it's a big no-no, but she loves having him snuggle up next to her, his soft skin, his little fingers winding around hers. The closeness is reassuring for both of them and it's such a small thing.

Today was another hard day at preschool. The teacher told her as Ava was buckling him into his car seat, and Ava was livid that they hadn't called her, hadn't given her a chance to come and pick him up, to make it all better. The teacher didn't see what happened, a squabble over some plastic blocks that ended up with one child hitting another. Max, in the middle, didn't get hurt but was upset. He stopped talking for the rest of the day, didn't eat his lunch, didn't want a snack. He did nap, the teacher said, brightening. As if that made it all better.

Ava listens to her son breathe, his breaths short and even. He's pressed against her, not trusting her to roll even an inch away before he reaches out for her again.

Ava sighs in the dark. This is the hardest part for her, the part that makes her turn away when she sees families where both parents are there and engaged, backing each other up and tag teaming. She belonged to a moms' group for a while but dropped out because she couldn't stand hearing the other women complain about their husbands and what they didn't do. What about what they *did* do, however small? It'd have to beat being on your own all the time, having it all come down to you and you alone. No one to talk to, to bounce ideas off of, to formulate a parenting strategy.

There's no room to get sick, to take a break, to have a major meltdown.

After an hour Ava is able to carefully slip out of the bed. She tucks pillows around Max and gently closes the door, leaving it open a crack. She needs to unwind, needs to put her unsuccessful day of job hunting behind her. The Jeep died again today, and fortunately someone was able to give her a jump. Her savings are at an all-time low and she doesn't know what she'll do when they officially run out of money.

She makes her way into the living room, to the corner farthest away from the bedrooms. She switches on a small lamp clipped to the side of the makeshift bookshelf and feels herself relax as she looks at the space around her. Her creative corner. It's small, but it's hers. It's the one place where she can lose herself.

Dishes of colorful, gleaming bottle caps are lined up on a shelf, waiting to be transformed. Ava sits down, turns on the small radio, and preps her worktable. When it's ready, she begins.

She places a bottle cap on a steel bench block and begins to flatten the edges with a rubber mallet. It's satisfying, especially after the day she's had, but it goes by fast—only a few seconds around the rim and then again on the other side. After ten minutes she has a nice pile and even though she could do more, she stops.

She's going to be making hair clips and

bookmarks tonight, and maybe a bracelet if she has time. A lot of the local gift shops are trying to source products locally instead of having them shipped in. Ava knows she probably can't make a living doing this, but it's something she can do on her own time and doesn't cost her a lot of money.

She's always had excellent fine-motor skills—it was one reason being a dental assistant came so easily to her—and there's a simple precision that comes with jewelry making. She has good technique and an eye for color, even though she can't put much into her inventory. She's gone beyond simple magnets and earrings, and has found ways to make bottle-cap jewelry look good.

Ava knows it would solve a lot of their problems if she could find a way to go back to work as a dental assistant, but the truth is she hasn't even tried. After Bill died, Ava wondered if people knew about what had happened. She felt certain that news of their affair circulated among the other dental offices in the area. Her own embarrassment kept her from applying at first, and now too much time has passed. Any dental office she applies to will want job experience and a recommendation, and there's only one person who can give her one, the one person Ava hopes she'll never have to see again. Bill's partner, Dr. Strombauer.

She reaches for a plastic shoebox, pops off

the lid. Inside she has bags of images, sorted generally by color, already cut in one-inch circles. She doesn't overthink this part, will use whatever calls out to her. A hummingbird, a music note, a man on a bicycle. She'll drop a few beads into the resin, knowing that they'll float around until the resin sets. Ava likes the randomness, likes how you don't know how it will turn out until it's all done. Ava chooses a handful of possibilities and fans them out on the table.

Her favorite part is next. Her fingers glide through a plastic container of beads, mostly glass, some lampwork, some seed, some crystal. They sparkle under the light, small bursts of color that seem so hopeful, so happy. *Look at us,* they seem to say. She scoops out a thimbleful and pours it carefully onto her bead mat.

She works quickly, quietly, her ear trained to the bedroom as the local Avalon station plays late-night favorites. A familiar song comes on and she stops, pliers in hand, as she listens and remembers. Smiles. Laughter. Love. This same song playing in the background, piped into the dental office from the stereo in back, a selection of hits that they got in the mail each month.

She misses Bill.

The thought stops her, paralyzes her. Ava forces herself to breathe, not wanting the emotion to take over, but not wanting to forget, either. She can't ever forget him.

Bill, the man she loved, the man who gave her Max. She wishes Bill could have seen his son, held him once, had a chance to brush his lips against Max's sweet brow. She wishes she could give that to Max, that little piece, but she can't. Bill died before Max came into the world. Max will never know his father.

Ava closes her eyes.

And it's not just Max, it's her, too. She wishes Bill was here, wishes he was still making plans with her, telling her it's going to be all right, that they're going to find a way, that things are going to work out fine—no, better than fine. Great. Beyond expectation. A new life for both of them, together. He'd said this, and she'd believed him.

So now . . . what? This aloneness is the hardest part for Ava. The separateness. Bill's mother, Max's biological grandmother, has made it clear that she wants nothing to do with them, so there is only one person left.

Ava has written her letters but hasn't received a response. Ava doesn't even know if she still lives in Avalon. It's been four years, after all, and maybe she's moved on, like Ava should, but can't. Or maybe it's still too soon, and Ava can't take a hint and leave well enough alone. If it was just about Ava, she'd already be gone, her bags packed. But it's not just about Ava—it's about Max.

The wire slips from the pliers and sends beads

flying across the living room. Ava gasps—she'd brought out the Swarovski crystals especially for this bracelet, wanting it to be the centerpiece of her collection. She watches as the crystals scatter in the air and then drop into the thick carpet, instantly obscured.

She drops to her knees, wills herself not to cry. She knows how life works, at least her life up to this point—if you wait for the other shoe to drop, it will. She isn't going to be like that anymore. She's going to think only good thoughts for her and Max. She's going to find a job, she's going to fix the car, she's going to find each and every crystal. She's going to do what she can to give him the very best life she can. And it's all going to be fine. Strike that—it's going to be beyond expectation. Good things. One miracle after another.

Yes.

For a moment Ava believes it so fully her eyes spot the first crystal, sparkling from within the deep pile. But when she reaches for it, it transforms itself into a piece of plastic, a small broken piece from one of Max's toys. And then she hears it, a small cry from her bedroom as Max discovers that she's not there. He calls for her, his voice sleepy and uncertain, and then full of panic. Ava knows the room looks dark and murky through his eyes, thick blurs that won't correct themselves into recognizable shapes until he puts his glasses on. Ava is torn, but only for a moment. She stands up, turns off the lamp and radio, plunging the apartment into darkness once again.

"I'm coming, Max."

Christopher Barlowe, 55
More Than Meets the Eye
Photography Studio

"Oh, you look great. Really, you do. You're going to love this! You're a natural and, wow, that's it, that's the look! That's a definite keeper. I think you're going to be happy with these. I really, really do."

Christopher Barlowe has been taking pictures and snapping shots since he was twenty, and some of his travel and creative work has shown up in magazines, won a few awards. In the past couple of years he's earned enough not only to support himself and his family, but to buy the lot next door and build a studio. He can walk to work in his pajamas, though he never has—he still gets up and shaves and dresses exactly as if he were going to his old place down on Main Street. He's proud of what he does, and doesn't take it any less seriously because his studio is less than sixty seconds from his kitchen.

When people ask him what he does for a living, he hands them his card. They see the collage of portraits on the back, see the word "Photographer" on the front and write him off as some guy who only takes senior portraits and wedding photos. He does that, too, and actually enjoys it, but there's so much more to the job than standing behind a lens.

Once he had an apprentice who thought getting into photography would be a way to make a quick buck. Christopher told him, "If you want to be good, you're not just a photographer. You're part psychologist, part sociologist. You have to understand your subject, help them feel good about themselves, about being in front of the camera. If they're having a bad day or feeling nervous, you have to help them feel better. They should leave feeling really good about the shoot, and about themselves."

The apprentice didn't listen of course. He started his own portrait business the following spring, offered cut-rate discounts and coupons, bragged about how good he was and how bad the competition was, including Christopher. He didn't make it to Christmas.

More Than Meets the Eye is still here, and business is thriving. No small feat since everyone has a digital camera or some kind of photo-editing software, and can easily order large prints online, even on canvas. For a while, business slowed to a stop and Christopher was worried, not sure if things would pick up again and if they didn't, what he would do. He loves Avalon—both he and his wife grew up here and now the same can be said for their girls—but things got dicey for a while.

The month he thought he'd have to close shop for good was the worst. He was in the old location looking at a stack of bills, wondering if this was it. It was very depressing and his wife had gone home crying, sad that they might have to leave and start over somewhere new. He was sad, too.

Someone knocked on his door then. He looked up and saw that he hadn't even remembered to turn the sign from CLOSED to OPEN, that's how distracted he was. He saw an umbrella and a bob of silvery-blue hair. It was one of the ladies from his neighborhood. Bettie Shelton.

He hurried to let her in. It had been raining outside that day, cats and dogs as it sometimes does in the spring, and she stamped her feet on the welcome mat to get all the water off her galoshes. She leaned the umbrella against the outside of the door.

"Just stopping by to give you this," she said. She handed him a stack of business cards. They had her name on them, along with her phone number and address. *Scrapbooking supplies,* it read, *for all your memory-keeping needs.*

"Um," he'd said, not sure what to do.

She pulled out a small business card stand adorned with fake jewels and ribbon. "It was a good day when they invented the glue gun," she said. "So, Chris, I'm thinking if you put these out for your customers and they buy anything from me, I can give them an extra five, make that ten, percent off. They just have to show the card. I have a little code in the corner, see? So I'll know the business came from you. I'll extend the discount to you, too."

He put her cards and stand by the small cash register. "I'll put them out," he said, "but you should know that I may not be in business much longer. People aren't spending money on items like photography anymore."

"What? Don't be ridiculous," Bettie scoffed. She looked around the studio, took in the pictures on the walls, the books of photographs in the seating area. "It's a matter of adjusting to the times, that's all."

"Yeah, well, if you figure out how to do that, let me know." Christopher turned his attention back to the mess on his desk, but not before he saw her scowl.

"What, you're throwing in the towel already? You haven't even begun to figure this one out." Bettie shook her head, obviously disappointed. "For instance, I've been noticing that more people are using stock images these days. You should as well."

"But everyone's doing that," he told Bettie. "I don't see why anybody would want to buy stock images from me when they can get them from lots of other places online."

"Holy smokes!" she retorted. "With that attitude I'm amazed you're still in business at all!" She pointed to one of his favorite photos on the wall, an image of a man with his grandson, sitting on a bench in Avalon Park. "Look at that. You capture not only the connection between the two of them, but *where* they are. That boy will always have special memories when he goes to the park—he'll always think of his grandfather. Or why not spend your free time taking pictures of landmarks around Avalon? I'm sure lots of businesses might like you to get photos for them, too. Proprietors standing in their doorways, for example. Like Hal at the butcher shop, swinging his cleaver. Or Mason Cribbs, driving his snow plow in the winter. Or Tessa Bridges when she's taking out a fresh loaf of bread from her oven. We're always telling people to buy local, maybe *show* them what buying local means, you know?" She played with the ribbons on her business card holder, trying to figure out how they'd look best.

Christopher was skeptical, but intrigued. What was he doing moping behind a desk, waiting for someone to call with business? He should be doing what he does best—standing behind a lens.

And then he got discouraged again. "But who would buy those?" he asked.

"I would," Bettie said, standing tall. "In fact, I'd like to commission you to take a photo documentary of me and my scrapbooking society. A few nice black-and-white photos from our meetings that we can save in our archives. I might also use them for Christmas cards."

Bells started going off in Christopher's head. Not warning bells, but the kind that let you know that inspiration is brewing.

Christopher thought about what Bettie said, about putting a face to a name, about encouraging small business owners to show their customers what they were about. He knew he could capture this better than anyone else. These people put their hearts into what they did. It was their passion. And it was up to Christopher to show that to everyone else.

He started with Bettie and the Avalon Ladies Scrapbooking Society. He took pictures at a meeting, then went to the homes of some members and took pictures of their craft spaces, their albums. The result was four more jobs, and he started shooting pictures for people who wanted to get grants for their nonprofit organizations, who were chronicling their businesses, who wanted compelling, well-shot images for their own marketing and promotional purposes. He used this same approach with his own business, setting up self-portraits so people could see him in action. Six months later, he was out of debt. Nine months later, he'd made almost as much money as he did the previous year. By the end of his second year, he'd had his best year ever.

Anyone can take a picture, and that's the truth.

But what he tells prospective clients is that not everyone can capture a person, or an image, or an emotion. There's a creative engagement that happens when you look through the lens. This is not a haphazard endeavor, but one that you enter into with great care and focus. You see what matters most, and then you snap a picture of it for all the world to see.

Chapter Six

Frances gazes dreamily at the pink petticoats, the white lace. She's standing outside Margot West's new store, a catchall gift shop selling beauty and body care, wooden toys, knitwear, and baby clothes. There's a sign in the window, AVON PRODUCTS SOLD HERE, and Frances is reminded of her own childhood, the round boxes of talcum powder her mother used to buy from their neighbor, Mrs. Granger. Frances herself had a small yellow pin, a bird whose tummy would pop open to reveal a small pot of lip balm. It was a silly thing but she loved it, and she wishes now she had more keepsakes from her childhood.

Brady is having a full-on conversation with himself, still on a sugar high after the ice cream cone from lunch. Frances couldn't help it—he didn't want the chicken fingers, didn't want the macaroni and cheese, refused a peanut butter and jelly sandwich. He pointed to another young child sitting in the booth next to them, a child who had already eaten her lunch and was now enjoying a chocolate cone with sprinkles. Nick and Noah were in school, Noah having started kindergarten this fall. So it's now just the two of them, Mom and Brady, having this time together. Frances didn't want to spoil it.

She had tried several times to talk to him about

his baby sister who was on her way to joining the family, but Brady had stared at her blankly, as if she were from another planet. *Baby who? Baby what?* his expression seemed to read.

Frances sighs. She should know better than try to put this on a three-year-old. She drew a picture the other day with him, making six smiling faces for their family instead of five. Brady had shaken his head and crossed out the smallest one, his fingers wrapped tightly around the crayon, then passed the picture back to her, satisfied.

He'll figure it out when she gets here, Reed had reassured her when she called him at work upset. *Let him be.*

Let him be, let him be. Frances had agreed but now, standing in front of Margot's shop, she has an idea.

"Brady, let's go get some things for Mei Ling's care package!" she exclaims, her voice more animated than usual.

Brady points to a toy train in the window. "Train! Train! I want to see!"

"Yes, a train," Frances says as she pushes the door open and ushers him inside. They're greeted with a blast of cold air and Frances catches a whiff of lavender. She feels herself begin to relax as Margot looks up and waves from the register.

"All blue-dot items are ten percent off today," Margot says. "And I have a special bath and body care promotion going on. Buy one, get one free."

"Thank you," Frances says as Brady makes a beeline for the train set in the window.

"That's just for display," Margot tells her. "Been in the family for years." She picks up a smaller wooden train set, painted in primary colors, tucked safely behind the cellophane packaging. "Look, a blue dot!" The look on her face is pure surprise, as if she had no idea.

Frances nods politely. "We'll think about it," even though she knows there's no way she's bringing another train set into their house.

Or airplanes or fire trucks. Or cars of any kind.

No more marble mazes or racetracks or Legos. Frances is going to clean out and ban the eight million golf balls Reed brings back from the golf course. Noah threw one at the oven door when he was four and it cost them $150 to replace it.

What else? No more mismatched play tool sets. No more rockets, guns (all gifts, not her idea), or Mr. Potato Heads. The boys have plenty, but Frances is ready for something more gender neutral. Something quieter. Prettier.

Her eyes drift to the miniature tea party kit. Real ceramic cups, teapot, creamer and sugar bowl, tiny spoons and saucers and plastic finger sandwiches. She wants to swoon.

"Those have no phthalates or BPA," Margot informs her proudly. "And I have these adorable petit fours dessert toys that would go with it beautifully. They're hand knitted by Maureen Nyer—the tops are made from felt. All locally made."

Frances gasps at a small chocolate cupcake dotted with white stitches that look like sprinkles. "Brady, look! It's like the real thing!"

Brady doesn't bother to look over, and instead concentrates on pushing the train through a tunnel.

"I'll get them all," Frances says, even though she knows she can't send them to China. Their adoption agency is very specific about what can go into a care package, but that's all right. She'll save it for when Mei Ling is actually here, add it to the growing collection of special items that Frances is putting aside for her.

Frances finds a few more items that can go into the care package—a small picture album, a doll, some fabric hair clips, a coloring book of Avalon Park. Mei Ling is in a foster home in Guangzhou instead of an orphanage, but Frances is pretty sure they don't speak English. She passes on the board books filled with ABC's and buys a couple of postcards of Avalon instead, hoping that Mei Ling will fall in love with this small town that will be her home.

Margot is ringing her up when a young woman enters the store.

"Hannah!" Margot exclaims. "I was wondering when you were going to come by with more brochures. People have been asking about your music classes, you know."

Frances watches as Hannah Wang gives Margot a hug. Hannah is somewhat of a celebrity, a former cellist with a famous orchestra in New York or Chicago, Frances doesn't quite remember. She doesn't know Hannah personally, but remembers her from the prior year when Avalon was baking friendship bread for a neighbor town that had been devastated by floods.

"I just added a master class," Hannah explains as she hands Margot a stack of brochures. "And another beginner's class, so I had to redo everything. This should last you awhile, though." She turns and smiles at Frances. "Hi, I'm Hannah."

"Frances Latham." They shake hands and Frances is struck by how graceful and refined Hannah seems to be. She looks like she's in her mid- or late twenties. Hannah has the figure of a dancer, tall and lean, her sleek dark hair pulled back in a simple chignon. "We actually met briefly last year. At Madeline's."

"The night we baked for Barrett," Hannah remembers, nodding. "That's right! It's nice to see you again."

"You too."

Hannah spies Brady by the wooden train set. "Is this your son? He's adorable."

"That's Brady," Frances says. "He's my

youngest. I have three boys, if you can believe that. Nick is eight and Noah is five. Brady here is three."

Margot lets out a low whistle, either impressed or from sympathy, but Hannah laughs. "I believe that your hands are full, that's for sure," she says. "My boyfriend is from a family of four boys so I know how crazy it can get. His mother's always telling me stories about how much trouble they used to get into when they were growing up."

"Hannah dates Jamie Linde," Margot explains. "He drives a truck for UPS." She takes Hannah's brochures and walks to the front of the store where a small table and community bulletin board have been set up.

"Jamie?" Frances gasps. "Of course we know Jamie! I just put his photo in our photo album!"

"Your photo album?"

"He dropped off the referral letter for our daughter, Mei Ling. Well, she's not our daughter yet, but she will be. We're adopting from China. I got a picture with Jamie when he delivered the letter the other day."

"I remember that!" Hannah exclaims, then blushes. "I hope you don't mind, but Jamie told me that there was a family in Avalon who was going through a Chinese adoption. I think that's wonderful, Frances."

"Us too," Frances says, grinning. It feels good to talk about it with someone. She's been careful in sharing the news, not wanting to navigate the barrage of questions, not wanting to get everyone's hopes up including her own, but now she feels almost giddy with relief. She's thrilled that someone else knows, and Hannah looks genuinely happy for her. "We're hoping she'll be with us by Christmas at the latest. I know it's only a few months away, but it feels like forever."

"I'm so excited for your family," Hannah tells her. "And it's just a matter of time—she'll be here before you know it."

Frances smiles, grateful. "Thank you, Hannah."

Hannah returns the smile. "I hope I'll have a chance to see you again, maybe meet your daughter when you bring her home."

Frances nods. "I'd like that, too." Her eyes drift to the geometric clock on the wall and she gasps. "Oh, I'm late. The boys will be coming home from school." Frances quickly gathers her things, wishing she could stay and talk some more. "Please tell Jamie we say hi."

"I will." Hannah waves as Frances bids Margot goodbye and ushers a reluctant Brady out of the store. The minute they step outside they're met with a blast of blazing heat, but Frances doesn't mind, not even when Brady whines and insists that she carry him the rest of the way, which she does. By the time they reach the car, both the bags and Brady are heavy and Frances is covered in sweat, but she's too happy to care. Talking to

Hannah about Mei Ling has made it all the more real. They've been approved, they have their referral, they have Mei Ling. Frances is going to have to practice saying that she has four children now, because Mei Ling is going to be Frances's daughter, and, like Hannah said, it's only a matter of time before she'll be coming home to Avalon.

Isabel stares at the envelope, postmarked Barrett. It's addressed to her, the handwriting unfamiliar, but in the upper left-hand corner, Isabel sees the return address, the name.

A. Catalina.

"Whatcha got there?" Bettie Shelton calls from next door. She's also checking her mail, and Isabel can see Bettie's mailbox is stuffed with catalogs and magazines. "Pen pal?"

Isabel doesn't respond, just closes the mailbox door with a slam.

She's climbing the steps to her porch when suddenly a worn board gives. Isabel grabs the handrail and struggles to keep her balance.

"I told you so!" Bettie tells her. "Good thing it didn't happen during the meeting, otherwise you'd have a lawsuit on your hands!"

Isabel shoots Bettie an annoyed look before putting her mail down to inspect the board. It's rotted through, the board soggy and weak. As Isabel glances around her porch, she sees the spot where Bettie stepped through last week, and a couple more soft spots, too. Bill used to take care of all this, pressure washing the porch annually, the weatherproofing, the staining. Suddenly, Isabel can see the sum of her neglect. The entire porch looks like a danger zone.

"I have two copies of *Crafters Today*," Bettie calls to Isabel. "Want one?" She waves the magazine in the air like a flag.

If Bettie thinks Isabel is going to forget about what happened the other night, she's sorely mistaken. Isabel's still finding miscellaneous ribbon and eyelets everywhere. She goes into her house and closes the door, feeling the house sigh along with her.

It's so quiet. That was the first thing Isabel had noticed after Bill left—how quiet the house suddenly was. Even if she and Bill were in separate parts of the house, doing their own thing, there were always footsteps, the sounds of shuffling paper, of running water. Simple reminders that you were not alone.

She walks into the kitchen, looking through her mail when her hand rests on the envelope, her name and address written in small, careful script. Isabel feels her heart clench.

It's the third one she's received since Bill's death. Whatever that woman has to say, Isabel isn't interested in hearing it.

She throws the letter into the trash and heads out the back door to the shed where she finds the crowbar. She marches to the front of the house and straight to the porch. A few minutes later, the rotten board is gone.

An hour later, Isabel's torn up her entire front porch without a clue as to what to do next. She steps back to survey her work, a bit appalled at the mess she's made, then tosses the crowbar onto the grass in defeat. It started with that single rotten board on the steps and then Isabel had gotten carried away, enjoying the satisfaction that comes with tearing something up, the creak of old nails reluctantly being pulled from the wooden framing, the boards cracking and breaking, brittle. At first she thought fresh planks of wood were in order, and she liked the idea of everything being new, not only the one busted spot. Except now she sees she's gotten in over her head and it's going to cost her double to find someone to finish the job.

A truck pulls up in front of her house. What now? Isabel watches as the woman she met at the scrapbooking meeting climbs out and heads up her walk, waving as she does so. Evelyn something. No, Yvonne. The in-house technician/plumber.

Caught off guard, Isabel waves back.

"Fixing your porch?" Yvonne calls as she approaches.

"Destroying it is more like it," Isabel says with a grimace. It all seems so hopeless. She wishes she could undo what she's done, but it's too late. "It seemed like a good idea when I started."

Yvonne grins. "I wanted to stop by to tell you that a lot of these old houses are having plumbing issues," she says. "You might want to have it checked out. Wouldn't want it to slow up the sale of your house." She nods at the FOR SALE sign.

"Well, it's not selling yet. Besides, I figure the new owners can take care of it."

"Yeah, I get it. I thought I should mention it, though—Bettie's was the fourth house this month. I'm going to tell all the other neighbors, too. All things being equal, if you've already addressed the problem it might make your house stand out from the others."

Isabel considers this, knows Yvonne has a point. "How much would this cost me?"

"There are plenty of plumbers who can take a look and give you an estimate, but you could probably take a look yourself and do your own assessment. You seem pretty handy."

"Me?" Isabel scoffs. "I'm the least handy person I know."

Yvonne peers up at the porch. "Could've fooled me. I see lots of remodels—you did a good job there. Framing's still intact." She looks at the boards on the lawn. "And you still have some pretty good boards there."

"Yeah, I figured that out a bit too late. Story of my life."

Yvonne raises an eyebrow but doesn't say anything.

"And," Isabel says abruptly, leaning forward, "I'm sorry, but I have to ask. How is it that a plumber has perfectly plucked eyebrows? I mean, is that a job requirement?" Isabel knows she's being blunt but she doesn't care. How do some women make looking good seem so easy?

Instead of being offended, Yvonne laughs. "Old habits die hard," she says. "I think my mother put a pair of tweezers in my hand when I was ten. I was trained to pluck away unsightly body hair the second I got it."

Isabel flops down on the steps. "I bet you work out, too?"

"My job is enough of a workout," Yvonne says. "But I swim at the Avalon pool whenever I get a chance. I'm thirty-two and it definitely takes more work to stay in shape."

"I hate exercising," Isabel says. Suddenly she feels old and frumpy.

"You probably burned a decent amount of calories pulling up those boards," Yvonne points out. "Beats the rowing machine, you know?"

"Yeah." Despite feeling sorry for herself, Isabel gives a small smile. "Hey, maybe I should reshingle my roof while I'm at it."

"Why not? You could remodel your kitchen, too."

"Or install a drop ceiling in my laundry room."

"Retile the bathrooms."

"Insulate my attic."

"Get new window treatments."

At this Isabel makes a face and the two women burst out laughing. "I don't even know what a window treatment is," Isabel says. "Curtains and blinds?"

Yvonne nods. "Basically anything that goes in, on, or around a window. My mother lives for window treatments." She gives a slight roll of her eyes. "It's sad, really."

The women look at each other and burst out laughing again.

"Isabel!" The two women turn to see Bettie Shelton standing in the frame of her doorway. "I certainly hope you plan to clean up that mess today. It's unsightly and I wouldn't want the neighbors to think your house has fallen to disrepair."

Isabel's finally in a good mood and she's not about to let Bettie get the better of her. "Bettie, I'm afraid that's not going to happen," she calls back. She gives a cheerful wave, something she's never done before. "I'm beat. Maybe tomorrow. Or after the weekend. By Halloween for sure!"

Bettie purses her lips and retreats into her house.

Yvonne looks a bit guilty. "She's a sweet lady," she says as Bettie slams her door. "She means well."

"Oh, you don't know her like I do," Isabel says.

"Did you forget that she commandeered my house Thursday night? Without my permission? And with your help, I might add?" There's an accusatory tone in her voice.

Yvonne frowns. "I know, I'm sorry. I had no idea. I thought you were friends."

"Yeah, well." Isabel walks over to the pile, gives one of the boards a kick. "I don't have a lot of friends."

The women are silent as they survey the pile of boards. Isabel's little demolition project has attracted a few neighbor kids.

"Hey lady, what are you going to do with all those boards?" A boy with a shock of red hair and a smattering of freckles leans forward on the handlebars of his bike. Jack or Jake, Isabel always forgets.

Isabel glances at him. "I haven't thought that far ahead. Why? You got any ideas?"

"We want to build a clubhouse," another kid tells her. "Over in Lucy Fitzpatrick's yard. She's got the biggest yard."

Isabel considers this. That would certainly solve her problem with the boards and Yvonne is nodding in approval of the idea.

"We could help if you like," Yvonne offers and there's a collective whoop from the kids.

We? Isabel shoots Yvonne an annoyed look but then thinks, what the heck. It's Saturday and it's not like she has anything else going on.

"Fine," she says, then rolls her eyes when Yvonne does a high five with the freckly kid. "But you should probably ask your parents first. And Lucy Fitzpatrick."

"They'll say yes," he tells her over his shoulder as they quickly bike away. "We'll be right back!"

Yvonne's phone rings and she steps away to take the call. Isabel starts to sift through the boards, putting the ones in better condition in one pile, the mediocre ones in another. Maybe she'll put in that composite decking, something low maintenance that can be sprayed down with a hose.

A shadow falls over her and Isabel says, "Do you think they want these rotten ones, too? If they cut around the bad spots they might be able to salvage the—"

"Isabel?"

Isabel looks up expecting to see Yvonne but sees a young woman instead, looking at her tentatively. Isabel tilts her head to the side, unable to place her, then stiffens when she realizes who it is.

Ava. Ava Catalina, her husband's dental-assistant-turned-lover. The woman responsible for changing Isabel's life forever.

Isabel sucks in her breath. She feels frozen in place, unable to move. Yvonne is still on the phone, her back to them, unaware that they've been joined by an unwanted third party. Isabel straightens up and holds herself tall, is pleased to see she has a couple inches on Ava.

She wants to stare Ava down, but something's wrong. The Ava standing in front of her is different. Gone are the colorful sea greens and sky blues. Ava's wearing a faded skirt that may have been red at one time, but now it's a dull shade of pink, a dusty rose. She's wearing a white T-shirt and plain sandals on her feet. Her nails are no longer painted but short and plain. And her hair—Isabel remembers it used to be a thick and lustrous chocolate, shiny and past her shoulders. Now it's cut short pageboy style, cropped close to her face. It's still annoyingly flattering but this is not the Ava Isabel remembers.

Ava takes a small step forward, clutches a cheap denim purse slung across her body. "I know you probably don't want to talk to me. I didn't want to show up this way, but I didn't think you'd answer your phone if I called. I sent you a letter . . ."

Isabel finds her voice. "That letter's in the trash."

"Oh." Ava swallows. "Well, I wanted to talk. I thought we should talk."

Isabel shakes her head. "I have nothing to say to you." She glances over at Yvonne who is still talking on the phone but is now looking at them, curious.

Ava follows her gaze uncertainly. "If now isn't a good time . . ."

Isabel steps forward. Ava shrinks back, her eyes wide. She's scared, Isabel realizes. *Of me.*

"I think you should go," Isabel says tightly.

Ava's hands are trembling as she unzips her purse. She pulls out a piece of paper. "Here's my number if you want to call. I'm also in the book . . ."

"Get off my property!" Isabel shouts.

The paper flutters from Ava's fingers. She turns and flees down the walk, down the street to where a green Jeep is parked. The windows are down and Isabel sees a child's car seat, the top of a child's head. Ava is crying as she fumbles for the door handle. She manages to pull the driver's door open and get inside. She makes a hasty U-turn, narrowly missing an oncoming car that swerves out of the way.

Isabel bends down to pick up the piece of paper. MAX AND AVA, it reads. And a phone number. Isabel folds the paper and tears it in half. Then again, and again, and again.

"Wow." Yvonne has come up behind her. "You weren't kidding about the friend thing." She shields her eyes from the sun as she stares at the Jeep disappearing from view.

Isabel turns to see the neighborhood bearing down on them. The kids are excited, chattering a mile a minute and arguing about who gets what.

In a matter of minutes her front yard is cleared of the boards, a parade of parents and children heading over to Lucy Fitzpatrick's house where someone has set up a small lemonade stand, twenty-five cents a cup.

Yvonne grabs her toolbox as Isabel tosses the scraps of paper into the air, expecting a breeze to carry them away, but instead they flutter to the ground. One torn piece of paper lands right side up.

MAX, it says.

Connie wakes up with a start. There's a thin bead of sweat on her forehead and the room is hot, almost suffocating. She doesn't like to run the air conditioner at night, opting instead for the ceiling fan, but she'd forgotten to turn it on before she went to sleep.

The digital clock by her bed reads 2:00 a.m. Connie kicks off the covers and lays there for a second, trying to cool off, but it's impossible. She gets up and feels along the wall for the ceiling fan switch and flicks it on. She moves to the balcony and swings the doors open, hoping for a breeze, but the air is still. There's a rustle in the dark bushes below her.

"Serena?" she whispers. She's built a sturdier fence, one with a gate Serena can't open, but Connie wouldn't put it past her. She discovered quickly how much fun having a goat can be.

Connie found an old green dog house in the shape of an igloo and cleaned it up, then put it in Serena's pen. Serena had seemed indifferent at first, but then Connie found her snoozing in it later that afternoon. It's since become one of her favorite things, and she'll hop on top with her little feet, queen of the mountain, and will call for Connie to come and play.

Now, Serena is oddly quiet and Connie wonders what kind of trouble she's gotten herself into. Connie whispers her name again and there's more thrashing below, but no goat. Connie hurries back to her room and opens the bedroom door.

In the hallway she bumps into Madeline, who jumps in alarm. "Goodness," Madeline says, clutching her chest. A thin robe is tied over her nightgown. "I heard something outside so I thought I'd go check. I think your goat may be out again."

"I know," Connie says. She hopes Madeline won't ask her if she's talked to the vet or put a GOAT FOUND poster up at the feed store, because she hasn't.

"Dolores says Walter is a light sleeper," Madeline says. "Here's hoping he's not out taking a midnight stroll."

At the mention of the Lassiters, Connie picks up her pace. She's anxious to get to Serena before Mr. Lassiter does.

Madeline flicks on the light for the back porch

and opens the back door. There's more thrashing and then the sound of someone muttering. A bleat—Serena's call—from the back of the yard, far away from where Connie and Madeline are standing. It's a bleat of warning, of alarm. Connie feels the hairs on her neck stand up.

She steps in front of Madeline and peers outside. "Hello?" she calls. Madeline has edged backward toward the phone on the wall, her hand on the receiver, ready to dial 911. "Hello?" Connie calls again.

The bushes give a shiver. Connie steps back warily, ready to run.

Bettie Shelton stumbles out of the bushes, small leaves strewn in her hair, dressed in her nightgown, dirty slippers on her feet.

"Darjeeling tea!" she snaps, then turns on her heel and disappears into the dark night.

Wally Miller, 62
Founder, Men in Aprons

"Okay, here's what we have: Mr. Jeffreys is putting in the shepherd's pie, Frank Arrington is doing the pickled tongue, Ronnie Stevens has his fried chicken, R.L. Yelverton has the fish muddle, Koji Takahashi is doing *tai chazuke*— did I say that right?—and Charlie Knox is putting in his squirrel Brunswick stew. Did I miss anything?" Wally Miller looks up from his notes and glances around the room.

R.L. raises his hand. "You forgot Winslow's dessert. He went down to visit his daughter in St. Louis but I'm sure he'd want to include it."

"Right!" Wally jots this down. "What was in it again?"

"Heavy cream with apple brandy—"

"—white raisins—"

"Don't forget the crystallized pineapple—"

"—and chopped nuts," Wally concludes. "Yes, I think that's it."

Jordan Adams raises his hand, looking abashed. He's a large man with a ruddy complexion, but the members of the group notice that the tips of his ears are tinged pink. He clears his throat. "I changed my mind. I'd like to include my jellied ham loaf, if that's all right."

The group claps him on the back, their mood

appreciative but somber. Jordan Adams is one of the newest members of the group, his wife having passed last year.

"That's great, Jordan. We'd love to have it." Wally gives him a kind smile. Jordan wipes his eyes with the back of his hand.

"Is oyster stuffing considered seafood?" someone asks.

"I don't see why not," Wally says. "Would you like to add that, Gerald?"

"Yes."

"Oyster stuffing," Wally writes. "Is that the one with the Worcestershire sauce? I think you made it last Fourth of July."

Gerald nods. "The fried bacon really gives it a pop."

"That it does. So, if I look back at what we have and what we've just added, it looks like we have one hundred twenty-seven recipes, two over our goal. We have ourselves a cookbook, gentlemen!"

There's a hearty round of applause as the men congratulate themselves. A couple bring out handkerchiefs and pretend to sneeze.

Wally closes the fat binder, stuffed with recipes they've shared over the years. He's feeling a bit emotional himself, not quite believing that they've done it. They've gone and written themselves a cookbook, and a book printer in Rockford is going to publish it and help them distribute it.

Bettie Shelton had suggested the cookbook five years ago, but the men weren't sure if they wanted any kind of publicity. When she pointed out that it would be more than a special memento, but something that could help other people in the same situation, they started thinking about it.

The group had come together as a fluke, a few men staying after the weekly grief support group to exchange recipes or talk about what a struggle it was to cook for one. They'd all lost a spouse or someone close to them who took care of the things they had taken for granted before, like cooking. Everyone burned pans that first year, set off fire alarms, ended up staring into a pot full of canned soup and feeling so lonely they felt invisible.

So Wally suggested that they swap recipes and help each other out. Nothing too intimidating to start, but an identical recipe and shopping list they could all share each week, so they could compare notes the following week. It took a while, but they got better, more adventurous. Wally can always tell someone is on the road to recovery when they start pulling out their late spouse's cookbook or their grandmother's yellowed recipe cards. Almost every one of those meals will bring tears.

For Boyd Robby, it was his wife's sausage cakes, fried in lard. For Otto Warren, it was pressed veal. David Combs kept them stocked with shrimp gumbo for weeks—he wouldn't give up until he got it right.

For Wally, it was the Spanish pork chops that Virginia used to make. Lay the chops in a baking dish with a slice of onion, a slice of pepper, a heaping tablespoon of uncooked rice, topped with canned tomatoes and season generously. Into a four-hundred-degree oven for forty-five minutes and you have a meal to remember. He can picture Virginia smiling at him from across the table whenever he eats it. He wishes he could turn back time and make those chops for her. He knows she'd be proud at how far he's come.

So that's really what their cookbook is all about. Not just food, but memories. Each person is writing a small story about the recipe, about something funny that happened, about the first time they made it, about what it means. It's about sorrow and joy, about the mishaps in the kitchen as well as the successes. But most of all it's about the women who left a few hapless men behind, men who've learned to pick up a spatula, tie on an apron, and cook for themselves.

Chapter Seven

Connie yawns and turns over, still sleepy. The morning sun casts patterns on Connie's bed, the sunlight filtering through lace curtains.

She opens one eye and looks at the clock. Eight o'clock. Eight o'clock! Connie sits up in disbelief, then quickly gets out of bed and throws on some clothes. All she can remember is stumbling back up the stairs after Bettie Shelton almost scared the living daylights out of them. She must have turned off her alarm when she came back to bed.

Connie brushes her teeth and adds some hair gel into the palms of her hands before raking it through her hair with her fingertips. She runs out of the room and down the stairs, slowing only when she nears the already bustling tearoom.

A few of the regulars smile and say good morning. Connie returns the greeting as she hurries into the kitchen where Madeline is frying up some eggs in a skillet. "Madeline, I'm so sorry. My alarm didn't go off and I must have overslept . . ."

Her voice trails off when she sees Hannah Wang emerge from the pantry, her arms encircling a basket of potatoes, an apron tied around her waist. She smiles pleasantly when she sees Connie, lifting her chin in greeting. "Good morning, Connie."

"Oh. Hey, Hannah." Connie watches her place the potatoes by the basin and begin to rinse them. Even though they sometimes ask Hannah to come in and help when they're busy, it's usually Connie and Madeline in the kitchen. She hadn't expected to see Hannah here.

"Hannah called early this morning to see if we needed any help," Madeline explains as she slides the eggs onto a couple of plates. "As usual, her timing is perfect. I thought you could do with a little rest, Connie, after our exciting adventure last night. You've been working so hard lately." But instead of looking at Connie, Madeline is beaming at Hannah.

"I like being busy," Connie quickly says. "I don't need a break."

"You haven't taken a day since you started," Madeline reminds her.

"I like working," Connie says. She turns to Hannah. "And I don't want to put you out."

"It's no trouble at all," Hannah says easily. She begins to peel the potatoes. "I love being here, it's like my second home."

Madeline adds several strips of bacon to the plates, then goes to Hannah and gives her shoulders an affectionate squeeze. "You are welcome here anytime. I love having you here, too."

Connie frowns as she watches this exchange. She knows that Hannah's schedule is open and flexible, that she teaches music to kids and adults but also has some money from her years of playing and performing professionally. Hannah doesn't need a job, but Connie does.

Madeline adds a sprig of parsley to each plate. "Now, let's get these breakfast orders out for the Johnsons at table nine. I'll get the pancakes going for table six."

"I'll take those out, Madeline," Hannah says, and Hannah and Madeline exchange another smile, making Connie feel like a third wheel. Hannah and Madeline have a relationship that predates Connie and it always seems like they have an unspoken understanding of each other. Connie watches as Hannah wipes her hands, then picks up the plates and heads out to the tearoom.

Once Hannah is out of earshot, Connie turns to Madeline. "Hannah doesn't have to stay if she has somewhere else to go," she says. She pretends to scan the day's menu even though she knows it by heart. "I mean, I'm here now." She ties her apron around her waist.

Madeline glances outside where Hannah's polite laughter can be heard over the din of forks scraping against the china dishes and random conversations. "Oh, I think she's happy to be here. The regulars seem happy to see her, too."

That's exactly what Connie is worried about. Connie frowns as there's a bleat from the backyard. "But we don't . . ." she begins.

Madeline reaches for a large mixing bowl filled with pancake batter and gives it a quick stir before ladling out a portion onto the griddle. "I think your goat is calling you," she says.

"Serena can wait," Connie says impatiently. "We have customers. I can take over the pancakes, Madeline. Did you say table six?"

Madeline shoos her away. "Goodness, I'm already here, Connie. Go take care of your goat or we'll be hearing her complain all morning."

For the first time since Serena's arrival, Connie feels annoyed by her bleating demands. She picks an apple from the fruit bowl and steps out the back door into the yard. It's early but it's already starting to get hot, another clear, cloudless day. She makes her way through the path in the garden until she comes upon Serena resting atop her igloo, her legs folded beneath her.

"What do you need? Water?" Connie unlatches the gate and steps inside. Serena's water bowl is indeed empty, but Connie can tell by the damp earth around it that Serena has tipped the water out herself. There's plenty of grass and she knows Serena isn't hungry, but she tosses her the apple anyway. Serena doesn't move, just watches the apple bounce off the igloo and roll onto the ground.

"What's with you?" Connie asks as she picks up the water bowl. She heads out to the toolshed to get the water hose. She glances back and sees

Serena still sitting on the igloo, a bored look on her face.

Connie quickly rinses the water bowl and fills it with fresh water, glancing anxiously back at the house. Why does Hannah have to stay? Connie and Madeline have developed a rhythm that she can tell is already off because a third person is in the kitchen with them. It's nothing personal against Hannah, and Connie appreciates the other times that she's stepped in to help, but this is their regular morning crowd. *Her* crowd. The success of the tea salon is due in large part to their ability to turn over tables when it gets full. It's a delicate balance between keeping existing customers happy while making room for new ones. If Hannah's going to linger by the tables and chat all day, it's going to affect their bottom line.

Connie hurries back into the pen and puts the water bowl on the ground. Maybe if she puts Hannah to work at baking some fresh loaves of Amish Friendship Bread, it'll keep her in the kitchen and out of the—

Connie stands up and stares at the empty pen in front of her.

Serena is gone.

Connie quickly scans the spacious backyard, looking in all the usual places Serena tends to go to. Nothing. It's possible that she's trotted into the house, which she's done on numerous occasions, but Connie did remember to close the back door and Madeline is handy with the broom. She could also be in the front of the house, greeting customers or scaring them away, depending on her mood. Or, and this last and most likely option fills Connie with dread, Serena has headed over to the Lassiters'.

Connie is muttering under her breath as she hurries over to their neighbors, hoping Serena will be in their yard. It's become a bit of a routine now, though Connie is tiring of it and she suspects the Lassiters are, too. But when Connie looks over the fence, Serena's not there.

Connie walks to the front of the tea salon, scans the street up and down. With a sinking feeling, she realizes that Serena could be anywhere. Nosing through garbage, checking out gardens, looking for new friends. Traipsing around Avalon without a thought for Connie, about how her morning—and Madeline's—will be wrecked if Connie has to go out looking for Serena. Again.

"Connie?" Madeline appears at the front door, wiping her hands on her apron. "The phone is ringing madly. It seems like everyone has decided to have a meeting this morning and wants some baked goods to go with it."

"Serena's missing," Connie says, and feels the heat of tears. She scans the street one more time.

"Yes, well . . ." Madeline doesn't seem surprised. "Goats are like that. This one, at least.

Come on in, there's no sense in fretting. She'll turn up."

"But what if she doesn't?"

Madeline looks grim at the prospect. "Well, then, she doesn't. But if that happens, we'll figure out what to do, all right?"

Connie wipes her eyes with the back of her hand, then reluctantly turns back toward the house. Serena doesn't understand cars or traffic, doesn't take well to instruction of any kind. Connie can picture her in trouble, and who would bother to help? She's just a goat.

They walk into the house. Despite her agitation, Connie is comforted by the smell of buttermilk pancakes topped with fresh berries and warm syrup. When she sees that Madeline's made up a plate for her, she smiles gratefully.

"Don't forget to eat," Madeline reminds her sternly. "Finish up these pancake orders and then get yourself a bite."

Hannah is standing in front of the wooden cutting board. "Connie, I've peeled the potatoes. How do you want me to cut them?"

Connie quickly pours the pancake batter into perfect disks on the griddle. "Use the mandolin to slice them—we'll be doing scalloped potatoes for lunch. I filled some muffin tins last night with a raspberry and blackberry mix and those need to go in the oven. They're in the fridge and there's a streusel topping there as well. Madeline, I was

126

thinking we could take a few bags of Amish Friendship Bread starter from the freezer out back and make those olive oil loaves everyone seems to like."

Madeline nods and says, "I'll go grab some." They usually keep a starter going in a glass container on the counter, but it quickly gets away from them. Madeline and Connie have found that it's easier if they slow the fermentation process every now and then by refrigerating their starter and freeze any excess when it's time to divide the batter. It leaves them with plenty of starter for recipes whenever they need them, without the daily hassle of having to care and feed it.

Connie serves up the pancakes, then quickly eats her own breakfast. She fills a few to-go orders and starts on another round of pancakes.

"I've forgotten how busy it can get!" Hannah remarks with happy exhaustion as she moves the now-baked muffins onto a cooling rack. She deftly slides several loaf tins filled with a rosemary lemon olive oil Amish Friendship Bread batter into the oven and closes the door with a flourish.

Madeline gives Connie a wink. This is their life five days a week, sometimes more if they have a special event, no break for the holidays. Two meals a day with dinner orders to go, just the two of them.

The breakfast crowd is starting to thin and it's

time to get ready for the lunch rush. Connie clears a few tables, takes an order, then sees Bettie Shelton coming up the walk. She's pulling an oversized portable luggage stroller stacked with her telltale scrapbooking plastic bins. She's looking spry and well rested, and Connie wonders if last night was a dream.

"Pot of Darjeeling," Bettie says loudly when she walks through the door. She surveys the room critically, looking for the best spot. She settles at a table near the window and begins to unlatch her boxes.

Connie pulls a tin down from the shelf then spoons a few teaspoons of loose Darjeeling tea leaves into a teapot. As she adds the hot water she watches Bettie make a show about her new stencil samples, engaging the tables around her.

Connie brings a teapot, strainer, and teacup to Bettie's table. "So . . . that was some night last night, huh?"

Bettie frowns. "What?"

"You know," Connie prompts. "Last night? It was really late? You were out . . ."

Bettie stares at her blankly. "Out? I don't know what you're talking about."

Connie isn't sure if Bettie was sleepwalking or just embarrassed at being caught. But Bettie is looking at her, waiting for an answer, making Connie shift uncomfortably. "Never mind. Big moon, that's all."

"I must've missed it. I'm early to bed except on scrapbooking nights." Bettie scans the blackboard where Connie's written the daily specials. "I think I'll take the pancakes," she declares. She gives a satisfactory nod, pleased with her choice.

Connie raises her eyebrows in surprise. Bettie is notoriously cheap and she's never ordered food before. "They're $5.99, Bettie. Plus tax."

"I can read, Connie Colls. One order of pancakes, and get me a pot of Darjeeling tea." Bettie picks up a packet of stencils and frowns. "These don't look like lilacs, do they?"

Connie points to the teapot on the table. "Bettie, your Darjeeling tea is right there."

Bettie's brows furrow as she takes in the pot of tea in front of her. "Oh. Of course." She gives a sniff of indignation but her cheeks flush as she squints at a stencil sample in front of her.

Connie retreats to the kitchen, wary, and puts in the order for Bettie's pancakes.

"Look what I got!" Hannah says a few minutes later when she reenters the kitchen with some dirty dishes. Tucked under her arm is one of Bettie's scrapbook starter packets. "She gave it to me for free, isn't that nice?"

"Nothing's ever free with Bettie," Connie informs her, but Hannah doesn't seem to be listening. Connie glances outside and sees Bettie handing out business cards liberally as she floats from table to table. Connie frowns. "Madeline, I really think . . ."

But Madeline's moved next to Hannah and the two of them are giggling as they watch Bettie zero in on a potential customer. "Hmmm? What was that, Connie?"

Connie lets a pan drop into the sink with a clatter. "Nothing." Maybe she just needs to take her break and check on Serena. But as she begins to untie her apron, she remembers that Serena isn't there.

Connie picks up the phone to call the Lassiters. To her dismay, Walter Lassiter answers.

"Hello?" he barks into the phone.

"Mr. Lassiter, it's Connie Colls. Serena got out of her pen this morning, and I'm hoping that you'll give me a call if you see her—"

"Good riddance!" he snaps. "I found hoofprints in my garden this morning and my hydrangeas look like someone took a weed whacker to them!"

"Really?" Connie hears the hopefulness in her voice. "I mean, I'm sorry!" She looks out the window toward the Lassiters' backyard. If Serena found a way to get over there, then there's a chance she's still lurking about.

"If I see that goat again, I'm getting out the hose. Or worse!"

Connie hastily hangs up and makes a note to bring a casserole over to the Lassiters' first chance she gets.

There's a racket in the dining room. "Where's my tea?" demands Bettie.

"I'll get it," Hannah volunteers.

"But I already got it for her," Connie says. She turns to Madeline and gestures to the teapot sitting in the middle of Bettie's table.

Madeline frowns. "Maybe she's out of hot water. Hannah, why don't you go check . . ."

"No, I can do it," Connie says quickly, and cuts Hannah off as she heads into the dining room.

Bettie is scowling as Connie approaches her table. "Hey Bettie," Connie says casually. She lifts the teapot and sees it's still filled with hot water. She makes a point of pouring the tea into the teacup in front of Bettie. "There you go. All set?"

Bettie stares at the teacup as if it's sprouted wings. Then she turns to Connie, her eyes flashing angrily. "I'm on to you, Connie Colls!"

"What?" Connie says, bewildered. Suddenly they have the attention of the tea room. Bettie is red in the face as she looks at Connie. In fact, everybody is looking at Connie. How did that happen?

"You can't fool me! Now please get me some Darjeeling tea!"

Connie grits her teeth. She storms back into the kitchen, past the inquisitive looks, and is about to slam the teapot onto the counter.

"Let me take care of that," Madeline says, rescuing the teapot before it becomes a heap of useless shards.

Connie takes a dish towel and balls it up in frustration. "What's wrong with her? This tea was perfectly fine!"

Madeline sets about putting fresh leaves into a new teapot and adds hot water. "Maybe she's preoccupied," she says, but Connie can tell that she's not convinced.

There's a bit of commotion as a woman races into the salon. "There's a stray goat outside! It almost got me!" She fans herself as someone pulls out a chair for her.

Connie hurries to the window and sees that it is indeed Serena, munching on some grass. She feels a flood of relief. "Serena!"

She hurries outside, set on reprimanding the wayward goat, and finds herself on her knees instead, her arms wrapped around Serena's neck. Connie knows she's a sight but she doesn't care. After a few silent minutes—her clinging to Serena, Serena oblivious and eating grass as usual—Connie takes hold of Serena's rope collar and leads her back to her pen. Madeline and Bettie are standing in the doorway, watching.

"Well," she hears Bettie murmur. "Who would have thought it would be possible to love a goat? I've never heard of such a thing."

Madeline's voice is quiet, full of understanding.

"I suppose that's what makes us human," she says. "We can love anything, even the impossible."

"These are lovely." Margot West, owner of Avalon Gifts 'N More, bends over Ava's portable display box. She picks up one of the sparkly vintage rhinestone rings rimmed by a silvery bottle cap and slips it onto her finger.

"I burnished the brass ring finding to a gunmetal tone," Ava explains, embarrassed by the praise. The shops in Barrett had turned her away so this compliment comes as welcome relief. "That's new. Everything else is upcycled."

"Upcycled? Is that like recycled?"

"Recycled items make items of lesser value, but upcycled items repurpose things for equal or greater value." Ava points to a large rhinestone gracing the center of the ring, an orbit of small silver balls encircling it. "That used to be part of a brooch that was cracked and missing smaller rhinestones. I found it at a garage sale. The silver ball chain had been cut too short at a jewelry store and was in a box of discards. And, of course, the bottle cap. It's an antique cap from Reisch Brewery, which used to be in Springfield, Illinois." It had been an unexpected find, and Ava still isn't quite sure what to make of it. It had been in the bag Colin had given her, but the brewery hadn't been around since 1966. It didn't make any sense that he would be serving beers almost half a century old. "Taken individually, the value isn't much, but putting it together significantly increases its use and overall value, plus becomes an entirely new creation."

Margot holds out her hand to admire the ring. "You could even wear it with evening wear!" The large rhinestone winks at them.

Ava beams. She loves when people get it, when they see exactly what she sees. "I designed it to be versatile. It could go with a little black dress or jeans and a T-shirt. It'll look wonderful either way."

"I agree. I may have to put this aside for myself." Margot peers down at the rest of Ava's items. "So you have three rings, ten bookmarks, and ten of those adorable hair clips." She looks at the price list. "Well, I think I'll take them all."

"All?" Ava can't believe it. "I mean, that's great. Thank you!"

"The packaging is wonderful, too," Margot notes. *"Free Hearts."* She taps the small cellophane packets with Ava's triptych heart logo hand-stamped across the top on creamy card stock, three hearts in a row. "Touching and sweet, very nicely done. I think I'll put the hair clips and bookmarks in a basket and maybe put the rings with the jewelry and body care items. Let's see how we do with that and go from there."

"Thank you," Ava says. "Um, terms are net thirty . . ."

Margot waves her hand. "You're here, I can pay you now. It'll save me the stamp. Just give me a moment." She disappears into a small room in back separated by a pink gingham curtain.

Ava is grateful for the moment alone, so no one has to see the huge smile on her face, her damp eyes. Her first real sale! It's not much but it's a start, and the woman is taking all of her inventory, which means Ava doesn't have to worry about knocking on any more doors until she has more. Which she'll start on tonight. In fact, she can't wait.

She hovers by the wooden toys, admires the train set in the window. It's a nice shop, filled with something for everyone. Maybe she'll bring Max here sometime and see if there's anything he'd like for his birthday. Ava checks the price tag on one of the toys and gives a start. Maybe not.

The door opens and an elderly woman tumbles in, pulling a luggage cart behind her.

"Mercy, it is hot today," she mutters, touching her brow. She sets her cart upright and then picks up one of the mosaic-tiled hand mirrors by the door and checks her silvery-blue hair. She sees Ava in the reflection, and tosses the mirror back into the box.

"Who are you?" the woman demands. She marches up to where Ava is standing and Ava doesn't know what to do. "Where's Margot?"

"She's, um, in the back," Ava stammers, taking a step back. "She'll be right out."

"Are you the new shopgirl?" The woman is squinting at her.

"No, I had some business with her. With Margot. The owner."

"I know who Margot is," the woman retorts. "I just don't know who you are." Then a look of recognition crosses her face. "Wait a minute. Didn't you used to work in Dr. Kidd's dental office?"

Ava feels the heat race to her cheeks, feels her heart pounding in her chest. She remembers most of their patients, but not this one, and at any rate she has done her best to avoid running into anybody who might remember her. She knows no one will want to hear her side of the story, and she knows it will never be right in the eyes of most people. Even Ava doesn't feel completely right with it but it is what it is, and she's trying to be okay with it, not just for her sake, but for Max's.

Margot emerges from the back room. "Here we are." She hands the check to Ava and grins at the woman. "Oh, Bettie! I have to show you what Ava brought in. So original!" She gestures for Bettie to follow her to the register.

Ava edges toward the door. "Well, I should be going," she says, folding the check and tucking it into her purse. She doesn't even bother to see if the amount is right, she just wants to get out of there. "Thank—"

"How clever!" she hears Bettie exclaim.

"And look! I have one on!" Margot sticks out her hand and shows off her ring.

"Of course you'd choose the one with the biggest rock," Bettie sniffs. "It's just as well. I like this rose one here, with the vines. What is that?"

"It's a vintage gold button," Ava says. Despite wanting to leave she can't help adding, "It's resting on a champagne-pink bottle cap, which reflects onto the button, giving the entire piece a rosy glow."

"Oooh." Bettie slips it on and gazes at her finger. "How much?"

"I haven't priced these yet," Margot tells her.

"Margot West, are you turning down a sale? What kind of businesswoman are you?"

Margot looks put out. "If you'll give me a minute, Bettie, I'll figure it out. Anyway, aren't you here to drop off those scrap packs?"

Bettie nods. "The last of the summer soda-pop colors. I'll have the fall packs ready next week. It's more of a service to Society members than anything, mind you. I'm not always available when they want materials in between meetings."

"Well, I'll have to mark them up so I can make some kind of profit," Margot points out. "As a proper businesswoman, you understand."

The sarcasm isn't lost on Bettie, who glances at Ava still hovering by the door. "Where are you going?"

"I need to get back," Ava says, her mind a blank. "I have errands, and . . ."

"Amateurs," Bettie says to herself with a shake of the head. She waves to Ava's inventory on the counter. "You have a potential customer here. *Me*. You need to work on your sales pitch, present yourself as the *artiste*. Get my drift?"

Ava nods but doesn't move.

"So . . ." Bettie prompts. "Any day now. I'm not getting any younger standing here, that's for sure."

"Her bark is worse than her bite," Margot says to Ava, beckoning her. "Come on over and tell her what you told me."

Ava hesitates, then walks forward, her chin tilted up. "The ribbons and findings are new," she says, "but all the other items are upcycled or repurposed. The beads on the hair clips are vintage—I took them off a beaded purse that had a broken clasp and ripped lining. Everything's been thoroughly washed and, where necessary, treated with a clear coat to prevent any further rusting. All of these pieces are original, one of a kind, and should last a long time."

Both Margot and Bettie are nodding.

"I've been experimenting with stacking bottle caps, too," Ava continues, encouraged. "To create a more layered effect, like petals on a flower. Instead of a centerpiece like a rhinestone or antique button I put a picture in the center and fill it with a clear resin. Then I'll add some petite glass beads and a word like 'love' or 'gratitude.' If these sell, I'll bring some of those in, too. They're small tokens or charms that you can tuck into a birthday card or your purse."

Bettie is looking thoughtful and Margot gets a knowing look in her eye. "Uh-oh," she says to Ava.

"You know," Bettie says, straightening up, her voice suddenly full of tender endearment. "I think these would be perfect embellishments for a scrapbook page. So original, so creative, and you could undercycle—"

"Upcycle—"

"—whatever you have in your scrap box. Bits of glitter, a photo, and so on. Yes," Bettie says, nodding her head as if they were all in agreement. "That's perfect. You'll come to a meeting and do a demonstration, and of course you'll have an opportunity to sell your items, too. It's common practice to take a bit of a commission, a nominal courtesy fee if you will, but I'm happy to waive it in this one case. And if you think about it, it's perfect because we creative types need to stick together. "

Ava hesitates. "The meetings are in Avalon?"

"Of course! It's the Avalon Ladies Scrapbooking Society, after all. I'm the founder and president, Bettie Shelton." Bettie sticks out her hand as if they were just meeting and haven't been in conversation for the past ten minutes. "And you are?"

"Ava," Ava mumbles, not wanting to say more than she has to. If the meeting is in Avalon, Ava is out. She was nervous enough coming to Avalon Gifts 'N More after the disastrous attempt to talk to Isabel Kidd last week. It had shaken her to her core, the vehemence with which Isabel had responded to her, the anger. Ava was ready for the cold shoulder or the evil eye, but never did she think there would be a scene, an outburst.

In the years Ava had worked for Bill, Isabel had always treated her with polite distance. When Bill left Isabel, Ava quit her job and made a point of staying out of the way. And then when Bill died a couple of months later, it had been Isabel who made all the funeral arrangements since she was still Bill's legal wife. The only words that had passed between them were Isabel's request that Ava not attend the memorial because Bill's mother had made it clear that she didn't want to see the woman she was holding responsible for Bill's death. The fact that she was carrying her grandchild seemed to make no difference.

Afterward, Isabel had sent Ava a letter. It was short but clear: a savings account had been set up for Max because that's what Bill would have done had he lived, but that was all Isabel was able to do. Ava was grateful, but now she knows it's not enough, and it has nothing to do with the money. But after Isabel had reacted with so much anger on Saturday, Ava's not sure she can risk running into her again.

No one else. No one else.

"I'm sorry, but I have to go," Ava says. She shakes both of their hands. "Thank you, Margot. And it was very nice to meet you, Bettie." She turns and heads quickly to the door.

"You'll come to a meeting sometime, won't you?" Bettie calls after her. "Second Thursday of every month. We have refreshments and everything. And the ladies are wonderful, I'm sure you'll love them!"

Ava doesn't say anything, just quickly steps into the muggy August afternoon.

"Tell me you're going to shower before we go out." Isabel is sitting on the porch swing of Yvonne's house, her nose wrinkled. Isabel is wearing her usual ensemble, a white shirt with a skirt and lightweight cardigan, white sandals. She had gone online the night after she'd painted her walls, in search of a pair of shorts, when she saw row after row of summer whites on sale. Every imaginable piece of clothing, all available in white. It was like Garanimals for adults, a mix-and-match wardrobe that a child could put together. Or a thirty-eight-year-old woman who didn't want to spend an ounce of energy figuring out what to wear. As Isabel was pleased to discover, when you have a wardrobe of white, everything goes together. "Or are we taking separate cars? And sitting in separate restaurants?" Isabel fans her hand in front of her nose.

Yvonne grins as she looks down at her splattered T-shirt and chinos, her scuffed work boots. When they helped bring over the boards for the neighborhood clubhouse, several of the dads couldn't keep their eyes off of Yvonne. Isabel found herself vacillating between annoyance and envy. Only Yvonne could make hard work look good. Isabel, on the other hand, looked like she'd run across a desert. Sweaty, her chestnut-brown hair droopy and listless, her face flushed red from the heat. Not a pretty picture, that's for sure.

But there was no doubt that it felt good, the act of building something after she'd torn up her porch, the triumphant feeling of completion and satisfaction when they were done. Isabel had never given it much thought, had never been one for dirty, manly jobs. In the past those tasks fell to Bill, not for any reason other than that's how it was. It seemed natural that Bill would clean the gutters or shovel the snow while Isabel scrubbed the house and fixed dinner. It wasn't anything they discussed—and it wasn't like Isabel really wanted to clean the gutters or shovel snow—but when Bill was gone everything just stopped.

Isabel is getting that there's no reason she can't do a lot of this herself. It helps having someone like Yvonne pave the way, a woman comfortable with tools and sweat, who doesn't worry about anything being too hard or intimidating.

"Women are great problem solvers," Yvonne had said. "We're naturally creative. So coming up with creative solutions is easy for us."

Isabel's admiration for Yvonne continues to grow, especially when she hears through the grapevine that her clients love her, that Yvonne isn't like some of the other local outfits that overcharge or take advantage of people. Yvonne is honest and does good work, gives the other plumbers in town a run for their money. Yvonne always has a smile on her face, is pleasant and polite, and makes Isabel laugh through her witty observations.

But Yvonne is also a bit of a puzzle, this plumber who could body double as a model and whom Isabel could never have seen herself befriending. Women like Yvonne aren't usually friends—they're competition. They're the ones guaranteed to steal the show—or the guy. If Isabel were still married to Bill, she'd feel uncomfortable with Yvonne, worried that she'd somehow be trying to seduce Bill, or that Bill wouldn't be able to keep his eyes off her. But maybe that's too obvious. It's not the gorgeous plumbers you have to worry about—it's the unassuming dental assistants who find a way to get pregnant with your husband's child.

Isabel tries to push the thought from her head, but it's hard. It's different from before, where Isabel would obsess about when it all started, could picture Bill in Ava's arms, would wonder about what they talked about, about where Ava lived. Isabel would torment herself dreaming up imaginary conversations, pictured them talking and laughing about her. Dumb, clueless, childless Isabel.

But now Isabel keeps replaying that day on her front lawn, at how pale and drawn Ava looked, how she'd stood there nervously, as if she had more bad news to break to Isabel. The tuft of hair in the backseat of the Jeep. Isabel doesn't want to think about it, but it's impossible not to. In fact, it's all she can think about.

"What's wrong with the way I'm dressed?" Yvonne asks now. She kicks off her boots before climbing the steps to her porch, pulls the elastic from her ponytail so her blond hair falls around her shoulders. "Come on. Let's go."

Isabel looks at her new friend dubiously. There's a stench coming from Yvonne that smells like a cross between a pool hall and a Dumpster.

Yvonne laughs before Isabel can say anything. "I'm kidding, Isabel! Of course I'm going to take a shower. Gotta pretty myself up for all those good-looking single guys in Avalon."

"I think there's only one," Isabel informs her dryly, "and he lives with his mother."

Yvonne unlocks her front door. "Well, you only need one," she says optimistically.

Isabel makes a face—she hopes Yvonne isn't one of those New Age positive types. "I already had one, and that was enough, thank you."

"Well, maybe you need another one," Yvonne says simply as she pushes the door open. "A good one." All Yvonne knows is that Bill left her for Ava and then conveniently died. Isabel didn't mention the baby, whose name keeps floating in front of her face. *Max.*

"Bill was a good one," Isabel says. "If you discount the cheating part." She follows Yvonne into the house and is instantly struck by the heady fragrance of gardenia. She spies a glass vase filled with fresh blooms near the doorway. "Maybe I should get a cat. Cats are good companions, aren't they?"

Yvonne laughs. She gestures to the living area just off the entrance, points down the hallway into the kitchen. "Make yourself at home. I'll be back down in a jiffy."

"Okay." Isabel looks around and sees that she's stepped into a picture-perfect house, something out of one of those trendy catalogs or magazines, *Pottery Barn* or *Martha Stewart Living.* Fresh blooms in vases are dotted everywhere, the furniture cozy but complimentary, nice artwork on the walls. On the one hand it fits Yvonne perfectly, and on the other hand it doesn't make sense at all. "Are you renting this place?"

Yvonne shakes her head. "I bought it. I'd been saving for a while and the prices in Avalon are pretty reasonable." As she's talking she peels off her dirty T-shirt and jeans so she's clad in only a sports bra and underwear. Isabel turns away, embarrassed.

"Sorry," Yvonne says. "I have to chuck my work clothes into the washing machine down here. I don't have people over much."

"Much?"

Yvonne laughs. "Okay. At all." She disappears into the kitchen and a few minutes later Isabel hears the washing machine agitating, then Yvonne bounding up the stairs.

Isabel circles the living room, notices how everything seems to be in its proper place. Everything is complementary, carefully thought out and considered, placed deliberately but with an air of casual nonchalance. A slant of late afternoon light falls on the small coffee table, the polished walnut finish warming the room and offsetting the lighter upholstery of the sofa and chairs.

Isabel's own front porch is still torn up, her living room bare and void of furniture. Isabel has no idea what to buy, has no interest in going furniture shopping at all. Maybe she should Garanimals her house. All white, all matching. A no-brainer.

Isabel falls into an overstuffed love seat, examines the slipcovers. They're perfectly pressed and Isabel wonders if Yvonne washes them herself and then irons them, or if she's just really neat. Maybe she sends them out. Who washes slipcovers? Dry cleaners? Why does Isabel even care?

Bored, Isabel pokes through the magazines laying in a wooden rack next to the love seat. A few fashion magazines, an outdoor fitness magazine, some trade magazines. A glossy lifestyle magazine catches her eye and she pulls it out. It automatically flops open to a page where a corner's been bent. The headline reads, "Crimson Harvest: The Fruit of One Family's Labor."

Isabel halfheartedly skims the article. It's about a privately-owned cranberry bog in Wareham, Massachusetts, hitting a record-setting year. Isabel turns the page and sees a series of photographs and in them, a familiar face.

Yvonne.

A young Yvonne, granted, in her teen years through her early twenties, but it's definitely Yvonne. In one, she is surrounded by members of her family who look exactly like her—radiant and blond, perfect smiles with perfect teeth. The pictures aren't posed studio shots—some are on the shore, another at a restaurant, one at what looks like a party on New Year's Eve—and yet everyone looks dazzling, their eyes on the camera, their bodies turned just right. The caption reads "The Tate Exchange: Keeping It in the Family" then proceeds to list Yvonne's name along with her family members, where and when the pictures were taken.

Isabel studies the pictures, tries to pinpoint what it is that makes them look so put together. When she takes all the pictures into consideration at once, she sees it.

Yvonne is rich.

Or comes from money. Plenty of it, from what Isabel can tell. Suddenly everything in the room comes into sharp focus—the quality of the furniture, the choice of books on the bookshelf, the paintings on the wall.

Isabel sees something else. In one of the pictures, the family is standing in a pond wearing fishing waders and surrounded by bobbing red berries. Yvonne is beaming like in all the other pictures, the only difference being that in this one, she has a simple diamond ring on her left hand. In small italics the date is ten years ago.

Isabel arches an eyebrow, looks around the room. So where is the wedding picture? And where is the husband?

"Ready to go?" Yvonne is behind her, already

dressed in a pink spaghetti-strap dress with flat sandals on her slim feet, her hair still wrapped in a towel. She shakes out her hair, towel dries it some more.

Isabel glances at Yvonne's left ring finger which is bare. Isabel has a million questions, and suddenly she finds herself grinning, relieved to discover that Yvonne has a history of her own that she doesn't want to share, much less remember. Isabel had been ambiguous about this friendship but now it's official: Yvonne has a secret, and that makes her tremendously more interesting to Isabel, who no longer feels like the elephant in the room.

Yvonne frowns. "What's so funny?" She walks to the hallway and drapes the damp towel on the stair post.

"Nothing." Isabel slips the magazine back into the rack. Maybe Isabel should ask for the full tour, crack open the medicine cabinet when Yvonne's not looking. Who knows what else she'll find?

"We could stay in and eat here," Isabel ventures. "You know, keep it casual." She darts another look at the magazine rack, wonders if she'll have a chance to read the article in its entirety.

"Sure, if Diet Pepsi and stale crackers are up your alley. I don't keep a well-stocked pantry and I have pots and pans in my kitchen that I've never used. Come on." Yvonne's tone is light, but Isabel can hear a subtle edge in it.

Isabel feigns indifference. "Okay, the Avalon Grill it is. I mean, if you're sure . . ."

Yvonne is already at the door, keys in hand, and for a second Isabel sees her face tighten, but maybe it's her imagination. A second later Yvonne bounds forward and grabs Isabel's hand, laughing, pulling her down the hall. They pass a mirror on their way out and Isabel is pleased to see she doesn't look as dowdy as she thought. While she's no Yvonne, she doesn't look so bad, either. Isabel's so caught up in the thought that she doesn't hear Yvonne mutter under her breath.

"Oh, I'm sure."

What did Isabel see? Yvonne couldn't tell for sure, but when she walked in Isabel had turned to her with a face full of curiosity, questions. She might have been flipping through the magazine, looking for a way to pass away the time. Nothing more, nothing less. Yvonne doesn't need to read into it, doesn't need to make it into a big deal. Even if Isabel saw the article, she might not have had time to put two and two together—Yvonne wasn't gone that long. Anyway, she'll know soon enough if Isabel saw something. People can't help themselves from asking questions once they know who Yvonne is.

But either Isabel is showing incredible restraint

or Yvonne's past isn't as intriguing as she thinks. They settle at the bar, both opting for a beer even though Isabel orders a "lite." They proceed in typical girl fashion to discuss what they should order for dinner.

"They do a mean beef brisket," Isabel says, perusing the menu. "Oh, and the artichoke dip! I'm putting on weight just sitting here."

"Go for it," Yvonne says, running her finger down the list of appetizers. "What about—"

"Whatever you say, please don't tell me you're getting a salad," Isabel says, a hint of warning in her voice. "Because I'm starving and it's bad enough you're wearing a dress that I couldn't fit into in a million years."

"You look great, Isabel. I don't know what you're talking about." Yvonne tosses the menu onto the bar. "And I *am* getting a salad. With dressing on the side."

"God, no. Really?" Isabel wrinkles her nose.

"Yeah, for my appetizer!" Yvonne laughs, reaches for her beer. "And then I'll get the catch of the day and the veggies. Comes with a massive side of pasta. And a bread basket."

"Where does it go?" Isabel demands. "That's what I want to know. All those carbs—are they somehow magically transported to someone else's body? Like mine? That would explain a lot."

"If you want to burn calories, get into

151

plumbing. I don't even have to bother with a gym membership anymore." One of the many perks of the job, Yvonne has discovered. Her arms have never been so toned.

"Um, Yvonne, I've seen plumbers, and they most definitely don't look like you."

"Some do," Yvonne insists.

"None of them do. You must have good genes."

Yvonne gives her a blank smile but doesn't respond. Instead she says, "What are you going to order?"

Isabel looks longingly at the menu. "I want the beef brisket. Of course I would be wearing white—we know how that's going to go. I can picture a chunk of beef falling off my fork and landing in my lap."

Yvonne reaches for a handful of bar nuts, picks out the cashews. "I didn't want to say anything, but you know it is past Labor Day. In case you wanted to wear, I don't know, any other color other than white. Unless you're making some kind of fashion statement?"

"I like white," Isabel says smugly. "It's straight-forward, it is what it is. I'm sick of all this teal, aquamarine, chartreuse or whatever business. Just call it blue, you know? Green. Yellow." She sighs. "Though I'll admit I wish I wasn't wearing white now so I could get that beef brisket."

"It's called a napkin. Get the beef brisket, Isabel."

"I'll regret it tomorrow."

"Sounds like you're regretting it already. Come on—life's too short."

Isabel sighs. "Life is too short so I should eat beef brisket? Maybe I should put that on a bumper sticker."

Yvonne grins. "Why not? Just don't make it a question. Make it a statement: *Life is short—eat beef brisket!*"

The women laugh as the manager, Arnold Fritz, emerges from the kitchen looking distraught. "Sorry, folks, but we have to close early tonight. I'm going to have to ask you all to leave."

There's a collective groan, the loudest one being from Isabel.

"How come?" someone demands.

"What about my skirt steak?" someone else wants to know.

"Can I still get dessert?"

"What about my beer? Can I finish my beer?"

Arnold holds up his hands. "It's a plumbing issue, folks. Nothing major, but it'll shut us down for the night. I can't get anyone to come out and take a look until the morning and I'm not comfortable having a full house under the circumstances. The waitresses will hand out rain checks—fifteen percent off the next time you come in. Sorry for your trouble."

There's more grumbling as patrons begin to gather their things.

"There's always the Pizza Shack," Isabel says with a sigh, tossing the menu aside. "Or McDonald's."

Yvonne notices the manager talking with the bartender. She eats another cashew, then slides off the stool and walks over. "You're having plumbing problems?"

Arnold nods. "Really slow drains. Company came out last month to clear the grease traps but something's going on. I'd rather lose a little business than have a major problem on my hands."

"Same thing happened at the last place I worked in Barrett," the bartender says. He starts to clear the discarded glasses on the bar, waves to a few customers as they pass by.

"I'd be happy to take a look," Yvonne offers. "No promises, but I can see if your grease trap is the culprit."

"The grease trap?" Arnold chuckles, amused. "While I appreciate your offer, miss, the grease trap is not some little doohickey inside the kitchen."

"I know what a grease trap is," Yvonne says. It doesn't bother her that the manager of the Avalon Grill assumes she doesn't know a thing about plumbing. "I'm a licensed plumber in the state of Illinois. Yvonne Tate, Tate Plumbing." She digs in her purse, a small glittery thing that seems a bit impractical at the moment, and hands him a business card.

"Let her take a look, Arnold," the bartender suggests. "In Barrett it backed up into the kitchen—it was a real mess, shut us down for two weeks. We had to have the health inspector come out again."

Isabel is behind her now, looking as flummoxed as Arnold. "What's going on?"

Arnold looks at her and back at Yvonne, who is holding out her hand. He shakes his head as he shakes her hand. "I'm not sure, but I think this little lady is going to look at my grease trap out back."

"This little lady is," Yvonne confirms, reaching for another handful of nuts. Isabel seems less enthusiastic but Yvonne tugs her along, following Arnold through the kitchen and out the back door.

It takes her all of five minutes to conclude that whoever pumped their grease trap did a lousy job. "If they pumped a month ago, it shouldn't be this full," Yvonne says. Isabel is next to her with her nose pinched. Generally restaurants the size of the Avalon Grill would need to have their grease traps cleaned four times a year, so missing a cleaning or doing a lousy job could end up with disastrous results. "Are they snaking the lines into the kitchen, too?"

"I thought so," Arnold says. "But obviously not. I don't want to bad-mouth anyone, small town and all, but I'm not happy with the company we're using. They're the biggest outfit around but I guess that doesn't mean they're the best."

"I'd look into another company," Yvonne advises. She doesn't do grease traps, doesn't have the tank or equipment to properly flush the lines or pump out the fats and other food solids that have to be treated after they're removed from the premises. But she knows what a clean grease trap looks like, and this isn't one of them. "You made the right call, Arnold. If left for too long you'd be looking at hydrogen sulfide gas, which is not only dangerous but could accelerate decay of the trap itself." If Arnold is able to get a company out first thing in the morning, it will take all of thirty minutes to get the grease trap properly serviced and maintained.

"Thank God, I was worried there for a second. I can't afford to lose this job and—" Arnold lets out a deep breath, offers them both a sheepish smile. "I guess there's always that not knowing, huh? If you made the right choice or not? It's a relief to know you made the right decision."

The two women look at each other, then look away, each lost in their own thoughts.

"Yeah," Yvonne says, and suddenly she can't wait to get out of there, to end this conversation, to crawl in between the sheets of her own bed, to close her eyes to this day that's beginning to fill with old memories she'd rather forget. "You're lucky. Because sometimes you never get to know."

• • •

"Fran, what are you doing?" Reed looks bewildered as Frances bursts through the door with the boys in tow, their arms laden with shopping bags. Reed puts down the book he is reading.

"Mom is nuts," Nick says, dropping his load onto the couch. "She bought everything in the store."

Frances shoots her oldest a look. At eight, Nick is already tall and gangly, still a boy but with occasional glimpses of becoming a young man. It's too fast, Frances used to think, but now she's just annoyed. "Nick, that's not true."

"It is true," Noah declares, lugging a large plastic bag behind him. "Me and Nick were bored. Right, Nick?"

"Yeah, whatever." Nick is quick to disappear to his room.

Brady trails in last, sucking on a lollipop. Reed scoops him up, then frowns. "His tongue is blue."

"Well, the lollipop is blue." Frances hurries to put things away before Reed can get a good look.

"Didn't Dr. Tindell say Brady needed to lay off the sweets?" he calls after her. "He already has one cavity."

"I know, I know. But they were giving them out at the shoe store. I couldn't exactly say no." The truth is that she could have said no, but it was easier just to give in. She gives her youngest a hopeful smile. "We'll go brush our teeth, won't we, Brady?"

Brady gives a solemn nod. Reed deposits him on the ground and Brady takes off for the living room. "Hey, champ, I need you to stay in the kitchen with that," he says.

Brady ignores him.

"BRADY." Reed's voice is loud but calm. Brady does an immediate 180 and heads back to the kitchen, plopping himself down on a stool as he finishes his lollipop.

Frances breathes a sigh. It's easier managing the boys when Reed is around, all the testosterone playing off one another.

Noah is tugging at a large garbage bag filled with something almost as tall as him. "Look, Dad!" He starts to pull it off before Frances can stop him.

Reed stares at it. "Um, Frances?"

Frances clears her throat. She hadn't meant to bring it in, but she'd lost track of what was where and who had what.

"A dollhouse?" he says, his voice louder. "It's practically bigger than our house! Where are you going to put it?"

Frances feels guilty, and then defensive. The plan was to move the home office into the living room but there's not enough space and they haven't had a chance to figure out how to make it work. The desk is next to the couch in the living room but the file cabinets are still in the office because Reed didn't want the younger boys getting into them. The office is already half full with a princess bed and canopy, a matching dresser, toys, and a closet crammed with clothes.

Noah crouches on his knees and peers inside. "The doors open and everything. And look!" He presses the small doorbell and there's a chime. "It works!"

Reed is shaking his head. "Frances . . ."

"Reed, I know," she begins, but then she can't help herself. "I saw an ad in the paper for a used dollhouse and I thought I'd take a look, just to get an idea. I wasn't planning on buying it, but then someone else showed up and wanted it because it's such a great deal and in good shape and . . ."

"Noah, take Brady and go play in the living room." Reed points, his voice firm. A couple seconds later, both boys are gone.

Frances slides into a chair. Their kitchen does seem dwarfed by the dollhouse, giving her a sense of being Alice in Wonderland. The euphoria that's followed her all day has dissipated and now she isn't sure where they can even put the dollhouse, much less all of the other things she bought. She wishes she could start over.

"I'm sorry, Reed. I know I've been getting a bit

carried away. I've had so much on my mind lately with Mei Ling coming . . ."

Reed closes his eyes. "Frances, we need to talk."

She stares at him. "You have to travel again."

"Yes, but that's not what I want to talk about. I want to talk about Mei Ling. About her medical report." A foreboding manila envelope is in the center of the table.

Frances swallows. "Is that it?"

He nods.

Frances reaches for it, then hesitates. "It's what we thought, right? What they originally said?"

Reed opens his eyes. "Do you want me to tell you or do you want to read it for yourself?"

She doesn't know. News, even bad news, is always easier when it comes from Reed, but Frances doesn't want to find out that way. Not for this.

She picks up the envelope but doesn't open it. "Reed, we're past the halfway point now. It won't be that much longer, and then she'll be with us. There are families that have been waiting much longer than us. Most China adoptions are taking five years, some are predicting up to ten. It's a miracle that this is even happening, you know."

"It's happening quickly because we agreed to take a waiting child," Reed says. "A special needs child."

"Not that cleft palate is special needs," Frances corrects. "And you saw her! She looked wonderful, the surgery had obviously gone well."

A shadow crosses over Reed's face. "Mei Ling didn't have surgery for cleft palate, Fran. That wasn't—isn't—her condition."

"What do you mean?" Frances frowns. She lifts the flap of the envelope and pulls out a thin sheaf of documents. The original medical report, written in Chinese, and the translation. Frances skims it, the color draining from her face. Her hand flies to her mouth and she finds herself gasping for air, unable to breathe.

"I'm sorry," Reed says, leaning toward her, but she pushes him away, shakes her head.

"No," she whispers. She's shaking.

"I called the agency as soon as I read the report. I'm sorry, but I couldn't wait. I had to know." He gets up and goes to the sink, pours her a glass of water. When he comes back, he crouches next to her. "Mei Ling has congenital heart disease. She's going to need open heart surgery, among other things, and even then her prognosis . . ." His voice trails off.

Frances shakes her head, still unable to believe it. "But how . . . I mean, I didn't—we didn't . . ."

"The agency doesn't know how it happened, but it happened. They assigned us a child with a complicated medical history that is far beyond what we said we were able to take on."

"Is there another family waiting for her? Or another child waiting for us?"

A pained look crosses Reed's face. "Frances, don't do this. This was a mistake, that's all."

"Is there? Was she supposed to be referred to someone else?"

He sighs. "No."

"Is there another child that was supposed to be referred to us?"

Another sigh. "No, but we're still at the top of the list and it shouldn't take long to get a new referral. The agency will straighten it out with the Chinese government so we're not penalized in any way because they gave us the wrong child."

At this Frances jerks up. "She is not the wrong child, Reed! She's ours. You know she is!"

Reed doesn't respond, but moves to the chair next to hers and falls into it heavily.

"You said you knew she was the one," Frances says, remembering his wet eyes, his goofy grin when they called their parents on the phone to give them the good news.

Reed closes his eyes and turns away from her. Reed has never turned away from her in the twelve years they've been married. Frances wants to burst into tears.

"I thought she was," he says. "But now I'm not so sure."

Frances feels as if she's being ripped apart.

162

How can this be happening? How can any of this be happening? "What are you saying, Reed?"

"I'm saying that we shouldn't accept Mei Ling's referral. I'm saying no, Frances. I'm sorry."

Abilene Gould, 26
Temporary Secretary

"Avalon Drywall, can you hold please? Avalon Drywall, can you hold please? Avalon Drywall, this is Abilene. How may I help you?"

"I'm looking for an Abilene Gould. Is she available?"

Abilene frowns. "May I ask who's calling?"

There's a guffaw. "Abby, it's me. Mr. Whatley. I'm yanking your chain, girl! Just wanted to make sure you were on top of the phones."

Abilene turns to glance back at her boss's office. Sure enough, there he is, laughing his head off. "Very funny, Mr. Whatley," she says, waving gamely.

She disconnects the call and punches the button for the first line. "Avalon Drywall, this is Abilene. How may I help you?"

"It's me again!" comes the familiar chortle.

She disconnects and punches another button, already filled with dread. "Avalon Drywall, this is . . ."

"You get an A-plus, Abby. You're an ace on the phones. Now if only people were actually calling. Come back here a moment, will ya?"

Abilene sighs and reaches for a pad of paper. It's her second temp job and the agency told her that Avalon Drywall is going out of business so the position is on a day-to-day basis. They don't have anything lined up for her after that so she's back to square one, circling ads in the newspapers and trying to squeeze in interviews whenever she can.

Dick Whatley is leaning back in his chair, balling up blank invoices and tossing them into the trash. "Score!" he shouts when he gets one in.

Abilene settles herself in the chair in front of his desk. "Yes, Mr. Whatley?"

"You're a smart girl, Abby. Noticed that the minute you walked in. So I'm sorry to tell you that today's your last day." He smiles but it's a struggle, his bravado gone. "I'm closing up shop tomorrow. Gonna pack everything up." He gestures to the walls where pictures and plaques of recognition and community service have hung proudly for years. "This was my father's business," he says, pointing to one photo. "He built it from the ground up. He managed to weather two recessions. I wish I could say the same." He picks up a framed photo on his desk and shows it to Abilene. "Those are my girls. My wife, Ann Marie, and my little girl, Tiffany. Though she's not a little girl anymore—she's sixteen. I haven't had a chance to put a new picture in."

"It's a nice picture," Abilene says politely.

"So, I know you've only been here a couple of days but I'm happy to write a recommendation, say that you impressed me from the get-go. It'd be the truth. I hope you find something that you like, something good." He starts piling the papers on his desk, then stops and looks around, suddenly overwhelmed. "I have to be out by Saturday. Thought it would be quick, you know? But I haven't been able to do much of anything. I've already sold the furniture and the file cabinets, most of my equipment. Movers come tomorrow to take everything where it needs to go. But my files and personal belongings—well, I've yet to make a dent in things. I guess I'll be up all night packing up and ferrying things back and forth over the next few days."

Abilene swallows, can see the sadness on Mr. Whatley's face. He's a portly man, a bit rough around the edges, but nice. She can see that at one time business was booming, that he held a position of respect in the community. He has a lot to be proud of, but in the face of the devastating close of his business, it's hard to see any of that.

"I'd be happy to come in and help you," she offers.

"Oh, I appreciate that, Abby, but I can't afford to pay the agency past today." He powers down his computer and the sound is so depressing they both slump down a little lower in their chairs.

Abilene forces herself to sit upright, fastens on a bright smile. "You wouldn't have to pay me," she tells him. "I don't have anything going on anyways. I'd much rather stay busy and I'd like to help you."

For a second his face brightens. But then he shakes his head. "No, no. It's my business, I should be the one to do the work."

"Okay, Mr. Whatley. I understand." But Abilene finds herself drawn to the pictures on the wall, to the framed dollar bill, to an autographed photo of Mr. Whatley and his father posing with the governor of Illinois. There's a timeline, too, and three different graphic renditions of how the logo has changed over time. Abilene can't imagine the despair Mr. Whatley must feel at having to take it all down and put it away.

And that's when it hits her.

A few weeks ago she'd stood outside the Pick and Save, relishing a yellow gumball. She'd come back from yet another disappointing interview and the globe of glass, filled with large, multicolored gumballs, beckoned her. She fished around in her purse until she came up with a quarter, then slid it into the slot and turned the knob. There was a satisfying crunch of machinery and then the sound of a gumball falling into the dispenser. Abilene opened the little door and popped a yellow gumball into her mouth. She felt, for the moment at least, a wave of simple happiness overcome her.

A petite woman with silvery-blue hair stopped

and pointed to the gumball machine. "Colorful, isn't it?"

Her mouth full, Abilene could only nod.

"I bet your generation has a lot of good memories about gumball machines," the woman said. "It's childhood at its best. Right up there with ice cream trucks and tree houses."

The hard sugary shell finally gave way and Abilene was able to speak. "I had a tree house growing up," she said. "My dad and I built it."

"You see?" the woman exclaimed. "That's what I'm talking about! Did you have a stamp collection, too?"

Abilene shook her head. "Not stamps. I had an eraser collection, though. And I liked Betty and Veronica comics. Double digests especially." She had smiled at the memory, remembered how she had over a hundred in all. What happened to them? Did her parents give them away? Abilene could have sold them—she kept them in mint condition, each one carefully stored in archival plastic sleeves. They'd be worth something now.

The woman grinned. "You're new to Avalon, aren't you? I'm Bettie Shelton, president of the Avalon Ladies Scrapbooking Society." She stuck out a hand.

"Abilene Gould."

"You should come to our meeting tonight. You'll meet lots of people, get some good ideas for how to preserve your memories in creative ways. It's usually fifteen dollars a month but I'd be willing to waive it in your case, seeing how you're new in town. You can't tell anyone that I've done that, though. Wouldn't want people to think I'm playing favorites." She continued to pump Abilene's hand up and down, beaming.

Abilene finally managed to extract her hand. "Thank you, but I'm not much of a creative person."

"What? Nonsense. But I tell you what—just come for the company, meet a few nice people. Tonight, seven o'clock. Here's my card." Bettie pressed an ornately embellished business card into Abilene's hands. "That's one of my fancy ones. I have six other styles."

"Oh, I don't know . . ."

Bettie waved away her excuse. "I hear some strawberries and Maalox calling my name— mercy, it's been one of those weeks. See you tonight!" She gave Abilene a friendly pat on the arm and disappeared into the store before Abilene could respond.

And so Abilene had gone to the meeting, had listened politely, had learned a little bit about scrapbooking and a lot about the town of Avalon. The other members had taken her under their wings and the word is out that she is looking for a job, but who knows how that will go. She hadn't planned on going back, but maybe she will, because she sees that there's a way she can help Mr. Whatley, one that will have a lasting effect.

"Mr. Whatley," she says suddenly. "Would you like me to help put some of these things together in an album? Sort of as a keepsake of the business?" She points to the pictures on the wall.

He cocks his head to one side, not comprehending. "You mean take them out of the frames?"

"Yes. No. I don't know. Maybe you could keep the originals someplace safe and we could make color photocopies to put in the album. I went to a meeting the other night that talked about this sort of thing, about creating a memory scrapbook. I'm still learning so I wouldn't be able to do anything fancy, but it might give you a nice record of what you and your father have done with the business. Would you like that?"

Mr. Whatley looks at Abilene, a slow smile breaking over his face. "Abilene," he says, calling her by her full name for the first time since she started working for him. "I would like that very much."

Chapter Eight

Yvonne picks through her jewelry box, looking for a pair of earrings. She prefers small gold hoops while on the job, but she lost one last week and she's thinking she should wear studs instead, something less likely to fall out of her ears. Of course the reasonable thing would be to be completely jewelry free, but what would be the fun in that?

Nothing too fancy, she tells herself as she looks through her choices. It's a handful compared to what she used to have, but it's enough.

She touches a pair of silver turquoise hearts and hears her breath catch. *Sam.* He'd given the earrings to her for her eighteenth birthday after he'd taken a trip to the Southwest with some buddies. It had been an eye-opening trip for him, had lit a desire to see more of the world beyond Wareham, to have a life beyond the cranberry bogs. His enthusiasm was contagious, and Yvonne felt certain that it would happen for him someday.

And then, well. Yvonne sighs, shakes her head. She knows that others might see the earrings as a painful reminder, but she doesn't. She was wearing them the day she left Wareham and hasn't worn them since. They comfort her, as do the simple pair of pearl earrings that used to belong to her grandmother. Yvonne misses them both.

Last year her oldest sister managed to get ahold of her, told her the news.

"Gramma passed," Anne had said briskly on the phone. "Stroke. Funeral's next week. I know you're not coming."

Yvonne had felt a stirring of nostalgia, of familiarity, but it wasn't enough to change anything. "No," she said. "I'll send flowers."

"Don't bother," her sister had said. "I already ordered some in your name. Carnations."

Yvonne hates carnations, and Anne knows it, but she didn't say anything. Instead they hung up and a month later a small package arrived with a folded copy of the program from the memorial service, the earrings carelessly tucked into a cotton ball. It was probably the only thing nobody else wanted, clamoring instead for the money, or the diamonds, or both.

Two simple pairs of earrings loaded with meaning, so much so that Yvonne can't bring herself to wear them anymore.

She finally settles on a pair of citrine ear studs when the doorbell rings. Yvonne glances at the clock—it's half past eight in the morning. She's due at a job in half an hour but she's already run five miles and had her breakfast. Yvonne tosses a few throw pillows onto the bed, then checks herself in the mirror once again before heading down the stairs.

She takes a look through the peephole but doesn't see anyone, just the sunny street that runs in front of her house, Mrs. Markowitz walking by with her dog. Yvonne opens the door and scans the street, but doesn't see anyone else. Then she looks down and sees a note tucked under the corner of the doormat.

It's a scrawl, written in haste.

Go home, it says. *You don't belong here.*

Yvonne feels her throat tighten. She picks up the note and gives a polite wave to Mrs. Markowitz who's looking at her with a frown. Yvonne balls up the note in her hand, then throws it into the kitchen trash.

She pours herself a glass of orange juice and wills herself to stop shaking. She has a busy day ahead of her—that's where her mind needs to be. Work. Work has always made it better, has helped her move out of her head and into her body.

Her cellphone rings and she hesitates for a moment. The area code is for Avalon, though, so she answers. "Yvonne Tate."

There's a lot of throat clearing before Yvonne hears anything. "Is this the plumber lady?" comes an uncertain voice.

"Yes, this is Yvo—"

"I'm sorry to call at the last minute, but I won't be needing your services today. Looks like everything's working fine now. Oh, this is Mervin McDowell of 1524 Plum Street."

Yvonne digs through her bag until she finds her job book. She flips to the page with Mervin McDowell's information. *Residential, stopped-up shower.* Well, quite possibly a little Drano fixed the problem, though it had sounded more serious than that.

"No problem, Mr. McDowell," she says. Yvonne's disappointed to lose the work, but it happens. "If you need any other—"

Click. He's hung up.

Yvonne stares at her cellphone, then slowly crosses his name off her calendar, makes a note on his page. Well, the upside is that she can move the rest of her appointments, end her day a little early. Every cloud has a silver lining, right? Maybe Isabel will join her for dinner. They can go out or see a movie or something.

She looks up her next appointment and gives them a call. "Hi, Mrs. McKenzie? Yvonne Tate of Tate Plumbing. I wanted you to know that I have an opening and can move you up to an earlier time."

"Oh, Yvonne!" Mrs. McKenzie sounds delighted to hear from her. "I was meaning to call you. It looks like we'll have to reschedule, if that's all right."

Reschedule? They were going to replace the water heater. The old one wasn't working at all, which means the McKenzies are in a house with no hot running water.

Yvonne looks at her calendar. "I have some time tomorrow," she says. It's a big job, not complicated, but it takes time to drain and remove the old water heater and install the new one, plus Yvonne was going to dispose of the old water heater at a steel recycle center almost half an hour away. "Or I can try to move some jobs around, try to get over there sooner."

"Oh, you know, I hate that you have to go through all this fuss. You know, forget about it. I'm sure we'll work something out. I can probably get Larry to figure it out."

Mr. McKenzie? Yvonne remembers him crashed out on the couch, his belly rising and falling as he snored away, thick Coke-bottle glasses askew on his face. No, Larry McKenzie most certainly will not be able to figure it out, nor will Mrs. McKenzie, who's a small, wiry thing.

"Thank you *so* much for everything, Yvonne," Mrs. McKenzie says before saying goodbye.

Now her schedule is really open, with only one job left. What the hell? Frustrated, Yvonne punches in the numbers for Isabel's cellphone.

"Hey, do you want to come over for dinner tonight?" she asks as soon as Isabel picks up. "I only have soup, but it's Wolfgang Puck, and pretty tasty . . ."

"Geez, hi to you, too. I'm about to go into a meeting—can I call you later?"

"You don't have a second to talk?"

"I do . . . and now it's gone. Here comes my boss—gotta run. Call you later." Isabel hangs up.

Yvonne is not an emotional eater but she wanders back to the pantry and grabs a bag of rice cakes. As she munches through one and then another, she tries not to get upset. It's just a couple of cancellations, albeit bizarrely on the same day, and nothing more. Yvonne finishes off one more rice cake and reaches for her phone again.

She calls her last appointment of the day, someone she hasn't met yet because he didn't want a quote, just someone to come over quick to help with a running toilet that's been keeping him up nights. He had been hoping she could do an emergency call last night, but she was already on another job and by the time she was done, she was too beat to head out again. Now, however, she dials his number with trepidation, wondering if he'll tell her that his toilet has fixed itself and that he doesn't need her, either.

"What a relief!" comes the reply when she tells Hubert Hill she's available to come by now.

Yvonne almost can't believe it. "Really?" she says. "Now is a good time?"

"Are you kidding? I was about to take a hammer to the thing this morning. Can you meet me at the house in half an hour? You know where it is?"

"Yes, I have the address. I'll see you there." Yvonne hangs up the phone with an air of satisfaction, draws a smiley face on Hubert Hill's page. *I knew it wasn't anything,* she tells herself triumphantly as she brushes bits of puffed rice into the trash. But the smile falls from her face when she sees the balled-up scrap of paper. She stares at it a moment, then lets the lid of the trash can slam shut.

Twenty-five minutes later she's standing on the doorstep of a handsome Queen Anne house a few minutes outside of Avalon. It had to be built around the turn of the century—the *last* century—and she wonders if they've had any issues other than a running toilet. The exterior is in pristine condition and painted a sunny yellow. She counts three floors and guesses that the first floor has at least nine-foot ceilings based on the location of the windows.

She rings the bell. A second later, the door opens and a huge yellow Lab bounds out, practically knocking her over.

"Whoa, there, boy!" she says as she ruffles his ears and the back of his neck. The dog nuzzles against her hand, panting happily.

"Sorry, he needs some manners. Toby, get back here." A hand reaches out to grab Toby's collar. Yvonne sees loafers and khaki pants out of the corner of her eye and quickly straightens up.

"A Lab with manners?" she says jokingly, then

finds she's rooted on the spot. Because Hubert Hill is not what she expected.

Gorgeous brown eyes, that's the first thing she sees. Dark brown hair, a navy blue polo shirt opened at the neck, khaki pants, nice belt. But his arms—Hubert's arms are muscular, not body-builder muscular, but lean and toned, like an athlete. And his smile—Yvonne suspects he's won over quite a few women with that smile alone. He's her age, maybe a couple years older.

Yvonne finds that she's blushing and quickly gets ahold of herself. "I'm Yvonne Tate."

"Yvonne Tate." Hubert says this slowly, staring at her. Toby is bucking against him, wanting to be set free so he can wreak havoc somewhere. "*You're* the plumber?"

Yvonne nods. It takes her a second to find her voice. "I'm the plumber."

Toby breaks free and tears down the porch, across the lawn. A squirrel, maybe, or a cat. Or quite possibly nothing at all.

"Um, right. Okay. Well, come on in. The culprit's upstairs. Master bath." Hubert steps aside and Yvonne steps in, a little too aware of how close he is when she passes him. He smells clean, like soap.

Yvonne has two choices: melt into a puddle on the floor or keep it together, get the job done, and get out of there. No eye contact, that's the key. Her legs feel rubbery, unreliable. She tries to stop herself, but can't. Her eyes drift to his left hand, to his ring finger.

Empty.

Hubert whistles for Toby. His whistle is confident, commanding—he could stop traffic with that whistle. Even Yvonne finds herself standing at attention.

Toby bounds back inside, debating whether to follow them up the stairs. Yvonne looks at the lace doilies and silk flowers crammed into fluted porcelain vases, the faded oriental rugs lining the pink plank flooring. The walls have glass-front cabinets and beautiful woodwork. It's lovely, but a little old-fashioned for her taste, and it doesn't seem to fit Hubert at all. "You have a lovely home," she says politely.

Hubert makes a face as they walk up the stairs. He looks like he's about to tell her something but instead simply says, "Thanks."

"Have you had any other issues with the plumbing?"

Hubert shakes his head. "We gutted the place about ten years ago, did a complete renovation, refinished the floors, the works. We put in a new septic system and R/O system, upgraded the water tank and heater. Everything's been running well until, um, this."

In the bedroom, Yvonne tries not to notice the floral linens, the puffy pink duvet, the shelves lined with china figurines of children and cats.

She sees pairs of men's shoes lined up next to the wardrobe. There's a stack of papers on the desk, the only messy area. Hubert grabs a cellphone sitting in a charging station and slips it into his back pocket.

So this must be his room. Huh.

The master bathroom is just as fluffy, with matching bathroom rugs, toilet seat covers, tissue box holders. A beautiful cast iron tub sits in the corner by a large window, overlooking the gardens.

Yvonne puts down her tools. So it's officially a bit weird, but whatever. Hubert is standing in the doorway, watching her.

She clears the top of the tank and lifts the lid, gives the toilet a flush. She watches the valve and sees that the ball and flapper aren't covering it completely. "It looks like you may need a new flapper," she says.

"What? No." Hubert frowns. "I had a guy here last week who replaced it."

"Last week? I don't think so." Yvonne peers into the tank. "I mean, you can see it's corroded around the edges. That's definitely not new."

Hubert looks into the tank. "Damn. I can't believe it."

"It's not as bad as you think," Yvonne says. "You should call this guy and have him come out again. He obviously didn't fix the problem. He should take care of this for free."

"Yeah, no kidding." He's shaking his head, disgusted, and Yvonne can tell that he's making some sort of mental note. "Anyway, I'd rather get this taken care of now. Can you do it?"

Yvonne fiddles with the chain, flushes the toilet one more time. "Sure. This shouldn't take me long. I'll remove the damaged part and take it with me to the hardware store so I can get the right fit. I should be done within the hour. Do you want me to do this now or do you have to get back to work?"

"No, now would be great. Yeah, definitely. I don't want to run the water bill."

Yvonne adjusts the float until she's satisfied with the water level in the tank, then turns off the water. She removes the flapper and dries her hand on the clean towel she has tucked into her belt. "All right. I'll be back soon."

They stand there for a moment, neither of them moving. What's happening? And then before she can help herself, the words slip out of her mouth.

"You're welcome to come with me if you want," she says offhandedly. "So you'll know what to do if this happens next time. You could probably fit it yourself. We can bring Toby, too. Take him for a little ride."

By the shocked look on his face, Yvonne can tell she's overstepped her bounds. What was she thinking? But then Hubert grins.

"Yeah, that'd be great—I should probably learn

how to do this stuff someday. Let me grab Toby's leash and I'll meet you outside."

When Yvonne gets into her truck she furtively dials Isabel's number. When it directly goes to voice mail, she quickly taps out a text to Isabel.

MET THE MOST AMAZING GUY! BUT I THINK HE LIVES WITH HIS MOM. WEIRD?

Hubert steps onto the porch, leash in hand. He shakes his keys and Toby bounds out. He gives Yvonne a wave. "I'll be there in a sec," he calls out.

Yvonne smiles brightly and furiously types another text.

ISABEL!! THIS IS AN EMERGENCY!! WE'RE GOING TO HARDWARE STORE NOW.

She's relieved when her phone pings back almost immediately.

HECK YEA IS WEIRD. DUMP HIM. IN MTG, TTYL.

Yvonne snaps her phone closed and sags against the seat. Great.

But when Toby and Hubert walk toward her, she can't help but smile. She's not marrying the guy, just going for a quick ride to the hardware store, and there's Toby to boot. She starts up the engine, then leans over and opens the door for them.

The next hour is arguably one of the best hours of Yvonne's life. Hubert is funny and smart, and of course there's Toby, who seems to know exactly what's going on between his owner and his new friend.

Yvonne wishes the job was more than a leaky toilet because it seems like only a matter of minutes before she's replacing the lid of the tank. "Well, you're all set." She takes her time putting her tools away.

Hubert gives the toilet one more flush. "You did it."

"It's not rocket science. And now you can do it, too, if it ever happens again." She hands him the old flapper in a Ziploc bag. "Though I'd try to get your money back from that guy if you can."

"Doubtful. The guy's a jerk." They both grin and then clear their throats, looking away, embarrassed.

They walk downstairs to the first floor. Yvonne is startled to see an older woman standing at the base of the stairs, waiting for them, her face disapproving.

A light cardigan is wrapped around her shoulders, and she's dressed in a blouse and calf-length skirt. Her graying hair is short and styled, tan heels on her feet. Jeweled reading glasses are perched on the edge of her nose and she looks serious, reminding Yvonne of an accountant.

"Hubert?" she says, her voice carrying a hint of warning.

"Mother," he says. Yvonne waits for an introduction but there is none. "She was just leaving."

He quickly ushers Yvonne out the door and walks her to her truck.

"Thanks again," he says. "You did great work."

"You're welcome." Yvonne hands him a receipt and her card. She decides against saying anything about his mother—it's not her business and who knows if she'll ever see him again. But then she blurts out, "Feel free to call me if you have any other problems."

"I will." Hubert glances at the house before looking down at her card. "You know, you don't look like an Yvonne."

She smiles. "Well, you don't look like a Hubert."

"Fair enough. Family name, there was no way of getting around it. But nobody calls me Hubert except for my mom—I go by Hugh."

"Hugh." Yvonne likes this. She reluctantly slides into the driver's seat and slams the door.

Hugh leans against the open passenger window. "So can I call you if I don't have a plumbing-related problem?" Behind him, Yvonne sees a curtain move. "Like for dinner?" His voice is low, almost a whisper.

A small thrill runs through Yvonne but she forces herself to keep her composure. "Sure," she says. "I'd like that."

"Me too." He smiles, then steps away from the truck and gives her a wave.

Yvonne fumbles for her earpiece, then quickly

dials Isabel's number. As expected, it rolls to voice mail, but Yvonne doesn't care.

"Isabel!" she breathes. "I think I have a date!"

Connie is peeling Granny Smith apples as she gazes out the window. It's still bright outside but their day is officially over, everything cleaned up, the next day's prep complete. It'll be a nice, quiet evening for her and Madeline, one that Connie is looking forward to.

Long strands of apple skins gather in a bucket at her feet. She'll take it to Serena later, a treat for good behavior. Serena's stayed out of trouble and been friendly to guests who wander into the backyard to see the garden. Even Madeline seems to enjoy having Serena around when she goes out to do a little weeding in the early morning.

Connie begins to core the apples. She's baking apple dumplings in an attempt to sharpen her kitchen skills. She's good at following directions and knows how to make everything on the tea salon menu, but she's not much of an innovator when it comes to food. She doesn't have the natural talent that Madeline or Hannah has, and even though she knows she can easily manage all the administrative aspects of her job, she wants to be more of an equal in these other areas, too.

Connie's okay with Hannah, but she can't help but feel a little left out whenever Hannah comes over. Hannah and Madeline have a friendship that goes beyond the tea salon, have an appreciation for music and the arts, something Connie doesn't know much about. They're both well traveled and will talk about places they've visited or things they've eaten, shows they've seen. They both speak a little French and will sometimes converse in short sentences, laughing as they do so. Connie finds it both intriguing and a little off-putting, too—they make it sound so easy, so everyday, so accessible. Connie doesn't have a passport—she's never even left the state of Illinois.

The phone rings as Connie begins to work the dough.

"Stay there, I'll get it," Madeline says when Connie moves to wipe her hands. Madeline puts down the *Avalon Gazette* and pushes herself up from the table. Her eyes flicker to the bowl of apples dusted in sugar and cinnamon. "Mmm. We may have to forgo dinner tonight and go straight to dessert."

Connie smiles but she knows Madeline is being polite. She had shown Madeline the apple dumpling recipe and saw her arch an eyebrow when she came across the last ingredient: a bottle of soda pop, Mountain Dew to be specific. Not exactly a high-rolling gourmet ingredient, but it sounded like fun, so she wants to try it.

Connie rolls out the dough. It's so odd that she's here, acting a bit like Suzy Homemaker when it's so far from who she is. In a way she was better suited at the Avalon Wash and Dry—she blended in there, the girl with the jet-black hair and shabby clothes, a girl who was part of the background. At Madeline's Tea Salon, however, Connie is the anomaly, the piece that doesn't quite fit. She was known for the first couple of months as the Girl with the Spiky Hair, and now she knows people refer to her as the Girl with the Goat. It's just as well—Connie can't imagine her life without Serena. She doesn't want to.

Madeline hangs up the phone. "Connie, that was Bettie Shelton. She'd like to use the sitting room for her scrapbooking meeting tonight. I told her I'd check the schedule and call her back."

Connie glances at the clock. "But it's already four o'clock!"

"I know, but she seems to be in a pinch and we don't have anything going on tonight. She says the group usually does a potluck dinner, so they don't need anything other than the space, though I'm happy to put out hot water and tea."

Connie grumbles as she starts to cut triangles in the dough. "She did this last month, too—tried to squeeze in at the last minute. And she'll want to come in for free, no doubt."

"Yes," Madeline admits. "But she did say the members would stay to help clean up afterward, and that she'll include two scrapbooking starter kits and albums, for us, for free. I have to admit

I'm intrigued—I've been thinking about making a scrapbook for Maggie. About Steven, her grandfather. I wish he were alive to see her—he'd be tickled by that sweet child." Maggie is Madeline's granddaughter, her stepson Ben's one-year-old daughter. Madeline and Ben had been estranged for years but reconnected this past December, and they've been in touch ever since. Connie knows it's a relationship that's precious to Madeline, but also fraught with old hurts and painful memories. She can also see that Madeline's already made up her mind, that Bettie and her friends will be descending upon the tea salon in a couple of hours.

The look on Madeline's face is both wistful and sad as she begins to wipe down the counters, fill the large hot water carafes, her nose wrinkling as it does whenever she's trying to keep herself from being overwhelmed by emotion. Connie sighs. Madeline is so good to her that she can put up with Bettie Shelton for one night.

"I'll make sure we have enough chairs in the sitting room," Connie says as she places an apple wedge in a dough triangle and pinches it closed. She places the dumpling in a baking dish and starts on another one. "And I guess I can put this on the buffet table for the ladies, too, if it turns out okay."

"Oh, Connie." Madeline offers an appreciate smile. "That's very generous of you."

"It's nothing," Connie says, already putting on her tea salon manager hat. "I can take care of everything if you want to go freshen up. At least we don't have to worry about dinner. Do I need to put out plates and utensils?"

Madeline shakes her head. "They'll bring paper products, so that will help tremendously with cleanup. Just the teacups, I think. They'll be needing the tables, too, so we'll let them sort themselves out between the sitting room and dining area. I'll give her a call back and let her know we'd be happy to host the group tonight." She hesitates for a moment. "I tried to speak to Bettie about the night we saw her in the backyard."

Connie nods, curious. "I mentioned it to her the day after but she didn't seem to know what I was talking about, or she was pretending not to."

Madeline nods. "That was the same response I got. I think old age may be catching up with us old ladies."

Connie finishes one baking dish and starts on another. "I don't think it's old age," she says after a moment. She isn't sure what it is, but there are plenty of women Bettie's age, Madeline included, who aren't running around in the middle of the night in their nightgown and slippers.

Madeline looks sad as she gazes out the window. "I know."

There's a bleat from the backyard. Madeline

glances at the clock. "Sounds like your goat is ready for a walk. Or dinner."

"Both, probably. I'll take care of her in a sec."

"Have you talked to the vet or thought of putting up any signs?"

Darn. Things had been going so well that Connie was hoping that Madeline accepted the fact that they would be keeping Serena, no more questions asked.

Madeline waits but Connie doesn't say anything. What's there to say? Instead, Connie gets up and goes to the stove, busying herself as she turns the heat on low under the small saucepan holding butter, sugar, and cinnamon.

"Connie?"

"Um, I know, Madeline. I was going to work on it, but I haven't gotten around to it yet." Connie keeps her back to Madeline, relieved she can't see her face, which is flushed.

"I know we've been busy, Connie, but I can't help thinking that someone may be looking for her. It's September—it's been over a month already. And she can't stay here forever—the Lassiters will make sure of that."

Connie nods, mute, stirring the melting butter with her wooden spoon.

"Would it be helpful if I called the vet?"

"No!" Connie spins around. "I mean, I'll take care of it, Madeline. I'd like to be the one to do it, if that's okay."

"Of course." Madeline studies her for a moment. "Are you all right?"

Connie takes a deep breath. "I'm fine. I'm just thinking about tonight and getting everything together before the meeting. That's all."

"If there's anything you'd like to talk about, maybe about Serena, I'm here. Okay?"

"Okay." Connie forces a smile but it quickly breaks so she turns back to the table. She carefully pours the butter mixture over the dumplings, aware that Madeline is watching her. A second later, she hears footsteps as Madeline heads to her bedroom.

Connie reaches for the Mountain Dew and cracks the lid open. There's a hiss, then the soda bubbles up, fizzling and threatening to spill over. Connie feels dread, can picture herself mopping up the mess, the apple dumplings ruined since she doesn't have any more Mountain Dew. The rest of the evening will be off, Connie always a step behind, one thing going wrong after another.

But the soda settles and sparkles, waiting. Serena calls out again and Connie lets out her breath. She pours the soda over the apple dumplings, then slips the baking dishes into the oven. She sets the timer for thirty-five minutes and tidies up, then picks up the bucket filled with apple rinds and heads toward the back-yard.

• • •

Noah's kindergarten teacher, Miss Howe, is on the phone, her voice rushed and despondent. "Mrs. Latham, I'm so sorry to bother you, but one of Noah's classmates, Baxter Pickett, is celebrating a birthday today and somehow the guinea pig got into the cupcakes while we were at recess."

Ew, Frances thinks, but instead says politely, "I'm so sorry to hear that."

"Yes," Miss Howe says. "The kids were upset and Newton needs to go to the vet. So I was wondering—would you mind picking something up for Baxter's birthday? His mother is at work and can't get away. You're at the top of the list for parent helpers this week."

Inwardly Frances groans—she doesn't want to leave the house. She's a mess, for starters, still in her pajamas and robe, peanut butter and jelly smeared on her sleeves. Brady is glued to the television, has been for the past three hours. Frances even let him eat his snack there.

Because what does it matter? These small details of life, the pockets of good moments here and there, the excitement of a class birthday party, the softness of a guinea pig, the snuggle of your young son. It's wonderful, but is it enough? Now, as Frances is on the cusp of seeing a life-long dream slip away, she wonders what's worse: not experiencing it at all, or having had the opportunity only to lose it altogether.

She and Reed have had endless discussions about Mei Ling, have shed tears, have argued the pros and cons. They've talked to other families who made the decision to adopt a child with extreme medical challenges like Mei Ling. Each story is a stab in Frances's heart. There are parents who say that as much as they love their child, they weren't prepared for the degree to which it's impacted their lives. The financial strain, the emotional toll, the attachment disorder that often accompanies these adoptions. Marriages falling apart, children who can't be consoled and lash out at anyone around them—siblings, parents, teachers, healthcare workers.

There are families who've had to find new placements for their adopted child, who knew they were in over their heads and sought another solution that would work in the best interest of everyone. These stories are the saddest for Frances, and she knows it will devastate her if she were ever faced with that same dilemma.

But this isn't that dilemma. She knows Reed is trying to cut this possibility off at the pass, to make sure they don't end up another sad statistic, but it's too late because Frances already feels attached to Mei Ling. She's seen a whole future with this child in their lives, whatever that might mean. Yes, there are worst-case scenarios, and Reed has already gone through each and every one of them. Frances, however, isn't going to go there. And because of this she and Reed are now distant, separate. The two of them have taken positions on opposite sides of the river and there is no in between, no common ground.

"Mrs. Latham?" Miss Howe's voice calls her back to the situation at hand. The class birthday party, the first of the year, the one Noah couldn't stop talking about before leaving for school this morning.

"I'll stop by the store and pick something up," she hears herself saying even though she really wants to crawl back into bed. She can pick up two dozen cupcakes from the Pick and Save, drop them off at the school, and be home within the hour.

"Oh, thank you!" Miss Howe's relief is so huge Frances almost feels guilty. "We'll do our celebration after lunch. His mother had made special cupcakes but I know that's too much to ask at this late hour. Baxter is gluten intolerant so regular cupcakes or cookies are out of the question, I'm afraid. Maybe pick up some fruit or cheese?"

Frances makes a face but agrees. It takes her a minute to change, anxious to get this out of the way. Brady is zoned out and easy to move into his car seat. Frances hands him a juice box and they drive over to the Pick and Save.

Standing amid the fruits and vegetables Frances is gloomy. What kind of birthday celebration is this going to be? Throw in the cheese sticks and it's nothing more than a glorified snack time. She wants to lob the apples into the aisles, scatter the red and green grapes onto the floor. Why does it have to be so hard? Why does everything have to be so damn hard?

"Frances?"

Frances turns and sees Hannah Wang coming up behind her, pushing a shopping cart. "Oh, hi, Hannah."

Hannah smiles. "It's good to see you again! How are you?"

Frances is about to lie and say she's good, but she can't. Instead her eyes fill with tears.

"Oh," Hannah says. She fumbles through her purse for a tissue.

"No, that's all right," Frances says, wiping her eyes with the back of her hand and sniffing. "Mei Ling's medical report. We . . . we got the wrong assignment. They gave us the wrong child." The words ring false in her ears. "Mei Ling has a serious heart condition along with other medical challenges. We have until tomorrow to respond but Reed wants to turn it down, wait for another child." The tears come again. Brady is facing forward in their shopping cart that's fashioned after a boat.

"I'm so sorry," Hannah says.

"And now I'm supposed to pick up fruit and cheese for a birthday party—a birthday party!—

195

at my son's school. The kid, Baxter, is gluten intolerant but Newton got into the gluten-free cupcakes and now he's sick and I'm here picking up fruit and cheese instead. Fruit and cheese!" She's practically hysterical.

Hannah's eyes widen. Frances is on a roll.

"Why can't they have cupcakes? I want to bake them cupcakes but I have no idea what a gluten-free cupcake is and I don't have enough time to figure it out. But what kid wants FRUIT on their birthday?" Frances gestures to the fruit around them. Brady cranes his neck from the front of the boat to take a look at what's going on. Frances catches her breath, blows it out. She slumps against the handlebars. "I'm sorry. It's been a hard couple of days. I just wish everyone could have what they want, you know?"

"I know. I'd like that, too." Hannah looks at the bananas in Frances's cart. "Did they ask you to bring fruit?"

Frances nods. "Baxter's mother had made gluten-free cupcakes but they don't sell them in the bakery. I think Noah's teacher thought it would be easier to make a fruit salad. Which I'm sure it is." She picks up a cantaloupe and gives it a halfhearted thump.

"How many kids?" Hannah asks.

"Twenty-two. Plus Miss Howe, the teacher."

"Cutting up fruit for twenty-three people isn't going to go a whole lot faster than baking two trays of cupcakes," Hannah says. She lifts a slender wrist and checks her watch. "I'd be happy to help, Frances. My mornings are slow since most of my cello lessons are after school or in the evenings."

"That's a nice offer," Frances says, "but I don't know anything about baking gluten-free cupcakes."

Hannah smiles. "I do." Her eyes cloud with concern for a moment. "But tell me first: Who's Newton and is he okay?"

The next two hours are a blur—Hannah efficiently leading them through the store, picking up ingredients as she explains how her neighbor is allergic to gluten but loves baked goods. At the Latham home, Hannah doesn't seem to notice the mess, the evidence of this morning's breakfast still on the table, the piles of laundry that need attending to. The recipe is quick and simple—butter, sugar, gluten-free flour, eggs, milk, and vanilla extract—and while the cupcakes are baking they whip up a homemade buttercream frosting. With Brady's help, they frost and top each cupcake with a generous handful of colorful sprinkles that Frances always keeps on hand. They don't talk about Mei Ling, about how Frances's life feels like it's falling apart at the seams. Instead they talk about food, about her boys, about the cello, even Jamie. Frances can tell they're in love and it makes her think about Reed and the chasm that's grown between them because of what's happened.

When Frances drops off the cupcakes she receives a heartfelt cheer from Noah's class. Noah is beaming with pride and Baxter is thrilled to be having a proper birthday after all (Newton was sadly absent having been rushed to the vet). As her middle son gives her a grateful hug, Frances feels something inside her shift. It's subtle. While she wouldn't call it a happy decision, she knows that it's the right one, at least for now.

She stops at Reed's office on the way home. It's too important to wait until dinner, and she doesn't want him unmoored any longer than he has to be. She spies him through the glass wall of his office, talking with a coworker, and is struck by how much she loves him. It makes her decision even more certain.

Brady is the first to call out. "Hi, Dad!"

Reed looks up, surprised. "Brady," he says, striding over to them. He lifts Brady from her arms, pulls Frances in for a kiss. He buries his face in her hair. She inhales him, this scent of her husband. It's only been a couple of days but she's missed it.

"I'm sorry," he says. "I'm sorry about Mei Ling. It hasn't been easy for me but I can only imagine how difficult it's been for you."

"I know," she whispers. He guides them back to his office, closes the door. Brady is instantly taken by the stapler and tape dispenser. Reed hands him some scratch paper.

"Let's talk about it more tonight," he says.

Frances shakes her head. "I think we've said everything that needs to be said."

Reed looks sad. "I know. But are you okay with it?"

She gives a small lift of her shoulders. "I don't know that I ever will be," she admits. "But I don't want to make a decision as big as this unless we're both on board and feeling confident. Really confident. And I accept that we're not there, as much as it breaks my heart. But our life is good. Really good. And I'm grateful for that."

Reed nods. "Me too."

Frances takes a deep breath. Her voice is shaky. "So I think we should let the agency know that we're turning down the referral."

Reed is silent.

"I also don't think I can go through this again. Maybe adoption isn't for us—for me, at least. I don't feel right bringing another child in when I'll be thinking about her and what could have been."

There's a doubtful look on his face. "Are you sure about this, Fran?"

She stares at him, her heart racing for a moment. "I'm sure. Are you not sure?"

He hesitates but then he says, "I'm sure enough."

They stare at each other. Frances takes her husband's hands, accepting his decision and her own even though she wishes it could have been different. This is still good, and she has to remember this and not let it tear them apart as it has other families. "I love you, Reed," Frances says simply.

"I love you, too, Fran." He leans toward her, kisses her gently.

"I'll call the agency in the morning," she says. "I want to be the one to do it." She feels her heart clench but there's a sense of renewed determination. "And then I want to get our life back to normal."

"Normal?" Reed chuckles as he gives a wry shake of his head. "No such luck. We left normal years ago." He brushes his hand along her cheek and Frances can tell he's sad, too. "I know you've been pushing yourself, and it's been a rough week. And I'm sorry that I have to leave tomorrow for Arizona."

"It's only a couple of days," she says. "I'll be fine."

Reed watches Brady as he pulls out the last of the Scotch tape, having successfully taped Reed's chair to his desk. "Hey, why don't you take a break from everything tonight? Call a girlfriend or go see a movie? I'll watch the boys."

Frances considers this. She's out of her pajamas, after all, so she may as well make the most of it. She doesn't want to bug Hannah who's already been so generous with her time today, but it's the second Thursday of the month and most of the moms she knows already have plans. The idea of being alone holds little appeal. "Thanks, but no one's available tonight. Everyone's been scrapbooking these days, and there's a meeting so they'll be going to that. They have a potluck dinner and then scrapbook for a few hours. It'll be late by the time they're all done."

"Why don't you join them?" Reed suggests. "That sounds like fun."

"Maybe." There are so many things that she should do first—clean the garage, pack away the summer clothes—that she feels a bit guilty at the thought of sticking pictures on paper.

"It'll be good for me, too," Reed says. "I miss hanging out with the boys. Maybe I'll take them to the arcade, challenge them to a couple rounds of air hockey."

"That sounds like the perfect activity right before bedtime on a school night," Frances says, but it makes her smile.

"I'll get them to bed, so you don't have to worry about it. Go to this scrapbooking meeting, Fran. Sound good?"

Frances looks out the window. Maybe the

change of pace will do her good, help her get her mind off things, steel her for the difficult conversation tomorrow. She went to one meeting a couple of years ago and it was fun. "Okay," she agrees. "That does sound good."

Trick McGaughy, 52
On-Air Personality and Radio Host, KAVL 94.5 FM

"This is Trick McGaughy and you're on KAVL 94.5 FM, Avalon. What's your question?"

"Hi, Trick. My mother-in-law is driving me nuts. We have a five-year-old boy and she keeps buying him toys and candy even though we tell her not to. It drives my wife crazy, which in turn makes me crazy. What should I do?"

Trick leans in to the microphone and steeples his fingers together. "How long have you been married?"

"About seven years."

"And your boy—how's he? Good kid?"

"Yeah, he's great. We don't want her spoiling him with stuff we don't agree on."

"Huh. Well, I think I have an answer to your problem. Ready? Here it is: GET OVER IT. She's doing exactly what a grandma's supposed to do. Consider yourself lucky that she's involved at all. Let's move on to our next caller . . . this is Trick McGaughy and you're on KAVL 94.5 FM. What's your question?"

"Hey, Trick. Just want you to know I love your show and your straight-shootin'-tell-it-like-it-is advice. It's helped me with each of my three divorces, and I appreciate it." The man's voice is gravelly and he coughs.

Smoker, Trick decides. Fifties or sixties. Probably got a paunch around his belly. "Flattery will get you everywhere," he says, pleased. "What can I do for you today, sir?"

"Well, I haven't had much luck with the ladies, as you can probably guess. But there's this new gal at work and I think there might be a spark . . ."

"Whoa, let me stop you right there. I think we both know how this is going to turn out."

The man protests, "But I'm telling you, this gal is different, Trick."

"She might be, but you're not. I don't think the problem is with the ladies, my friend. I suggest you take a little alone time, maybe pick up a hobby or two. What about fishing? You like fishing?"

"Not rea—"

"I suggest you spend your money on a good reel and learn to do a little catch-and-release. That's where you let the fish go after you catch them. Might be a good lesson for you to carry into your romantic life—I'm not so sure you want another divorce under your belt. It shortens your life span. Next caller, you're on the air with Trick McGaughy . . ."

Trick has a one-hour slot including the occasional commercial, so he takes his time listening to the rest of the callers and doling out his sage advice. It's the same old thing—boy-friends who won't commit, bosses intimidating employees, stressed out babysitters, love affairs gone awry, wives catching husbands watching illicit videos on the Internet. The problem across the board is relationships, which is why he's single and has been for a long time. He'll take loneliness over drama any day.

His producer, Damian Moon, taps his watch and points to the board. One caller to go and then they're done. Easiest job in the world. He'll head home, throw in a frozen pizza, watch a little TV.

". . . and you're listening to KAVL 94.5 FM with Trick McGaughy. Ask me your questions, I'll tell you no lies. What's your question?"

"I would like to know what your credentials are for giving people advice!" comes a snappy voice over the studio speakers.

Trick looks at Damian who shrugs his shoulders. "Just this thing between my ears called a brain," Trick says. "I try to use it when other people can't seem to find theirs. Most people have too much therapy—I'm their quick and easy alternative to a better life." *Ha, take that, lady!*

"A better life? Quick and easy? What planet are you living on? I don't think it's a good idea for you to trivialize people's issues!"

"Hey, they call me, I don't call them. And I don't hear anyone complaining." In fact, Trick has a stack of fan mail that says the opposite.

"*I'm* complaining, young man! A woman in my scrapbooking club called you, quite distressed about a debate she'd been having with her husband over a new car. They're retired, they have no debt, and you told her to stop being a tightwad and to loosen up, that life's too short. Well, I'll have you know that she took your advice to heart and cashed in one of her IRAs so they could buy this new car. Which her husband drove straight into a tree because the man is as blind as a bat. Thank goodness he didn't hurt himself or someone else!"

Trick vaguely remembers the caller, maybe two or three months back. "Lady, I am not a financial analyst and I don't work for the DMV. I tell it like it is. I'm giving out my opinion, that's all. And you should probably consider the fact that since the car was new, it might have saved his life. If they'd bought an old clunker, it might have folded up like some old accordion." Damian gives him a triumphant thumbs-up and Trick grins.

"Oh?" the woman says, her voice loud. "Is that what you think, Mr. Big Shot?"

Mr. Big Shot. Trick squares his shoulders even though she can't see him. "Yeah, that's what I think. And I think you should mind your own business, lady. People have a hard enough time in life without having other people butt in. People like you are the problem, not the solution. If your friend doesn't like the advice I gave, *she* should be calling me, not you."

"I'll have you know that one of the great blessings in life is to have people around you who care," she counters huffily. "Did you call for help when his car hit the tree? Drive his wife to the hospital, arrange a phone tree so people could offer good wishes and send food over? Are you the one sitting in the hospital room with him? Cleaning their house? Talking to the insurance company? Making sure their cat is fed?"

Trick shifts uneasily in his chair. "Lady, I don't even know these people."

"My point exactly." There's a smugness in her voice. "Now, I know people will keep listening to you no matter what I say. I know you live alone and keep to yourself. That's no way to live, Mr. McGaughy. We all need people. So I'll be coming by the studio—"

Trick looks at Damian in alarm. He doesn't do personal appearances and he most definitely does not want to put a face to any voice. "Don't come by the studio—" he begins.

"—and dropping off my card, along with some materials so you can come to a meeting of the Avalon Ladies Scrapbooking Society and meet some of the people who listen to you. And this time, I think you should listen to them. You might learn a thing or two about real life and be able to give out more thoughtful advice in the future.

And since I know we're live on the air, I have all your listeners as my witnesses, and the ladies of the Society will be making it their mission to call you until you come to a meeting."

"I'm not coming to any meeting and that's all we have time for today. This is Trick McGaughy and—"

"—and Mr. Moon, your mother and I go way back. She's a fine woman and a member of the Society, too. We'll be expecting *both* of you at our meeting tonight."

Damian looks panicked and hits the button to queue the music, but it's too late. The damage has been done.

Trick pulls the headphones off his ears and stares at Damian. "What was that?"

"Man, she told my mom?" Damian says with a shake of his head. "That's low."

"Well, I'm not going," Trick says stubbornly. He doesn't like being coerced like this. This is why he doesn't interact with people directly unless it's absolutely necessary.

"Did you hear her?" Damian looks chagrined. "You have to! Plus I don't want my mom on my case—she's already threatening to kick me out."

Trick is disgusted. "I don't know what you're doing living at home anyway—you're forty, Damian."

"Hey, it's free rent, man. Not all of us get to be big radio stars. Plus she has cable . . ."

Trick just shakes his head.

". . . and she's my mom." Damian looks down. "She's been lonely since my dad died. Marcia got the house after my divorce and I didn't have a place to live—it works out well for both of us. It's kind of nice, actually." He looks up at Trick. "Look, I'd consider it a personal favor if you'd go, Trick."

Trick makes a face. He's worked with Damian for about ten years, but he doesn't mix his personal life with his work life. And a scrapbooking meeting? Trick doesn't even know what that is. "Sorry, buddy, but I have plans tonight."

"No, you don't. And Trick, I'd do it for you." The look on Damian's face is serious, and Trick knows he's right.

"Fine," Trick finally grumbles. "I'll go." He breaks into a grin when Damian claps him on the shoulder in happy relief.

"You're a good friend," Damian says, and Trick looks at him in surprise. He doesn't keep company with anyone so this is a label he isn't used to. "My mom always brings this meatball corn stew that's really good. I'll tell her to make extra for you. Hey, you've never even been over to our place! Why don't you stop by before the meeting? I'll give you directions. You know, I bet those old ladies will have tons of questions for you. This might even be kind of fun!" Damian is babbling like a teenager.

Trick's not so sure about that, but there's no backing out now. As for fun, well, Trick's annoyance is turning a bit into admiration—it's not every day he has a caller who can steamroll him like that, and he has to admit that he's a bit curious to meet this lady who sounds like someone's grandma. Trick thinks back to his own grandmother, now long gone, and just as feisty.

"Meatball corn stew," he says with a nod. "All right. I'm in. What time do you want me there?"

Chapter Nine

"This is so typical," Isabel complains as she stirs her tomato soup. She drops in a handful of croutons, wishing she'd thought to pick up some real food before coming over. Yvonne never seems to have more than soup and rice cakes in her pantry. "You find the only available guy in Avalon, and of course he's a looker."

"Make that with a capital L." Yvonne is glowing.

Isabel shoots her an annoyed look. "But he does live with his mother," she reminds her.

"Yeah, the jury's still out on that one. But maybe he's got a good reason, like she's sick or something." Yvonne's brow furrows. "Although she looked pretty healthy to me. So that's probably not it."

"Maybe he's gay," Isabel suggests a bit too hopefully.

"Nice try. I don't think so." Yvonne is smirking.

Isabel points her spoon at Yvonne. "I got it. He's the devil in disguise."

Yvonne rolls her eyes.

"What? I'm saying it seems a bit too good to be true, you know?" Isabel has lived in Avalon long enough to know that even though the town is growing as retirees and small families move in, it's still not a place where good-looking single men tend to flock to. "What did he say he does? For a living?"

"Some kind of family business. We didn't have time to get into it." Yvonne stirs her soup dreamily. "Anyway, one date won't hurt. And maybe if it goes well and we decide to go out again, we could double date." She looks at Isabel. "Hey, that would be fun!"

"Now I know you're joking." It's bad enough that Yvonne is oozing giddiness like a schoolgirl, but Isabel doesn't want to get roped in, too.

"I'm serious. Look at it this way: we double date, you can check him out, save me from certain disappointment. Unless, of course, he turns out to be as perfect as he looks."

"Doubtful."

Yvonne can't be dissuaded. "You never know," she sings as she scoops up Isabel's almost-empty bowl.

"Hey, I wasn't finished with that!" Isabel protests, spoon still in hand.

"We both need to be eating better," Yvonne declares, dropping the bowls into the sink. "Let's go out and get a salad." She plucks the spoon from Isabel's hand and tosses it into one of the bowls.

Isabel pouts. "In case it's escaped you, *I* don't have anyone I need to stay in shape for."

"It's not just what we eat, Isabel. I'm talking about making changes from the inside out."

"Oh great. Next you're going to tell me you're a lifestyle coach."

"I'm serious, Isabel. We've both been in a bit of a rut lately, kind of going through the motions with life. Maybe we should be doing more to feel better for ourselves."

"I don't want to do all that for some guy," Isabel says. "I did that with Bill, and look where that got me."

"We wouldn't be doing it for some guy," says Yvonne. She turns off the water then sits down next to Isabel. "We'd be doing it for ourselves."

Isabel shakes her head, unconvinced.

"Look," Yvonne says earnestly. "I want to feel good about myself . . ."

"From the inside out. I got it."

". . . *so I can do more with my life.* I got into the trades because I wanted to make a difference, and for some reason I've been so caught up in my day-to-day life that I forgot about that. This might be a way for us to connect with ourselves again."

Yvonne is so earnest that Isabel bites her tongue, refrains from cracking another joke about breaking out the white sage or doing some weird dance in the moonlight. And it's true that she stepped on the scale the other day and nearly toppled over. She's been a rail most of her life, not lean and curvy like Yvonne, but she's put on small pockets of weight here and there, and it's been discouraging. And she used to love to cook—simple meals, at least, but her cooking was something that Bill used to love and compliment her on. Maybe that's why she doesn't bother anymore—she can't stand being in the kitchen or preparing any of her favorite dishes that used to be Bill's favorites, too. Isabel has been eating out for a long time, and could afford to continue eating out a little while longer, but she's realizing that maybe she's hungry for something else.

"Fine," she says grumpily, because she's not at all sure how this is going to go. She hopes it doesn't entail any kind of schedule or calorie counting, both of which she has little interest in. "And by the way, *if* we were to double date, did it occur to you that I don't have anyone to take on this alleged date?"

"Oh, don't worry about that," Yvonne says blithely. She reaches for a pad of paper, starts making out a shopping list. "Guys like Hugh always have friends. I'm sure one of them will go out with you."

"Gosh, thanks, I feel so much better now."

Yvonne laughs just as her phone rings. She checks the display, then grabs Isabel's arm. "It's Hugh! Should I answer it?"

Before Isabel can say anything, Yvonne presses the RECEIVE button and composes herself. "Yvonne Tate," she says, her voice a mixture of sexy allure and fake boredom.

Isabel watches as her friend goes through a round of animated conversation, laughing at something or other. *So this is what dating looks like,* Isabel thinks, feeling a twinge of envy. It's been so long that she's forgotten. Bill had been her first real love, and then they'd married. She hadn't planned on ever being with anyone else. Unlike him, obviously.

This whole Ava thing would have been easier if there hadn't been a child. The child was the wild card, the unfair advantage. Isabel, who'd had three miscarriages after years of trying and fertility treatments. Bill had wanted a family, and even though he swore the pregnancy was unexpected, it seemed a little too convenient. And now Isabel is alone, husbandless, childless, even ex-husbandless, with only Yvonne to count as a friend. What's the likelihood there will be someone out there who will want to date her?

"Oh, Hugh." Yvonne is giggling.

Isabel's never gotten used to this, the banter that goes on during the courting period. She sees it all the time at work, can spot a blooming office romance a mile away. There's the flirting and small private signals that people think no one else can notice but it's the opposite—it's so obvious you could set your watch to it. *I'll meet you in the break room in 5. XOXO.*

"This is a bad idea," Isabel says the minute Yvonne hangs up. "I've changed my mind."

"You can't change your mind, I've already started our shopping list," Yvonne says calmly, holding up the piece of paper.

"The only thing you wrote on there is our names, Yvonne."

"Well, it's a start. Hey, do you want to know what Hugh said?"

Not really, but she knows Yvonne is going to tell her whether she wants to hear or not, so she shrugs and says, "Tell me."

"He says that Toby missed me after I left."

Isabel pretends to vomit. Yvonne swats her, laughing, just as Isabel's cellphone begins to ring.

"Well, well. Isn't this interesting?" Yvonne says as Isabel reaches into her purse. "Maybe someone's calling to ask *you* on a hot date."

"Ha-ha," Isabel says, but it's curious. Nobody other than her boss or Yvonne uses this number. Isabel looks at the display but doesn't recognize the number.

"Tell him you like chardonnay and long walks on the beach," Yvonne whispers as Isabel says hello.

"Isabel!" comes the screech. "I hope to God you're not being a potato couch!"

A potato couch? What? Isabel checks the display again, then puts the phone back to her ear. "Who is this?"

"I'm at Madeline's and we're about to start our

meeting, but I forgot to bring my pop-up glue dots. You'd better hurry."

Bettie. Yvonne is leaning against her, curious, trying to listen. Isabel swats her away. "How'd you get this number?" she demands.

"The keys are under the mat, and the dots are in the large box on the shelf labeled ADHESIVES." There's some mumbling on the other end and Isabel hears Bettie say, "Oh, thank you, Tess, but Isabel has it all taken care of."

"Bettie, I'm not even home . . ."

"The girls and I will be waiting. It looks like we have a full house tonight. See you soon!" Bettie hangs up before Isabel can respond.

"Unbelievable," Isabel mutters. She recounts the brief conversation to Yvonne, who listens with interest.

"Well, obviously you have to go help," Yvonne says with authority.

"No way." Isabel sits in her chair, arms crossed. "I'm not her lackey."

"No, you're not. You're her neighbor." Yvonne flicks off the kitchen lights, grabs her purse. "Come on. I'll go with you. It'll be fun to see everyone again."

Isabel grumbles as she gathers her things. "And you know what else she said? She accused me of being a potato couch."

"You mean couch potato?"

"She said potato couch."

"I'm sure she meant couch potato. She's probably got a lot on her mind, trying to get ready for the meeting while coming up with a solution for the Glue Dot Dilemma. What is a glue dot anyway?" Yvonne holds open the front door.

"Who knows. Some overpriced scrapbooking thing, no doubt."

"The only thing worse would be the Case of the Dried Out Inking Stamps."

"Or the Which Sequins to Choose Affair." At the meeting in Isabel's home, Mrs. Wingert had spent a full half hour deliberating on the right assortment of sequins for her project, fretting that she didn't want to make the wrong choice.

"Fuchsia or teal?" Yvonne remembers, laughing.

It takes the women less than five minutes to drive to Isabel's neighborhood. Isabel looks next door at her own home, dark and lonely, then turns up Bettie's walk with Yvonne at her heels.

Isabel surveys the welcome sign on Bettie's door. WARNING: THIS HOUSE IS PROTECTED BY AN AVID SCRAPBOOKER. She sighs and bends down, lifts a corner of the doormat and then the other.

"There aren't any keys here," Isabel says. She picks up the doormat and gives it a good shake. Bits of dirt and crushed leaves fall down.

Yvonne tries the front door. "Locked," she reports.

The two women look up and down Bettie's porch. There's an old wrought iron bench, a few dying potted plants. A two-foot stone statue of an angel is tucked into the far corner, its nose chipped, and covered with cobwebs.

"I wonder . . ." Isabel says as she walks over. She sneezes when a cloud of dust rises as she rocks the angel from side to side. "This thing weighs a ton."

"Look!" Yvonne exclaims, and then Isabel sees it. A glimmer of steel. A key.

Isabel picks up the key. "That's an odd shape," she says, frowning. "It looks too small."

"Try it anyway," Yvonne suggests.

Isabel tries to slip the key into the lock but it won't fit. "Nope," she says. She looks at Yvonne. "What should we do?" She puts the key back under the angel and wipes her hands.

Yvonne is chewing on her lip, a look of uncertainty on her face. "Well, okay. Here's the thing: I can probably get us into the house but I'll have to use some unconventional methods."

"Does it involve a rock and a window?"

"Of course not!" Yvonne gives her an exasperated look.

"Okay, okay. Just hurry."

Yvonne goes to her truck and comes back with her tool chest. She rummages around and then holds up what looks like a couple of wires. She turns to the door and starts to jimmy the lock. A few seconds later there's a click, and Yvonne turns the knob and pushes the door open.

Isabel stares at her. "What are you, a thief? Do you have a record?"

"Don't be ridiculous. I studied to be a locksmith, too, that's all. Learned a few tricks of the trade. Now come on."

The women don't get past the foyer.

"Oh my God," Yvonne says, struck. "What happened?"

Isabel looks around, speechless. It's as if a hurricane has come through and upended everything. The house looks ransacked—items strewn everywhere, books and mail on the floor, craft items spilling off the tables and shelves. "I don't know," she manages to say.

Yvonne reaches for her phone. "Should I call the police?"

Isabel shakes her head. "The door was locked, remember? Nobody broke in here." She gingerly takes a step forward, then slowly begins to make her way around Bettie's house.

Isabel has only been in Bettie's house a few times, but it's always been neat as a pin. Bettie is one of those organized people who keeps every-thing in well-labeled, matching boxes. But now everything is in disarray. In the kitchen, Isabel notices the dishes piled up in the sink, plates of half-eaten food scattered everywhere. Isabel has to pinch her nose to block out the stench.

"It wasn't like this when I came here to fix her sink," Yvonne says, bewildered. "What was that, a month ago? Something's seriously wrong here."

That much is clear. But Isabel doubts it has anything to do with anyone other than Bettie.

Her cellphone rings again and Isabel sees it's the same number as before. "Bettie?"

"Isabel, where are you? Did you find the dots? We're about to start the meeting, but there's no way I can do my segment on 'Scrapbooking Secrets' if I don't have them!" Bettie sounds indignant.

"I'm looking for them now," Isabel says, gesturing to Yvonne to start looking. "But, uh, I'm having a little trouble finding them."

"Oh for goodness' sake. Are you in my craft room? It's toward the back of the house, near the laundry room." Bettie hangs up with a click.

"You're welcome," Isabel mutters.

They pick their way to the craft room, which is in marginally better shape than the rest of the house. After a few minutes, Isabel finds the box labeled ADHESIVES but finds everything except for adhesives inside.

"Maybe we should stop by the store and buy some," Yvonne suggests.

"We don't even know what we're looking for," Isabel says, opening every box. A few minutes later, she holds up a box labeled FIBERS triumphantly. "Pay dirt. Glue sticks, glue guns, instant decoupage sealer, rolls of washi tape and . . ." She reads off a clear packet filled with adhesive foam cut in the shape of circles. "Pop-up glue dots!"

Yvonne is gagging as she holds up a half-eaten package of powdered donuts dotted with mold before dropping it in a trashcan that's already overflowing. "We don't need to diet—I've officially lost my appetite. Forever."

Isabel nods toward the door, still unable to make sense of everything around her. "Me, too. Let's go."

"The September meeting of the Avalon Ladies Scrapbooking Society is now in order. Please take your seats, ladies."

Ava sucks in her breath. There are so many people here, so many women who look familiar, a few whom Ava remembers. She wishes she hadn't said yes to Bettie Shelton, who had called to invite her to the tea salon for dinner. She had foolishly assumed that Bettie wanted to buy some inventory or get a few ideas, and she was so encouraged by the news that Margot had almost sold out of Ava's jewelry that she had said yes without really thinking about it.

Max is covering his arm with stickers. "Look!" he says to Ava, who puts a finger to her lips.

"Shh," she whispers, but smiles and pulls him onto her lap. Bettie had a small packet of stickers and paper ready for him when they walked through the door.

Ava hugs Max tighter to her. He's excited to be out, has enjoyed being fawned over by the ladies of the scrapbooking club. She's relieved not to be alone, and she's planning on using him as an excuse to get out of there. *Bedtime,* she'll say apologetically to Bettie the first chance she gets.

She waits impatiently as Bettie goes through the minutes of the last meeting, makes some announcements.

"Tonight I want everyone to think outside the album," Bettie is saying. "Memories can happen anywhere. It's not just the big events, but the small moments, too. Scrapbooking isn't about making things pretty on the page, but about how you feel, about the details in life that are special, that feel good. Invite others to take an emotional journey with you. Using textures in your layouts is one of the fastest ways to get people there." She frowns and scans the room, then mutters, "Isabel better show up with those glue dots soon."

Startled, Ava looks around. Did Bettie mean Isabel Kidd?

"So, since we're talking about texture today, I'm pleased to introduce our surprise guest, Ava Catalina. She's the owner of Free Hearts, a bottle-cap jewelry company."

Despite her anxiety, Ava feels herself flush with

pleasure. Owner? Company? It sounds so official, so real. Bettie nods toward her and the women turn around and start clapping.

"And her son, Matt . . ."

"Max," Ava corrects politely as Max smiles on cue. "Thank you for having me," she adds to everyone. There are approving nods and smiles. No one seems to know who she is, and it feels good to be noticed in a way that doesn't involve disapproving snickers or scowls.

"We'll have Ava up after the break," Bettie says. "I'm also pleased to announce that I'll be hosting a beginner's scrapbooking primer in ten minutes for you newbies. As for the rest of you, Madeline has given us full use of the sitting room and dining area, so find your work space and let's start scrappin'!" There's a *bang* as she hits a wood block with a decorated mallet, making Ava jump.

There's a small cheer as the women stand up and quickly start arranging themselves. *After the break,* Ava thinks with dread. Maybe she can talk to Bettie, explain that unfortunately she won't be able to stay so late because of Max's bedtime.

"Don't forget to use your punches!" Bettie calls out to everyone. "And make the most of your chipboard alphas—this is a great time to break them out if you've been holding back!"

"Oh my God," Ava hears a murmur behind her. "Let's drop this off and go."

"Five minutes," another voice begs. "Did you see those cute tags Bettie has in this month's scrap pack? They're *embossed,* Isabel."

"I'm going to pretend we're not even having this conversation," comes the annoyed reply.

Ava gives a quarter turn, then freezes when she sees who it is. It *is* Isabel Kidd, and she's with her friend. They're a formidable pair, confident and pretty, though Isabel clearly looks put out. Ava shrinks in her chair, buries her face in Max's hair as she tries to come up with a plan.

"FINALLY!" she hears Bettie say. "I thought you'd never get here! You can put them over here. And you brought Yvonne, how lovely!"

As the women walk away, Ava scoops Max into her arms and hurries toward the exit.

"Oh, isn't he adorable?" A woman carrying a box of tea bags stops to give them a smile. Ava recognizes her as the owner of the tea salon.

"I'm Madeline," the woman says. "And this is Connie." She nods to the young woman behind her. Connie is holding a china platter filled with small pastries.

"I'm hungry, Mommy," Max says, looking up at Ava. He wouldn't eat when they first arrived, too enthralled by all the commotion. Ava had only picked at her food, unsure of what was happening, still reeling from the shock that her "dinner" with Bettie included thirty other women toting small luggage carts filled with paper.

"There's still plenty of food on the buffet," Madeline says. "I think the ladies plan on grazing all night. Help yourself."

"We need to be going," Ava says quickly. "But thank you."

"I'm hungry," Max says again, and there's a hint of a whine.

"Here," Connie says, handing Max a pastry, then looks at Ava guiltily. "Oh, sorry, I should have checked with you first. Is it okay that I gave that to him? It's an apple dumpling." They watch as Max shoves the whole thing into his mouth.

"Moruh," Max says, his mouth full.

Ava sighs. "It's okay," she says.

"There you are!" Bettie exclaims, hurrying up behind them. "Ava, I was thinking that it would be so much fun if you could talk about how to use bottle caps in our layouts, or maybe as a separate do-it-yourself project with leftover paper scraps. I know the ladies would welcome your ideas."

"Well, I haven't had much time to think about it," Ava says, wanting to get out of there before Isabel sees her. "And you know, Max is tired . . ." She nods apologetically at her son who's reaching for another apple dumpling. He smiles at them, looking anything but tired.

"Oh, he looks like he's having fun!" Bettie says, producing another package of stickers. "Look what I have, Matt!"

Max reaches for it and then says again, "I'm hungry."

"Perfect!" Bettie cries. "Connie can take him to get some food, can't you?"

"Actually . . ." Connie begins but Bettie gives Max a tickle and in the same motion manages to extract him from Ava's arms and plop him into Connie's while passing the apple dumpling platter to Madeline. Both Madeline and Connie have their arms full as Bettie drags Ava away.

"Now, I'm going to do a quick 101 for you and a few other new members."

"I don't scrapbook . . ." Ava begins.

"Exactly!" Bettie nods her head as if Ava has proved her point. "Everyone says that, but the truth is that everybody scrapbooks in one way or another—you just don't know it. It's my job to give you the right tools to make it easier to preserve those special memories. Don't you want to have something nice for Matt?"

"Max . . ."

"They grow up so fast, and we're all so busy these days. Scrapbooking a little bit here and there ensures that we remember the moments that matter most. It'll be something he'll treasure when he's older." Bettie smiles. "Don't you want that for him?"

What a low blow. Ava hasn't even put together Max's baby book, doesn't keep a journal of any kind. She's been meaning to do something, but every time she begins to sift through the photos, it feels hard and overwhelming, incomplete. She doesn't know where to begin and at the same time is afraid of leaving something out, knowing already that the biggest piece isn't there.

"Now, you don't have to worry about anything right now. Just listen and play—that's what I tell everyone. Listen and play, and see where it goes from there. You'll be amazed at what happens when you have pretty patterned paper and card stock looking back at you! It's like something opens up inside. Come on!" Bettie tugs on her arm.

"Bettie, I can't." Ava untangles herself from Bettie's grip and holds her ground. "I'm sorry, but I can't go back in."

"Why not?"

Ava hesitates. "Because there's someone there who would be very upset if she saw me."

Bettie stops and stares at her. "Who? I know every lady in there and I can assure you that you'd be welcome."

Ava shakes her head. "I don't think so."

"I'd stake my life on it," Bettie declares. "Now who is it?"

Ava swallows. She can tell that Bettie won't let up unless Ava tells her. "Isabel Kidd."

"But why would Isabel . . ." There's a long, drawn-out pause as Bettie stares at Ava. In the instant when Bettie puts two and two together, Ava can almost see the lightbulb go off.

She explains, "As you know, I used to work for her husband, Bill, in the dental office. We were together for a year before he died. Max is Bill's son." There's a rush of heat to her cheeks when she says it out loud, but it's freeing, too. A relief. It's the first time she's actually said what had happened, who Max is.

"Oh lordy lord lord lord," Bettie mutters. She chews her lip as she shakes her head. "Well, of course! I have to say, I am gobsmacked. Didn't see this one coming, no, I didn't."

"I'm sorry about the presentation," Ava says. "Maybe I could leave some samples with you and—"

"Just when you think you've seen it all," Bettie continues with a shake of the head. "It's funny how life works, don't you think? I certainly don't blame you for not wanting to stay. If I were in your shoes, I'd certainly be tempted to run away, too. There's no other solution, now, is there?"

Ava stiffens. "I'm not running away. I just don't want to cause her any more unhappiness."

Bettie pats her arm soothingly, as if she were a small child. "Of course not. Now let's get you out of here before Isabel sees you. She's all worked up for some reason or another—you certainly wouldn't want to get in her way tonight!" She begins to steer Ava toward the front door.

"Wait, I have to get Max . . ." Ava begins when Isabel and her friend walk into the foyer.

"Yvonne, we're going," Isabel is saying darkly as her friend protests. She stops talking when she sees Ava.

Ava wants to run, but she can't get her legs to cooperate. They're like jelly, threatening to buckle.

"Well!" Bettie says, clearing her throat. "This is certainly awkward." She looks between the two women.

Neither Ava nor Isabel respond.

Ava feels Isabel's eyes boring into her, searching, accusing. Resentment and anger are shimmering from her like heat off a sidewalk. Unlike Isabel's outburst in front of her house, this is worse. Much worse. Isabel seems different somehow, more prepared, more powerful, and Ava can sense every emotion running through Isabel's body. Forgiveness and understanding, however, are nowhere in the vicinity.

"You," Isabel says. She turns to her friend. "It's *her.*" She spits the word out, like a threat.

Ava glances at Bettie, who seems both concerned and a little enthralled. The hubbub of women and activity continues around them as if everything were normal, as if Ava weren't concerned for her safety and well-being. At the moment she doesn't know what Isabel might do, she just knows she should get out of there before she has a chance to find out.

Isabel's friend puts a hand on her arm and

says in a quiet voice, "Come on, Isabel. Let's go."

"NO." Isabel is rooted on the spot, her hands on her hips. Ava can almost picture Isabel wearing a cape, an avenging superhero, wind blowing in her hair as she's about to take down a villain.

"Isabel," Ava says. "I'm sorry, I—I didn't know you were going to be here. But I'm leaving now."

Bettie purses her lips but doesn't try to persuade Ava to stay. Even Isabel seems satisfied with this, her glare a little less hostile, her stance softening a little, the tightness easing up.

For a second Ava thinks it might all be okay, that she might get out of there, when she hears Max's laughter and the sound of small footsteps running up behind her.

"Mommy!" he exclaims, and launches into her arms. "I have a goody bag for us!" He holds up a brown paper bag tied with a ribbon. A yellow letter *M* is taped to the top. "It's my Happy Meal! The *M* is for Max!"

Connie and Madeline appear behind him, smiling.

"He's so cute," Connie says. "He said he wanted to share it with you so we decided to fill a to-go bag. He found that ribbon and chipboard *M* on the scrap table."

"Swap table," Bettie corrects, then reddens when she remembers what's going on.

Ava doesn't look at Isabel, her cheeks hot. She says hastily to Connie and Madeline, "Thank you."

"No problem," Connie says.

"Max is a delight," Madeline agrees. "He's welcome here anytime." She smiles pleasantly at Isabel and her friend. "Hello, I'm Madeline Davis."

Bettie clears her throat. "This is *Isabel Kidd* and Yvonne Tate." She blinks frantically at Madeline, like she's sending Morse code with her eyes.

Yvonne shakes their hands but Isabel isn't paying attention to any one of them. The bluster seems to have gone out of her and her face is drawn and pale.

"Well, goodbye," Ava says, and begins to make her way toward the front door.

"This is Max?" Isabel asks. She steps in front of them, stopping them.

Ava clutches Max to her, turns him away from Isabel. She's no longer scared for herself, her own fear dissipating and replaced by a new one as she realizes what this could mean. Bettie and Yvonne are holding their breath while Connie and Madeline look uneasy, aware that something awkward is taking place.

Max pushes his glasses up the bridge of his nose. "Hello," he says.

Ava is holding her breath, too. If she has to, she'll fight. Push back, push her out of the way. Burn the bridge once and for all.

But Isabel doesn't even seem to notice Ava. Her

eyes are on Max, and Ava can see them filling with tears.

"My God," Isabel breathes. Her hand comes up to her mouth, her eyes wide and wet. "He looks just like Bill's baby pictures."

"Really?" Bettie squints and stares at Max. Connie and Madeline inadvertently look at him, too. "Even with those glasses?"

"Bill had strabismus as a kid, but he had surgery and got it corrected." Isabel's voice is a whisper. Ava feels her heart give a leap at this news.

Bill had it, too. Just like Max.

"Stra-bis-what?" Bettie asks, but Isabel is shaking her head, unable to answer.

"Strabismus," Ava says quietly. "Misaligned or crossed eyes. Max's isn't too bad so he won't need a procedure, but he has to do regular exercises to strengthen the muscles in his eyes."

"It's probably hereditary," Bettie says, and then stops when she realizes what she's said. "I mean . . ."

At hearing this, Isabel seems to jerk back to her old self. She straightens up and clears her throat, wipes her eyes. "I have to go." She spins and leaves before anyone can say anything, almost bumping into someone walking into the tea salon.

"Isabel!" Yvonne calls, but she's already gone.

"Let her go," Bettie says, reaching out to touch Yvonne's arm. "Give her some time."

233

Yvonne watches her friend disappear, worry etched on her face, but doesn't go after her.

Ava feels terrible. She isn't quite sure what to make of this turn of events. It was her plan to leave, but Isabel beat her to it. She doesn't know what to do now. Max wiggles in her arms, grinning happily, oblivious. She holds him tighter, still processing the information that Bill also had strabismus. She'll have to tell Max's doctor, not that it will make any difference, but it can go into the file as a note. *Hereditary predisposition.* One more thing that Bill and Max share, something Ava can't wait to tell him once they get home.

"Excuse me." The woman who just walked in stares at the cluster of women, at Bettie, Madeline, Connie, Yvonne, and Ava. "My name is Frances Latham and I'm looking for the scrapbooking meeting. Am I late?"

Bettie checks her watch and gives it a tap, grateful for the interruption. "You're right on time."

Chapter Ten

"Scrapbooking is part preservation, part visualization," Bettie begins. She's standing in front of a round table where Connie, Yvonne, Ava, and Frances have gathered. Max is helping Madeline straighten up in the kitchen. Connie told her she could do it but Madeline shooed her out, wanting some alone time with Max. Connie knows she misses her granddaughter and that this young boy is like a balm, helping to ease Madeline's longing.

Connie fidgets in her chair, wishes she could be in the kitchen as well. It had just sort of happened, her sitting here. They were all standing awkwardly in the foyer after Isabel had run out, a little stunned and unsure of what to do, and Bettie had been quick to herd them into the sitting room and plunk them into chairs.

"People scrapbook for all sorts of reasons," Bettie continues. "And there are all sorts of ways to do it." In one hand she holds up a thick album with a plastic protective cover, in the other a smaller handmade album held together with two round binder rings and all sorts of decorative fabric, ribbon and paper sticking out of it. On the table other sample albums are spread out in front of them in all shapes and sizes.

Frances Latham raises her hand. Connie sees

her around town every now and then, knows that she's a mom who's always rushing around with her kids, the kind of person who participates in every Avalon fund-raiser or charitable event. She's come into the tea salon a few times, usually as part of one of these special events, never on her own. Connie knows there are lots of women like Frances, women who find it hard to make time for themselves because they're always doing things for others. She makes a note to have special ten-percent-off coupons that they can hand out to Society members the next time they come in for tea, maybe with a special surprise treat on their first visit, a small pot of jam tied with a ribbon or a cluster of fresh lavender.

"My problem is I don't know where to start," Frances admits. "I have so many pictures, it's overwhelming to think about organizing everything. And our pictures are scattered everywhere—some are still in the envelope from when I picked them up from the store! If I have to go back and start documenting everything after the first year my kids were born, they'll be in college before I'm done."

There's laughter. Ava is sitting next to Frances and tells her, "I haven't even done my son's baby album yet."

Frances sighs. "Tell me about it."

"I don't have any kids," Yvonne says. "But it seems a bit indulgent to scrapbook about myself."

Connie wasn't planning on saying anything when the words slip out of her mouth. "I don't have anything to scrapbook about," she says. "I hardly have any pictures from my past."

The women look at her questioningly and Connie wishes she hadn't said anything. But Bettie continues, unconcerned.

"Ladies, scrapbooks are about *memories*. It goes beyond the photographs." She holds up a funky album made of old menu covers. "This one is from Tilde Smart, the lady over there. A few years ago she put together an album filled with menus, napkins, and other memorabilia from restaurants she used to eat at with her college roommate, Sweeney. She has pictures in here, too, but a lot of it is writing, like a journal. Tilde wrote down every memory, every silly joke, any detail she could remember. Sweeney had been diagnosed with cancer, you see, and Tilde wanted to give her something she could take to the hospital when she had treatments. Something to make her smile, take her mind off of what was happening.

"When Sweeney passed, the family sent this back to Tilde. And look." Bettie opens to a random page and shows it to the women. Connie sees two different sets of handwriting. "Sweeney had written her own memories in there, too, next to Tilde's, while she was going through chemotherapy. You can only imagine how Tilde felt when she first opened this and saw Sweeney's handwriting, saw the funny doodles in the margins, a poem Sweeney wrote at the end. Tilde treasures this album. It's part of who she is."

Bettie shows them several more albums. "You get to choose what goes inside," she tells them. "It doesn't have to be in chronological order, it doesn't have to be anything other than what you want it to be. And if you don't have pictures, find other images or words or colors that evoke the memory. Connie, what's one of your favorite memories?"

Connie squirms, again in the hot seat. "I don't have one," she says.

"Not one?" It's clear Bettie doesn't believe her. "A birthday? Christmas? Camp? Anything!"

Images flicker through Connie's mind, but not one of them is worth sharing. "Sorry, I've got nothing."

"Well, what about now? What's something you enjoy doing now?"

"The tea salon," Connie says without hesitation. "And Serena. My goat."

"Ah-ha!" Bettie snaps her fingers. "There you go! An album filled with pictures of you and Madeline, of the tea salon, of some of your favorite menu items. You could even include tea bags, or recipes, or pressed flowers or leaves from the backyard. The salon's business card. Pictures of customers. You could even take the loose tea and stitch in a clear plastic pocket right into your album! And Selena . . ."

"Serena . . ."

". . . I'm sure you can find lots of goat information on the Internet. You could jot specifics about her breed, what she likes to eat, what she likes to play with, funny stories."

"I do that already in my journal."

"So you *are* already scrapbooking!" Bettie looks around at the women, triumphant. "A scrapbook is like a journal except you're adding a stronger visual element. In addition to the words, you're letting the colors of the page, the texture even, remind you of special moments with her. You could even photocopy a page from your journal and put it in the scrapbook, or expand your journal to include more visual pieces. You don't have to scrapbook in a special album—your journal will do just fine."

Connie hadn't thought of that. Her journal is filled with sketches, and occasionally she'll tuck in a small piece of memorabilia, like a movie ticket stub or inspiring word torn out of a magazine. She looks at the fat makeshift album on the table and pictures her journal transformed, with small fabric loops stapled to the page to serve as tabs or dividers.

"There are so many ways to do this, you are only limited by your imagination," Bettie continues. "Choose an event, like a birthday party or a graduation, or even a girls' night out. Scrap about that. Or think about something you want in your future, a new job or new house, and scrap about that. You could scrap a gift for someone special, like Tilde did."

"If it's so simple," Connie asks, "then why all the fuss? Why do we need all this?" She waves at the tables next to them, piled with paper and punches and glittery embellishments.

"The stuff of inspiration, dear," Bettie says. "You can't bake a pie without some basic ingredients, now can you? And the more you have, the more options available to you. Who knows what you'll come up with? Plus, and you might want to sit down for this, Connie . . ."

Connie wrinkles her nose. "I *am* sitting down."

"It's fun." Bettie grins at them. "FUN!"

Yvonne is nodding. "Fun," she repeats, and Connie can tell Yvonne is already hooked.

"I could use some fun," Frances mutters.

"I don't even know what fun is anymore," Ava says quietly. "But I'll take whatever I can get."

Fun? Really? Connie had never thought of scrapbooking as fun. It always seemed to be more of a weird obsession or retailing ploy, but now as she looks around the room, she notices that everyone is relaxed, laughing, enjoying themselves.

"There's no way to get it wrong, and so many ways to get it right," Bettie tells them. "Even if you tie or bind all of your birthday cards together, for example, and tuck in a few pictures or words here and there. Voilà, you're done! You're no longer saving a bunch of cards, but you've taken a moment to imbue it with thoughts and memories. I promise you that in ten years, you'll be glad you did."

Bettie passes out several cellophane packets around the table. "Here's the September scrap pack—lots of fun goodies inside! You don't have to use my kits, of course, but I strongly advise that you choose archival safe materials whenever possible, and that includes any glue or tape. You want your hard work to withstand the test of time, and acid is most certainly *not* your friend."

Connie picks up a packet. Inside are several sheets of scrapbooking paper and card stock, a small clear envelope of buttons, brads, and eyelets. Five different kinds of ribbon and yarn are wrapped around a cardboard tag. There are also small paper frames, embossed tags, clear vellum squares with different words and sayings. A full page of alphabet stickers in a typewriter font and a half sheet of decorative border rub-ons.

"Can I get two?" Yvonne asks. "One for me and one for Isabel?"

"The best value is if you have a membership to the Society," Bettie says. "Only fifteen dollars a month. You get all Society news, discounts on products and classes, the monthly scrap pack which is otherwise $9.99, and unlimited support by me. 'Turning moments into memories,' that's the Bettie Shelton motto and the heart of the Avalon Ladies Scrapbooking Society!"

"I'll join," Frances instantly says. "Where do I sign?"

"Can we trade for some bottle-cap products?" Ava asks Bettie a bit anxiously.

Bettie is nodding as the women bring out their wallets and eagerly open their packets, *ooh*ing and *aah*ing over the contents inside. Connie has to admit that it looks even more appealing once everything is spread out, feels herself drawn to a sheet of black-and-white-checkered paper. Her eyes drift to a sparkly black pom-pom, then a sheet of velvety green card stock. The blue rickrack. Suddenly her mind is swimming with ideas, the items rearranging themselves on a journal page. *Serena,* she thinks. *It would be nice to do a scrapbook of Serena.*

"Connie?" Bettie has an eyebrow raised, nodding to the unopened pack sitting in front of her. "You and Madeline each get a kit for free, plus a starter album. Remember?" She slides the pack closer to Connie until it practically falls into her lap. "You can choose your album now. They're right over there." She points to a sales table filled with merchandise in the corner of the room.

Connie looks to the sales table, Bettie's voice

fading into the background. Albums of different shapes and sizes are propped up across the table, and Connie watches as a couple of women linger and browse there, picking up item after item.

It wouldn't kill her to take a look. That pink frilly album? No way. On second glance, it's a baby album anyway. There's a puffy album with lemons and peaches stamped on the front, and others with polka dots and stripes, rainbows, solid leather or picture windows. Pass, pass, pass, pass. Connie's eyes skim the table, bored, and then she sees it.

A fat square black album with what looks like black lace and graffiti on the cover. Silver fabric tags poke out of the pages, and the entire album is held together with metal binder rings and tied with a stretchy silvery cord. It seems so out of place among the colorful, ornate albums on the table, the black sheep, a misfit.

Perfect.

As Connie rises from her seat, one of the women standing by the table reaches for the album.

"Look at this!" she exclaims. "My niece would love it. What's this called—urban grunge?"

"I don't care for it," her friend informs her. "It perpetuates bad behavior, I think."

"Oh, you're just being a fuddy-duddy. It's a new generation, Eleanor."

Connie hurries over as the woman picks it up. "Hi, sorry, I'd like to get that if you don't want it." She resists the urge to reach out and pluck the album from the woman's hands.

The woman gives her a smile. "Oh, I'm sorry, but I'm getting it for my niece's birthday. Maybe ask Bettie if she has any more?"

"No more," comes a prompt reply from the beginner's table. "Now let's talk about layering!"

"This one's nice," Eleanor says, thrusting a garish lime-green fabric album decorated with paper flowers into Connie's hands. "Green is going to be big this fall."

"I did hear that green is the new black," her friend agrees.

Ugh. "Thanks, but I think I'll keep looking." Connie puts the album back on the table and casts another look around. There's nothing else that holds her interest, not even close. Connie tries to hide her disappointment as she veers away from the beginner's table and makes her way back to the kitchen.

"How's it going?" Madeline asks, handing Max a wooden spoon. It looks like she's put him to work, stirring yogurt and letting him add granola and dried fruit. She gives Connie a wink as she nods toward Max. "He's cooking, aren't you, Max?"

"Yes!"

"Nice," Connie says. She pulls out a chair and flops down. "So when is this scrapbooking meeting going to be over?"

Madeline glances at the clock. "Another hour. You're not having fun?"

Connie tries to shrug. "It's not my thing." Despondent, she drums her fingers on the wooden table.

"That's too bad," Madeline says. There's a wistful look in her eye. "I have to say, though, that I'm inspired. I've decided that I am definitely going to chronicle Steven's life for Maggie. I'm going to do everything I can to share as much as possible about her grandfather. And grandmother. I'll have to ask Ben to help me fill in the details. Do you think he'll mind?"

Connie thinks back to Ben's last visit, over Easter. How they'd hidden eggs in the backyard for Maggie to find, even though she was too young to know what was going on. How she squealed with delight whenever Madeline produced a colorful egg from underneath a bush or from behind a tree. Connie remembers watching Ben's face, the mix of emotions, of gratitude, of love. The entire time he and his wife, Karen, were here was spent in the kitchen, talking with Madeline as she cooked.

"I don't think he'll mind," Connie tells her. "In fact, I think he'd really like it."

"Oh, I hope so," Madeline says. She gives Connie a sheepish look. "I don't want to overstep my bounds."

Connie runs a finger along the smooth grain of

the wood. "You won't," she says. "I think finding ways to show someone you love them is pretty cool. It's the one thing I wished I had more of when I was growing up. Someone to show they cared."

Wordlessly, Madeline comes around the table to give Connie a hug. Connie hugs her back, feels her disappointment about the album slipping away. She's received more hugs from Madeline in the past year than she's had in the past ten. She'll never tire of it.

"Excuse me?" There's a knock on the frame of the doorway. The two women from the sales table are standing there. Connie can see the black album already tucked into a kraft-paper bag.

"Trudy, Eleanor, come in," Madeline says. She wipes her eyes and steps back, gives Connie's arm a squeeze.

Trudy Hughes steps forward. "We wanted to drop this off." She looks at Connie and pats the package in her hands. "You said you wanted this if I didn't?"

Connie feels a small leap of hope. "You didn't get it?"

Trudy smiles. "I've decided to give my niece a gift certificate. Let her choose her own album for herself. Or, as Bettie likes to say, let the album choose her." She holds out the paper bag. "I think this chose you, yes?"

"I still like the green one," Eleanor Winters mutters.

"So you get it," Trudy tells her. She turns her attention back to Connie. "Anyway, here you go. Enjoy!"

Connie takes the bag, feels the crisp crinkle of paper as her fingers curl around the album. She pulls it out and touches the cover, the texture of the lace, the ribbons.

She clutches it to her chest and tries not to look too happy, but it's impossible. A wide smile breaks across her face. "Thank you." Already she knows that the first page will be a picture of Serena. Maybe she'll do one of those film strips with four images and run it along the side. Or a hoofprint. Could she get a hoofprint? Maybe Serena could step in ink and trot across the page.

Trudy adds, "And Bettie wanted me to tell you that our special segment will be starting soon. Something about bottle cups."

"Bottle caps," Eleanor corrects her.

"I'm pretty sure she said bottle cups," Trudy says.

"There are no such things as bottle cups, Eleanor. She's been jumbling her words lately, haven't you noticed?" Eleanor purses her lips. "Well, let's go. I think I'm going to get that green album for myself." She looks at Madeline and Connie and straightens up. "Green is the new black, you know." She avoids looking at her friend.

Trudy giggles. "See you back outside!" The women leave.

"That is a lovely album," Madeline says, admiring it. She smiles. "It suits you."

"I know." Connie pages through the album. It's a fairly simple album filled with black card-stock pages, but there are also random tags and overlays, little bits and bursts of sparkle here and there. Not a lot, but enough. Just like Connie. Suddenly she can't wait to get started. "I think I'll go back to the meeting. Is that okay?"

Max is holding up the bowl of yogurt toward Madeline. "Try?"

Madeline laughs. "Of course! And take notes. In the meantime, I'm going to get Max and myself a couple of spoons."

Isabel sits in her car in her driveway, stares at her darkened house. Next door the lights in Bettie's house are blazing, the automatic timer having kicked on, an attempt to stave off intruders.

Isabel's eyes trail along the fence line circling Bettie's backyard, practically in line with their own. She and Bill had put the fence up shortly after they moved in, in anticipation of the children who would one day come.

It's not that Isabel really wanted kids. That is, she wanted them as much as the next person, had planned to take that natural step into motherhood like other married women her age. She hadn't thought about it much, hadn't expected it to be a problem. But when it didn't happen, it became about what she didn't have, what she couldn't have. The baby, then Bill.

Isabel slides down in the driver's seat. She doesn't want to go inside her house. What exactly is she coming home to? Canned soup, white walls, her own loneliness?

She leans her head against the window. She could live in her car. Sell the house, sell her things, live out of her little hybrid coupe. It gets forty-five miles to the gallon and it'd be a heck of a lot cheaper than her mortgage. The seat reclines and she could shower at the gym. Keep her files in the trunk, do her laundry at the Avalon Wash and Dry, eat out. The proceeds from the house sale would give her enough cushion that she could take a leave of absence from work. Tour the country. Head to the ocean.

And then what? Eventually you have to have someplace to come back to, a place to call home, a place to hang your hat. It's the unwritten rule of life. You grow up in one tribe, your family, and then strike out on your own to build another. It's what people do.

Everyone, that is, except Isabel. Even Ava has managed to do this. An interrupted life with Bill but still she has Max. Isabel hardly has any friends. Even Yvonne, as wonderful as she is, has managed to find a boyfriend. Everyone on the path to finding a home and filling it with the people they love.

In the waning light, Isabel looks at the FOR SALE sign, at her dilapidated porch that has yet to be fixed. Who would want to buy this place? The grass in the front yard is spiky and dry, the hydrangeas brown and shriveled. Even the windows in the house look sad and droopy, the porch frowning its disapproval.

Isabel gets out of the car. They never bothered with a sprinkler system ("*I'm* the sprinkler system," Bill would joke as he dragged out the hose and tossed the oscillating water sprinkler into the middle of the lawn). Isabel can't remember the last time she bothered to water the lawn. She digs around in the shed until she finds what she's looking for.

When the rusty sprinkler is connected to the hose and Isabel turns on the spigot, there's a reluctant sputter, like an indignant old man being force-fed his dinner. For a second she thinks the whole thing might explode and she steps back, expecting the worst.

But then a stream of water spurts from the first nozzle, and then the next. Soon a cascade of water is washing over the dry grass. It hits the sidewalk in small patters, cooling the warm concrete. Isabel stands there for a moment, watching.

Max. She remembers the baby announcement,

the picture taken a few days after his birth. There were similarities, yes, but the truth is it could have been any blue-eyed, big-eared baby.

But the little boy standing in front of her tonight was a miniature Bill. A little Bill, a junior Bill. Bill & Son. Isabel remembers Bill's baby pictures, buried somewhere up in the attic, knows how real this connection is. She thinks of Lillian, Bill's widowed mother, who'd made it clear that she had no interest in Ava or "the child," both of whom she held responsible for the dissolution of Bill's marriage and subsequent death. But if she could see Max now, Isabel is certain Lillian would feel differently.

Because Isabel feels differently. Not toward Ava so much—her supposed henpecked, I'm-a-stressed-out-mom-with-my-hands-full state doesn't fool Isabel one bit—but Max is a different story altogether. It messes everything up.

A fan of water hits her as the oscillating spray rotates. It's refreshing, but it startles her. She touches her cheek, surprised by the wetness, and then realizes that it's not water from the sprinkler, but her own tears.

"What's a guy got to do to get a girl's attention these days?" Hugh's voice is teasing over the phone, and Yvonne laughs.

"Sorry, I ended up at a scrapbooking meeting

251

last night," she says. "It ran late." She fiddles with a clevis screw.

"What are you doing now?"

"Fixing Mr. Gaulkin's kitchen faucet." Yvonne turns up the volume on her earpiece and starts to remove the mounting nuts and washers from under the sink. "Once I get rid of the old one I'll need to thread the water supply lines into the inlets of the new faucet."

"I love it when you talk plumber. What are you doing after?"

"I was supposed to see a movie with Isabel but she's not up for it. Hey!" she brightens. "Do you want to go on a picnic in Avalon Park? You, me, and Toby?"

Hugh hesitates. "Uh, I'd like to but I can't. Family thing."

It's the third time in the past two weeks. "Another one? You seem to have a lot of those." She pictures Hugh and his mother seated at opposite ends of the large maple table in the dining room, sipping on their soup, asking each other to pass the salt.

"Yeah, well," Hugh clears his throat. "Hey, the movie idea might work after. Late show?"

Yvonne uses a razor to scrape at some old putty. "Sure."

"Okay, I'll text you later."

They say goodbye and Yvonne turns her attention back to the job in front of her. Secretly she was hoping Hugh would join her for dinner, but it's no big deal. Maybe she'll go for a run through the park.

Yvonne finishes her work, then chats with Mr. Gaulkin for a few minutes before heading home. She's eager to change into her running gear. She'll do a three-mile run, grab a salad on the way back, then shower and send out a few invoices. By then it'll be time to meet Hugh.

She wishes they would go on a real date. So far it's been very buddy-buddy with a sprinkle of romance thrown in, but she noticed that Hugh is not a fan of public displays of affection. Their dates are limited to errand running and late-night movie watching, or just relaxing at Yvonne's house. Not that she minds, but for once she'd like to get dressed up and hit the town. Go on a proper date, talk to each other over the glow of candlelight, have a waiter refilling the wine and checking to see if there's anything else they need.

They haven't been dating long so it's much too early for Yvonne to propose anything like a road trip or short getaway. Still, she's curious to see what Hugh might be like once he's out of Avalon. "Mommy issues," Isabel said a little too gleefully when Yvonne voiced her concerns. Yvonne doesn't think so, but then again, Hugh is a grown man living with his mother. A temporary thing, he told her, because he'd just moved back to Avalon after being in Denver. In a way, it's sweet—he's a good son who wants to spend time with family. Nothing wrong with that.

Yvonne sighs as she pulls her truck into the driveway. She knows she's reaching, but she doesn't want to overthink it, doesn't want to pick it apart for no good reason. And she's having fun. It beats the first twenty-two years of her life, which were marked with obligations and responsibilities and expectations. Yvonne was never a bad girl, never rebelled like some of her friends who couldn't stand the expectations that came with family money and social standing, but that didn't mean she liked being told what she could or couldn't do, or who she could or couldn't be friends with.

Sam Kenney. Even his name set him apart, relegated him to staff before he was old enough to work. Her best friend since the third grade, even after she was sent to boarding school in Connecticut for high school. Her parents tried to discourage the friendship, but they weren't there to monitor the mail, to stop the late-night phone calls from the hallway pay phone, to prevent him from coming over and sneaking her out of the dorm on weekends.

And then, when she was in her senior year at Smith, Sam predictably started working the cranberry bogs alongside his father and brothers. Yvonne came back during fall break, right around harvest time, and her father drew a line in the sand. She was a Tate, they had a reputation to uphold, they were the pillars of this small community and Yvonne could not "run around with that Kenney boy" anymore. It was a ludicrous request, and of course Yvonne refused. Her mother, who'd been tight-lipped throughout all of this, demanded to know if they were "involved." It might have been out of spite that Yvonne proposed to Sam, both literally and figuratively, that they get married. She even went down on bended knee. He had cracked up, but then said yes.

She graduated from college, turned down a plum job at a magazine in New York thanks in part to her mother, and came home to Wareham. It was clear her parents thought that she'd thrown everything away, but they surprised her by insisting that they host the wedding. Yvonne had protested at first, preferring something simple.

"No," her mother had said flatly. "You'll give us this, at least."

Sam had been the one to convince her to let it go. It was a small thing, he reminded her, and then they'd have the rest of their lives.

The rest of their lives.

Funny how a simple friendship can grow into true love. Being with Sam was always good for Yvonne—he made her feel real. Yvonne knew she would be walking away from money and opportunity, and Sam had been concerned about what she would be giving up, but it was a small price to pay for what she was getting in return.

Freedom. Love. Happiness.

And then, their wedding day. Yvonne woke before the alarm, dawn having not quite broken. She stared at the billowing white dress hanging on the closet door. The catering crew was already setting up.

She knew something was wrong by the knock on the door. The small square of an envelope, her mother's stationery even though it was Sam's handwriting. An apology, short and sweet, the goodbye. Her mother came to her room a few minutes later, and Yvonne knew this had been her doing.

"Where's Sam?" she'd screamed, but her mother shook her head.

"He's gone," her mother told her. "And he's not coming back. And good riddance, because it was only about the money, Yvonne. Your father offered him a sizable sum, and he took it. And left."

Yvonne didn't believe it. Couldn't believe it. She jumped into her car and drove to Sam's house, where his father was waiting for her with a cup of coffee, his face tired and weathered from years of working outdoors. He didn't have to say anything for Yvonne to know it was true.

Sam was gone.

Driving home, Yvonne realized that her life

would always be this way. Her parents showing her who she was and what she could or could not have, no matter what the cost. They wanted to humiliate her into submission. But it was more than simple embarrassment, Yvonne knew. They wanted her hurt. Hurt so she could see the cost of love, and that in the end, it would always be about the money.

She left her car by the side of the road. When she saw the plumbing truck, she stuck out her thumb. His name was Harold Stroup. He was sixty and ready to retire, had been in the business for over forty years. When he smiled the edges of his eyes crinkled. They talked as they drove away from her past and toward her future.

Now, Yvonne lifts her toolbox out of her truck and heads into the house. That was ten years ago, a lifetime ago. The first few years were the hardest, trying to make her own way and finding that life was harder when she didn't have the resources available to her that she was used to. But she managed, and she saved. When she was ready to buy a home of her own, she looked for a small town where she wouldn't have to pay an arm and a leg. She found Avalon.

She should tell this all to Hugh, not to mention Isabel, but Yvonne doesn't want to go there. She knows what happens when people find out about her past, about her family. The questions start and they don't stop, and then they start treating her differently, even if they don't mean to. The money thing gets in the way, and then it gets awkward and uncomfortable. She's had friendships and relationships end because of it, ex-boyfriends who wonder if maybe she should reconnect with her family, if she's absolutely sure that she's been cut from the will. When she says yes, there's the wavering and then the eventual breakup. It never starts because of the money, Yvonne realizes, but it usually ends because of it.

Yvonne is about to put her key in the lock when she notices that the front door is slightly ajar. Odd. She gives the door a push, and it slowly swings open.

From the doorway, everything looks as she left it. Nothing seems to be missing or broken. Someone breaking in wouldn't be so discreet, would they? Plus it's still light out. Who would risk coming into her house in broad daylight, much less through the front door?

Yvonne hesitates, unsure of whether or not to go in. She may be fearless, but she's not stupid, and something doesn't feel right.

"Hello?" she calls out, and half expects someone to reply. But no one does.

Should she call the police? What would she say? Maybe she didn't close the door all the way when she left—she was in a rush this morning to get to the elementary school on time, to fix a busted water main. She was excited to get the call, after weeks of sluggish business and unexpected cancellations, and it was very possible that she wasn't paying attention.

It's a plausible explanation, and there are probably others, too. So why does Yvonne suddenly feel scared?

Lamar Henderson, 72
Retired Teacher

Lamar Henderson is in his living room playing the weekly Sudoku in the *Avalon Gazette*. He pencils in a 4 beneath a 1 when he hears a panicked cry from the driveway.

"Help! Lamar, oh Lamar, come quick!"

It's his wife, Alice. There's something about the urgent tone of her voice—no, not urgent, but desperate—that makes Lamar throw down the paper and rush to the door, almost tripping over their cat, Precious.

Lamar fumbles with the lock as Alice cries out again for help. He throws open the door, half expecting to see Alice lying on the ground with a twisted ankle or clutching her chest in pain.

"Lamar! Thank goodness!" Alice gasps when she sees him. She's buckling under the weight of several large shopping bags, their contents threatening to spill over the sides. He hurries forward to catch the bags as Alice's arms give way.

Several spools of ribbon fall out of one bag and roll toward the walkway before settling on their sides. Bright oranges and sunny yellows, pinks with white polka dots, crinkly blues, luscious purple stripes. Ribbons in every color of the rainbow. Lamar stares at them and a long-forgotten memory comes up—paper strips of sugary candy dots, his favorite treat as a young boy, so many summers ago.

"Alice, did you make it back from Rockford in one piece?" comes a holler from across the street. Alice and Lamar turn to see Tubby Jenkins wiping her hands on her apron before giving them a wave.

"Yes! But I couldn't find those heart cabochons that Mary Winder has. Came across some alphabet ones that are adorable, though. I picked up a set for you, too. They have a nice epoxy dome on top."

"Bless you!" Tubby exclaims. "I'm finishing up a pie. I'll be by in an hour with a couple of slices and you can show me what you got."

Alice waves as she picks up wayward ribbon spools as she heads into the house. "We're going to fry in this heat if we don't get in the house," she tells her husband. "Don't forget the bags in back!"

It takes Lamar almost ten minutes to bring everything in. Alice has changed into a house-dress and is standing by the kitchen sink, washing her hands and bubbling with excitement. "Oh, good, I can't wait to see what I got!"

Lamar stares at her in disbelief. "You don't know what you bought?" he asks. He peers into one of the bags as his stomach gives a grumble. "Is any of this food?"

"Food? Don't be ridiculous. It's scrapbooking supplies. And I know what I bought, I just want to see everything again. I'm going to convert the guest bedroom into a crafter's paradise!" Alice beams as she peers into the first bag.

Lamar frowns. "But where will the kids stay when they come to visit?" They have two children, all grown up with children of their own. Six grandchildren in all.

"Oh, we'll figure it out. They only come two weeks out of the year—there's no point in leaving the room empty for the other fifty. Besides, you have a home office in the second room and a wood shop out back. Why can't I have a little space of my own?"

Lamar feels a small rise of panic as Alice begins to pull things out of the bags: thick stacks of patterned paper, empty storage boxes, large puffy albums, scissors with colorful handles, jar after jar of small metal things. She's even bought some kind of machine that looks like a cross between a printer and a toaster.

"Isn't this clever?" she's saying as she zips and unzips the matching nylon carrier. "I can't wait to show the girls at the next meeting!"

"Doesn't Tubby have one of these?"

Alice waves his comment away. "Lamar, I can't keep borrowing everyone else's die-cutting machine—it wears on the blade, it's just not fair. Plus I plan to do a fair amount of scrapping from here on out so I'll need the right tools. It's not like you don't own every hammer, wrench, or power tool this side of the Mississippi."

"That's different," Lamar protests. "Those things are practical. Necessary."

Alice stops for a second and puts her hands on her hips. "For what? A couple of footstools, a squirrel-be-gone bird feeder? I don't see you putting a new roof on the house anytime soon. You putter just as much as I do, Lamar. Don't deny it."

She's got him there. He watches Alice pull out a strip of paper several feet long before he realizes in horror that it's a shopping receipt. "We're gonna go broke, Alice!"

Alice swats him. "Oh, hush. Almost everything I bought is on sale or had a coupon. I'll have to get a little creative with our food budget for the next few months, that's all. It'll be fine." She pulls out a box that looks like it has a hair dryer inside. "Oh, and I got this for you."

"For me?" Lamar looks at it, puzzled. *Heat embosser,* he reads. He doesn't know what it is but it looks like something that could go in his shop.

Alice nods. "It's for you to give to me for our anniversary next month. Skip the dinner out—I'll make something nice here. Skip the chocolates, too—Tubby and I are going to start Weight Watchers at the end of the month." She hands him several small jars of sparkly powder. "This goes with it. You can wrap it all up and give it to me then."

"But it won't be a surprise," he says, frowning. He hasn't had a chance to think of a gift yet, but he would have. Eventually.

"I'll pretend," Alice says. "It's not like I haven't before. And, really, this will make me very happy. I love you, Lamar, but I don't need another bottle of perfume I'll never use."

Lamar gives one of the small jars a shake. Snowy glitter, he thinks. Well, he's a man and he doesn't understand these things—he's long since given up trying to. And Alice is right—he hasn't come up with a good gift for her in years. She's saved him a trip to the drugstore at least.

"Well, all right," he says reluctantly, because there isn't anything else for him to say. He pokes his head into another bag and lets out an exclamation. "How much ribbon do you have in here?!"

"You can never have enough ribbon," Alice informs him, her face lighting up as she gasps in delight at her discovery of another purchase she'd already forgotten about. She's happy, there's no doubt about that.

Lamar picks up a spool of red rickrack and weighs it in his hand, remembering an episode on one of those home-shopping channels a couple of years ago. A lady had a whole room dedicated to gift wrapping, with rolls of gift wrap suspended on wooden dowels. It was some sort of expensive storage system that cost over a hundred dollars. Lamar had scoffed, saying it would take him half an hour and less than ten bucks to make the same thing. Alice had laughed.

Lamar listens to his wife hum their favorite song as she heads to the fridge. Lamar smiles. *Three coins in the fountain, each one seeking happiness.* Sinatra. Best song ever.

"Now, let's see what we have," Alice says, surveying the contents. "I can make you a turkey sandwich with a side of potato salad. Oh, good, we still have some of that passion fruit iced tea left over. I'll pour you a glass." She removes the items from the fridge, then stops for a moment, gazing toward the ceiling, lost in thought. "You know what I'm going to do for my first project in my new craft room, Lamar? I'm going to put those photos from your retirement party together— they're just sitting in a box. And all those nice cards people wrote! They said such kind things about you, remember? I'm going to include those, too."

His retirement party. Lamar hasn't thought about that in years. Now that Alice has brought it up, he remembers those cards, too. There was one from Jake Spencer, a young teacher whom he'd taken under his wing. Jake had written a long and heartfelt note, thanking Lamar for inspiring him to become a better teacher. Other teachers and students had lots of kind words for Lamar, too. Lamar loved teaching, loved what he did, and reading those words of appreciation made it all worth it.

"Of course," Alice adds thoughtfully as she spreads mayonnaise onto a slice of bread, "I may have to put the cards in cellophane sleeves if they're not acid-free. I'll have to ask Bettie about that." She pauses, making a mental note, then nods, satisfied.

Lamar doesn't know what his wife is talking about but he walks over and gives her a peck on the cheek and she smiles. For the first time in a long time, he knows exactly what he's going to give Alice for their anniversary. He'll wrap up that heat embosser thing and those jars of whatever, but he's going to surprise her with something else, too. He's going to build a rack where she can store all of her ribbons, just like the lady on that show. Given the number of spools in this bag alone, he'll need three dowels at least, maybe even four. May as well make it five for good measure. He'll mount it on the wall so Alice can access them easily. Maybe he'll add some shelving for all this paper, too.

"Your sandwich is ready!"

Lamar grins. *Yes.* The minute Tubby comes over, he's going to slip out to his shop and start drawing up plans.

Chapter Eleven

Frances slides a photo of Brady into a two-inch-square punch and gives the lever a firm squeeze. There's a crunch as a perfectly cropped photo pops out of the punch window and lands in her palm. Frances grins and adds the photo square to her growing pile, then reaches for a picture of Noah and does the same.

Frances is making a favorite-things album for each of the boys. Favorite foods, favorite toys, favorites places, favorite sayings, favorite clothes. She's going to laminate the pages of the albums for the younger boys, hopes it stands up to years of handling. She wants it to be something they'll keep for a long time, maybe even long enough to share with their own children.

She has a few other albums planned: family vacations, birthday parties, and Christmas to start. They have some family albums, of course, where she stuck in photos whenever she had time, but Frances always has to narrate each one, explain what's happening or recount a funny story. With her new scrapbooks, she won't have to. She'll journal on each page and include ticket stubs and birthday cards and airplane boarding passes. The story will be right there on the page for anyone to see.

She's addicted, she'll admit it. The day after the

scrapbooking meeting, Frances went to the library and checked out every book she could find on scrapbooking and memory keeping. She pored over every page, made lists of supplies and equipment, went shopping. She subscribed to several scrapbooking magazines, went to eBay to bid on huge lots of scrapbooking supplies by people who were giving it up. Those were her favorites—the boxes filled with a jumble of paper and embellishments, stickers, rub-ons, punches, and scissors. It was fun to sort through everything and delight in the randomness of it. Some people included more than what was listed, deciding in the end that it was better to get rid of it all, so Frances always had a surprise or two— a mini craft iron in one, a set of gel pens in another. It was almost too much, but Frances figures she can always use them for projects with the boys, too.

Frances knows that as fun as this is, she needs it, too. She needs to keep busy, she needs to find ways to occupy her time and mind so that what's happened (or rather, didn't happen) doesn't consume her. She knows scrapbooking isn't going to fill the hole that's left from Mei Ling, but it's made her realize how much she has, how much she's grateful for. And that's worth something, isn't it?

Reed passes by the kitchen table on the way to the fridge. She can tell by the way his brows furrow that he has something on his mind, but he doesn't want to talk about it.

"Guess what?" Frances says, hoping to distract him. "We won't ever have to buy a greeting card again. I'll be able to make whatever we need. Birthday, holiday, sympathy cards, anything!"

"That's great," Reed says, distracted. He rummages through the fridge but comes up empty-handed. He heads over to the pantry. He opens the door and flicks on the light. Frances hears bags of chips and pretzels being moved around, boxes of cereal being shaken. After a moment, the light flicks off and Reed is standing there, still empty-handed, and looking irritated.

Frances frowns. Reed looking for food is not a good sign. He only eats when he's stressed, and even then only in the worst situations. The last time Frances saw him like this was when her father died a few years ago. They'd been close, the perfect father and son-in-law pairing, and his passing had devastated him. He gained almost fifteen pounds during that time.

"Are you looking for anything in particular?" she asks. She sorts through a stack of journal cards, choosing one for each photo. They're made of simple card stock with colorful borders and lines to write a sentence or two. She almost hates to use them, they're so pretty.

"No," Reed says. "I just feel like a snack or something."

Frances glances at the clock. It's past nine at night. The boys are in bed. Reed never eats past seven.

"We have yogurt," she begins, when Reed snaps, "I don't want *yogurt,* Frances." Both irritation and disgust are in his voice.

"Oh," she says, a little stung. "Okay." Reed doesn't have much of a temper, so Frances isn't sure what to do. She ducks her head and pretends to be absorbed in organizing the pictures on the page. She wrinkles her nose when she feels tears prickling her eyes.

Reed runs a hand through his hair. "I'm sorry," he finally says. He pulls out the chair next to her and drops into it. He reaches for Frances's hand and she flinches at his touch. "Fran, I'm sorry."

"It's okay." She shuffles some pictures around, not even sure what she's looking at.

Reed leans back in the chair and stares up at the ceiling. "We need to get rid of Mei Ling's stuff. It's just sitting in my office—I can barely move in there. And there are things in the garage, too. I'd feel better if we could clean it all up and get it out of here."

Frances bites her lip. She's thought about it, too, but she can't bring herself to part with anything yet. It's only been three weeks since they turned down the referral, and she wants to let it sink in. Plus she doesn't know what to do with everything—it somehow doesn't feel right to sell it or give it away. "I wish we could send it all to her. We got it for her, after all."

"You know we can't do that," Reed says. "If you want, I'll take care of it. I want it all out of here. It's too much of a reminder . . ." His voice trails off and he shakes his head.

"I know." Frances finally stops pretending to work and looks at her husband, at the unhappiness in his face. She knows that he's right—as soon as it still might be, they need to move on. "I'll start going through everything this weekend. I could . . . sell some things, I guess. Donate the rest. It'll feel good to give them away to some children who could use them. Maybe a hospital, or . . ."

Reed is looking at her pile of photographs. He picks one up of Nick at two, clutching a raggedy-looking stuffed dog with a missing eye. He used to take it with him everywhere. "God, I forgot about that thing. What did he call it?"

They both pause, remembering, and then speak at the same time. "Struffy," they say in unison, and smile.

Reed picks up another photo, this one of Brady taken last year. He's banging away on a tinny-sounding toy piano that Frances had found at a thrift store for a dollar. Noah "accidentally" broke it by sitting on it. "I can't believe I'm saying this, but I actually miss that piano." Reed used to throw pained looks Frances's way whenever

Brady would play it, but now a small smile is tugging at the corner of his mouth.

Frances laces her fingers together and rests her chin on top of them, her elbows on the table. She points to one of Noah potty training. He's wearing a cowboy hat and nothing else. "He loved that hat. I didn't have any other pictures of him wearing it, which is weird if you think about it. He was *always* wearing it."

Reed laughs, and the sound of his laughter seems to break through something that's been lingering between them, tight and unyielding. Frances feels her shoulders drop and realizes she's been holding her breath all this time, taking small bits of air only when she needs it. She lets herself exhale, and smiles.

"I want to save that for the slideshow at his wedding," Reed says. He fans out the rest of the photos. "Wow, you have a lot of good ones here, Fran." He lifts one of the photos. "This is one of my favorites—the one of Nick at the Fourth of July display when we were visiting my parents. I think he was three at the time?"

"Yep. And he kept his hands over his ears for the rest of the week," Frances says. "He was worried the fireworks might start up again any moment. We had to feed him because he wouldn't put his hands down to hold a fork."

They both chuckle. Frances thinks about something Bettie said at the last meeting, about scrapbooking being a form of therapy. Maybe it's not for the people making the scrapbooks, but for those looking at them, too.

"I wish . . ." Reed begins, but then his voice catches in his throat and he shakes his head.

"What, Reed?"

But her husband won't speak, just wordlessly thumbs through the photos, his face a mask of pain.

Frances looks down at the piles of pictures, confused. These are all happy pictures, with smiles and people laughing, nothing unpleasant or difficult here. Maybe it's the occasional glance of his father, still a picture of health as he stands next to the older boys holding matching fishing rods. But somehow Frances doesn't think that's it.

"Do you want to talk about it?" she asks.

Reed shakes his head. "Not really." He taps another photo. "That was a great trip—our first family vacation after Brady was born. Yosemite." There's that small smile again, and Frances feels relief.

"We were ambitious," she remembers. "That was a *very* long car ride." With enough crying, yelling, and complaints along the way. Never again, they'd both vowed, but of course as soon as they were home they started planning the next family vacation.

Maybe that's what they need. "Hey," Frances

says suddenly. "What do you think about taking a family vacation? We haven't taken one for the past couple of years because of . . . well, anyway, it could be a short getaway, a break from our day-to-day. What do you think?"

Reed looks appalled. "No," he says, surprising her. "I mean, not right now. It's been such a roller-coaster ride, I just want things to settle back down."

"Okay." Frances feels a pinch inside at the memory of the past couple of months, the best and worst months of her life. She forces a smile. "Well, I guess the first order of business will be to find a new home for Mei Ling's things. We'll feel better then, because we did the best we could, Reed. You know if there were any other way, we would have considered it. But there was none. Right?"

There's a long pause, but then Reed looks at his wife and Frances finally sees it—a determination, an absoluteness. He takes her hand and gives it a firm squeeze. "Right."

Ava waits in her car, trying to tune her radio but finally giving up. She's four cars away from pulling up to the school in the designated drop-off zone where a teacher will escort Max to the car and buckle him in. New rules, they told her. They didn't want parents clogging the exit during dismissal, anxious to take their children home.

Instead the parents are being asked to line up like children themselves, one after another, waiting for a teacher to wave them forward.

The Jeep gives a shudder and Ava prays it won't overheat. It needs a major tune-up, the radiator flushed, new brake pads. The treads in the tires are wearing thin. A couple more months, the guy told her, which takes her right into winter. The sooner she can get these problems taken care of, the better—but how?

After the scrapbooking meeting, Ava received a large order from Bettie for simple bottle-cap embellishments that members could buy and add to their layouts. Now that she knows more about scrapbooking, Ava knows exactly what she can do. Girl themes and boy themes, vacation themes, birthday themes. She'll flatten these caps so they'll add texture without sticking out too much from the page. She's also thinking about making an album kit with six or seven bottle-cap bookmarks for different pages. She'll set it all up and give people the supplies they need to put their own pictures in the center of a cap.

Margot at Avalon Gifts 'N More also placed an order for more bottle-cap jewelry, and there's another gift store in Rockford that wants to do a trial of her collection as well. That's what she's calling it now: the Free Hearts Collection. It sounds so legitimate, like she's a real designer.

But while it's helping with their expenses, it's far from enough, especially since she now needs to invest in more supplies to fill all these orders.

They can't keep scraping by like this. She can't find a good full-time job that'll give her some flexibility with Max, and all the part-time jobs don't pay well. It seems like a waste to keep trying to do something new when she already has a marketable skill—her training as a dental assistant. It's easy work, and Ava was good at it. The plan had been that Bill would eventually open his own solo practice, separate from Randall Strombauer, and Bill and Ava would work together. They would be married, it would be their business, a family business. But when Bill died, that dream evaporated. A lot of dreams did.

For the past four years Ava's tried to reinvent herself, has tried to start their life from scratch. Maybe if it was just her she could do it, but it's not just her. She has Max, and he deserves more than what she's been able to give. When Ava realizes this, she knows what she has to do. She's going to have to see Dr. Strombauer and ask him for a recommendation.

The last time she saw him she was packing up her things, the Monday after Bill broke the news to Isabel. It was her last day. Dr. Strombauer knew now that they were seeing each other, but that didn't stop him from cornering her in the break room. He stood so close she could feel his breath on her neck, could smell the alcohol from one too many drinks at lunch.

"Things are looking up for you, aren't they, Ava girl?" He'd given her an even smile, but she could hear the edginess in his words.

She couldn't find her voice, afraid if she spoke her fear would give her away. But she forced herself to stand tall and look him in the eye. It was hard, and still he towered over her. In the end she was the first to look away.

A finger trailed down her bare arm, making her shiver. "Bill coming over later? That must be nice. What are you going to do, make him dinner? Or something else? Because I sure am hungry, too." He leered at her.

Ava was grateful for the box between them, the one that held a handful of personal items. She gripped the edges tightly, didn't say anything. The receptionist was gone for the day, and Bill was at the lawyer's. Everyone else was gone. They'd had a full day of patients and Dr. Strombauer hadn't said more than a few words to her. Until now.

"Obviously the two of you have been planning this for some time. Sneaking around—I have to say, I'm impressed. I didn't think he had it in him. Though it makes me wonder if Bill has plans to sneak around on me, too, you know?" His stance was threatening now, and suddenly he knocked the box from her hands. It fell to the floor, spilling its contents everywhere.

And then he was pressing against her, crushing her against the wall, his hands wrapped around her wrists, the tips of their noses touching. He was going to kiss her, she was certain of it, and he wouldn't stop there. Every worst-case scenario flashed through her mind. Ava was terrified, wanted to scream, but who would hear her?

And then she thought of the baby.

That's all it took. Ava found her strength, her anger. She did the only thing she could think of.

She bit him.

He had hollered and reeled back, his hands cupping his nose. Ava had been too busy grabbing her purse to know what had really happened, and then she was pushing open the door of the emergency exit, the alarm shrieking. She ran to her car, her hands shaking so bad that she could barely get the keys into the ignition, but she did.

She didn't tell Bill what had happened. She meant to, but she didn't know what he would do, didn't trust him not to confront Dr. Strombauer and possibly hurt him, destroying his chances for his own business. She only said that they'd had a disagreement, that she ended up leaving her box at the office. Bill brought it home the next day and Ava noticed a few things were broken or missing, but none of that mattered. She was just glad she'd never have to go back to that office, relieved she'd never see him again.

Now, however, things are different. Bill is dead. She has Max. Randall Strombauer owns Bill's share of the practice. If anything he owes her this one simple thing.

A long honk from an annoyed parent in the car behind her shakes her from her reverie. Ava manages a wave and edges up a car length, sighing as she puts the car back in park. She can see Max standing in line by the door, lunchbox in hand, waiting for his turn, too. She tries to smile, but she suddenly feels sad. The memory of that long ago time, or maybe it's this moment, where she and her son have to wait for someone to tell them when they can be together.

Connie sits on a bale of hay in Serena's pen, watching the goat doze in the shade of her dog house. Connie doodles in her journal, finally drafting the sign that she'd promised Madeline she would make.

"Goat Found," she writes. *"Female. Friendly. Playful. Masterful escape artist. Please inquire at Madeline's Tea Salon."*

Connie adds a few colorful flowers around the border, draws teacups nestled inside of roses. She sketches Serena's face peeking out from behind the Lassiters' hydrangea bush. She'll make it nicer on the computer later, and include an actual photo of Serena as well, but at least now she can tell Madeline that she's working on it and that might buy her a few more days.

Her new scrapbook album sits on the desk in her room, still void of pictures. Connie doesn't know where to begin, doesn't know what to put inside. She took the photographs from her suitcase and started to lay them out on the page, and then got nervous about gluing them in, making it permanent. She's not sure what the album is about anymore. Is her past more important than her future?

Her thoughts drift to her parents, to her mother especially. Connie already finds that she's forgetting things, that she can't quite picture her mother as clearly as before. Maybe because no photo albums exist, those memories are now lost forever.

What does Connie remember? Her mother being impetuous, the way her spur-of-the-moment ideas would become infectious, the way she could cajole Connie and her father into agreeing to just about anything. "A road trip!" she'd suggest, even though Connie's father had to work the next day. Or the time they'd chased down an ice cream truck for three blocks to get a Cherry Bomb they could share.

After Connie's father died, Mary Beth Colls seemed to sink into herself. If they were out, Mary Beth put her best face forward and like magic, it seemed to work. They'd laugh, they'd have a good time, and Connie would think that maybe her mother would be okay after all. But then they'd come home and she would deflate, shrinking into herself, becoming silent and morose. Connie watched her take the pills that helped her sleep.

"Oh, Connie," she murmured one night as they lay on the couch together, watching TV. "You're so much like your father. You're both so strong. Fearless. You can do anything." There was a shakiness in her voice.

"You too, Mom." Connie was thirteen.

Mary Beth had shaken her head, pulled Connie closer to her. Her lips brushed the top of her daughter's head. "No, Constance. I'm not." Then she'd pushed Connie away and told her it was time for bed.

In the morning Mary Beth was still asleep when Connie went to school. Connie had tiptoed out quietly, leaving a plate of toast and scrambled eggs warming in the oven for her mother when she woke up.

But she never did.

Connie feels Serena bump up against her. She puts her nose up to Serena's, who is looking at her unabashedly. "You love me, don't you Serena?" Connie asks.

Serena lets out a happy bleat, then nudges Connie toward the gate. She was planning on putting pictures of Serena in the album, too, but now that she has to look for Serena's original owner, Connie's not so sure that's a good idea. An album full of loss. Talk about depressing.

Another bump. Connie leans forward and buries her face in Serena's neck. "Stay with me," she whispers. "Okay?"

Serena gives her a nuzzle, a sure *yes* if Connie ever knew one. Encouraged, Connie puts down her journal and reaches for Serena's leash. "All right, let's go for that walk."

Adele Christensen, 75
Homemaker

Any immigrant will tell you that memories are more important than things. When Adele Christensen and her husband came to America, there was much they had to leave behind. They did it all for the dream of America, for a new life, a better life.

When they came from Denmark in 1965, they had two suitcases and less than $500. Adele was pregnant with not one child but two, a boy and a girl who were later born in Philadelphia.

Adele's husband worked two jobs and went to night school while she raised the children. It was hard, but they did it, and after six years her husband graduated from the university. Adele admired his dedication—he was up every morning at 3:00 a.m. and home just before midnight—and then he went on for his master's degree. It took him another five years and then he was offered a very good job with a company in Rockford, Illinois. A year later they were able to buy their house in Avalon.

They were careful with their money. Adele did what she could to stretch their budget, to be practical yet creative. She saved what she could, not only money but paper bags, tinfoil, plastic wrap, rubber bands—anything that could be used again. She didn't believe in waste and she didn't believe in extravagance. The children were always complaining that their clothes were too old or not fashionable, but Adele was unwavering about these things.

Once they had a huge fight about school lunches. The kids wanted to eat lunch from the cafeteria like their friends instead of bringing the frozen cheese sandwiches Adele made every Sunday for the week. Her husband sat them down and told them they had a choice: take it or leave it. End of discussion.

They paid off the house early and when her husband retired their bank account had grown multifold. They had plenty for their retirement and enough to take the whole family on a nice trip once a year.

When her husband passed, Adele's children wanted her to come and live with them. She refused. Her friends thought she was crazy— their children didn't invite them to live with them, she was lucky to have such generous children. And she was grateful for them. But Adele was still perfectly capable of taking care of herself and this was her home. Everything Adele had was in these four walls. All she had to do was look around and see her husband, see what they had accomplished, see what their children and grandchildren had accomplished. Adele feels more joy than sorrow walking in and out of her simple home—why would she leave this?

Then, last year, her son and daughter came home for Thanksgiving with their families. They were wearing jeans and sweatshirts and heavy jackets, an uncomfortable look on their faces. Adele didn't worry about it, just fussed over the grandchildren and took out the pastries she had bought on sale at the Pick and Save.

Then, an hour later a big truck put a Dumpster onto her driveway.

Adele watched as everyone—except her—started to go through the things in the garage, the closets, the attic, under the sinks. Everything was put out on the lawn in the bitter cold, and occasionally they would ask her about this and that but then deciding with their spouses what to keep and what to throw out. They said they were trying to make things easier for Adele.

"Mom, you have four ice buckets," her son said. "Nobody even uses ice buckets anymore."

She'd forgotten completely about those ice buckets but brightened at the sight of them.

"One was a gift from the Andersens on our thirtieth anniversary," she told him. "One we won in a raffle, another was a Christmas present from your godmother. The fourth . . . well, I don't remember where the fourth one was from but I like it. I want to keep it."

Her son told her she was too sentimental and

put them in the donation pile despite Adele's protests. "You won't even know they're gone," his wife, Jane, promised. "You didn't even know you had them, remember?" They shooed Adele into the living room and planted her in front of the TV even though there was nothing she wanted to watch.

The hours ticked by. Adele was worried they wouldn't finish before it got dark and she could tell they were worried, too. *Was one Dumpster enough?* they murmured among themselves. Soon they were no longer including Adele, their actions brisk and efficient, mumbling and laughing as if she couldn't hear them.

"They're antiques," she heard her daughter say when they came into the kitchen for a break. "And they're in pretty good condition. Maybe take them to an antiques store?"

"What about auctioning them online?" her husband suggested. "You can set a reserve to make sure it at least sells for a minimum price."

"What are you talking about?" Adele asked anxiously.

"Nothing," her son said. "Does anyone want to order a pizza?"

When everyone else was eating dinner, Adele managed to sneak into the garage from which she'd been banned. It was cold but that's not what made a shiver run through her. There were piles of things everywhere, her whole garage turned inside out. Then she felt her heart seize—in the middle of the chaos were the two suitcases that brought them to America. The leather was worn and the latches were rusty. There was a layer of dust and she wiped it away with a wrinkled hand, remembering how carefully she had packed their bags on the day they left Esbjerg to begin the journey to a new land. Adele picked up one suitcase by the handle and then the other—they were both empty but still a bit heavy—and walked back into the house and into her room. She locked the door behind her.

Her children knocked and knocked. Was she all right? Why had she locked the door? They tried to explain that the waste management company would be coming first thing in the morning. They said they didn't tell her because they knew she wouldn't agree, that because she wasn't going to live with them they wanted to make sure the house was clean and safe.

It wasn't an apology exactly, but Adele softened, knew in her heart that this was true. They had gone about it all wrong, but they meant well. She unlocked the bedroom door and told them she was keeping the suitcases.

They finished throwing things away and reorganizing, then they left two days later. When Adele looked around, she saw that her house was no longer her home.

There were new towels, new racks, new

containers. Everything labeled and stacked neatly, like a store. The familiar musty smell was gone, and a pungent scent of artificial oranges wafted through the rooms. Adele couldn't find her can opener and then saw they had bought her an electric one and placed it on the counter, all shiny and new. She went into the garage and saw nothing but her car.

Back in the living room, she tried to turn on the TV for the first time since they'd left and found two new remotes. Her son-in-law had thrown away the old videocassette recorder and video-tapes and replaced it with something fancy. They had to return to the city for work so he didn't have time to show her but said Adele could go online or he would help her at Christmas. A month away.

Outside it started to snow. Adele stared out the window and watched the fat flakes drift lazily to the ground. She knew that by nightfall the ground would be covered, and she was filled with a desire to cover everything, to hide all of this newness from view so she could remember her house like before. She went and opened the front door then returned to the living room, wrapped herself in a blanket, and sat down.

She was like that for a long time, welcoming the numbing cold.

Then, the crunch of footsteps. The shadow of a woman standing in the doorway. Adele couldn't see who it was but the light from the street shone from behind her and she thought, for a second, that the woman was an angel. "Adele," she said, and Adele jumped, thinking that maybe it was her time to join her husband in heaven. She stared at the figure in the doorway, and then it stepped forward and Adele saw that it was Bettie Shelton, the woman who lived on the next block.

Bettie stamped the snow from her boots and closed the door. She squinted at the shoe rack by the door, labeled INDOOR, OUTDOOR, and SPECIAL OCCASION.

"I had no idea you were so organized," she said.

"I'm not," Adele told her. "My children and grandchildren were here. They cleaned up everything."

"Yeah, I saw everything being hauled away," Bettie said. "I wondered if you were moving or dead." She came over to where Adele was sitting and pointed to the magazines, fanned in alphabetical order. "This is like my dentist's office. Do you have the latest issue of *Time*?"

Adele managed to lift her shoulders in a shrug.

Bettie ran her fingers over the magazines, selected one at random and began flipping through it. "So, seeing how you're still alive, and how you seem to have some time on your hands, might I interest you in any scrapbooking supplies?

I just got a new shipment and I over-ordered. It's not worth sending back so I'm offering them to anyone who might be interested."

Adele shook her head.

"I have some wonderful new borders and paper stock."

Adele shook her head again.

"I'm offering them for *free*, Adele."

This got Adele's attention. She'd seen the scrapbooking kits in the store and knew they could be expensive. It seemed unnecessary when you could buy a set of three photo albums from the drugstore for half the price. But Adele didn't say anything, just sat there shivering even though Bettie had long closed the door.

Bettie arched an eyebrow, frowning. "It's a fifty-dollar value, Adele. Even if you don't want it, you could give it as a gift. I'll go get it." She left before Adele could protest.

Bettie returned fifteen minutes later. In her hands was a lovely woven bag filled to the brim with paper, ribbons, fancy scissors, all sorts of jars and canisters. Adele didn't know much about scrapbooking, but she knew the value of things. This was certainly worth more than fifty dollars.

"What a relief to get rid of these," Bettie said. "I'm running tight on room myself. You're doing me a favor, Adele." She placed the bag in Adele's lap and it was deliciously heavy.

Adele reached inside and pulled out a sheet of

stickers. They were travel stickers, similar to the ones on her suitcase, some even in the shape of a suitcase. She touched them carefully and suddenly felt overcome with emotion.

"How about some coffee?" Bettie asked. "I noticed you got some fancy new machine on your kitchen counter. From your kids, no doubt. Come, let's give it a whirl."

It took them a while to figure out how to get the new coffee machine to work, but they did. Afterward they sat at the kitchen table and Bettie spread everything out, explained what each item did. They took out Adele's stack of photo albums, so numerous that she rarely looked at them, and selected photos that could go into a single book that would capture the moments Adele wanted to remember most. Her wedding day. Coming to America. The day her children were born. Her husband's graduation. Their home. The grandchildren. Anniversaries. Birthdays. Family vacations. Bettie Shelton helped her do this, and when Adele finished her first album a month later, her children wanted a copy and then asked her to help them make their own. So she did.

Adele and her children never talk about that day, because there's nothing to say. She knows they were doing what they thought was best, just as she had always done for them all these years. Whether they were right or wrong did not matter, because Bettie showed her another way to save the things that mattered most, the memories she wanted to keep. Adele became an avid scrapbooker, and Bettie Shelton became her good friend.

Chapter Twelve

Isabel keeps one eye trained on the small clock in the upper right-hand corner of her computer. In ten minutes she's home free, another workday over. She doesn't know what's worse—staying here in this poor excuse for a job or being home and waiting until it's time to go to bed.

They'd had another ridiculous sales meeting, one in which her recently graduated twelve-year-old boss (really closer to twenty-five but you can hardly tell the difference) set new sales goals. Either the kid's on drugs or his daddy, founder of KP Paper & Son, offered him a bump in his allowance if he could figure out how to get more corrugated paper products out into the world.

Why is she even here? It had started as a part-time job, a way to keep busy while Bill was at work, an attempt at a career she wasn't interested in. Bill wanted her to work with him at the dental office doing administrative paperwork, but aside from sounding dull and unnecessary, Isabel thought that having her own thing, her own job, was somehow important.

What did she know?

So now she's here, having her own thing and doing her own thing, and hating it. She would have quit except she needed the money after Bill died, and she doesn't know what she would do if she ever left this job. Work for another paper company? Get another job in sales? In the end it just seemed easier to stay.

Isabel sees Jimmy Beall sauntering over, making stupid paper jokes along the way. By the time he makes it to her desk, everyone in his wake is shaking their heads.

"Hey," he says, leaning into her cubicle. He pretends to fiddle with her stapler. "What did the paper say to the pencil?"

Isabel keeps her eyes on her computer screen. "I don't know."

" 'Write on!' " Jimmy guffaws. "I use that all the time with my clients—they love it."

"I doubt it," Isabel mutters, but Jimmy doesn't hear her.

"Hey, I got another: Knock knock!"

Isabel stares up at him. "Jimmy, I think someone's calling you. From *way* over there."

"One more," he begs, not falling for it. Obviously Isabel isn't the first person to try that one on him. "Come on. Knock knock!"

She sighs. "Who's there?"

"Jimmy."

Argh, she thinks, but goes for it anyway. "Jimmy who?"

"Jimmy your number, let's go out for pizza!" Jimmy grins, tossing the stapler back onto her desk and knocking over a pencil cup in the process. "Oops, sorry. But do you get it? Jimmy sounds like gimme . . ."

Isabel retrieves the runaway pens and pencils. "Yeah, I got it."

"So, what do you think? Do you wanna grab a pizza after work?"

Jimmy, with his thinning hair and pronounced gut, twice divorced. How is it that a guy like this even gets to get married twice?

Isabel feigns regret. "Gosh, Jimmy, I'd love to but I already have plans." She offers him her brightest, fakest smile and decides her workday is officially over.

Jimmy looks disappointed. "Shoot, really?"

"Yup." Isabel grabs her purse and her car keys. "I'm attending the opening of my garage door. See you tomorrow, Jimmy."

Isabel makes one quick stop at the grocery store, where she picks up something for dinner and dessert. When she pulls into her driveway, she's surprised to see a man standing on her lawn, looking up at the house. A woman is sitting in the car, which is still running. She's checking something on her phone, her face a mask of tolerant impatience.

"Can I help you?" Isabel asks as she pulls the grocery bag from her car.

The man walks over. He's in his mid-thirties. "Hi, is this your house?" He's dressed as if he's come straight from work.

Isabel nods. "Yes." She slams the trunk shut.

The man motions to the sign on the lawn. "How much?"

Isabel tries to remember. "It was on clearance, so I think it was $4.99. It's metal, which is great, because it holds up well in the weather . . ."

The man gives a smile. "No, I mean for the house. We'd like to take a look if we can."

"Oh." For a second Isabel is stunned into silence. Someone is interested in her house? Her first reaction is to lie, to tell him that her house is no longer for sale. But why would she do that? So instead she tells him the first number that comes to mind, a number slightly higher than even she had originally considered.

The man gives a small nod, thinking. "How many bedrooms?"

"Three," Isabel says. She tries to remember the state of her house. Underwear on the floor? Kitchen sink full of dirty dishes? "And two bathrooms. There are two roomy living areas, though, and a small sun porch out back. If you want to give me a few minutes to straighten up, I can show it to you now."

"That would be great." He turns to call to the woman in the car. "She can show it to us now!"

The woman snaps her phone closed and turns to give a long look at the house. She gives a halfhearted shrug, then reaches over to cut the engine.

Isabel hurries into the house. Prospective buyers! He hasn't said anything about the front porch yet, or the lack of it. Maybe she won't have to bother with it at all, just knock a few hundred off the sale price and let him take care of it. All she'd have to do is pack and move.

As she quickly wipes down counters and picks up stray trash, Isabel feels her spirits rise. It's a sign that things are about to change, she's sure of it. When she's satisfied that the house is in fairly decent showing shape, Isabel goes back to get them and brings them inside.

Isabel has never considered herself much of a salesperson, which is one reason she hates her job. But suddenly she finds herself pointing out small features in the house that she knows will appeal to them.

"Furniture," the man is saying, surveying everything carefully. "Will any of it be for sale?"

It only takes Isabel a moment to answer. "It's all for sale," she tells him. "Even the towels and linens, if you want them."

"I'd rather get our own," the woman says. "We already registered for them, anyway." Isabel sees a diamond ring on the woman's hand but no band, and notices that the man's not wearing a ring. Yet.

"It's a straightforward plan," Isabel says. "Everything on one floor, no stairs. Fenced backyard, too. Great for kids . . . I mean, if you're planning on starting a family."

There's a silent exchange between the couple and finally a small smile breaks out on the woman's face.

"Yes," she says. "We are."

"What about the porch?" the man asks. "Was there a problem?"

"What? Oh, no," Isabel says, blithely waving her hand. "A couple of boards were old and I decided to replace the whole thing. Although if you'd prefer to finish it up yourselves, I could take that off the sale price."

The woman is shaking her head. "I definitely want that fixed before we move in. It's not going to work for me if we have to do it ourselves." She frowns.

"No problem," Isabel says brightly. "I was planning on having someone come out and take care of it soon anyway." She'll flip through the Yellow Pages the minute they're out the door.

She walks them back to their car, answering a few more questions about the neighborhood. Out of the corner of her eye, she can see Bettie moving throughout her house.

"The neighbors are great," she adds hastily. "And everyone is always around to lend a helping hand."

"It's a great house," the man says, nodding. "We've relocated to the area for work and have been looking for the right place. If you want to send me the papers, I'll take a look and we can go from there. I can get you whatever information you need if you're running a credit report." The man holds out a hand. "I'm Dan Frazier. My girlfriend—I mean, fiancée—is Nina."

"I'm Isabel Kidd." They shake hands. Then Dan and Nina get into their car and leave. Ohio plates are on their car.

The minute the car turns the corner Isabel lets out a squeal. She sold her house. *She sold her house!* Isabel can't quite believe it and of course nobody's signed anything yet but for all practical purposes, she's sold it.

She can quit her job. She can tell her boss and Jimmy Beall to shove it, she can take a cruise around the world. Isabel is ready to dance a jig right there on her lawn.

Next door Bettie Shelton's front door opens. Perfect timing. Isabel can picture how it would have gone down if Bettie had come out a moment earlier. Well, there's no point in worrying about that. It couldn't have gone any better than if she had planned it.

She watches as Bettie steps onto her porch, an electric fan hat on her head, gardening shears in hand. On her feet are green plastic clogs.

Other than that, Bettie is buck naked.

Bettie does a stretch and gives Isabel a solemn nod. "Finally starting to cool off!" she hollers. "This October air is bracing, isn't it?"

Isabel claps a hand to her mouth. On the one

hand, she could pretend everything is normal and let Bettie make a fool of herself. It would certainly be fair payback after all these years. But as Isabel watches Bettie whistle and begin to clip the hedge near her front door, she realizes that at any second Bettie is going to bend down and treat them all to a posterior view of her privates. Before she knows what she's doing, Isabel has crossed the lawn and draped herself over Bettie's naked body.

Bettie tries to fend her off, annoyed. "Isabel Kidd, what in the world . . ."

Isabel looks around. Everyone is home now, the work and school day over, milling about as they take care of their lawns or prepare for an after dinner walk. Isabel grabs the welcome mat and uses it to shield Bettie from the view of passersby who are gawking from the sidewalk. "Bettie, did you forget something? Like clothes?"

Bettie snorts and then looks down. "Oh boy."

Isabel keeps her eyes averted.

Bettie tosses her hedge clippers aside and grasps the welcome mat, stiffly wrapping it around her body. "Excuse me," she says primly, and steps back into the house.

Some of the neighborhood kids are gathering on the sidewalk and giggling. "Beat it," Isabel tells them. A few of the kids roll their bikes a few feet back but nobody leaves.

"Oh, they're just watching what you're doing,"

Bettie says, reemerging from her house in a brightly colored muumuu and wool scarf. She gives them a cheerful wave, which sends the kids into a chorus of giggles.

Isabel raises an eyebrow. "I'm not doing anything," she says. "I think they're hoping to catch more of your little show."

Bettie sputters. "Well, I never . . ."

"Hey!" Isabel snaps at two whispering boys leaning on their bikes. "Show's over! Go home!" Isabel recognizes one of the boys from down the street, the redheaded mastermind who managed to rally the whole neighborhood to put up the clubhouse in Lucy Fitzpatrick's yard. The boys roll their bikes back again but don't leave.

Bettie frowns in disapproval. "Isabel Kidd, you're not being very friendly."

"Don't you have some gardening to do?" Isabel gives her a pointed look until Bettie picks up her hedge clippers. She can't resist adding, "Besides, it looks like I'll be moving soon. I just got a full-price offer on my house." She doesn't mean to gloat, but she can't help it.

Bettie takes a long look at Isabel and then at her house. "No kidding. Well, good for you," she finally says. She starts clipping a clump of evergreen near the doorway. "American Boxwood. Hardy stuff. Bill helped me put this in, remember?"

"Vaguely." Isabel wonders how much she

should ask for the furniture. They'll be saving her the trouble of selling it herself, and she'll be able to use everything until the last day she's there. She decides that she'll give them a good price, throw in a few things for free, too.

"Impervious to cold weather, pests, and disease resistant. Yes sir, this was a good recommendation." Bettie snips at a stray branch near Isabel's feet. "How is Bill these days, anyway? I don't see much of him anymore. I still need to thank him for helping me with my gutters last winter." She clips another branch.

It takes Isabel a moment to register this. Bill? Isabel looks up at Bettie's gutters and sees that they're rusting in spots, stuffed with leaves and other debris. One section is sagging heavily while another looks brittle and thin. Bettie probably hasn't had anyone else work on her gutters since Bill died.

Bettie prattles on, unaware of Isabel gaping at her. "Ingrid Olson is so jealous that Bill's always helping me out. So handy around the house *and* he's my dentist! He always gives me extra toothbrushes and those little tubes of toothpaste for free, too. I tell him not to bother with the floss, because life's too short, you know?"

"Bettie," Isabel says slowly. "Bill passed away. He was hit by a truck. Remember?"

Bettie stops and stares at Isabel. "What?"

"Bill. He died. Four years ago."

Shock fills Bettie's face. "Bill isn't dead. That's a horrible thing to say, Isabel!"

"I think that maybe you should see a doctor . . ."

"I'm not the one who needs to see a doctor—you are! You're the one who thinks your husband is dead!" Bettie throws the hedge clippers into the bushes and marches into her house, slamming the door behind her.

Now what? Isabel has lived next door to Bettie all these years and she doesn't know who she should call. Bettie knows everyone in Avalon, but Isabel isn't sure who'd be considered a close friend. This is a private matter, something that only someone close to Bettie should know about. Isabel doesn't even know if she has any family anywhere—it's never once come up in conversation.

Isabel wonders if she should knock on the door and then decides against it. What would she say? Bettie's confused and upset, and it's not like Isabel's going to break out the obituaries to prove Bettie wrong. Isabel turns back to her house, unsure of what to do.

"Wow," she hears the freckly redheaded kid say to his friend as they begin to pedal away. "That was better than TV!"

"That should do it," Yvonne says, standing up. She's at the Avalon Cut and Curl where she's installed and plumbed their new pedicure massage chair. She runs the water, hot and cold, then drains it. Mavis Lipinski, the owner, beams.

"Oh, it's perfect! I don't know how to thank you, Yvonne."

Yvonne smiles and hands her an invoice. "This should do fine, Mavis." She begins to pack up her things.

"But I want to do something more. I mean, you rushed over after Hillshire Plumbing canceled and saved us in a pinch. And we have back-to-back pedicures scheduled tomorrow!" Mavis scrunches her face, then snaps her fingers. "How about a pedicure? You can be the first one in our new chair!"

Yvonne sticks out a foot, clad in a heavy work boot. "Thank you, Mavis, but I'm not exactly wearing the right kind of shoes today. I'll schedule something in the future and bring my flip-flops."

"What about a manicure?" Mavis offers.

Yvonne studies her nails. She wouldn't mind a manicure, but it's pointless. Her work is too hard on her nails, so it's easier to keep them short and buffed, polish-free. She wiggles her fingers and Mavis laughs.

"Well, so much for that," Mavis says. Then her face brightens. "I know! We just got in a fabulous gel mask that we've been using for all our facials. It has real rose petals in it. *So* hydrating and it tones the skin—oh, I promise it'll be worth it!"

Yvonne snaps her toolbox closed. She's done for the day, but that's not a good thing since it's only two in the afternoon. Her jobs have slowed to a trickle, cancellations coming in left and right. She still hasn't figured out why. A little treat might be nice.

"Okay," she finally agrees.

Mavis claps her hands. "Perfect! Come on back to the aesthetician's chair and we'll get you set up."

For the next ten minutes Yvonne's face is cleansed, massaged, inspected, and then finally covered with a thin layer of gel. A warm eye mask smelling of rose water is placed over her eyes, plunging Yvonne into darkness.

She lets out a slow breath. She can hear women buzzing around her, talking, gossiping, laughing. The Cut and Curl is small, with one side for beauty and nails and the other for hair, so it's easy to hear everyone and everything. Yvonne feels safely invisible, comfortable in the company of these women but grateful she doesn't have to say anything. She feels herself relaxing for the first time in days, relishing the quiet time.

She overhears women talking about their children, about the latest celebrity news, about talk of a new restaurant coming to town. Someone pans the latest community theater production, saying the lead was overly dramatic and not even from Avalon, but from a neighboring town instead. There's a whispered conversation about an affair, about a teenager being sent off to juvenile detention, about upcoming vacation plans. And then she hears, unmistakably, her own name come up in conversation.

"She was just here," someone is saying. "Pretty girl, but I've never heard of a girl plumber before. It's strange, don't you think?"

"Maybe she's one of those lesbian types," another person suggests.

"Well, I have it on good authority that she's seeing one of the Hill boys," someone says. "Odd, isn't it?"

There's a murmur of assent.

What's so odd about it? Yvonne wonders. So she's a plumber. Big deal. Plumbers are entitled to a little romance, aren't they? She feels the skin on her face pull as she replays the conversation in her head. Hill boys? Hugh has brothers?

"Sleeping with the enemy," someone else titters. "I hope she knows what she's doing. Remember what happened with Fred Mackie?"

There's a round of *tsks* and sighs. "Such a shame," someone says sorrowfully.

Yvonne can't stand it anymore. She pulls off the eye mask and sits up. "What happened with Fred Mackie?" Her face is tight from the gel and it comes off more biting than she intends. The women eye her in surprise, then look away in embarrassment when they realize who she is.

Mavis comes rushing over with a hot towel and promptly dumps it on Yvonne's face. "No talking, ha-ha! Let's soften this up and then we'll wash it off." Yvonne can hear her hissing reprimands at the other women.

Yvonne wipes the mask off her face with the towel and hands it back to Mavis. "Who's Fred Mackie?" she asks again.

"Fred Mackie was a handyman," Mavis says. "He did all sorts of jobs—"

"He was wonderful," one woman says. "And so reasonably priced. And they chased him out of town!"

"Remember when my basement flooded?" Another woman is reading the bottom of each bottle of nail polish. "Oh, I can't decide—Passion Pink or Romance Red? Anyway, I don't know what I would have done without him. Our sump pump was broken and he came over in the middle of the night to take care of it."

"He installed the shelves in my garage," someone else remembers. "And helped us get some new shingles on the roof when my husband was recovering from hip surgery. You should definitely go with the Romance Red, Nettie."

"He did a lot of plumbing, too," Mavis tells Yvonne. "We used him a lot because he was a jack of all trades. He could fix anything."

One woman with a head full of foil nods her head. "But then Hillshire Plumbing got wind of it.

307

Fred was doing a lot of plumbing jobs, and they didn't like him getting all the business."

"Hillshire's been in these parts forever," Mavis explains. "Been in Joan's family for several generations. She used to have us do her highlights, but she hated sitting in the chair, didn't like the chitchat. I think she's finally let the gray kick in."

"You can't fight Mother Nature," a woman says, patting her silvery head that's being blown out. "But I happen to like my grays. Gets me a better seat on the bus."

Another woman with her hair wrapped up in a towel is flipping through a magazine. "A couple of years ago Hillshire Plumbing started having problems, so that's when they decided to go after the little guys who were doing well, like Fred."

"And Hank Carter . . ."

"And the Woodsen brothers . . ."

Yvonne looks at the women. "What do you mean, go after the little guys?"

Mavis looks guilty. "They offered lower prices. Free inspections and estimates. They came by and gave us all sorts of goodies—" Mavis nods to a calendar on the wall. "Pens, keychains, those little flashlights. Basically it was hard to say no."

Yvonne has a business card, and that's it. "But you called me," she points out.

Mavis nods. "Because they called this morning to cancel. I was like, excuse me, but you can't cancel because we already have a full appointment book! I couldn't believe it. They couldn't have cared less and weren't going to send someone out until next Wednesday. I told them no way, I'd find someone else, and hung up. It's like they drove everybody away just so they could get our business, and then they don't even show up to do the work!"

Normally this sort of thing doesn't bother Yvonne, because it is just business. It's all about supply and demand, customer service, pricing. If someone has a plumbing emergency, they're going to go through every number in the book until they find someone who can help them.

But why is everyone still looking at her funny?

Mavis dabs a cotton ball over Yvonne's face, something cool and crisp that makes her skin tingle. The silver-haired woman has finished with her hair appointment but isn't budging from her chair. "You are being careful, aren't you?" she asks in a low whisper. "You have protection, right?"

There's a tittering among the women. Mavis is furiously shaking a bottle of moisturizer, her eyes cast upward to avoid eye contact with Yvonne.

Yvonne pinks, unsure of how her sex life became the topic of conversation. "That's a bit personal, don't you think?"

Mavis clears her throat loudly in warning to the ladies. She begins to spread the moisturizer on

Yvonne's face in a sweeping motion. "Just relax now . . ." she croons in an obvious attempt to change the subject.

Yvonne touches Mavis's arm. "Mavis, come on. What's going on?"

Mavis sighs. She wipes her hands on a towel and helps Yvonne sit up, casting a nervous glance around the salon. "We're not talking about *that* kind of protection. We heard rumors that they roughed up Hank Carter when he came out of the pharmacy. Pushed him around, scared him a bit. You don't know with those Hillshire Plumbing folks, that's all. Maybe carry some—I don't know—pepper spray or something, just in case. I don't think they would go so far as to actually hurt you, but who wants to find out, right?"

Heads are bobbing in agreement.

"You should get one of those Taser things," Nettie suggests a bit too enthusiastically. "I always wondered what it would be like to Taser someone. Show a perpetrator that, and I bet they'll head in the other direction, you know? *Zap!*"

"That's enough, Nettie," Mavis says, shooting her a look. "We don't want to scare her."

"It probably doesn't help that you're a girl," someone else says. "If anything that probably makes them madder, right?"

"I never thought about that!" someone gasps. "Oh, do be careful!"

Yvonne doesn't know if the ladies are right or just bored and in the mood to come up with some dramatic worst-case scenarios. Either way, tiptoeing around with a container of pepper spray much less a Taser is not how Yvonne does things. She thinks about the note, the open door, the cancellations. She doesn't know what's been going on but she's sure as heck going to find out.

"I find it hard to believe that one more plumber in Avalon is going to make that much of a difference to them, but I'm going to go over and introduce myself." Yvonne gathers her things. "Does anyone know where their office is?"

Mavis fishes around in a drawer and comes up with a tape measure. She taps the plastic casing. "That's their address."

Yvonne nods. "Okay, thanks. Who do you think I should talk to?"

The women suck in their breath, and the look on Mavis's face is pure pity.

"Oh, my dear," she says, reaching out to give Yvonne's arm a sympathetic squeeze. "It's Hubert Hill, Joan's son. He's the president of Hillshire Plumbing."

Frances is shaking out the laundry and folding the boys' clothes into neat squares on top of the dryer, separating them into daytime piles and nighttime piles. Frances loves the smell of fresh laundry, loves to pull clothes out of the dryer, soft

311

and warm. She knows many women find house-work tedious, and while there are certainly jobs around the house she'd be happy to give up, laundry isn't one of them.

She hears the rumble of a truck outside the house, then the sound of the truck backing into their driveway.

"Mom, come look!" Noah hollers excitedly as he races by. Brady runs after him.

"Don't go outside!" Frances is worried that the driver of the truck won't see two little boys running up behind them. "Reed, can you get the boys?" she calls. There's no response.

"What's going on?" Nick asks, striding by with a soccer ball tucked under his arm. "What's that big truck doing in our driveway?"

"It's Goodwill here to pick up some things." Frances clears her throat, forces a smile. "Where's your father?"

Nick shrugs. "In his office, I think." He tosses the ball into the air and heads toward the garage.

"And make sure your brothers stay out of the way," Frances reminds him as Nick grumbles, "Yeah, yeah."

Frances scoops up the boys' laundry and heads to their bedroom. "Reed, Goodwill is here," she calls out. She quickly puts the clothes away and hurries to the office where all of Mei Ling's things have been packed in boxes, ready to be donated.

Reed is there, sitting at his desk, staring at the oversized dollhouse. Frances cringes every time she sees it, and it'll be a relief when it's gone.

"I still can't believe you bought this," he says. There's a sad smile on his face. "I mean, it's huge. It's completely too big for this house. I don't know what you were thinking."

"I know, I know," Frances says. She reaches into one of the boxes and picks out a small crocheted croissant from the tea set she bought from Avalon Gifts 'N More. She considered saving them to see if Brady was interested in any imaginative play, but his response was to throw one of the petit fours into the toilet.

"Just look at this thing," Reed continues. He gets up and starts opening and closing the doors and windows, peering into the small closets. "There's even an ironing board, for God's sake!"

"OKAY." Frances picks up a box of clothes. "I get it. I know I got carried away, but I couldn't help myself." She heads to the door, put out that he's still nitpicking over the dollhouse. "Grab that box there, will you? I think it's her puzzles and books."

"I can't do it," Reed says suddenly. He looks up and his face is stricken. "I can't do it, Fran." His voice breaks.

For a second Frances is caught off guard, and then she's quick to put the box down, to go to him. She crouches down, taking his hands in hers. She hadn't realized that this had taken a toll on him, too—Reed seemed so settled and definite in his decision, so clear even if there was a tinge of regret. To see the look of misery on his face now makes her sad at what could have been, and at the same time, she loves him all the more for it. "You don't have to do anything," she says. "I'll take everything out, or have them come in and help."

"No," he says, shaking his head. "I've changed my mind. I don't think we should give her things away." He runs his hand along the roofline of the dollhouse. "She would have loved this, Frances. You were right to have bought it."

"Reed," she says. She's unsure of what to make of this. "We can't keep these things. You were right—we need to let it go, we need to let Mei Ling go." Her voice trembles, but that doesn't change the way she feels. Frances has struggled to accept their decision for the sake of Reed and the boys, and she's managed. Barely. She's still unable to sleep at night, tossing and turning as she pictures Mei Ling waiting for a family that most likely will never come. A child with such an intimidating medical history makes it difficult, both financially and emotionally, for anyone to say yes.

But still, anything is possible, and Frances still hopes for her, still prays that there is enough room in somebody's life to include this little girl.

"Somebody will be grateful for these things," she tells Reed, hoping this will make it easier.

But that seems to agitate him more. "But these are *her* things," he says again, running a hand through his hair. "They belong to Mei Ling." He turns to look at Frances. "You know how you've been making those scrapbooking albums for the boys? It kills me to think that she won't have one. Like that birthday book you've been making for each of them. I want to see her blowing out the candles on her cake, Fran. Opening presents. Just like the boys."

Is Reed having a nervous breakdown? Frances doesn't know what to do.

"Mom?"

Frances turns, startled. Nick is staring at them, his brothers behind him, oddly quiet for once. "Those guys are waiting outside."

"I know," Frances says as Reed turns away. "Tell them a couple more minutes, okay? Offer them some water?"

Nick pokes through the box by the door. He lifts out a small pink jumper. "Didn't Grandma send this?"

Oh, this isn't helping. She sees Reed's shoulders heave, and she can sense that something is about to happen, that whatever fragile peace Reed has made with their decision is about to shatter.

"Go outside, boys," she says, a little desperately, just as Reed is overcome with large, racking sobs.

The boys don't move, frozen in place at the sight of their father crying.

"Why Daddy crying?" Brady asks.

"Because he's sad, dummy," Noah tells him.

"Don't call him dummy, dummy," Nick scowls. He gives Noah a small push.

"Don't push me!" Noah pushes Nick back, a much harder push despite his five years and significantly shorter stature.

"Cut it out!" Nick hollers as Noah readies another push.

Brady starts to cry, overwhelmed by the turn of emotions. Frances knows they're unnerved at the sight of Reed so upset—it's disconcerting to see a grown man cry, especially your father. She pulls Brady into her lap, then puts her hand between Noah and Nick, resting the palm of her hand on Noah's chest. It's the only thing that will calm him down when he's riled up, and she can feel his heart racing, his small, angry breaths.

"It's okay, boys," she says. She's decided that she's not going to hide what's transpiring between her and Reed, because it's such a big thing. It's a big thing that's affected their family in a profound way, and the boys have a right to know what's going on. "You know how we said that the adoption with Mei Ling didn't work out? Well, your father is still sad about it. Me too."

"So why don't we adopt her then?" Nick asks. He's still holding on to the jumper, and Frances can almost picture him holding Mei Ling as she wears it. She feels her own tears coming.

"She has serious heart problems," Frances says. "Among other things. She's a child who has a good chance of getting very, very sick someday." She doesn't add that there's the very real possibility of Mei Ling getting so sick that she could die as a result. "She may need medical care that your father and I can't give her."

"So if we got sick, you couldn't take care of us?" Noah asks, an uncertain look on his face.

"No, of course we would," Frances assures him quickly.

"But what if we were really, really sick?" Noah persists. "Like her? Could you still take care of us then?"

"Yes," Frances says firmly. "Yes, Noah. You don't have to worry, okay?"

Nick looks perturbed. "So if you can do it for us, why can't you do it for her? It's not her fault she's this way."

Frances stares at her oldest son, at the unexpected wisdom that came from his eight-year-old lips. She feels something click into place, the missing piece that's been causing her heartache since they made the difficult decision to turn down Mei Ling's referral. She knows she and Reed have already agreed, have already looked at the numbers, at the overwhelming impossibility of it all. But if it were any of the boys, they would find a way. Of that Frances has no doubt.

"Yes," she says slowly. "You're right. It's not her fault she was born with these challenges." Because that's all they are: challenges. Everyone has something, and while some are bigger than others, you never know what the next day will bring. It could go either way—anything is possible.

Frances holds her breath and turns to look at Reed, who is looking at Nick with shiny eyes. His face is ragged but Frances sees a glimmer of relief, of joy. "You're right, son," Reed says, echoing her words. "You're absolutely right."

What does this mean? Frances clutches his hands, wants to burst out in laughter and tears. "Reed?" she says.

"Yes, Fran," Reed says, and he stands up, brushing his hands on his jeans, wiping his eyes. "We're going to do it. I'm going to call the agency and get our daughter back."

Herb "Buster" McMillan, 57
Truck Driver

At 3:00 a.m., Herb "Buster" McMillan's alarm clock goes off.

Brrnng! Brrnng!

It's an obnoxious, jarring sound but it gets him out of bed, rouses him from the four or five hours of sleep he's been lucky enough to get. It'll still be dark out, the same as when he went to bed, but he'll flick on the light and let himself drop to the floor. He'll count out fifty sit-ups, then an equal amount of push-ups. He'll get up and grab his clothes from the wooden valet, already clean and laid out from the night before. He'll dress on the way to the bathroom, from the top down, so that by the time he reaches the sink, he can toss his pajamas into the wicker hamper before he does a quick shave and brushes his teeth.

At first glance Buster looks like any other tanker yanker, slightly paunchy with a weathered face from years of being on the road. He'll be out three hundred days of the year, sometimes for two or three days in a row with no sleep, no exercise, the sun blazing through the windshield during the day and the nights long and dark. He's careful, though, and he'll sneak a nap if he needs to because there's nothing worse than hauling a loaded fuel tank and closing your eyes one second too long. Everyone has a horror story, but fortunately Buster's learned from everyone else's mistakes. He's never had a fire, has never rolled his cab or tanker, has never dropped at the wrong station. He has a few golden rules that he follows: never hurry, always trace your lines, and get it right the first time.

Buster has albums filled with places he's visited, but the ones he carries with him at all times are filled with pictures of Avalon. The small two bedroom house that's his, free and clear. Avalon at Christmas, his favorite time of the year. Avalon Park, where he'll go to feed the birds after grabbing a cup of coffee. Summer barbecues in his backyard with his neighbors and a few buddies he went to Avalon High with, back in the day. Buster's found that people are just as interested in him as he is in them, and sharing these pictures is the best way to let them know who he is and where he's from.

His home is his sanctuary, so whenever he's on the road he brings a little bit of Avalon with him. The albums keep him grounded and he likes sharing them with people, even if it is a little goofy and sentimental. You never know when someone might want to see them. Like this past spring, when he was driving from Dayton to Miami. He decided to stop for coffee a few hours out of Ohio. He fell out of the cab like a klutz and sprained his ankle. It was the first time anything like that had ever happened to him.

In the emergency room the nurse had passed him his duffel bag when one of the albums fell out. She picked it up and they started talking. He showed her the pictures, embarrassed at first and then with pride. She laughed at his stories while his ankle was being wrapped and then she told some of her own, staying a couple hours past her shift.

"A dog trainer," she confided in him. "I love being a nurse but I'm good with animals, too. Dogs especially. I think it would be fun to do that, you know?"

"You should do it," he told her. "Try it, at least. Maybe in your spare time and see what happens."

She blushed. "Oh, I don't know. It seems more like a hobby, not a real job."

"I bet there are people out there dying for someone like you. People who are having a hard time with their pets and need some help. If you get good I bet you could charge whatever you want."

She smiled. "You think?"

He nodded. "I think it's great that you know what you'd love to do. Most people don't even have that." He smiled and felt a flutter in his gut. He saw them taking long walks and holding hands and sitting in front of a crackling fire in the dead of winter. He cleared his throat, feeling his own cheeks grow hot. "You should go for it," he said again. "What have you got to lose?"

They exchanged information and he didn't think he'd ever hear from her again. But a few days ago he got a letter with a business card inside and a picture of a little dog jumping through a hoop. "Puppy training and socialization classes by Alicia." That's her name—Alicia Rodriguez. Alicia with the most beautiful brown eyes, long lashes, and a smile that will knock your socks off.

Lately he's been thinking that maybe he's ready to go out on his own, be the master of his own schedule, build in a little more free time for himself. He wants to enjoy his home more, wants to spend some of the money he's been saving up. And who knows—the last time he walked through Avalon Park, he saw plenty of people with puppies and dogs. Maybe he'll invite Alicia up for a visit, if she's interested. She already said that Avalon looked like the kind of place someone would be happy to call home. Maybe he's being presumptuous that she'd want to see him again, but it can't hurt to ask.

After all, what does he have to lose?

Chapter Thirteen

Connie whacks at a patch of wild dandelions that are threatening to take over the garden. It's early on a Saturday morning and the October air is cool. She has a full day of food prep ahead of her, and she needs to return some calls to people who want to book the tearoom for an upcoming event.

The tea salon is becoming popular with wedding planners who like to recommend the space for bridal luncheons or small engagement parties. Connie's designed a paper tea packet that brides can customize with their name and wedding date. She can add a quote about love or marriage, or put a title like "Love Is Brewing" or "The Perfect Blend." It's a simple thing that adds a personal touch, and when tied with a satin ribbon looks as professional as the ones that cost an arm and a leg.

Connie pulls the dandelions up by the roots, tossing them into the growing pile next to her. She knows Serena will eat them, the flowers and leaves, at least, and it would be so much easier to let her roam free and help keep the weeds in check. The only problem is that Serena won't restrict herself to the weeds, instead going for anything green and edible. Madeline doesn't want her to bother patrons or create a problem for the neighbors. In short, it's this or nothing.

Connie glances at the goat. Serena looks conked out even though it's too early in the day for her to be tired. She wishes there was more space for Serena in the pen, but since they converted the backyard for additional seating and a small lounging area for customers, it's not possible. Connie can hear Madeline remind her that the property's not set up for livestock, and that there could be a zoning issue, too.

"Have you asked around yet?" she'll ask casually. It's not nagging exactly but Madeline's not giving it up, either. The thought that Serena might no longer be a part of her life is unbearable, but Connie doesn't want Madeline or Walter Lassiter getting involved, so she finally sat down and printed out copies of her MISSING GOAT sign.

"Leave some in the tea salon," Madeline suggested yesterday. "In case anyone wants to put it up in their place of business, too. The more people who see it, the better."

So Connie had reluctantly left a pile on one of the tables in the entryway along with their take-out menu and business cards. So far no one's taken any. She's counted them out, twenty in all, and each time she goes by, she counts them again. Still twenty. She feels encouraged each time she sees the small stack, knows Madeline can't say she isn't trying to get the word out.

"So what's wrong with your goat?"

Connie looks up and sees Walter Lassiter

peering over the top of the fence. He gives a nod toward Serena, who ignores them both.

"Nothing's wrong," Connie says as she digs out some crabgrass. "She's just tired."

"Nope," Walter says. "She's sick. Maybe she ate something she shouldn't have."

"Sick?"

"Look at her. Something ain't right." He jerks his thumb toward the pen.

Connie bites her lip. "You're saying that, Mr. Lassiter, because you want me to get rid of her."

"Of course I want you to get rid of her!" he snorts. "Are you just figuring this out? She doesn't belong here. *She's a goat.* She belongs on a farm or in a zoo. Has she even been dewormed?"

Connie looks at Serena, who's lying listlessly in her doghouse. She doesn't hop on top anymore, which Connie finds odd. She figured Serena was pouting because Connie couldn't play with her as much as she'd liked.

"Goats can have all sorts of parasites," Walter continues. "They need to be vaccinated. After all, this is a neighborhood, with people. Do you see any other goats around? No."

Do you see any other fussy neighbors around? Connie wants to retort. *No.*

But she doesn't say that, just stands up and wipes the dirt from her hands. She gathers up the weeds and dumps them into the small wheelbarrow she uses to garden. "Well, I'm trying to find the owner," she says. "But if I can't find them, then . . ."

"Then I guess you'll have to find another home for her," Walter finishes. The look on his face is all business now.

"That will be up to me to decide," Connie says. She doesn't want him thinking she's easily bullied.

"No, missy. City ordinance. I don't want to have to bring this up at the next town meeting, either. It's bad enough you have all these people coming and going . . ."

"The tea salon is a legitimate business," she interjects.

"But keeping a goat in a residential area, even if you have a commercial license, isn't. I looked it up, missy."

"My name is *Connie,* Mr. Lassiter."

"I'm telling you this first, missy, because I know you're doing your best and I appreciate the casseroles. But the minute I do a sit-down with Madeline, that goat is history. Again, nothing personal. I don't have any intention of spending my retirement years living next door to a goat. There's enough commotion going on as it is."

Connie is suddenly weary. "I hear you, Mr. Lassiter."

"And I'd get that goat to a vet, if I were you. Something's not right with her." He grunts and heads back to his house.

Connie pushes the wheelbarrow toward the trash and compost area, then goes over to Serena's pen. "Hey, girl," she says. She unlatches the gate and walks in. "How are you feeling?"

Serena gets up and walks over to Connie, nuzzling and leaning into her. Connie looks around and sees that she's due to rake out the pen again, lay down some new straw. She read that male goats stink up their pens but female goats aren't so bad. It's just manure, after all, and it's good for the compost heap.

Serena wanders away, then flops down, forlorn. Connie hesitates. They have a busy day ahead and then a busy evening with a monthly book club meeting in the sitting room. There's no time for Connie to squeeze in an emergency visit to the vet.

Inside the kitchen, Madeline is covering a large container of fruit salad with plastic wrap. "I was hoping for a quiet morning but we already have quite a few call-ins. I also thought we'd be able to serve a butternut squash soup for the daily special but now I'm thinking we should use up the tomatoes instead . . ."

"I think Serena's sick," Connie blurts out. She scrubs her hands in the sink, suddenly anxious. "She hasn't been herself lately."

Madeline puts the fruit salad into the fridge just as the oven timer goes off. "Yes, I was noticing that myself." She slides on her oven mitts and opens the oven door.

Connie reaches for her apron, then stops. "What should I do?" she asks Madeline.

"Depends." Madeline pulls out a baking tray of blueberry Amish Friendship Bread scones and sets it on a rack to cool. "What do you want to do?"

"I want to take her to the vet," Connie says. She lines up the empty butter dishes on the counter. "But there's no time. And I can't leave you here alone."

"Oh, *pshaw,*" Madeline says. "I did run this place for a while on my own, you know." Then her face lights up.

"Hannah!" she exclaims, snapping her fingers. "We could call her and see if she's available to help us today. I'm sure she'd be delighted."

Again? Connie grimaces. She's been paying closer attention to the times Hannah joins them in the kitchen and was dismayed to discover that Hannah has the same sensibilities and preferences as Madeline in the kitchen. No Mountain Dew dumplings for her.

"I can take Serena later," Connie says, reaching for the apron again. She doesn't want Hannah coming in to help. Call her insecure, but she just doesn't.

Madeline gives her a stern look. "Put that back," she orders, referring to the apron. "And I'm calling Hannah. You call the vet and get your goat squared away."

"But . . ."

The bell over the door tinkles as the first customers trickle in. "Taking care of an animal comes with certain responsibilities," Madeline says as she heads out of the kitchen to greet them. "Go and make sure she's all right."

But when Connie calls the vet, the receptionist tells her Dr. Ballard is completely booked.

"Please," Connie begs. "Could he just take a quick look? I need to know that she's all right."

The woman sighs. "Well, if you come now I can try to squeeze you in between appointments."

"Thank you," Connie says with relief, already reaching for her keys and wallet. "I'll bring her right over."

She updates Madeline before heading to the backyard. Serena looks up with mild interest as Connie approaches, and Connie feels hopeful that everything will be fine. She's probably worried about nothing. She'll get Serena into the car, drive to the vet's, get some vitamins or whatever, and come right home.

Twenty minutes later, Connie is still standing in the driveway tugging unsuccessfully at Serena's leash as she tries to get her into the car. Serena seems to know what's going on and wants no part of it.

Hannah walks up, her purse slung over her shoulder, her long dark hair pulled back in a sleek ponytail. She's dressed in khakis and a pressed white shirt, ballet flats on her feet. "Hey, Connie," she begins, and then stops when she sees Serena. "Oh."

"I'm . . . trying . . . to . . . take . . . her . . . to . . . the . . . vet," Connie grunts. She finally collapses against the car in defeat.

Hannah glances at the tea salon, then back at Connie, her eyes filled with concern. "Do you need help?"

No, Connie wants to say, but she doesn't have much of a choice so she nods.

"Okay." Hannah slips off her purse and looks at Serena uncertainly, unsure of what to do. "Do you want me to push? From, uh, behind?"

"That would be great. Steer clear of her kicking zone, you know, in case." But even with Connie and Hannah at opposite ends, Serena doesn't budge.

"Oh, come on now," Madeline says, stepping out of the tea salon, looking exasperated. "We have work to do." She holds up a bran muffin. "Let's go, Serena!" She tosses the muffin into Connie's car.

"I don't think . . ." Connie begins, but then Serena breaks away from her and hops into the backseat.

Madeline looks satisfied. "There we are! Now let's get inside, Hannah, I need your help in the kitchen. Connie, you better get on your way

330

before she polishes off that muffin and starts in on your upholstery."

Connie gives them a wave, then carefully backs out of the driveway. Serena finishes the muffin before they've reached the end of the block. She starts to stand up, wobbling as Connie takes a corner a little too sharply. She looks unhappy at being inside the car and starts butting the door in an attempt to get out.

"Serena, sit!" Connie commands, even though she knows Serena doesn't know what that means. Fortunately, like most things in Avalon, the veterinarian's office is only a few minutes away.

As promised, the receptionist has penciled her in and after half an hour leads them to an examination room. While they wait, Connie glances at the pictures on the wall. Dr. Ballard looks to be about sixty, his hair all gray, a kind smile on his face. He's standing next to a horse while wearing a short-sleeved shirt and necktie. There are other pictures, too, with different animals and owners. Connie can tell that he loves what he does.

So when a young man with dark hair walks into the room wearing a white lab coat with "Dr. Elliot Ballard, DVM," Connie is confused.

"Where's Dr. Ballard?" she asks.

"I'm Dr. Ballard," he replies. He looks at her and gives her a friendly grin, and Connie feels her cheeks flush. When he holds out his hand, Connie goes to shake it and feels a tingle that shoots straight up her arm and into her chest, resonating throughout her body. For a second her mind is a blank—she forgets about Serena, about the tea salon, about everything. All she can think about is the man standing in front of her and notice that her heart is doing flip-flops in her chest.

He smiles at Serena. "So what seems to be the problem?"

"I'm not sure," Connie says. She glances at a mirror on the back of the door, relieved to see that she doesn't look as flustered as she feels. "I'm sorry, but you don't look anything like your pictures."

"That's because those pictures are of my father—he retired last year. But you can call me Eli. Most people do." Eli looks at his chart. "So you haven't been in before, Connie?"

Hearing him say her name sets off that tingling sensation again. She shakes her head.

"Usually I refer farm animals to Doc Handley," Eli says. "He handles the larger animals and livestock. I see more of your domesticated animals—dogs, cats, the occasional parrot or turtle. Though I have been seeing quite a few chickens lately . . . Anyway, I'm happy to take a look and refer you to him if necessary."

"Thank you." The thought of having to get Serena back into the car and to another vet is overwhelming.

"We used to have goats when I was growing up, LaManchas and a few Pygmies. Always wanted a Nubian, though." He checks Serena's eyes and ears.

"I figured that's what she was," Connie says. "But I wasn't sure."

"They're great goats," Eli says. "But they can be a handful. I'm surprised she's not kicking up a fuss." He checks her hooves. He runs his hands over Serena's coat, her throat, her underbelly, her legs. "Hmm. She eating well?"

Connie nods.

"I'd like to draw some blood. I should get a fecal sample, too. I'll have one of my lab assistants come in and help. I'll also check her mouth for any ulcers and do a physical to see if there are any lumps or sore spots."

Connie swallows, hard. If there's anything wrong with Serena, she doesn't know what she'll do.

Eli notices her unease and pats her arm, his touch warm and comforting. "Don't worry. She seems healthy but I'd like to get her checked out. Sound good to you?"

Connie finally finds her voice. "Yes."

Eli turns back to Serena. "She's a nice-looking animal. What's her name?"

"Serena."

"Serena. It's Latin, right?"

For the first time in her life, Connie wishes she'd gone to college. "I don't know."

"It means serene, but you probably knew that.

Connie is Latin, too, short for Constance. Means steadfast." Eli puts on his stethoscope and listens to Serena's heart and lungs.

"You speak Latin?" Connie asks, impressed and a little intimidated. She only knows a handful of words in Spanish that she's picked up from television or the movies.

Eli drapes the stethoscope around his neck and rubs Serena's back. "Not really. I studied it for four years but it's not like there are a lot of people who speak Latin in Avalon. Or anywhere, for that matter."

There it is again, that grin. Connie figures he's a few years older than her, mid- or late twenties, but she likes that he doesn't take himself too seriously. He seems like the kind of person who would be a good friend, someone nice to hang out with. When he looks up at her and catches her eye, Connie feels herself flush.

She can't believe how unnerved she is. It takes all of her willpower to bring her back to the situation at hand. "So I was worried about her," she says, feeling heat rush to her cheeks. "She doesn't seem like herself."

Eli nods. "Well, it could be several things, but I won't know until I get the bloodwork back. If you'd like, we can keep her over the weekend for observation. It'll give me a chance to see how she does, if there's any change in her behavior. She seems to be pretty agreeable, though."

"But that's why I brought her in," Connie says. "She's not usually so agreeable. She tends to get into things. Like my neighbor's garden."

Eli chuckles. "That sounds like a goat to me," he says. He glances at the clock. "I'm afraid I have to get on to my next appointment. Why don't you let her stay until Monday morning? You can pick her up first thing. If anything comes up before then, I'll call you. Sound good?"

Connie feels a twinge of discomfort as she glances at Serena. "I don't know," she says. "I mean, will she be all right?"

"She'll be fine. I have dogs in here that are bigger than Serena. It's quiet now, so we'll be able to give her some attention." He looks at a clipboard on the table. "Is this the number to reach you at? Madeline's Tea Salon?"

Connie nods, still feeling a bit numb. "Maybe I should bring her back with me," she ventures, feeling lost at the thought of Serena not coming home with her. "I mean, in case she gets freaked out or . . ."

"It's up to you, Connie," Eli says. "Whatever you want to do is fine." The compassionate look on his face is all she needs to make up her mind.

"Okay," Connie says, because she knows that Serena will be in good hands. She takes a deep breath. "You'll call me if she needs anything?"

"I've already committed your number to

memory," Eli tells her, and then he flashes her one more boyish grin before leading Serena out of the room.

It's early Sunday morning and someone is pounding on Isabel's front door, pressing the doorbell one too many times. She gropes for her alarm clock but it falls to the floor and bounces under the bed.

Isabel groans but manages to get up and stumble down the hall, half awake, half asleep. She takes a look through her peephole. There's a man, a cup of steaming coffee in hand, whistling as he looks up and down her porch. Perplexed but curious, Isabel opens the door.

"Good morning!" he says, turning to look at her. A tool belt is fastened around his waist and he gives her a broad grin.

"I hope that coffee's for me," Isabel mumbles. She rubs her eyes and sees a white truck parked on the curb. *Braemer Patios and Hardscapes*, she reads. "What time is it?"

"Eight o'clock, on the dot," the man says. "Just like you said. You had me worried there for a sec—I thought nobody was home."

Isabel shoots him an annoyed look. "That's because I was sleeping, Mr. Braemer. I said eight o'clock on the dot, *Monday*."

The man knits his brows. "I could have sworn you said Sunday."

Isabel gives a yawn. It's not like she's going to go back to sleep now. "I didn't, but never mind," she says.

Ian Braemer straddles the porch framing as he gives it a quick once-over. "Looks like we're talking a few tongue-and-groove porch planks," he says.

Isabel nods, watching him sip his coffee. Maybe she's still half asleep, but she can't remember the last time she noticed someone, much less someone of the opposite sex, sipping coffee. It's oddly mesmerizing.

"Mrs. Kidd?"

"What? Oh. Porch planks, right. I haven't had a chance to figure out if I want to use wood or try those composite boards . . ."

"Wood," Ian says firmly. "Definitely wood. The composite decking is more trouble than it's worth, and it'll look shoddy after a while. I've installed them for a few clients and no one's happy with them. That's just my opinion, of course, but I wouldn't use composite anything on my house. They're a complete rip-off." He actually looks worked up.

Isabel grins, awake now. "Gee, tell me what you think, Mr. Braemer. And really, don't hold back."

He gives her a sheepish look. "Sorry. I don't want people wasting their money, that's all. I can give you some composite quotes if you want."

337

"Are you kidding? We'll go with wood. How long do you think it would take?"

"I need to take some measurements, figure out supplies. You want me to prime and paint as well?"

Isabel nods. "Sure, why not?"

"What color?"

She's about to say white when she remembers this will no longer be her home. "Whatever will match with the house," she says.

"Okay, no problem." He flicks out a business card and hands it to her. "Oh, and I can pick you up a coffee while I'm out, too. Black?"

Isabel looks at him. Ian Braemer looks about her age, his face tan and leathery from being in the sun. He's wearing a long-sleeved plaid shirt and jeans, work boots, a faded black baseball cap with the unmistakable White Sox logo. Tufts of brown hair peek out from underneath his cap. His eyes are a bright blue.

"Thanks, but I'm okay," she says. "I mean, I can make my own coffee. I just didn't know you were coming by today, that's all."

"No problem," he says good-naturedly. "So I'll measure and see you in a bit, Mrs. Kidd."

"Just call me Isabel," she tells him. "I'm not married anymore."

Another grin. "Okay, Isabel. And you can just call me Ian."

When Ian Braemer returns an hour later, he has

a young man in his teens with him. "My son," he says proudly. "Jeremy. He'll be helping me get your porch sorted out."

The boy raises one hand in mute greeting then shoves both hands into his jeans pockets. Isabel likes him immediately.

"So how long do you think it will take?" she asks. She wishes she had something to offer them. Bagels or pastries. Lemonade, maybe.

"Getting the planks in place shouldn't take too long," Ian says. "An hour or two, tops. But the priming and painting will take a while. I have to prep the boards, prime them, let them dry, then finish with a coat of paint, hopefully today. I picked up a nice shade that matches your trim. I'll come back the day after tomorrow to put on a second coat. And then, if you want, I can come back again to do a third coat to make sure that . . ."

"Three coats," Isabel hears herself saying quickly. "Definitely three coats. I mean, you know, just to make sure it's done well for the new owners."

"Okay. Three coats it is." Ian smiles at her and turns to head back to his truck. Isabel's eyes drop to the back of his jeans. Then she reddens and turns back into her house.

For the next couple of hours, she hears Ian and Jeremy talking and laughing, the sound of planks being dropped, a nail gun. There's an odd comfort in hearing someone working on her house, and she's suddenly struck by a memory, a feeling, a flash of remembrance.

Bill.

She's thought of him countless times over the years, whether she's wanted to or not, but today is different. There's no anger, there's not even sadness. It's more of a longing. Isabel feels a tug on her heart as her emotions tumble forward, no longer hiding behind the filmy veil that she's used to filter all her memories of Bill. This time, she lets them come, doesn't try to push them away, doesn't try to distract herself. She doesn't try to forget.

She misses how it would take him forever to mow the yard and even longer to edge the lawn. Bill would wash the cars then wax them with care. He'd trim the hedges, check the gutters and downspouts, rake the leaves into neat piles. Isabel used to complain that he was a perfectionist, until he told her that he just liked doing it. He liked being outside, so opposite from Isabel who considers herself a homebody. He said that it was the perfect complement to being indoors with patients all day.

She misses the smell of his body, his sweat, the way his hand felt in hers. Isabel misses having a body around, yes, but the truth is she also misses Bill. His goofy sense of humor, his easy companionship, his kindness. He was steadfast and patient, and she never appreciated that until he was gone.

Things might have been different if they'd been able to start a family. And yes, she'd been depressed for a long time. Who wouldn't have been? They talked about fostering, they talked about adoption, but their hearts weren't in it. For a long time they weren't able to look at each other, always averting their eyes not because they didn't care about each other, but because it was too painful.

To learn about Ava had been a shock, but it had been a double whammy because Ava was pregnant, too. There had been disbelief, then anger. As the days became weeks her emotions hit highs and lows but eventually settled on the plateau of guilt.

Guilt because she couldn't give Bill a child, as if it were somehow her fault. Guilt because she'd been so difficult and closed off that past year. Guilt because she'd yelled terrible things at him when he left. And then guilt when he died, as if she had somehow been responsible for making him turn down the wrong way on that one way street. Guilt because she forbade Ava from coming to the funeral. He may have been living with Ava at the time, but the divorce wasn't final and Bill was still her husband. It was always possible that he might have come back to Isabel, too. Always possible.

But not likely.

Isabel knew miracles happened in other marriages, that somehow couples could find their ways past affairs and broken trust. For a long time she thought that there might have been hope for them, but now she's not so sure. The truth is their marriage had been stuck in neutral for a long time. She never saw it as a bad thing but it wasn't until Bill left that she realized it wasn't enough.

The doorbell's ringing. Isabel takes a deep breath, then goes to answer it. Ian Braemer is standing on her new porch, proud.

"Looks great, doesn't it?" he says, waving his hand down the length of her porch. "We're going to start painting but I thought you might want to take a look, take a little walk on it. Nice, huh?"

Isabel steps carefully out onto the wood. "Wow," she says. She's been living so long with the bare framing that she almost forgot what it was like to have it be so solid, to have a floor beneath her feet. Suddenly it looks so spacious. And, a porch swing. She can see it now. Right over there, to the left of the window so it doesn't block the view from inside the house.

"A porch swing would be nice," Ian says, his hands on his hips. "You could put it right here." He opens his hands and points to the exact same spot Isabel was looking at.

Isabel walks the length of her porch, leans against the railing, takes in the view of her front yard from the comfortable shade of the patio. It's nice. She turns and can picture herself leisurely stretched out on a whitewashed swing, reading a book, a glass of lemonade nearby.

And then she remembers that her house is for sale, maybe even sold.

"The new owners can put it in," she says to Ian. Next door she sees a movement in one of Bettie's windows, a flicker of the curtain, then nothing.

"Okay, then," he says. He motions to Jeremy, who's sitting in the car with headphones on, his head bobbing to the beat. "Hey, son, break's over!"

There's something about the way Ian calls to Jeremy that makes Isabel want to crawl into bed and pull the covers over her head. *Son,* she thinks as she goes back into the house. Such a simple word. Words she'll never speak, nor will Bill.

Son.

Chapter Fourteen

"You seem qualified," Dr. Creighton Marks is saying. He's flipping through Ava's job application, nodding as he goes. "But you haven't been working as a dental assistant for the past few years. Why is that?"

"I wanted to stay home with my son," Ava says, giving him what she hopes is a confident smile. "He's in preschool now, so I'm ready to get back to work."

"Strombauer and Kidd," he reads. "I think they have a new name now. Strombauer Dental Associates, I believe. Shame about Dr. Kidd. He was a nice man."

Ava swallows, wonders how much Dr. Marks knows. His office is in Laquin, on the opposite side of Barrett and a town away from Avalon. Far enough away that she's hoping he hasn't heard any of the gossip, doesn't know who she is. "Yes," she says. "He really was."

"Everything looks good. My assistant is getting married and moving to St. Louis in a month, so the timing is perfect. The last step is your reference check. My wife will kill me if I don't do my due diligence, so I'll give Dr. Strombauer a call as soon as we're done." Dr. Marks smiles as his eyes flicker to the framed photo on his desk. "She's the real boss around here—sometimes I feel like I'm the one working for her." He chuckles.

Ava laces her fingers together in an attempt to keep from fidgeting. "I haven't talked with Dr. Strombauer lately. I don't even know if he remembers me since it was over five years ago."

Dr. Marks nods. "Well, if you want to give him a call and let him know I'll be getting in touch, that'd be fine. I'd like to do this sooner rather than later so I can tell my assistant we've found her replacement."

Ava swallows. "Okay," she says. "I'll let him know to expect your call."

They shake hands and she leaves, holding it together until she's safely tucked into her car. The minute she closes the door, she starts to tremble.

She thought she was up for it, thought she'd be able to ask Randall Strombauer for a reference if it came to that, which it has. But now she doesn't know if she can do it. She'd easily take a million stare-downs from Isabel instead. One minute on the phone with Dr. Strombauer is filling her with fear.

It's not that he knows the truth, that he knows enough details to humiliate and intimidate her. It's because she's never felt safe around him, even though he never crossed the line until that last day. Innuendos, yes, and suggestive, obnoxious flirtation, but he always seemed to keep his distance, seemed to like watching her from afar, liked to see her squirm under his scrutiny. It was always uncomfortable and a bit creepy, but Ava always felt safe because Bill was there.

Ava needs this job with Dr. Marks. He's a nice man, and she can tell he'd be pleasant to work for. It doesn't hurt that the pay is much higher than she'd expected and there's a nice benefit package to boot. In short, she can't afford to pass this up. She's going to have to call Randall Strombauer.

In her apartment, she sits at the kitchen table, her eyes resting on the telephone. She still knows the number by heart. It takes her five tries before she's able to dial the number without hanging up.

"May I ask who's calling?" The receptionist doesn't sound familiar. Mrs. Clarkson had worked for them for years, had been hired on the day Bill and Randall opened the practice. Now the voice is younger and less friendly, clipped.

"Ava Catalina."

She's put on hold, Muzak playing in the background. Ava takes small breaths, wills her heart to stop racing. Enough time has passed that maybe she's making this into something bigger than it is. Asking for a job reference, that's all this is.

"Dr. Strombauer here."

At the sound of his voice, Ava feels herself

shrinking back. He sounds exactly the same, more gruff, more impatient.

"Dr. Strombauer, it's Ava Catalina." When there's no response, Ava clears her throat and tries again. "I used to be a dental assistant in your office a few years ago?"

"Ava!" His voice is suddenly friendly, as if he's just placed her. "Now this is a surprise. How are you? Doing well?"

His exuberant greeting catches her by surprise. "Yes," she says. "I know you're busy, but I'm looking to start work again as a dental assistant and I'd appreciate it if I could count on you for a job reference."

"I see. Where are you living now, still in Avalon?"

The question is innocent enough, but Ava suddenly shifts uncomfortably in her chair. "Um, no," she says.

"Barrett, then? Got some nice dental practices over there, I think."

She decides to avoid the question altogether. "So, um, would it be all right if I give them your name and number so someone can call you?"

"Sure," he says, and it seems like he's dropped it. His voice is friendly again, no longer prying. "No problem. Who might be calling, so I can tell Tina to put them through when they call?"

"Dr. Creighton Marks," she says without thinking, then realizes her mistake.

"Creighton!" comes the delighted crow. "Now that's a name I haven't heard in a while. Still living in Laquin, is he?"

There's no way around it, she realizes. He'll be able to figure it out, no matter who calls. At least he doesn't know where she lives, doesn't know about Max. She looks anxiously at the picture on the table. "Yes."

"Well, I'll take care of it. I'm sure Dr. Marks will *love* you."

There is no mistaking the scorn in his voice. Ava doesn't know what this means, but she manages a quick thank you and hangs up.

She knows that employers have a legal obligation to only offer the facts of previous employees—if they were on time, their job title, things like that. But Ava also knows that in a small town these rules don't apply. She knows that Dr. Strombauer is smarter than that, knows that he has a sharp lawyer in Chicago who is just as aggressive as Dr. Strombauer and who gives him advice that lets him dance as close to the edge as he can without falling over. That was always Bill's complaint, that his partner could talk his way out of anything, that he always seemed one step ahead of Bill whenever they sat down to talk about the business or review the financials. Bill was smart, but Dr. Strombauer was savvy, even crafty, and had encouraged Bill to agree to several shortcuts in the dental practice that soon became problematic for Bill. When Ava had first started working there, the strained relationship between the two dentists was evident, but Bill wasn't ready to change anything.

Until Max. When Ava told him about the pregnancy, fearful that he'd be upset, fearful that she'd be alone, his response had surprised her. She hadn't asked him for anything, hadn't expected anything. She treated their time together as a gift, and she treasured it. She saw his kindness right away, his heart, but it wasn't until the last year that anything had happened. It had been unexpected and quiet, not at all like how the beginning of an affair would seem. There was no moment of weakness, no alcohol, no sob stories being passed between the two of them. Instead it was a flash of kinship, an instant recognition of someone understanding—and appreciating—who you are. There was chemistry, too—there had been since the first day she started working there—but it wasn't until that day in the break room, when he handed her a cup of coffee before she had the chance to ask. Their eyes met and they both saw it.

They fit. They fit together like two pieces of a puzzle, two seemingly disparate people who didn't look like they'd be a couple yet complemented each other nonetheless. Bill with his easygoing attitude and unassuming demeanor that hid an undertone of frustration about the tedium of his life, about his desire for more. Ava with her optimism and unwavering belief that life was meant to be happy. Joyful. That anything was possible.

They wanted the same thing—to be happy. Never did she expect they would grow so close that she couldn't imagine her life without him. Not once did she expect that he would leave Isabel. Ava was hopeful but she also knew the realities of life. She thought that this stolen moment was just that—a moment that would come and eventually go.

When she discovered she was pregnant, it all fell apart. She was emotional, scared, suddenly filled with fear for her future. Maybe it had always been there, dormant and lurking behind her supposed happiness, but now it was out in the open, looming like a storm cloud, gray and threatening.

When he said he wanted to be with her, with the baby, that he wanted a new life where things could be fresh and new and alive, the truth was she had her doubts. She loved Bill unequivocally, but she couldn't help wondering if this was all just a phase for him, a midlife dissatisfaction with where he was and where he was going. She wondered if it would pass. Bill had a long history with Isabel, a marriage that seemed borne more of friendship than romantic love, but still there was that mutual respect, the years of shared memories and experiences. Ava knew how this would look to anyone on the outside—an older man, a younger woman, a baby on the way. Too cliché for words. She actually tried to talk him out of it.

But Bill was resolute, determined to finally "do right" by everyone. Telling the truth to Isabel, staying with Ava, ending the partnership with Randall. The day he told her it was done, that he'd told Isabel and Randall, that he and Ava could finally and openly create a life together, she'd felt disbelief and then unbridled joy. They started planning for the future, full of hope and excitement for what was to come.

And then, the accident.

Ava was at the apartment. Bill had been running errands, had called to say he was on his way home. Home to her, to their small nest.

When the phone rang hours later, she picked it up, worried but also ready to tease him for being late. But it wasn't Bill. It was Isabel, calling from the hospital, her voice flat and void of emotion. She delivered the news fast and without preamble. Ava had slid onto the floor in shock.

At the hospital, everything happened so fast. Ava had no role, no paperwork to fill out, no doctors to talk to. Isabel was still the wife, the person whom the police had called even though the divorce was days away from being filed. They had no idea who Ava was. Ava had no legal rights, no voice in the decision making. Her relationship with Bill was not acknowledged.

And his mother. Ava remembers how Lillian Kidd had collapsed in the waiting room shortly after seeing her son in the morgue. Ava hadn't meant to stay, aware of Isabel ignoring her, but she couldn't leave Bill until she knew what was going to happen. When Bill's mother realized who she was, she started screaming at Ava. It took two orderlies and a nurse to calm her down, and it was then that Isabel said that Ava should go.

Ava winces at the memory, at the reminder of how her life has been stripped away, bit by bit, since that day. For Max, it's the only life he knows, but for Ava, she knows what could have been.

"Stop it," she tells herself, because she isn't going to do this. She isn't going to slip into a well of self-pity, she is going to get them out of this. She is going to turn things around, she is going to get them on solid ground.

She picks up the phone again and dials the number for Dr. Marks's office. When the receptionist puts her through, Ava smiles even though she knows he can't see her, forces her voice to sound upbeat and positive, exactly like the kind of person you'd want working for you.

"Hello, Dr. Marks? It's Ava Catalina. I wanted to let you know that I spoke with Dr. Strombauer and he's expecting your call whenever you—"

"Hi, Ava. I just spoke with him, actually." The warmth from Dr. Marks's voice is gone and he sounds wary. Or is it her imagination?

She clears her throat. "Oh, okay. Well, if you have any other—"

"Unfortunately I had another applicant come in with more recent job skills, so I'm afraid I won't be able to offer you a position at this time. We'll keep your résumé on file, however, and let you know if we have any future openings. Thank you for calling, Ava."

And he hangs up.

Ava stares at the dead phone, hears the drone of the dial tone. She knows as well as Dr. Marks that he won't be calling her. She doesn't know what Dr. Strombauer said, but she knows he is the reason she didn't get this job.

Ava slams the phone into the cradle. She stares at it, her chest heaving, her eyes stinging with tears.

Then she shoves the whole thing onto the floor.

She jerks the cord out of the wall, hears the plastic crack from the outlet. Ava is not an angry person, she has never had a temper tantrum about anything, but now she feels wave after wave of despair and frustration, each one bigger than the last, overtaking her. She will never get another job as a dental assistant. She sees that now, sees how Randall Strombauer will ruin her chances any time she needs a referral. She hasn't worked anywhere else. Which means the one chance she had of actually supporting them has just evaporated.

Her small kitchen suddenly feels confining, limiting, insufficient, infuriating. Ava spins around, seeing all the flaws, the peeling paint, the chipped linoleum, the cabinets that don't hang right. The mismatched dishes, the mismatched glasses, the random forks and spoons and knives that don't go together. At first Ava had seen it as eclectic and fun, each different and unique, but now she sees it as a collection of junky stainless steel and cheap china, a poor attempt at hiding the truth.

Ava doesn't think, just grabs a trash bag and starts to shovel everything inside—the hopeful secondhand bakeware, the slow cooker, the pots and pans. For what? They will never need more than two plates and two sets of utensils, because they never have anybody over. Bill will never walk through that door and the other mothers shy away from her at preschool, suspicious of the young single mom. She has no friends. Her family hasn't spoken to her since they found out she was pregnant by a married man. She had moved to Avalon for the job, then moved to Barrett after Bill died. She is alone. Alone, that is, except for Max.

At the thought of her son, Ava feels the anger drain from her body, leaving her weary and sad, a heavy trash bag in her hands. She could put everything back, but what would be the point? It's not going to change anything. She wishes, for once, that she could let it all go and let her life officially fall apart, but she can't. She has to think of Max, because she is all he has.

She is sobbing now. Max will grow up with no one other than Ava to teach him what he needs to know, and she knows that is not enough. *She* is not enough. Max deserves more—he deserves to have a father, grandparents, aunties, uncles, playmates, and friends. People to advise him and counsel him and love him. People he can turn to and count on. Ava needs those people, too. People who will help her make good choices and not try to sabotage her efforts to make a better life for her and her son.

Like Randall Strombauer. Ava sniffs and wipes her eyes with the back of her hand. Her life is where it is because Ava was slow to adapt to their circumstances, waiting for a solution to present itself. She'd been tentative, hoping that people would meet her halfway but now she knows that if she wants anything, she'll have to go out and get it herself. And right now she wants to know what Randall Strombauer said to Dr. Marks, which she is certain was either inappropriate or a lie. A phone call demanding the truth won't yield anything.

She grabs her keys and purse. She has two

hours before she has to pick up Max, which leaves her with just enough time. She hurries out the door, dragging the trash bag behind her so Max won't see it when he comes home.

But by the time she pulls into the parking lot of Strombauer Dental Associates, Ava has cooled down enough to have second thoughts. Exactly what is she trying to accomplish here? He's not going to apologize—Randall Strombauer is not the apologizing type. Nor is he going to admit that he's done anything wrong. If anything he'll find a way to twist it around, make Ava feel like she's the one who's stepped out of line.

Ava grips the steering wheel to steel herself. She knows that he ruined her chances with Dr. Marks, but it's not just that. It's about what happened in the break room all those years ago, the thing she never told Bill but wished she had. Not because she would have wanted him to do anything, but because she needed somebody else to know that it really happened.

She's tired of being afraid—of life, of other people's opinions, of making mistakes. She doesn't want to let other people's words or actions or decisions dictate how she'll feel about herself, about Max, about her life. This realization is enough for her to pull her keys from the ignition, open her car door, and walk through the door of Strombauer Dental Associates.

Inside it looks the same as she remembered.

There's new paint on the walls, new carpet, some plants, and a large aquarium against the wall in the waiting area. It's homey and comfortable, the last thing Ava would have expected.

"Can I help you?" the receptionist asks, looking up. She's blond, young, and pretty. No surprise there.

"Is Dr. Strombauer in?" Ava asks, forcing a bright smile.

"He's with a patient. Do you have an appointment?"

"He's expecting me," Ava lies. When the receptionist gives her a skeptical once-over, Ava adds, "We spoke earlier today. He told me about you—Tina, right?"

The receptionist looks doubtful but gets up and heads to the back. There are a few customers reading magazines in the waiting area. Ava remembers how she used to love coming to work, used to love walking through these same doors. It's strange standing here now, as if nothing has changed.

"Ava?" Randall Strombauer opens the door from the examination rooms and steps into the reception area. He's dressed in scrubs with protective eye goggles resting atop his head. He has more gray hairs but he's just as fit and trim as she remembers. The expression on his face is guarded. "What are you doing here?"

"I wanted to follow up on our conversation, Dr.

Strombauer," she says, lifting her chin. "About Dr. Marks calling for a recommendation?"

There's a flicker of surprise and then a slick grin. "Don't worry. I took care of that."

Ava clenches the strap of her purse. "You lied to him."

"I gave him my honest impressions, that's all." His eyes flicker up and down her body, making her cringe. He drops his voice as he leans toward her. "Look at you. Motherhood sure does take a toll on a woman. If Bill could see you now, he'd probably be a bit disappointed, don't you think?"

Ava is speechless, her cheeks red hot.

He glances around before grasping her hand as if to give it a shake, pulling her close to him. He whispers, "Be nice, Ava. I'm a fair man—you play nice with me, I'll play nice with you. Give you that recommendation you've been wanting. Think about it." He releases her hand and claps her on the shoulder like she's an old friend.

It takes her a moment before she looks around to see if anyone heard him, but no one seems to have noticed their conversation. When she turns back, Randall Strombauer is gone, the door to the back closing with a soft click.

"Excuse me, but you can't go back there . . ." the receptionist protests as Ava throws open the door and storms down the hallway. She recognizes one of the dental hygienists, Sally Gillespie, but continues until she reaches the examination room at the end of the hall.

Randall Strombauer is already inside, a dental mask covering his nose and mouth, a spoon excavator in hand. A patient is stretched out in the chair and a dental assistant is taking notes.

"Who do you think you are?" Ava demands, her voice taking on a slightly hysterical peel. "You can't treat people this way, Dr. Strombauer! You can't make up lies about them or try to ruin their chances at a better life."

He doesn't even bother to look up. "Get her out of here," he says to the woman standing next to him, holding the patient's chart.

"Sorry, but you're not supposed to be in here . . ." the dental assistant begins.

Ava ignores her. "You can bully me all you want, Dr. Strombauer, but I know the truth. I know what kind of a man you are."

There's a stir as the patient spits out a roll of cotton. "Ava?" the elderly woman says. "I declare, is that you?"

Ava feels her cheeks pink as she recognizes the woman in the chair. "Oh, hi, Mrs. Weber. Got, um, another cavity?"

"You know me and sweets. I do try, though. Gum lines are receding, too."

"Sorry about this, Mrs. Weber," Dr. Strombauer says briskly, pulling down his mask. "Miss Catalina was leaving."

"No," Ava says, crossing her arms. "I don't think so. I'm not finished talking yet."

"Look," he says. His voice is cool, patient, but there's a dangerous glint in his eye. "I'm sorry you're down on your luck, but you made your bed. With Dr. Kidd, to be specific. I'm not about to bail you out of whatever mess you've gotten yourself into." He grits his teeth and Ava can see that he wants to say more, but he glances down at Mrs. Weber and knows he can't. Ava knows she might never get a chance like this again.

Her voice shaking, Ava says, "On my last day here, you cornered me in the break room. You knocked a box out of my hands. You tried to kiss me. I bit you so I could escape."

It's a huge relief to say the words aloud. She's aware that Mrs. Weber and the dental assistant are looking at her in shock, but Ava doesn't care anymore. It's the truth.

She continues, her voice louder. "And what you just said to me in the waiting room, about playing nice with you so you'll be nice to me, is disgusting. I want you to know that I haven't forgotten what you did, and that you don't intimidate me anymore. I won't bother asking you for a job recommendation in the future, but I'm not going to pretend what happened didn't happen. I'll tell the truth to anyone who wants to know."

"Lies," he says, but Ava sees him hesitate, unsure.

She taps her nose. She nods toward him. "Did you need stitches?"

His gloved fingers automatically rise to touch the bridge of his nose where there's a faint scar from where Ava bit him.

There's a stunned silence as the other women turn to look at Dr. Strombauer. Ava suddenly feels lighter, freer. There's nothing more to say so she simply turns and leaves, her head held high as she walks past the other patients and staff of the dental office.

In the parking lot the sun is shining, and Ava stops to take a deep breath, giddy with disbelief. Even though it doesn't change anything, Ava feels different. She stood up to Randall Strombauer and said what needed to be said. She did it.

Ava climbs into her Jeep, triumphant. Maybe she'll splurge and take Max out for dinner. Something simple and inexpensive, but a treat nonetheless. She slips the key into the ignition and gives it a turn.

Nothing.

She tries again, but to no avail. The engine doesn't give any sign of life.

On any other day, this would be what it's always been in the past—a reminder that Ava's life is far from perfect, that she will always be scrambling to do the things that seem to come so easily for other people. But Ava doesn't feel that way, not anymore. She takes a breath, settling in her seat as she figures out what to do next. Call a tow truck, yes, and then . . .

Sunlight bounces off a shiny black car, making Ava squint. She raises a hand to shield her eyes as she looks across the parking lot at a sleek sports car. It's waxed and buffed to a shine, completely out of place in a town like Avalon. She knows it's his car without even reading the license plate: STROMI.

Ava feels good now, she does. But she can think of something that will make her feel even better.

She's grinning as she goes to grab the trash bag from the trunk of her car.

"Hugh!" Yvonne is standing outside of his house. She picks up a handful of gravel and throws it at his window. "Hubert Hill, get down here now!"

The front door opens and Hugh's mother, Joan, stares incredulously at Yvonne.

"What on earth do you think you're doing?" she demands.

"Getting your coward son to come down and talk to me," Yvonne says. She wipes her hands on her jeans and strides forward, her hand outstretched. "We've never formally met. I'm Yvonne Tate, of Tate Plumbing. But wait, you probably know that already, don't you?" She withdraws her hand.

Joan Hill purses her lips, her mouth a thin, hard

line. Yvonne can see the family resemblance in the nose and chin and wonders if Hugh's brothers share the same features. It turns out he has an older and a younger brother. Yvonne can't help but wonder what else Hugh has that she doesn't know about.

Looking back, Yvonne now sees what she missed—the odd behavior, the strange timing of their get-togethers, his insistence that they play everything by ear. She didn't think twice about the fact that they'd meet at her house and never his. They never talked about his mother or the way she treated Yvonne that day they met. Still, she had no reason to be suspicious or think that anything was wrong.

But there was always a sense that Hugh was trying to make up for something. He wore a look of sheepish apology whenever he was late or if he started to say something and then stopped. She thought he was being considerate but now knows it was nothing more than guilt, plain and simple.

When Yvonne had come home after the Cut and Curl, she'd gone straight to her computer. She did a search for Hillshire Plumbing in Avalon, Illinois, and it came up immediately. It wasn't much of a website, but on the ABOUT US page there was a picture of Hugh, surrounded by his family and a motley crew of Hillshire employees. It was a small comfort to see that some of the details he'd told her were true—where he went to school, what he studied—but there was no mistaking the fact that he'd chosen to leave out the most important detail of all, that he was at the helm of his family's plumbing business.

Yvonne had tossed and turned all night, working herself into a state. How could they have been seeing each other for almost five weeks without a hint of this? Of course, Yvonne hadn't pressed him about his family's business or what he did for them, and he never brought it up. She assumed he set his own hours and wasn't accountable to anyone other than himself. Besides, the conversation was usually about Yvonne, about her work or what job she was on, and she was more than happy to talk about clevis straps, dual sewage systems, and inline water filters. She was showing off a little, yes, but Hugh seemed genuinely intrigued. She'd been flattered that he was so interested in her and her work.

How foolish she'd been. She found herself repeating the same mantra when Sam had left.

How could she not have known?

The moment daylight broke on the horizon, Yvonne jumped out of bed and dialed Hugh's number. When he answered she told him that they needed to talk, but he told her he had a busy morning and promised they'd talk later, that night at her place. Yvonne tried to protest, but finally Hugh cut her off, saying that he had to go. He hung up before she could say anything else.

Yvonne saw red.

Her next call had been to Isabel, who was on her way to work. Yvonne spoke quickly, the words tumbling out of her, and Isabel never once said *I told you so* or made Yvonne feel foolish. She didn't have to—Yvonne was doing a fine job on her own.

"Don't do anything crazy," Isabel warned her. The minute Isabel said that, Yvonne knew exactly what she was going to do.

"Hugh!" she hollers again now. She hears a bark and Toby comes tumbling out of the house, tail wagging. He bounds past Mrs. Hill and skids to a stop right in front of Yvonne.

Okay, so Toby's not so bad. Yvonne drops to her knees and rubs his ears, thinking, *Hugh doesn't deserve a dog like Toby. A pot-bellied pig, maybe. Or a snake. Maybe a rat.*

"Hey, boy," she says. He licks her face, happy to see her.

"You need to leave right now," Joan Hill tells her, crossing her arms. "Or I'm calling the police."

"Be my guest," Yvonne says, standing up. "Because I've been meaning to tell them about some of the anonymous notes I've been receiving lately. Maybe I could gather up some other plumbers, say, Fred Mackie or Hank Carter. What about the Woodsen brothers? We could all do lunch."

Toby lets out a delighted bark and Yvonne nods. "Yeah, I think that's a good idea, too. We should definitely invite Sergeant Overby from the police department, too."

To say Hugh's mother looks furious would be an understatement. Yvonne expects her to erupt like Vesuvius at any moment.

There's the sound of footsteps pounding down the stairs and a second later Hugh appears in the doorway, a towel around his waist, his hair wet. He's barefoot and there's water on his shoulders and torso. Yvonne can tell that he's just stepped out from the shower.

"Hubert!" Joan Hill looks appalled. "Go inside and get some clothes on!"

"What's going on?" Hugh demands, stepping onto the porch. "Yvonne, what are you doing here?" His eyes dart toward his mother and then back at her, indicating that it's not okay that she's standing there.

Yvonne doesn't budge. "Getting ready for your busy morning, Hugh? Got a full plate over at Hillshire Plumbing? Family board meeting, maybe?" She glares at him.

"Oh." Hugh stops as he realizes what's going on. His face is tight and he lets out a deep breath. "Mother, go inside, please."

His mother shakes her head. "I told you it was a mistake to get involved," she mutters.

"Not now," he says. "I need to talk to Yvonne."

Joan Hill lifts her chin but walks back into the house, closing the door with a slam.

Hugh grips his towel as he steps forward. "I was going to tell you," he begins.

Yvonne crosses her arms in front of her chest. "When?"

"Soon. We were having such a great time and I didn't want to ruin it." There's a short pause and then he amends, "For you. I didn't want to ruin it for you."

Yvonne turns and heads back to her truck, disgusted. Why do guys do that? Toby follows her, his tongue hanging out, thinking they're about to go for a ride.

Hugh catches up to her. "Look, I came back a few months ago to help my mother. The company's been struggling . . ."

"Yeah, I heard about how you've been 'helping.' What are you planning to do next, throw a rock through my window?"

Hugh's face reddens, telling Yvonne that he knew all along. "I'm trying to change all of that. But it's not easy . . ."

"Says the CEO."

"*In title.* I mean, yes, I was given the title when my father died three years ago but it's strictly a public relations thing. I never wanted to be involved with the family business but I didn't have a choice. My mom thought I could offer a fresh perspective, and my brothers said I needed to pull my weight with the company . . ." His voice trails off and he looks frustrated, at a loss. He runs a hand through his hair, which only serves to make him look even more sexy. "I was going to tell you, Yvonne. Really. It was never the right time."

"That's a convenient excuse. Next you'll be telling me you're married. Or gay."

"No and no," Hugh says, then he frowns, straightening up. "Wait. Seriously? Gay?"

Yvonne doesn't answer, glowering at him instead. "What was I, Hugh? Research?"

Hugh looks so pained, it's almost comical. "You know that's not true," he protests. "I mean, maybe at first, but certainly not now."

"What about the day we met? When you called me for your plumbing 'emergency'? Was that some kind of test?"

Hugh shakes his head. "No. Our own guys couldn't get out until the end of the day and you know I'm hopeless with this stuff. My mother thought it might be a good opportunity to check out the competition."

"A good opportunity." Yvonne shakes her head. "I can't believe I didn't see this coming." She reaches for her toolbox and pushes past him. She heads back toward the house.

"Wait, where are you going?" Hugh asks in alarm.

"I'm going to get back that flapper I installed for you," she calls over her shoulder.

"What? You can't do that! Besides, we paid you for that service."

"I'll give you a refund."

She's almost at the door when Hugh catches up with her. "Yvonne, stop this! You're acting like a child!" He grabs her toolbox.

Yvonne tries to wrench it from him, but Hugh is stronger than she realizes. After a fruitless struggle, she gives up and is horrified to feel her eyes wet with tears. "I really liked you, you know," she finally says.

"I liked you, too. It's just . . . my family . . ." He gives a helpless shrug.

Yvonne waits for him to say more, but he doesn't. "You're an adult, Hugh," she says. "You can make your own choices about your life. You don't have to prove anything to anyone."

Hugh looks scornful. "You don't understand."

They hold the toolbox between them. Yvonne takes a step toward him. "I understand more than you realize," she begins, but Hugh looks away.

"Yvonne, you're a plumber," he says. "And a damn good one. We'd be lucky to have someone like you in our company. But I lead a different kind of life than the one you lead." He has his CEO voice on now, one that Yvonne hasn't heard before. He looks at her almost pityingly. "My life's not as simple as yours. I wish it was, but it's not."

It's a thinly veiled insult. Yvonne can't believe she's hearing this.

"Given what's happened, I don't think we should see each other anymore," he continues, as if he's doing her some kind of favor. "I didn't mean for it to get this complicated. I'm thinking we should end it now."

"Don't give yourself too much credit, Hugh," Yvonne retorts. "I have a feeling thinking isn't exactly high on your list of to-do items."

He glares at her, abruptly letting go of the toolbox. The unexpected weight causes the handle to slip from Yvonne's fingers, and the toolbox crashes onto the porch, bursting open and scattering wrenches and nuts and bolts everywhere. Hugh jumps back as a copper pipe cutter lands dangerously close to his bare feet.

"Hey!" he yells, as if she'd done it on purpose. For a second Yvonne almost wishes she had. Jerk.

She bends down and begins to gather everything, refusing to look at him. All dates should start this way, she thinks, with the arguments and disagreements. Forget the courtship and the butterflies—she'd rather see a person's true colors up front. It would save everybody time and heartbreak.

Hugh doesn't offer to help, just waits impatiently. When Yvonne finally snaps her toolbox closed, there's the sound of a pickup truck coming up the road. Two men are sitting in the front, serious looks on their faces. Even from a distance Yvonne can see that the brothers do in fact share the same nose and chin as Hugh and his mother. "Oh look," she says. "Company."

"Just go," Hugh says, squaring his shoulders as the pickup rolls to a stop. The men jump out, slamming their doors with an air of importance. They're about the same height as Hugh, but brawnier. Their faces are set as they saunter up the walk. Joan Hill is standing on the other side of the window, phone in hand.

"Don't worry, I'm leaving," Yvonne says. She looks at her hands, which are spotted with small grease stains. "Just let me wipe my hands before I go. You won't be needing this, will you? Thanks."

And she yanks the towel from around Hugh's waist as she heads down the walkway to her truck.

Connie comes down the stairs, silver bracelets running up and down her arm. Hannah is in the foyer, talking earnestly with Madeline.

Hannah again. Normally she'd be put out but at the moment Connie doesn't mind. She just wants to get on her way.

"I have to go and get Serena from the vet," she tells them. "I won't be too long." She checks herself in the mirror, rubs her lips together to

371

make sure her lip gloss still looks good. She's about to walk out the door when she sees that Madeline and Hannah are looking at her funny. "What's up?"

"Well," Madeline begins, casting a nervous look at Hannah. "It looks like all your GOAT FOUND posters are gone. Someone must have decided to help you out and put them up around town. Hannah saw one at the pharmacy."

"Clyde Thomas put it right up in the front window," Hannah says. "You can't miss it. And I heard people talking and laughing about it at the Pick and Save." She quickly adds, "In a good way, I mean."

Connie feels as if she's been doused with cold water. "Oh," she says. She looks to the empty spot where the flyers used to be.

"Sweetheart, it was probably going to happen sooner or later," Madeline says, striding forward and putting an arm around Connie's shoulder. "We have to find Serena's owner. We're not equipped to take care of a goat."

Connie jerks her head up and down. "Yeah, I know." But she feels like crying.

"Hannah and I can cover today, so why don't you get Serena and maybe see if there have been any leads?"

"What if we can't find her owner?" Connie asks. "Or her owner doesn't want her?"

Madeline nods, the thought having crossed her

mind as well. "I don't know," she says honestly. "We won't be able to keep Serena here, though. Walter Lassiter is going to file a formal complaint next week. Dolores told me this morning. She feels bad, but he has his mind made up. Apparently he's been keeping notes and building a case against us, or against Serena at least. Even if it turns out we're free to keep Serena, I'm not so sure she could stay here. I'm sorry, sweetheart."

On the way to the vet's office, Connie tries to look at the bright side of things, but she can't.

In all the years that Connie has been on her own, she's never asked the question that she's asking herself now. Why her? Why her and not someone else? Why was she the one who had to lose her parents, who had to go to foster homes, who had to work harder than anyone else for the same basic rights for life—food, shelter, freedom—while people all around her never thought twice about it? She's never begrudged anyone but suddenly she resents everyone, even Madeline.

If Madeline loves Connie like she says she does, she wouldn't be asking her to give Serena up, would she? She'd try to find a way. How is Serena all that much different than a dog? Like Eli says, there are dogs that are bigger than her.

The vet's office is crowded when Connie finally walks in. There's a boy with his turtle, a man with a Jack Russell terrier, and a woman with a cat in a carrier.

The receptionist, Della, frowns when she sees Connie. "Hmmph," she says with a sniff. "I'll let Dr. Ballard know you're here." She gets up from her chair and marches into one of the examination rooms.

Eli will understand what she's going through. Connie knows her feelings for Serena don't make sense to people like Madeline or Hannah or Walter Lassiter, but veterinary medicine is Eli's field of choice. He knows animals, he loves animals, he's even had goats. Just like Connie.

Eli sticks his head out of the room. She gives him a bright smile, anxious to see a friendly face, but he doesn't seem to notice. "Come on back, Connie."

When Connie steps into the room, Eli is sitting on a stool, looking grim. Serena is nowhere to be seen. Connie feels a flash of apprehension.

"Where's Serena?" she asks. "Is she okay?"

"Oh, she's fine," Eli says. "She's in the back." He holds up a piece of paper. "This showed up in the office this morning."

It's her flyer. Connie swallows. "I made those to see if I could find her owner. I found her wandering around in the park one morning."

Eli doesn't say anything, just waits.

"I was coming back from the farmer's market and there she was, eating some grass by a tree,"

374

Connie continues uneasily. "She followed me home."

Eli looks at her. "Anything else?"

"She had, uh, a rope tied around her neck, but she had chewed through it." Connie squirms, discomfited.

"A runaway goat?" Eli suggests wryly.

Why is he looking at her so suspiciously? "Yes," Connie says. "Something like that. I mean, that's what I assume."

"But no one keeps goats in town," Eli points out. "How did she end up in the park?"

Connie shrugs. "I don't know. I found her there."

"You've had her since early August?"

"Yes," Connie says, then she frowns. "How did you know?"

Eli continues as if he hasn't heard her. "Have you heard of Doherty Farms?"

It sounds familiar, but Connie shakes her head.

"It's a working farm about forty minutes south of Avalon. They have a petting zoo that's open to the public, and they do hayrides, birthday parties, that sort of thing. They've been around for ages. I used to go there as a kid."

"That's nice . . ." Connie begins, but Eli holds up his hand. He's not finished.

"Apparently two months ago someone broke into the pens one night and took off with one of the Nubians. Broke some fencing in order to get her." The look on his face is stern.

Connie stares back at him. "Are you saying that I stole her? From a farm? Why would I do that?"

Eli's gaze is steady on her. "I don't know. Did you take her, Connie?"

"No!" Connie can't believe this. Who would steal a goat, for Pete's sake? "I made up those signs, after all! Why would I have done that if I'd stolen her?" Her cheeks are hot with indignation.

Eli's shoulders drop and he looks relieved. "That's what I told Rayna. She's pretty upset, though. Serena's pregnant, you see, and—"

Connie gasps. "Pregnant?"

"She was six weeks when she was taken, so she still has a ways to go—the normal gestation period for a goat is about one hundred fifty days. Still, Rayna was worried."

"Is she sure Serena is her goat?" Connie asks. "I mean, this is Illinois and there are lots of farms outside of Avalon."

"Rayna chips all her animals," Eli says. "So I checked. Found it right by her tailbone, in the tail web. It's Rayna's goat, all right. She goes by the name Daffodil."

"Daffodil?" Connie makes a face. She can't picture Serena as a Daffodil.

Eli laughs. "I like Serena better, too."

"So is she okay? Was there anything wrong?"

Eli shakes his head. "No, I think she was just homesick. Goats are herd animals, they're sociable. They need to be around other goats."

Connie feels guilty. "Yeah, that's what I've been hearing. So she was lonely."

He nods. Then he adds, "But she checked out fine otherwise. Pregnancy is fine, too. But listen, Connie, you may be in a bit of trouble."

Connie feels herself getting anxious again. "Why? I didn't take her."

"I know, but the fact of the matter is that Serena was taken and right now you're the only person who knows anything about it. Can anyone verify your story?"

"Yes," Connie says, nodding vigorously. "My employer, Madeline Davis. She was there when I brought Serena home. And she knows I never go anywhere. She'll be able to verify that I was home the night before."

"Just tell that to the police officer and I'm sure they'll get it straightened out," Eli says, standing up.

"The police?"

At that moment Della opens the door and points an accusing finger at Connie. "There she is, Officer."

Officer Joey Daniels steps into the office, followed by a woman wearing jeans and a pale pink button-up shirt, boots. Her gray hair is pulled back in a bun. Her cheeks are sun-chapped. She takes in Connie's all-black attire, her spiky hair.

"I want to press charges," she says in a faint voice.

"But I didn't take her!" Connie protests. "I found her. I'm the one who made up the signs!"

"You had her for almost eight weeks!" the woman cries. "Nobody saw these signs until today! You only brought her in because you thought she was sick. Fun's over, huh?"

Connie looks at Eli in disbelief. "You believe me, right?"

"Rayna, let's calm down," Eli says. "Everyone's worked up and I do believe Connie. She has no reason to lie about this. I think she's sincerely concerned about Serena's—I mean Daffodil's—welfare."

"I don't care," Rayna says. "I have been worried sick about Daffodil, and to think that something might have happened to her . . ." She shakes her head.

"I'm going to have to ask you some questions, Connie," Officer Daniels says. "And there was some property damage to the Dohertys' farm. Can you come down to the station?"

Connie nods, numb. She's never been in any kind of trouble, even when she was in all those foster homes. "Can I at least see Serena before I go?"

"No!" Rayna is livid. "I don't want you near her, ever." She turns to Officer Daniels. "I want to file a restraining order against this woman."

"Mrs. Doherty, let me talk to her first," Officer Daniels says. "This may be a big misunderstanding."

"Yes," says Eli.

"Doubtful," sniffs Della.

"Let's go, Connie." Officer Daniels nods to the door. "We'll sort this out at the police station."

"May I take Daffodil now?" Rayna asks Eli.

He hesitates, glancing at Connie, then nods. "You can bring your truck round back," he tells Rayna.

Connie follows Officer Daniels out the door and through the busy waiting area. Animals and humans alike turn to look at her, their faces curious. Officer Daniels' squad car is out front, and everyone up and down the street is watching them.

"Do I go with you or follow in my car?" Connie asks in a small voice.

Officer Daniels turns to Connie. "You're not under arrest," he says. "But don't take any detours, okay?"

Connie's hands are shaking as she fumbles for her keys. Officer Daniels flips on the lights to the squad car. The siren blares as she follows him to the police station.

Chapter Fifteen

Ava sits on the hard bench, her face twisted with worry.

"I have to pick up my son from preschool," she tries to tell a passing officer, but the officer keeps walking.

"Excuse me," she calls to another officer but the officer shakes his head.

Ava glances anxiously at the clock. There's a scuffle as the double doors burst open and a pretty blond woman is escorted in, her hands also in cuffs, a triumphant look on her face. After a second Ava recognizes her as Yvonne, Isabel's friend, the woman she met at the scrapbooking meeting.

The officer seats Yvonne next to Ava on the booking bench with a stern reprimand. Yvonne looks at Ava in surprise, notes the cuffs around Ava's wrists as well. "Oh, hey," Yvonne says. "Ava, right?"

Ava nods. "What are you in for?"

"Disturbing the peace. You?"

"Destruction of property."

Yvonne nods. They watch as two officers confer between the desks, glancing at the two women.

The doors swing open again and Madeline bursts through, a worried look on her face. "Sergeant Overby!" she calls out, and then stops when she sees the women sitting on the booking bench. "What in the world?"

Ava and Yvonne offer guilty smiles. "Hi, Madeline," they say.

"Goodness, what are the two of you doing here?" she asks, when Sergeant Robert Overby emerges from a room in the back of the small station.

"Are you here about Connie?" he asks Madeline.

Madeline nods. "Where is she?"

Sergeant Overby comes over. "She's in the debriefing room—she'll be done soon. What do you know about that goat of hers? She said you were there when she brought her home."

"Yes," Madeline says. "She'd gone to the farmer's market and found her there."

"Did she say what her intentions were? Apparently some flyers went up today, but why did it take her so long before notifying anybody about the goat's whereabouts?"

Madeline knits her brows. "Is Connie in some kind of trouble?" she asks.

Sergeant Overby looks grim. "She's in some kind of trouble, all right. She's been accused of theft—goat-napping, to be precise."

"But that's ridiculous!" Madeline exclaims. She's about to push past Sergeant Overby when he holds up his hands and shakes his head.

"I'm afraid not, Madeline. Rayna Doherty is

pressing charges. Someone broke into the petting zoo about eight weeks ago. There were skid marks everywhere—a busted fence and trough—and they took off with one of Rayna's goats. This one was pregnant, too. Did it in the middle of the night, scared everyone."

"I can assure you that Connie would never do such a thing," Madeline says vehemently.

"Can you vouch for her whereabouts the night before?"

"Of course." Madeline casts an anxious look at Ava and Yvonne. "She was home, with me."

"Are you a light sleeper?"

Madeline stiffens. "Average, I'd say. Bumps in the night wake me up."

Sergeant Overby nods. "Early to bed?" he asks.

Madeline's face is a blank.

Sergeant Overby sighs. "No offense, Madeline, but this happened just after midnight. Connie could have easily slipped out, gone to the Dohertys' farm, stashed the goat, then brought her around in the morning. You wouldn't be any the wiser."

"If there were skid marks everywhere, couldn't you match the tire tracks with Connie's car?" Yvonne asks. Everyone turns to look at her in surprise. "That would resolve it once and for all, wouldn't it?"

"This is Avalon, Ms. Tate. We don't plaster tracks unless foul play is suspected."

"You didn't suspect it then but you suspect it now?" Ava asks. She looks at Yvonne for support. "I mean, tire tracks and a broken fence sound like foul play to me."

Yvonne and Madeline are nodding while Sergeant Overby looks flummoxed.

"So if there's no way to match up the tire treads," Yvonne continues, considering this aloud. "What about checking her car for any damage? Even if she had it fixed up you'd be able to tell, right?"

"Yes!" Madeline says. "Her car is right there on the curb and I know it hasn't been in any sort of incident, ever. Connie is a very conscientious driver."

Connie emerges from the debriefing room looking shaken. Officer Juanita Tripp is behind her. When Connie sees Madeline she rushes forward.

"They didn't even let me say goodbye!" she cries as Madeline puts her arms around her. "They think I stole her!"

"Connie, we're going to inspect your car now," Sergeant Overby says. Connie sniffs and nods. They watch as Officer Tripp goes outside.

Sergeant Overby looks at Ava and Yvonne with a shake of his head. "Please tell me you weren't planning on booking these women," he says to Officer Daniels with a sigh. "Get those cuffs off of them, for Pete's sake."

Officer Daniels looks up with a frown. "Sergeant, Ms. Catalina dumped a trash bag full of diningware into a convertible sports car without provocation," he reports. "Pots, pans, plates, bowls, glassware, forks, spoons, and *knives*." He lingers on the last word, eyebrows raised knowingly.

Sergeant Overby isn't impressed. "And?"

Officer Daniels checks his notes. "Ms. Tate publicly humiliated a member of the Hill family and caused excessive damage to their front porch."

"First of all, there's hardly a dent on that porch," Yvonne says. "And second of all, I needed to wipe my hands on something and it turned out the towel around his waist was all he had on."

Ava giggles. Even Sergeant Overby gives a chuckle.

Officer Tripp reappears in the station and hands Connie back her keys. "No marks, sir," she says.

Sergeant Overby nods. "Connie, you're free to go," he says. He grabs the handcuff keys from Officer Daniels and quickly removes the cuffs from Yvonne and Ava. "We still need to talk to each of you."

"Can I go first?" Ava asks anxiously. She quickly apologizes to Yvonne. "My son is in preschool and I'm already late—really late—to pick him up. They charge a lot for after-school care and I don't want him to be worried."

"Do you have anyone else who can go in your place?" Sergeant Overby asks.

Ava shakes her head. "It's just me . . ." she starts to say, when she remembers. When she was filling out the paperwork for the school, it was mandatory that she list an emergency contact. She didn't have anyone, didn't have any names or phone numbers to put down except for . . .

The door swings open and Isabel walks through, Max in her arms.

"Max!" Ava cries in relief, rushing forward.

"Mommy!"

"Isabel?" Yvonne breaks into a grin.

"Yvonne?" Isabel looks bewildered as she looks between Yvonne and Ava. "Ava? What the heck is going on here?"

Ava is kissing Max's face as he squirms and giggles. "How did you know I was here?" she asks breathlessly. She holds her son tight, so grateful that she can't help smiling at Isabel.

But Isabel doesn't return the smile.

"I didn't know you'd be here," she says. She thumbs in Yvonne's direction. "I came looking for her. But I'm glad to see you because I have a question." Her eyes are hard as she leans in. "What in the hell were you thinking by listing *me* as your emergency contact?"

"I tried to tell you," Ava begins, stammering, but Isabel isn't paying attention. She's crouched down so that she's eye level with Max. He's cowering behind Ava's legs, startled by Isabel's harsh tone.

"I'm sorry, Max," Isabel says, her voice tight but gentler. "I was surprised to see your mom and I got a bit carried away. But I'm happy to see she's okay."

Ava can't tell if this is a lie or the truth. But Max seems to relax.

"Max, let's go outside for some fresh air," Madeline suggests, and looks to Ava for approval. Ava manages a nod. Connie holds out her hand and Max takes it, and the three of them leave the station.

"Again," Isabel says. Her voice is lower but Ava can tell she's furious. "You put me down as your emergency contact? Your *backup?*"

"I never thought they'd ever use it," Ava confesses nervously, "and I didn't know who else to put down. I wrote about it in the letters I sent you . . ."

"I never read those letters."

Ava swallows. She can feel Isabel's eyes on her and, unnerved, turns to Yvonne. "I know it was wrong to put her down without her permission, but I didn't know what else to do. The school wouldn't let me submit the paperwork without a name and number." Ava bites her lip and finally turns to face Isabel. "I'm sorry, but the truth is, you're the only person I really know. The only person I trust with Max."

"You don't know me," Isabel informs her hotly. "You don't know me at all. How do you think it makes me feel to get a call saying that I have to go and pick up a boy who's my husband's son? My dead husband's son? Whatever gave you the idea that you could trust me with him?"

"Because he's Bill's," Ava says in a small voice. "I know you would never hurt Max, because you loved Bill, too."

Isabel is sputtering, unable to form whole words. Yvonne clears her throat, touches Isabel on the arm. "Let's talk about this later."

"And you!" Isabel turns to her friend. "Why weren't you answering your phone?"

"Hugh's mother called the cops on me," Yvonne explains, a bemused look on her face. "They caught up with me a couple blocks away from the house, sirens blaring and everything. To hear her tell it, I took off with her grandmother's silver instead of a nubby department store towel. Officer Daniels almost drew his weapon! It was quite the spectacle—I'm sorry you missed it."

"I told you not to do anything crazy! I called Hugh to make sure he wasn't cut up into little pieces on his front lawn and he told me what happened. He did not sound happy. I came over thinking I'd have to post bail or identify your body in the morgue!"

"Now you're exaggerating."

Isabel looks exasperated. "Yvonne, you don't

storm up to somebody's house who's threatening you. You don't know anything about them, you could have been hurt."

"Hugh's a wimp and his doughnut-loving brothers are the reason people make fun of plumbers." Yvonne says defiantly. "Anyway, it's all over now."

Isabel turns back to Ava. "What's your story?"

Ava hesitates. "I dumped everything but the kitchen sink in Randall Strombauer's Maserati."

Isabel gives a start and Ava can tell this catches her by surprise. "Randall Strombauer? Why?"

"I won't be able to get another job as a dental assistant because of him," she says. "He ruined my chances of getting a job, a really good job, and he'll do it again, I know. I went to confront him and he tried to blackmail me, told me that he'd treat me nice if I treated him nice. I went to my car and took the bag of things I was going to donate and dumped it in his car instead."

"Randall Strombauer," Isabel murmurs. "I never trusted him." She looks at Ava. "I always thought you'd take up with him, but obviously I got that part wrong."

"Bill said you weren't happy," Ava blurts out. She shouldn't be saying this, not here, but she doesn't know when she'll get another chance. "And you didn't seem happy whenever I saw you, even though you were always nice to me. If I'd known . . ."

Isabel is glaring at her again. "What? You wouldn't have slept with him? Had his child?"

Ava pinks as Sergeant Overby clears his throat. "Okay, ladies, I think we're good here. Ava and Yvonne, you can go."

Officer Daniels looks up from his paperwork. "But Sergeant . . ."

"Go," he tells them, and then turns to Officer Daniels. "You get another pot of coffee on. I'll deal with the Hills and Dr. Strombauer."

The women exit the police station. Madeline and Connie are singing "Itsy Bitsy Spider" with Max under the shade of a walnut tree.

"Isabel . . ." Ava begins.

"I don't want to talk to you right now," Isabel tells her. The anger is gone, and she sounds tired, like it's all too much and she just wants to go home.

Ava hates to ask but she doesn't have any other choice. She doesn't want to go back to the dental office and risk seeing Randall Strombauer again. "I'm sorry, but I have a favor to ask."

"You've got to be joking."

Ava gives her a helpless look.

"Fine." Isabel sighs. "What is it?"

Ava hesitates then asks, "Could you please give me and Max a ride home?"

The doorbell is ringing. Frances is in the kitchen, her hands sticky with dough. "Nick, can you get that?" she calls.

"I'm busy," comes the reply from the living room. Noah and Brady are sitting at the kitchen table, fighting over a video game that has something to do with birds and pigs.

"Nick, come on," Frances says.

There's no response.

Frustrated, Frances quickly dampens a paper towel and wipes her hands as she heads toward the front door. Noah and Brady follow her, intrigued. They pass Nick lying on the couch, a baseball cap askew on his head.

"Don't you have homework?" she asks, grabbing the TV remote and turning it off.

"I already did it," he says. The baseball hat falls off his head as he gets up and follows her to the door. Frances notices that his cowlick is sticking up and attempts to smooth it with her hand.

"Mom!" he protests, batting her hand away. "Stop! It's embarrassing!"

"Who's looking?" she wants to know, and it takes all of her willpower not to try to smooth it down again. She'll have to talk to Mavis at the Cut and Curl to see if there's another way to cut it so it doesn't stick up so much.

When she opens the door she's surprised to find Hannah standing on her doorstep holding a platter of what looks like chocolate brownies.

"Oohhh," all the boys say in unison. Even Frances feels her taste buds at attention.

Hannah laughs. "I'm sorry to stop by unannounced, but I wanted to share these with you and I don't have your number."

Frances steps aside and waves her in. "We'll have to change that. Come on in!"

"I made a batch of gluten-free quinoa chocolate breakfast bars for my neighbor," she tells them as Frances navigates them through the typical Latham detritus on the floor. "And I thought you might be interested in trying them after our last experiment together."

"The kids loved them," Frances tells her. "Suffice it to say the first classroom party of the year was a hit, thanks to you. I wanted to call you and tell you but I didn't have your number either. I meant to look it up in the phone book, but . . ." Her voice trails off, embarrassed.

"Don't worry," Hannah assures, putting the platter on the kitchen table. "It was the same for me. One thing after another. I don't feel like I got a break until today."

They stand in the kitchen, grinning at each other. The boys are mobbing the table, Brady's hands already trying to sneak under the plastic wrap.

"I know it's close to dinnertime, but is it okay for them to have one?" Hannah asks, peeling back the wrap.

"Yes, but ladies first," Frances says. She reaches forward to pick up the first bar. She takes a bite. "Oh, this is good!"

Hannah nods, breaking off a small piece for herself. Nick has already finished his and is reaching for another.

"Nick, manners!" Frances reprimands. "And what do you boys say to Hannah, by the way?"

"Thank you," they dutifully reply.

Frances sighs as she wipes the crumbs from her fingers and heads back to the kitchen counter. Hannah follows.

"It looks like you're baking, too," she says, noticing the floury dough on the counter.

Frances shakes her head. "Not exactly," she says. She holds up a Chinese cookbook. "I thought I'd try my hand at Chinese cooking for Mei Ling, so I'm trying to make scallion pancakes. You fry them in the frying pan. Have you ever had them before?"

"*Cōng yóubǐng*? Sure, my mom used to make them when I was growing up. It's one of the things I miss most about my childhood." Hannah studies the recipe, nodding. "I've never made them before, but this sounds right."

"You've never made them?" The surprise in Frances's own voice embarrasses her and she quickly adds, "I mean, not that you would have any reason to make them . . ."

Hannah laughs as she pages through the cookbook. "I know it seems strange. I cook *poulet au porto* more often than a pot of rice. I prefer tisanes over traditional black leaf teas. But this food is part of my heritage and I grew up eating it. I guess I don't cook it because I'm so used to it. And the truth is I prefer European cuisine." She gives a smile as she looks at the bowl of chopped scallions. "This is bringing back memories I've forgotten about. My mother died when I was young, and I still haven't had a *cōng yóubǐng* that could match hers."

"I'm so sorry about your mother," Frances instantly says.

"Oh, it was a long time ago," Hannah says reassuringly, shaking her head. "It's a nice memory, not a sad one. I'd forgotten, that's all. I hope you'll save a piece for me when you're done."

Frances grimaces as she looks at the mess in front of her. "Well, I'm not sure I'll end up with something edible. The instructions are so confusing. It says to roll it up, then roll it in a coil and then roll it out again. Do you think I need to do that coiling and everything?"

"It's easier than it sounds," Hannah says. "But you definitely need to do it. It makes it flaky and easier to tear it apart when it's done. That was my favorite part. I used to watch my mother making it all the time, but eating it was heaven."

"Okay, that's it. You realize that I'm not going to let you leave this kitchen without helping me." Frances hands her a rolling pin. "You're too valuable a resource. In fact, there's a good chance

I'll never let you leave this house." She nods to the kitchen table where the younger boys are watching Nick show them how to play the video game. They each have a breakfast bar in hand and they're leaning into each other, talking among themselves, not fighting or bickering. "Happy, quiet boys? What did you put in those bars, a sedative?"

Hannah goes to the sink to wash her hands. "My secret weapon is . . ."

The women look at each and say at the same time, "Chocolate!"

As they roll out the dough into small discs, sprinkling sesame oil, scallions, salt, and white pepper, Frances tells Hannah about the quilt that she's making.

"Don't laugh," she warns Hannah. "I'm going to try and say it in Chinese but I'll probably butcher it."

"I'm ready," Hannah says solemnly.

"Okay." Frances takes a deep breath. "I'm making Mei Ling a *bǎi jiā bèi*." She says each word slowly and clearly, then waits for Hannah's response.

By the look on Hannah's face it's clear it doesn't ring a bell.

"*Bǎi jiā bèi*," Frances says again. "A One Hundred Good Wishes quilt?"

"Oh," Hannah says nodding. Then her nose wrinkles. "Sorry. I still have no idea what that is."

"It's a custom in northern China to welcome a new life by inviting one hundred friends and family members to contribute a fabric square to make this quilt. It's symbolic of blessings and good luck. I'm going to make a scrapbook with pictures of everyone who contributes to the quilt along with a sample cutting of their fabric."

"I love that idea!" Hannah says. "I'd love to contribute a square if that's all right."

"Of course it's all right," Frances says. She frowns, perplexed. "But you really haven't heard of it before?"

"No. But you were saying it right—*bǎi* means one hundred, and *bèi* or *bèizi* means quilt. And the middle word—*jiā*—means house or family. So that makes sense." Hannah begins to roll up one edge of the dough.

Frances imitates her. She watches as Hannah carefully rolls it into a coil, then flattens the coil with the palm of her hand. She passes it to Frances, who rolls the disk into a pancake once again, noting the pretty spiral pattern in the dough.

"Maybe it's not a real thing," Frances says, as she puts the pancake aside and reaches for another coil. "Maybe it's one of those customs made to sound Chinese. I mean, the only references I could find to it were at adoption sites. Maybe Chinese people don't even do this."

"Does it matter?" Hannah asks. "I think it's

wonderful that you're making an effort to help Mei Ling and your family stay connected with her Chinese heritage, but the thing that matters most is that she's surrounded by people who love her and who want the best for her. Your boys are lucky to have that. Any kids would be lucky to have that. I know Jamie feels that way about his parents. Like you, his parents are outnumbered and things are crazy but Jamie and his brothers know that their parents love them deeply."

Frances knows Hannah is right, but she also can't help thinking that she should do more, especially for Mei Ling.

"It seems too neat," Frances says. "An American family adopting a little Chinese girl who needs people to love her. I've told you that Mei Ling has a complex medical history and I feel like so much of it is out of our hands. This, however, is something I can do something about. Cultural differences do exist for us and I want to bridge that gap for her as much as possible. I don't want her to lose touch with her heritage. But is it enough? Love is only part of the equation, you know? And I don't want her to have an identity crisis when she's older. I don't want her to be confused about who she is."

"I don't know if there's much you can do about that," Hannah tells her. "I mean, I'm still trying to figure out who I am, and I'm twenty-nine. I think it's kind of a work-in-progress thing. I'm not so sure it's something you can do for her. Everyone has to figure it out for themselves. It's a part of growing up."

Frances sighs. "I'm not even sure who we're talking about anymore, Mei Ling or my boys."

Hannah gives her a friendly nudge. "We're talking about your kids," she says. "All of them."

Frances looks at the clock. Reed will be home soon, and she's planning to make a chicken stir fry with snow peas and mushrooms to accompany the scallion pancakes. "Any chance I could convince you to stay for dinner?" she asks. "I'd love for you to meet Reed and I promise not to make you cook anything else in this kitchen. At least not today."

Hannah laughs as she reaches for a pinch of flour. "I'd love to."

MISSING GOAT RECOVERED
Reported by Edith Gallagher

AVALON, ILLINOIS—Rayna Doherty of Doherty Farms was reunited with one of her goats after it was abducted from her farm in the early hours of August 3rd.

"We heard a ruckus in the middle of the night," Doherty tells the *Gazette*. "We ran outside and saw the taillights of a car leaving the farm for the main road. When we checked the barn, one of our goats was missing. We were very concerned, especially since she's pregnant."

The missing goat, Daffodil, has supposedly been in the backyard of Madeline's Tea Salon during this time.

"I woke up one morning and saw that they'd put a goat back there," said neighbor Walter Lassiter. "I told my wife, they'd better not be planning on keeping that animal there for long, unless there's going to be goat stew on the menu." Lassiter claims the goat has inflicted almost $65 worth of damage to his garden and landscape.

"I went to Madeline's to meet a girlfriend for lunch," Geneva Burch said, a regular customer at Madeline's Tea Salon. "And that goat was out front, roaming free, and almost attacked me. I was shocked that Madeline would put her customers at risk."

Shirley Hamilton agrees. "I thought she'd taken leave of her senses, but then I learned that it was Connie's goat. That's how it was explained to me, that the goat belonged to Connie. And I thought, well, who knows what young people like these days. And Connie has always seemed a bit different. I had no idea the goat had been stolen."

Connie Colls is the Tea Salon Manager (see picture to the left) and is currently under investigation for the alleged goat-napping though formal charges have yet to be filed. She declined an interview request by the *Gazette*.

Sergeant Robert Overby of the Avalon Police Department offered the following statement. "We are in the information-gathering stage at the moment—nobody is under arrest. The important thing is that Daffodil has been returned to her owner."

The perpetrator caused some property damage to Doherty Farms. Anyone with information regarding this incident is asked to contact the Avalon Police Department at 555-2390.

Chapter Sixteen

Yvonne looks at the crumbling concrete, at the dying shrubbery lining the common courtyard. It's one of those apartment complexes that seems to be tired and sagging, and Yvonne feels depressed just being here. She grabs the wobbly handrail and takes the stairs two at a time, then scans the numbers until she finds the apartment she's looking for. She wipes her feet on the welcome mat, smiles at the small mobile hanging by the door, the only splash of color and whimsy in this place.

"Yes?" the woman says. Her hair is short and cropped close to her head, a look of defeated surrender on her face. Clinging to her legs is a young boy with large glasses. He peers at Yvonne and she smiles.

"I'm Yvonne Tate of Tate Plumbing. You called about your garbage disposal?"

"Yes . . . oh." The woman stares at her, and Yvonne suddenly recognizes her.

"Ava?" she asks.

"Yvonne? I didn't know that—this—was you. You're a plumber?"

"Plumber by day, scrapbooker by night," Yvonne says.

"Come in," Ava says. "I'm sorry, I would have cleaned up more . . ." She's flustered at discovering Yvonne at her door.

"Don't worry about it," Yvonne reassures her, following Ava into the dingy apartment.

It's small but neat. The dining room table is set for two and there's a wicker basket filled with papers and bills. A laundry basket piled high with clean but unfolded clothes sits on a threadbare couch. The shades on the window are partially drawn, letting in a slant of sunlight. Yvonne is tempted to throw the windows open, to let in some fresh air.

"I turned it on this morning and it made this awful sound," Ava is saying as she leads Yvonne into the kitchen. Max trails after them. "I was going to call my landlord but he's already threatening to evict us . . ." Ava stops. "I'm rambling. Anyway, I thought it would be best if I figured out what was wrong on my own, first."

"I understand. Let's take a look." Yvonne flips the switch for the disposal and an awful grinding sound fills the kitchen. Max yelps then claps his hands over his ears.

"He's normally in preschool," Ava says, pulling him toward her and covering his hands with her own. "But my car wouldn't start this morning so I kept him home." She looks at Max and smiles. "Boy, it's loud isn't it?" But when she looks back at Yvonne, her face is filled with dread. "Is it broken? It is, isn't it?"

Yvonne gets the sense that Ava is used to having things break down or fall apart on a regular basis.

"It's something," Yvonne says, "but I don't know what. It sounds like you have a meat grinder trying to churn up an automobile or two. Or maybe a spoon or fork found its way down there while you were doing your dishes." Yvonne flicks the switch again and the grating metallic sound makes them all cringe. "Hey, maybe it's buried treasure!"

Ava lets out a small chuckle and pulls Max close to her.

"Buried treasure," Ava sighs. "That would be nice, wouldn't it, Max?"

Max nods. "We could be pirates," he says solemnly, his first words since Yvonne's been in the apartment. Yvonne grins as she opens her toolbox and opens the door beneath the sink.

"Yo-ho-ho," she says, pushing aside bottles of Drano and other random cleaning supplies. Yvonne grabs her offset wrench and inserts it into the bottom of the garbage disposal unit. She gives it a crank clockwise—the flywheel seems to be moving freely, but it's obviously dragging quite a bit of debris around or something that has broken into a million little pieces judging by the sound.

"I'll need to turn off the power for the disposal," she says, standing up. "Where's your fuse box?"

Ava points down the hallway. "In the bathroom, behind the door."

A few minutes later, Yvonne has found the

problem—she's fished out more than ten metal bottlecaps. If she didn't know Ava, she would have figured her for an alcoholic.

"What the . . ." Ava looks puzzled, then gasps, a red flush in her cheeks. She looks down at her son who is cringing behind her. "Max! Did you do this?"

Yvonne begins to put the disposal back together again. She inspects the lower mounting ring and tightens a few bolts, listening.

"Max, I'm talking to you," Ava says, getting down on one knee so she's eye to eye with him. "Did you put mommy's bottle caps in the sink?" Her voice sounds stressed.

From the corner of her eye, Yvonne sees a small nod.

Ava catches her breath. "Okay," she says. She takes both his hands gently in hers. "Okay. I know they're fun but you have to ask me first next time, okay? Mommy needs those for work, but I can find something else for you to play with. And I need you to be careful around the sink—I don't want you to get hurt." She stands up and pulls Max close to her, kisses the top of his head.

Yvonne remembers now that Ava does some kind of bottle-cap jewelry. "Do you want to keep these or should I throw them away?" Yvonne asks, holding out the mangled bottle caps in her hands.

"Oh, I'll keep those," Ava says quickly. "I

might be able to salvage them somehow. Create something different, who knows." She picks one up and Yvonne sees that it's different from the others—this one has small glass beads and a pretty design in the center even though it's been scratched and scraped up in the disposal.

"Pretty," Yvonne says.

Ava blushes. "Thank you. So how much do I owe you?"

"Nothing," Yvonne tells her. "I didn't have to do much of anything. My hands aren't even dirty."

Ava looks doubtful. "You don't need to give me any special treatment, Yvonne. You have to charge me something."

Yvonne puts her things away and goes to turn the electricity back on. She doesn't feel comfortable taking money from Ava, maybe because she knows her by extension and can see that Ava's hard-pressed to pay for anything. "It's not a big deal and I would have done the same if you were someone else. No special treatment, honest." She crosses her fingers behind her back.

"Well, a tip then," Ava insists. "Let me get my wallet."

Yvonne tries to protest. "It's really not necessary . . ."

"I'll be right back."

When Ava returns, she holds out a few bills. But there's something else in the palm of Ava's hand.

"This is to thank you for being so nice," Ava says. "I mean, only if you want it—please don't feel like you have to take it."

Curious, Yvonne leans forward for a look. It's a bracelet made of five bottle caps, all different beer and soda brands but in different shades of green. The centers of the caps are filled with different-colored glass beads floating in a clear epoxy. Two of the bottle caps have one word each to make the phrase: CREATE YOURSELF.

"Wow, this is nice," Yvonne says. "And green's my color!" She slips it on her wrist and it's a perfect fit.

Ava laughs. "It looks good on you. I'm glad you like it."

"I do. Thank you." Yvonne smiles. "So you're all set." She presses the extra bills back into Ava's hands. "Look, the bracelet is already a very generous tip. Use this money to buy a sink protector. I'd feel better knowing that little fingers—or bottle caps—keep their distance from the garbage disposal."

Ava gives her a grateful smile, and for a second Yvonne sees her eyes get shiny. "Thank you, Yvonne."

Max has joined them in the kitchen again and Yvonne is almost tempted to offer them a ride—to school, the store, wherever—but she knows it could hurt her friendship with Isabel. She also knows that it's a small Band-Aid to a much bigger problem, and that sometimes it's best to leave well enough alone. She gives Max a high five and then says goodbye.

Connie enters through the backdoor of the tea salon and goes to the sink to wash her hands.

"Well, it's done," she says, her voice breaking. "It's like she was never here."

Madeline looks to the backyard. The fence, hay bales, and doghouse are gone.

Connie comes to the table and drops into a chair. Pictures of the Dohertys' farm were sent over by Sergeant Overby, pictures that Serena's owner, Rayna, had submitted to the police station and the *Avalon Gazette*. Madeline and Connie have looked through the pictures, stared at the deep tread marks in dug-up earth, a broken fence, a trough split in two. It's a wonder nobody was hurt, and no wonder that the owner of the farm, Rayna, is upset—Connie would be, too.

"I feel like I should do something," Connie says. "I don't know what we're waiting for. Maybe I should say I did it so this whole thing can end."

"Absolutely not. You didn't do anything wrong, Connie," Madeline reminds her firmly as she lines the bottom of a pie dish with pastry dough. "Let the police finish their investigation. That's their business—we have plenty of things to do ourselves."

"I wish I'd taken more pictures," Connie says. She closes her eyes, which are swollen from having cried through most of the night. "I thought I'd have more time. I didn't think it would happen so fast. I didn't think it would happen like this."

"Oh, Connie." Madeline goes over to give her a hug, but Connie doesn't feel comforted.

She knows that most of the town of Avalon thinks she did it. It feels that way, at least. Even their regular customers look at her questioningly, their eyes darting away when she turns to face them. Business seems to have slowed to a trickle, people avoiding the tea salon until things can get sorted out.

But what if it doesn't? Connie doesn't want what's happened to affect Madeline, affect the tea salon. Connie called Hannah yesterday, asked her to fill in here and there over the next few days. She's going to show Hannah where everything is—where things are stored, the lists of food staples and recipes, the computer files and ledger. She'll mention the projects that need attention, like getting the fireplace cleaned and having the thermostats in the ovens checked. She doesn't want to make Madeline or Hannah suspicious, but it feels better to know that someone else can step in and take over, just in case.

"It'll be fine," Madeline says, trying to sound brave for both of them, but Connie can hear the worry in Madeline's voice. She closes her eyes but still the tears find a way of leaking out and spilling down her cheeks.

Isabel stares at the stack of boxes lined up in long, tall rows in her garage, almost touching the ceiling. The garage is so full she can't even get her car in. It's daunting, and even Yvonne seems intimidated as she lets out a low whistle.

"This is all from your attic?" she asks, amazed.

Isabel looks at the side of one box scrawled in Bill's messy handwriting. *Manuals*, she reads. She moves it to the side, creating a small pile for the new owners. Somewhere there are blueprints of the house, something the previous owner had left for them. Bill had been delighted and would pore over each oversized page, taking in every detail, nodding in agreement at the placement of electrical outlets and wiring, complaining about the side door being cut too close to the water heater. Isabel would tease him, say that he was channeling his inner engineer.

"I cleared out the closets and cabinets in the house, too," she says now. The prospective buyers are coming by next week to take another look at the house now that the porch is done. She wants them to be able to envision their own things in the house, wants to get rid of all the clutter and who knows what she's let accumulate over the years.

If things go as planned, she could be out of the house by the end of November. It's hard to believe that she might be ringing in the new year someplace other than here.

Yvonne opens one box and counts six identical flashlights, still in their packaging.

"That was Bill," Isabel tells her. "He liked to buy things in bulk. Said it was a better deal."

"Yeah, but only if you use them," Yvonne says. She looks around again and shakes her head. "You should have a garage sale. Don't even bother to unpack everything, just charge fifty dollars per box, sight unseen."

It's not a bad idea—after all, Isabel's made it all this time without ever looking in these boxes— but she can't.

"No," she says. "I told Lillian, Bill's mother, that I'd give her anything of Bill's she might like to keep. I always meant to go through everything, but I never did. I didn't want to see any of this, you know? But I owe this to her. She was always so good to me, and she was supportive of our marriage, even when things fell apart."

"She sounds nice," Yvonne says.

"She is." Isabel tugs on a piece of packing tape, wonders how Lillian's doing. They exchange the occasional card or phone call, but they have less and less to say. She knows that Lillian is still racked with sorrow. "But Bill was her only son and when he died so unexpectedly, she lost it. It was only a few months after Bill's father had died, so it was a rough time for her. She was like a completely different person. You should have seen her tearing into Ava at the hospital." Isabel shakes her head at the memory.

Yvonne clears her throat. "Speaking of Ava . . ."

Isabel doesn't like the tone of Yvonne's voice. It's one part caution, one part determination. Isabel can feel a sales pitch coming from a mile away, and she knows one is about to come from Yvonne.

"We weren't speaking of Ava," she says curtly. "We were speaking of Bill's mother, Lillian, and why I can't dump this stuff without seeing if there's something here that she'll want." Isabel flips through the manuals in the box and finds other documents stuffed in there as well—old tax returns, insurance papers. It's going to take her forever to go through everything.

Yvonne isn't deterred. "I'm saying that maybe you should give Ava a break. I get how awkward and weird this whole thing is, but I think she's reaching out to you, Isabel. Maybe just find out why, you know?" Yvonne gives her friend a hopeful look. "Maybe not be so quick to shut her down?"

Isabel closes up the box and reaches for another. "I'm glad the two of you had time to bond during your ten-minute incarceration," she retorts, "but it's not that simple."

"Maybe not before," Yvonne says. "But now I think that's exactly what this is. Things have changed, Isabel, and something is going on with her. I get the feeling that she doesn't have anyone else. Anyone other than . . . you."

Isabel snorts. "Just because she doesn't have any friends is not a good reason to put me down as her emergency contact. I still can't believe she did that."

Yvonne looks at her. "I can."

"Well, it's bizarre and completely inappropriate." Isabel rips the tape off a sealed box and finds a stack of sweaters she stored years ago, still wrapped in a plastic dry cleaner's bag. Isabel tears the bag and pulls out a yellow argyle sweater with green and blue diamonds. It smells of mothballs and dust but is in otherwise good condition, as if she'd put it away for the summer. "It's like she's doing this on purpose, dragging me into the drama of her life to show me that she's still here, that she has Max."

"I don't think she's doing this on purpose," Yvonne says. "And she's not this terrible person. I don't know what was going on in your marriage when she got involved with Bill, and I know it came from out of the blue . . ."

Isabel pulls out a navy cable-knit sweater with an alligator motif—one of Bill's old favorites. "When I look back, I can see that he was unhappy. But he didn't say anything to me at the

411

time, so I thought that was normal. Highs and lows in a marriage. We still got along and we weren't fighting—in fact, I don't think we ever fought, not even in the end. And it wasn't like I hated him or he hated me. We were . . . existing." Isabel runs her hand along the neckline of the sweater, remembering how Bill would complain that it was too tight but wear it anyway. It's not unlike her marriage. It was something that didn't quite fit but Bill wore it dutifully, at least until Ava came along. "I guess that wasn't much of a marriage, huh?"

"I don't know," Yvonne admits. "I never knew Bill, and I don't know how you were together. But I know there are all sorts of marriages out there, just like I know there are all sorts of families out there. There's no 'one size fits all.' I think what matters most is that there's love and happiness, you know?"

If it were anyone else, Yvonne's optimism would grate on Isabel. But instead it makes Isabel think. Even though Yvonne is being a loyal friend to Isabel, it's clear she doesn't dislike Ava, either. Yvonne is cheerful despite what has happened with Hugh and his family, doesn't seem to be stuck in the past like Isabel. Yvonne has found a way to be happy.

Maybe Isabel should, too.

She lets out a deep breath. She's never done this before, but she's also never had a friend like

412

Yvonne before. "So," she finally says. "What do you think I should do?"

Yvonne doesn't answer right away. She's halfheartedly rummaging through a small box and pulls out a single brass cufflink. It's tarnished but Isabel can see that it's engraved with Bill's initials—WSK. William Samuel Kidd. Bill's parents gave them to him when he graduated from college, and he wore them religiously until French cuffs went out of style. Isabel wonders where the other one is, if he lost it or took it with him when he moved out.

Yvonne studies the cufflink, then gently puts it to the side. "You know what I think, Isabel. It's the same thing you've been thinking about for a while, too."

Isabel stares at her in disbelief. "I finally ask you for advice and you lob it back into my court. Unbelievable." She drops the sweater into the box, frustrated.

"You don't need my advice, Isabel. You need someone to say it's okay to do what you want to do."

Isabel gives one of the boxes a kick, discouraged, and then leans heavily against the wall. "And what's that?"

Yvonne comes and stands next to her, her hands in her pockets. "To reach out to Ava and Max." She gives a sad smile. "I know what it's like to feel bad about loving someone. It's the worst kind

413

of feeling, Isabel, because in your heart you know one thing, but everyone else is telling you something different. And then you betray yourself by listening to them instead of yourself."

Isabel doesn't say anything.

"I almost got married once," Yvonne says. "Sam was my best friend. We grew up together. But his family worked the bogs while my family owned them—your typical mismatch from different sides of the tracks. It didn't matter to me, of course—I was in love. And I believe Sam loved me, too. But in the end my father offered him money—a lot of it—if he would break it off and leave the Cape. Sam did, on the morning of our wedding. I never saw him again. He never even said goodbye. Last I heard he got married about five years ago.

"When I look back now, I see that it wasn't just about me and Sam. It was about his family, too. I know my father and I'm sure he gave Sam and his family some kind of ultimatum, a threat."

"God," Isabel says. "That sucks. I'm sorry, Yvonne."

Yvonne shrugs. "Sam made a choice that allowed his parents and sisters to live a different life. I was willing to walk away from the money, but for Sam and his family, money equaled freedom. So I guess I'm saying that things are not always as they seem, Isabel. What happens has consequences that sometimes exceed what we can see. And I think that's what you have with Ava and Max."

"So what are we supposed to do, have sleepovers?" Isabel complains. "Do each other's hair? Reminisce about Bill?"

"Maybe."

"Maybe she wants money. Or maybe she wants me to absolve her of what happened. Well, I won't." Isabel crosses her arms.

"You don't have to do anything you don't want to do," Yvonne tells her. "I just know that you're not as closed off about Ava and Max as you claim to be. And because of that, and because I'm your friend, I want you to know that there's nothing wrong with striking up a conversation and seeing where it goes, especially since you might be moving soon. This may be your last chance."

Isabel can't picture how this will go. Awkward, that's for sure. More tears, mostly likely on Ava's part. Weird politeness, possibly the occasional curt word from Isabel if she can't resist. But Max?

Isabel hasn't told Yvonne everything about the call from Max's school, about how she answered the phone, confused at first, and was then struck with terror that something awful had happened to Ava. Why hadn't she picked up her son? Had she deserted him? Had she been in an accident? It had taken Isabel all of five seconds to leave the office and rush to the school, uncertain of what to do next. Who to call? Where to take him? Did they have any other family, any other friends? She didn't know where they lived. She didn't know anything more than Ava's last name.

But when she saw Max sitting there, alone in an empty classroom with a wooden puzzle, all her questions and fears evaporated. He had wet his pants. The teachers hadn't noticed, halfheartedly wiping down toys and complaining about this parent or that parent. All Isabel could think about was getting him out of there. Getting him out of there and then figuring out what to do.

Since the teachers hadn't bothered to change him, Isabel didn't bother to argue. She showed her ID, found the spare set of clothes he had at the school, borrowed a car seat, and got them out of there.

"I'm Isabel," she'd told him when he looked at her with his big blue eyes. "Your, um, mother asked me to come and get you."

"Mommy," he said at the mention of Ava, and Isabel saw his lower lip tremble.

"Yep," she said in what she hoped was a light and airy tone. "And she's so proud you waited patiently. Maybe we'll get an ice cream cone to celebrate, okay?"

He had nodded and seemed to relax. Then a barrage of thoughts filled her mind: Did he have any food allergies? Had Ava taught him about stranger danger? Was there another preschool she could send him to? Did he even know his home phone number? And then the more immediate question at hand.

Where the heck was Ava?

Isabel called Yvonne but there had been no answer. She drove by Yvonne's house, pointing out points of interest to Max along the way, and finally bit the bullet and called Hugh. She'd had to hold the phone away from her ear, he was yelling so loud. It had been easy from there, another five minutes to the police station, and then the surprise of seeing both Yvonne and Ava sitting on the bench, a look of guilt and pride on their faces, each for their own reasons.

But it was more than just surprise—it was relief. Max reached for Ava and for a second, all three were in an unexpected embrace as Max went from one set of arms to another. Isabel doesn't know if Ava felt it, but it doesn't matter—she knew that pang in her gut, felt something ring true. She knew in that moment that if they needed her help, Isabel was going to give it.

After she had dropped them off at their apartment, a dingy hole in a not-so-nice area of Barrett, things got complicated again. A war of emotions, of right and wrong, of fair and unfair. Isabel felt trapped, her clarity gone.

"I don't know what to do," Isabel finally says. "And I'm mad at Bill for leaving me to deal with all this. This is his mess, not mine."

417

"Don't look at it as messy," Yvonne advises. "Look at it as life. Not Bill's life, not Ava's life, not even Max's life. It's your life, Isabel. It's all up to you to decide what you want."

Isabel gives a small nod, wishing it wasn't up to her. "I think I need a drink," she says. "Let's take a break."

They open the side door, walk into the house, and gasp. There, sitting at Isabel's kitchen table, is Bettie. She's dressed but her hair is in curlers even though it's the middle of the afternoon. She's upended Isabel's trash onto the table and is picking through it carefully.

"Look at what I found!" she tells the girls, holding up an old bottle of pale pink nail polish. "It's practically full!"

"Bettie, how did you get in here?" Isabel demands, and then she sees her Hide-a-Key sitting on the table next to an empty tissue box.

Yvonne gives Isabel a pointed look as she begins to sweep the trash back into the bag. "Let's clean up a bit," Yvonne starts to say but Bettie swats her away, her face indignant. She doesn't seem to recognize Yvonne at all.

Then Bettie turns to Isabel, her face flushed with pleasure. She holds up a plastic tube. "And look at this: a rejuvenating clay mask, all natural! I could use some rejuvenating, that's for sure." She pops off the top and begins to squeeze the tube but nothing comes out.

"Bettie, that's old," Isabel tells her, taking it from her grasp. "I was cleaning out the cabinets in the bathroom." She motions for Yvonne to start cleaning up again. "I'll get you a new one, okay?"

"Get us a new one, you mean," Bettie says, grabbing bits of trash and paper as Yvonne tries to quickly shovel it back into the bag. "We have to do it together, like the old days. Right?"

"Um, right." Isabel gives Yvonne another bewildered look. "So Bettie, what are you doing here?"

"I'm baking," Bettie says matter-of-factly. "Wanted to bring some goodies to the scrapbook meeting on Thursday. I don't like last-minute baking—too stressful." One of her curlers is slipping out of her hair and Isabel notices that there's dirt underneath Bettie's nails.

Isabel glances at her oven. The dial is pointing to OFF, but she goes and checks it anyway, almost expecting to find a pan of uncooked batter sitting inside. But when she opens the door, the oven is empty.

Yvonne has removed all the trash and taken it to the garage. Isabel pulls out a chair and sits next to Bettie who's humming as she smooths a crumpled advertisement for a credit card.

The door accidentally slams when Yvonne comes back into the kitchen, and Bettie jumps. Her eyes grow wide and then she looks around, confused. "Am I home?" she asks.

Isabel feels her breath catch. "This is my home," she says. "You live next door."

Bettie looks at her, suddenly annoyed. "Well, I know that, Isabel!" She stands up, almost knocking her chair over. "Goodbye."

"Bettie, wait," Isabel begins, but Bettie is gone.

"We need to call someone," Yvonne says, frowning. "Her doctor, maybe? Or maybe we should take her to a hospital and see if we can get some answers."

Isabel nods, already reaching for the phone book. "I'll call Dr. Richard," she says. "He'll know what to do." She starts dialing and looks at Yvonne, her heart pounding. "What's happening?"

Yvonne shakes her head. "I don't know. I've never seen her like this before."

"I have," Isabel says, struck by the realization that while she knew something was wrong, she's waited too long. She presses the phone against her ear. "I should have done something, but I didn't. I thought that maybe she was being difficult, or absent-minded . . ."

Yvonne walks to the kitchen sink. "I have to wash my hands," she begins, and then she looks out the window, a horrified look on her face. "Isabel, call 911!"

Isabel rushes to the window. Gray and white smoke is billowing from windows in the back of Bettie's house. Orange and yellow flames lick the curtains, overtaking the back rooms. Isabel thrusts the phone at Yvonne and runs out the back door.

Isabel cuts across her backyard into Bettie's. Bettie's back patio is cluttered with debris and random household and garden items. Isabel touches the handle of the sliding door, finds it cool to the touch.

And locked.

"Bettie!" she calls, pounding on the glass. Flames seem to be coming from the kitchen and the back of the house, but smoke is everywhere. Isabel can see the piles of magazines in the hallway, already on fire.

Somebody else must have seen the fire because Isabel can hear the sirens but they're not close enough. With all the junk strewn throughout the house it won't take long before everything is ablaze. And Bettie. Where is she?

Then Isabel sees her through the window, in the front living room, her face already blackened by the smoke, walking toward one wall, then the next one, and round again. "Bettie!" Isabel cries. She picks up a heavy garden gnome and hurls it through the patio door.

The sound of breaking glass is deafening. Isabel scrambles through the glass and hears small explosions, snaps, and crackles. There's a layer of smoke wafting toward the front of the house. There's a *whoosh* and Isabel suddenly finds herself surrounded by flames.

"Bettie!" she calls, pulling up her shirt to cover her nose. She runs forward, tripping, kicking things out of her way.

Bettie turns in the direction of Isabel's voice. "Isabel!" she cries. "I can't find my way out!"

Isabel feels an unbearable heat on her back—there's a wall of flames blocking the patio exit. Isabel looks around, coughing, disoriented until she sees the front door. She grabs Bettie and pulls her forward, stumbling over piles of magazines and mail, miscellaneous scrapbooking items, trash. She manages to open the door and pull them through.

Yvonne is on the sidewalk and sprints forward toward them, as do several other neighbors. The fire trucks have arrived, along with an ambulance. Firemen race past them dragging long fire hoses. Two EMTs escort Bettie and Isabel to the back of the ambulance where they're immediately given oxygen and inspected for burns and smoke inhalation.

Isabel feels her arms and stomach smart—she has first- and second-degree burns that run up the length of her left arm and on her stomach. Bettie, thankfully, has none, but her face is black with smoke. Her eyes are wild behind the oxygen mask.

"It's okay," Isabel tells her, pulling off her own mask so Bettie can see her face. "It's me. Isabel."

The fire chief, Abraham Garza, approaches them. "Are you ladies all right?"

Isabel nods her head but Bettie looks at him, confused. "Abe?" she says.

Chief Garza smiles. "That's right," he says. He glances at the EMT who gives him a slight nod. "How are you, Bettie?"

"I haven't had a chance to call Imogene since the last scrapbooking meeting," Bettie says, her face a bit like a raccoon's. The ends of her hair are singed from the fire. "I wondered how she was liking that new circle cutter she bought. She was going to make coasters for the family reunion, I believe."

Chief Garza smiles. "She has most of them done," he says. "They sure do look nice, I have to say."

One of the firemen comes up to them. "Chief, it looks like the fire started in the kitchen," he says.

"Thanks, Ricky." Chief Garza turns back to Bettie. "Bettie, do you remember if you were cooking anything in the kitchen?" he asks.

"No," Bettie says.

Isabel coughs, her throat burning. "Bettie, you told me you were baking. Remember? For the scrapbooking meeting?"

"That's right!" Bettie exclaims, an excited look on her face. "I wanted to make a sugar-free crumble. There are some diabetics in the group, you know, and they have to watch their sugar intake. We always have so many delicious things they can't eat, so I thought I'd make something special. I used rhubarb. Is it time to take it out?"

"Uh, I think it might be done," Isabel says, glancing at Chief Garza.

An EMT escorts Bettie to a stretcher and has her lay down. They attach a clip with a wire to her finger, carefully put the oxygen mask back over her mouth and nose. A second later, Bettie's eyes flutter closed.

Isabel gasps.

"She's okay," the EMT reassures her, pointing to a monitor. Bettie's pulse is steady. "She fell asleep. That happens sometimes."

"We're going to take you over to the hospital in Freeport," Chief Garza says to Isabel. "Just relax and someone will be with you in a minute. Can you stay with her?" he asks Yvonne. Yvonne gives a fervent nod and steps closer to Isabel.

Isabel takes another hit of oxygen. They watch as the flames take over the roof, the firemen aiming their hoses through the windows and doorways. She thinks of everything in the house, of Bettie's life, going up in smoke.

Going, going, gone.

FIRE DESTROYS LOCAL HOME
Reported by Edith Gallagher

AVALON, ILLINOIS—A kitchen fire quickly set a local Avalonian home ablaze this past Sunday, according to local fire officials. The house belonged to longtime Avalon resident Bettie Shelton, who lives alone. Shelton, 77, was home when a fire broke out in the kitchen. Shelton was trapped in the home and rescued by neighbor Isabel Kidd.

"They were both very lucky," said Avalon fire chief Abraham Garza. "It's dangerous to run into a burning house, but she saved Ms. Shelton's life."

Shelton's house was gutted from the fire, which was a two-alarm blaze. She is currently staying with friends and appreciates the outpouring of support from the community.

Shelton is also president of the Avalon Ladies Scrapbooking Society. This Thursday's meeting has been moved to Madeline's Tea Salon.

Chapter Seventeen

Ava knocks on the door, carefully balancing a tuna noodle casserole. Max is holding a Tupperware container of chocolate chip cookies and a clump of weedy-looking flowers that he insisted on picking at the park.

Ava knows she may be pushing it, but she can't help it. Standing up to Randall Strombauer changed something inside of her and one thing's for sure—she's going to do her best to be as honest and open as possible, no more shirking away. Ava will never forget Bettie's unexpected kindness, her willingness to help, and she wants to offer some sort of support, even if it means being subjected to Isabel's wrath and obvious disapproval. It's true that she promised Isabel never to bother her again or show up unannounced, but this is about Bettie.

The door opens and Ava gasps, unprepared. Max presses against her legs, uncertainty etched on his face as well. The person answering the door is wearing a bathrobe with her hair twisted up in a clip, a clay mask on her face.

"Oh, it's you," comes the tight voice that Ava knows belongs to Isabel. "Come in."

Ava and Max step warily into the house. For Max, it's because the lady answering the door is unrecognizable and a little scary, but for Ava, it's because it's the house Bill used to live in. Her Bill, Isabel's Bill, Max's father Bill. She almost expects to weep in recognition but sees that the house is practically bare. There are no pictures, nothing that speaks of Bill or even Isabel. The furniture is spare and everything is neat and clean. It feels . . . neutral. Not good, not bad, but okay. Ava realizes she's gawking and quickly reminds herself why they are here.

"I wanted to drop this off for Bettie," she says, holding up the casserole. "I didn't know where her friend lives so I hope it's okay that I'm leaving it here." She follows Isabel into the kitchen and gives a start when she sees Bettie at the table as well, also wearing a face mask.

"Hello!" Bettie says, her voice also tight. "Look! We got these new rejuvenating masks at the drugstore. My skin already feels like butter!" She carefully touches the dried clay on her cheekbones. "Of course we might need a chisel to get this off my face. Isabel, do you have a chisel?"

"I'll look for one," Isabel says as she bends over the sink, splashing water on her face. When she looks up, the mask is gone and her face is glowing. "Wow, you're right," she marvels, using her fingers to press into her cheekbones. "Just like butter." She scrunches up her face and Max giggles.

Ava pushes him forward but Max steps back,

shy. "The flowers and cookies are for you," Ava says to Isabel. "From Max." She's still not sure what to expect, but Isabel hasn't kicked them out yet so she ventures, "And me. To thank you for picking him up. It . . . it meant a lot to us—me—that you did that."

Isabel gives her a long look as she pulls a headband from her hair. "Yeah, well . . . I was completely caught off guard. You should have asked first."

"Would you have said yes?" Ava asks.

Isabel thinks about this. "Probably not. But still you shouldn't have done it."

"I know," Ava says. And then she adds quietly, "But like I said, you were the only person that I could trust."

Isabel looks flummoxed. "I still don't get it. You'd think I'd be the last person on your list."

Ava gives a small shrug. "But you're not." And it's the truth.

Isabel just sighs and takes the casserole from Ava, then bends down to accept the cookies and flowers from Max. She smiles at him. "Are those for me? To remind me of our fun adventure last week?"

He nods and holds everything out. "Auntie Isabel," he says, then buries his face again in Ava's legs, embarrassed again. Isabel smiles but straightens up, quickly turning her back on them as she places the food on the table.

"Time to get your mask off," she says briskly to Bettie, and Ava sees Isabel do a quick dab at the corner of her eye. "Eula will be here in ten minutes to pick you up and take you home."

"My home?" Bettie asks, her voice hopeful.

"No, her home. You're staying with her and Buddy, remember?" Isabel wets a washcloth with warm water and begins to moisten the clay on Bettie's face.

"Oh, right." Bettie's face contorts as she remembers. She sighs. "It was nice of them to offer me a place to stay, but I miss the ol' neighborhood."

"You're only two blocks away, Bettie."

Bettie ignores her. "And it's so noisy over there," she complains. "Buddy snores like a freight train, it keeps me up nights. Have you ever lived with someone who snores?"

"Yes," both Isabel and Ava say. There's an embarrassed pause as this sinks in. Isabel turns beet red as she begins to wipe Bettie's face with rapt attention. Ava is horrified.

"I mean . . ." she starts to say. "That is . . ."

"Oh, forget it," Isabel says with a flick of the washcloth. She lets out a breath. "I mean, it's not as if I hadn't figured that part out." She gives a slight nod in Max's direction. "Exhibit A."

Bettie is still chattering, oblivious. "And Eula, well, I love her but let's face it: She has gas like nobody's business." Bettie tilts her head back so

Isabel can wipe under her neck. "I appreciate the charity but I have to say that I can't wait until I can move back home."

Ava and Isabel exchange a look. When Ava drove up she saw the skeleton of a house that remained next door. There is nothing for Bettie to move back to. She watches as Isabel rinses the washcloth and wipes Bettie's face again.

Ava reaches into her purse and brings out a muslin bag. There's a pleasant tinkle as she gives the bag a shake. "Bettie, look what I brought. I finished those bottle-cap embellishments we talked about." Ava opens the bag and pours the bottle caps onto the table, more than fifty in all. Bettie gasps in delight and even Isabel leans forward, entranced. Ava can't help but feel proud.

"Wow," says Isabel, picking one up. The awe in her voice makes Ava smile. "What are these?"

"I make bottle-cap jewelry in my spare time," Ava says. "I've sold a few pieces at Avalon Gifts 'N More and a few other boutique gift shops. Bettie asked if there was a way she could incorporate them into different scrapbooking layouts and I came up with these." She holds one up, a burst of oranges and yellows. "I'm calling them scrap caps. They're recycled bottle caps, but each one has a different word or image inside. I've added small beads in some and glitter in others. They're fun embellishments you can put on a page or in a handmade card. I also have blank ones so you can put a one-inch round picture in, too."

"These are wonderful!" Bettie exclaims, running her hands through them. "What are they for?"

"They're for your scrapbooking club," Ava says again. "You asked me to make them?"

Bettie gasps. "You make these? They're wonderful! What are they for?"

"For your . . ." Ava's voice trails off. She looks at Isabel, who confirms her silent question with a nod.

Bettie is looking at Ava with curious interest. "Have we met?" she asks. "Bettie Shelton, founder and president of the Avalon Ladies Scrapbooking Society. You should come to one of our meetings sometime!" She leans forward conspiratorially, "It's fifteen dollars a month and that includes the monthly scrap pack, but you can come as my guest and I'll give you one for free." She puts a finger to her lips and smiles. "But don't tell anyone!"

"I won't," Ava assures her. She reaches forward and plucks a bright pink bottle cap and hands it to Bettie. "You should keep this one. I was thinking of you when I made it."

"Memories," Bettie reads. "Oh, that's nice. Look, Isabel!"

Isabel nods. "Nice," she says. She holds up the

square of washcloth. "I'm going to go put this in the washing machine. Ava, do you want to help me?" Isabel jerks her head in the direction of the laundry room and gives Ava a look that she can't quite decipher.

Ava sees that Max has climbed into the chair next to Bettie and is running his hands through the bottle caps with her. Their laughter makes her smile. "Um, sure."

In the laundry room, Isabel tosses the washcloth into the sink. "Just so you know," she says. "Bettie has vascular dementia."

Ava feels her breath catch. "Oh, no."

"Dr. Richard diagnosed her a year ago. She's known for a while but she hasn't told anyone—he said she was determined to keep it private."

Ava remembers Nana, her father's mother. She recalls the vacant looks, the eyes focusing elsewhere as if seeing something in the far distance, visible only to her. There's a lump in her throat as she tells Isabel, "My grandmother had Alzheimer's. She couldn't live alone. She died in a long-term-care facility. I always wanted to do more to help her, but my parents wouldn't let me."

"Bettie supposedly has long-term-care insurance, but everything was destroyed in the fire so I don't know who the provider is. I have no idea what she had or what might be missing. I'm sure we can eventually figure it out, but it'll take time." Isabel runs her hand along an empty shelf, inspects it for dust. "And I'm moving soon. I have an interested buyer in the house, and there's nothing left for me here."

Ava feels the color drain from her face. "Leave? But you can't . . . you can't . . ."

"Oh, no," Isabel sighs as Ava furiously tries to blink back tears. "No waterworks, please."

"I'm sorry." Ava sniffs. "I mean, I wasn't expecting . . ." Her nose starts running and she wipes it with the back of her hand. *Pull it together,* she tells herself. *Don't let this be Isabel's last image of you, crying next to a stack of towels.*

But then Isabel reaches for a large box sitting on top of the dryer. "This is for you. Well, Max mostly. It's some things of Bill's I thought you should have." She pushes the box toward Ava.

Ava sniffs again as she looks inside. It's a random assortment of things, but Ava feels her heart catch in her throat. Bill's old yearbooks, a cufflink, some sweaters, a paper he'd written in dental school. There's an antique razor and brush with mother-of-pearl handles.

"Bill loved that set," Isabel tells her. "It used to be his father's but we had it stored up in the attic. I know Max has a ways to go, but in case, when he's older . . ."

Ava throws her arms around Isabel and starts crying in earnest. It's all so wonderful, and there's so much of it, things that she knows Max will treasure forever. "Thank you, Isabel!"

She feels Isabel stiffen at her touch, but she's not pulling away, either. Ava feels a mechanical patting on her back.

"Okay, okay," Isabel says awkwardly, and Ava is surprised to hear a catch in her voice, too. "I'll probably have a few more boxes later. I have some albums somewhere with Bill's baby pictures— they look a lot alike."

"They do?" Ava releases her and steps back, wipes her eyes again. She's a mess. "Really?"

"Let's just say you can tell they're father and son. Without a doubt." Instead of looking angry or uncomfortable, Isabel looks sad. "Anyway, this whole scrapbooking thing with Bettie, and the fire . . . I want Max to know his dad. You too." Isabel looks at her. "There's a lot about Bill that you probably never got a chance to know. Good things. Funny things. You'll find some of it here." She touches the box.

"But . . ." Ava looks through the box again, sees Bill's graduation certificates, letters from his parents, golf balls, music CDs, an expired passport. Small and personal mementos that she knows they'll treasure. "Don't you want any of this?"

Isabel shakes her head. "I have all the memories I need, including those I wish I didn't." She gives a small shrug. "But Max doesn't have even that."

Ava lifts a paperweight from the box. It's a glass penguin with a silly expression on his face, and it makes her smile. "So will you be moving far away?" The thought of Isabel leaving is almost unbearable, but Ava doesn't know what else she can say.

Isabel shrugs. "I have no idea. I'll be staying with Yvonne as soon as the house sells, until I figure out what to do next." Isabel nods at the paperweight. "That's classic Bill. The occasional random kooky thing. He loved that penguin. I almost can't believe he left it behind, but I don't think that was what was on his mind when he left."

Ava's voice is a whisper. "Thank you," she says again.

Isabel starts to head back to the house, then hesitates at the door. She turns to face Ava. "The scrapbooking meeting is this Thursday at the tea salon. Bettie has her good days and her bad days, but either way I'm sure she'd appreciate it if you were there."

Ava nods. "We'll be there. If that's okay with you."

Isabel doesn't say anything, just gives a small, silent nod before returning to the kitchen.

Whatever unseen embargo had been on Yvonne is now lifted. It's been less than two weeks since the incident at Hugh's house, but news has a way of traveling fast in a small town. Yvonne's days are packed again and her client list has swelled. She's scheduling jobs out over the next month, unable to fit everyone in at once. She's even received a résumé from another plumber new to town, a young guy still figuring out the ropes. He's interested in apprenticing with Yvonne until he can get his feet on the ground. Yvonne's never considered this, always content to work on her own, but if things continue like this some help might be nice.

One of her clients made a comment that she should teach classes. Nothing too hard, the woman had quickly added, but a basic introductory class.

"A do-it-yourself class," her client had said. "It's empowering to know that we can do it ourselves. And we're women, to boot!"

Yvonne likes the idea, and maybe in the new year she'll look into it. She knows that there's a lot of talk right now because she stood up to the Hillshire bullies, but she knows it might have gone differently if she hadn't been involved with Hugh. Maybe she would have filed a complaint or written a letter to the editor of the *Gazette*. A weak, most likely ineffective means to get her point across, to save her business. There was a chance that by the time everything got addressed and resolved, she'd be on her way to the next town, hoping it wouldn't happen again.

No, under the circumstances she'd acted just right. She didn't back down. The charges were dropped, though Yvonne doesn't know if it was Sergeant Overby or Hugh's influence over Joan Hill. Sergeant Overby, most likely. Hugh's not likely to stick his neck out for anyone, least of all Yvonne.

Yvonne wrinkles her nose as she drops her keys into the small bowl by her door. Talk about a coward. She can't believe she was so taken by him, and maybe that was the problem. She was so enamored by the possibilities that she couldn't see him for what he was. She saw only what she wanted to see—someone who might be able to step into her heart and be a part of her life.

Yvonne strips out of her work clothes and tosses them into the laundry, then goes to take a shower. When she emerges, fresh and clean, she walks to her jewelry box, drops her rings and earrings inside. She pauses when she sees the silver turquoise hearts resting on their sides, patient. Yvonne touches them, feels a rush of emotion.

Sam.

She never bothered to look for him, and she only heard about his marriage when Claire, her other sister, had called five years ago with the news that she was pregnant. It had been a subtle bomb, dropped at the precise moment when

Yvonne thought that things might have changed enough for her to go home for Claire's baby shower.

"They were here visiting Sam's father," Claire reported, delighting in Yvonne's stunned silence.

Yvonne knew then that the call really wasn't an invitation to the shower, but an opportunity to make sure that Yvonne knew her family was always watching, always ready, for any chance to show her who was in charge. They would always be one step ahead of her, quashing any chance of Yvonne's happiness.

Yvonne picks up the earrings, twirls the posts between her fingers. "Good luck charms" was what Sam had called them. The turquoise was a symbol of friendship. Yvonne was wearing them on her wedding day, a day where she suddenly found herself without a fiancé, without a friend. Hardly the good luck charms he'd promise they'd be.

But it did get her out of the Tate family dynamic once and for all. Even if she goes back now, it'll be on different terms, not because she knows her family's agenda better, but because she knows herself better. Yvonne gets to call her life her own, which is more than she can say for her mother or sisters, both of whom married men who are now working for her father. In a way, Yvonne was set free.

Yvonne unscrews the back posts and carefully

slips the turquoise hearts into her ears, one at a time. She tucks her wet hair behind her ears and gazes at herself in the mirror, then smiles at the woman smiling back.

"Sweetheart, I think you're being hasty," Madeline is saying. "And under the circumstances, leaving probably isn't such a good idea right now."

"I'll be back," Connie says. She can't look Madeline in the eye so she pretends to be absorbed in folding a sweater and then adding it to the pile. "I think some space would be good for me, that's all. Suddenly this town feels too small. Everyone's looking at me funny, like I'm a criminal or a hoodlum or something."

"I can understand that," Madeline says. "Except that you're not packing for a small trip, Connie. You're packing everything." She gestures to the empty drawers in the dresser, the dangling hangers in the armoire.

"I feel better if everything's with me," Connie says. "Old habits die hard."

"But . . ." Madeline's eyes look sad.

"And I don't want you to worry about everything that's happened with Serena. I mean, Daffodil." Connie begins to clear the shelves, stacking her journals in a box. She sees her black scrapbooking album, the one adorned with lace and graffiti, the silver tags still new, the pages still empty. She decides to leave it. "I'm going to take care of it."

"Connie, do you honestly think I care about that? Things will get sorted out one way or another, of that I am certain." Madeline perches on Connie's bed, anxious. "I know everything must be so distressing right now. Are you sure you don't want to talk? Or maybe I can find someone neutral for you to talk to . . ."

"A therapist?" Connie shakes her head. She's had her fair share of them and she's done. "No, I'm all right, Madeline. I just need a little time away. And I don't want to be here when they have the scrapbooking meeting this week—I'll feel like a sideshow freak. You know everybody will be looking. There's already a drop in business because I'm here."

"That's not true . . ." Madeline begins to say, but then her voice trails off.

Connie wishes she could tell Madeline the truth, that she is leaving and that she isn't coming back. That she has taken all of her savings out of her bank account, savings that have grown substantially over the years, and that a check is already on its way to Rayna Doherty to pay for all the damages to the farm and some, even though it's not Connie's fault. She doesn't want it to end up in Madeline's lap and she wants to make sure Serena's taken care of. Her baby, too.

Madeline might be sad at first, but she won't

miss Connie for long. Connie has already called Hannah, saying only that she'd be grateful if Hannah could help out for a while. She and Madeline will establish a new rhythm in the kitchen, and they'll be able to talk about music and art and all the fancy things that Connie knows little about. It'll work out better for everyone if she's gone.

"I'll be fine, Madeline," she promises, and she hears the strength in her own voice, her own words. She will be all right, come what may.

Madeline leaves, reluctant, and again Connie has to refrain from running to her and throwing her arms around her, telling her everything. But she doesn't.

When she's finished packing, she stands in the doorway and looks back at the room. Her room, her refuge for the past year. It's by far the nicest place she's ever lived, a place that feels as close to home as Connie's been able to get. She turns to leave.

Hannah is in the foyer, an apron already tied around her waist. She looks at the two suitcases in Connie's hands. "Hey."

"Hi." Connie looks away, blinking rapidly.

"Need a hand?" Hannah asks. Connie shakes her head but Hannah has already grabbed one of the suitcases from her.

They walk in silence out the door. Connie pops the trunk and Hannah helps to load the suitcases.

"So, I guess this is it," Hannah says. It's clear she knows exactly what's going on.

"What?" Connie says, trying to laugh. "I'll be back."

Hannah looks at her. "Promise?" she asks.

Connie swallows, unable to answer.

Hannah touches her arm. "Don't leave. It'll crush Madeline and you didn't do anything wrong."

Connie looks at Hannah, at her earnest face, at her perfect clothes. She knows it's not Hannah's fault, but Connie still can't help but feel a little resentful. "Maybe it's all true, Hannah, that I stole Serena because I'm lonely. I'm obviously reckless because of the way I'm dressed and the fact that I grew up in a bunch of foster homes." She slams the trunk closed and gives Hannah a defiant look.

Hannah isn't fazed. "Connie, nobody believes that you took Serena, and if they do they obviously don't know you. Look at what you've done with your life. You're smart and creative. You have this uncanny ability to take a good thing and make it better. There are a lot of people who believe in you. And you're going to throw it all away because of this little bump in the road? That doesn't sound like the Connie I used to be so jealous of."

Connie gapes at her in disbelief. Hannah? Jealous of her?

Hannah laughs. "Oh, don't be so surprised. You showed up last year and took over everything in the tea salon, came in at a time when Madeline needed help. Everything changed for her after that—you helped make her dreams come true. And you were the one that made the Amish Friendship Bread drive last year a success. I was filled with admiration but envy, too. You're so young but you know who you are. I'm still trying to figure that out for myself. I look at you and think, I want that courage for myself. And I know I'm not alone in thinking that."

"Then why is everyone being weird?"

Hannah shrugs. "Because the whole thing is weird. It's not you, it's the situation. Plus with the fire—everyone is on edge. But people who believe in you are looking to you for how to react. If you're anxious or nervous, they will be, too. If you're okay with it . . ."

"They'll be okay with it, too. I get it."

"I hope so," Hannah says, and then she catches Connie in an unexpected embrace. "Because this town won't be the same if you're not in it." She steps back and gives Connie a smile, then turns to head back into the tea salon.

Chapter Eighteen

The temperature in Avalon is dropping. Halloween is just around the corner, scarecrows and pumpkins adorning porches, wispy tissue paper ghosts gracing windows and doorways.

Frances is at her sewing machine, two half-sewn costumes on the ironing board, Mei Ling's growing quilt hanging on the door to the pantry. Nick refused a homemade costume this year, saying he was going to go as a skateboarder instead. T-shirt, jeans, sneakers, knit hat, skateboard, done. Frances tried not to look disappointed, but she can't help it. She's made a costume for him every year since his birth.

"Mom," he says as she ticks off possible costumes. Pirate, skeleton, wizard. "That's kid stuff."

Well, he's a kid, isn't he? Frances is perplexed by her growing boy, by her inability to anticipate his every need. She thought she was good at this. It was easier when he was little, and she's not having the same problem with Brady or Noah. But Nick is growing from boy to young man and Frances isn't sure what to do.

"I'm sorry," she says as soon as Hannah answers the phone. She explains her dilemma. "I remember you said that Jamie is from a family of boys, and I thought I could get some tips. I'm really feeling lost here."

"I'm not sure there's much I can do to help," Hannah admits. "But I'd be happy to introduce you to Sandra Linde, Jamie's mother. She's wonderful, and you have a lot in common."

Sandra invites them over for coffee. As she and Hannah walk up to Sandra Linde's house, Frances sees the battered basketball hoop but none of the odds and ends of boyhood that are so easily found at her house. Tricycles littering the lawn; the odd assortment of rubber balls, baseballs, soccer balls; a forgotten toy; dried out paint cups; even Brady's shoes. There's all the junk her boys have picked up throughout their day, too. A forgotten frog in a glass jar, makeshift swords, a bucket full of rocks. She knows Sandra's boys are much older, but for some reason Frances figured there would be evidence of their boyness still.

When Sandra answers the door and invites them in, Frances sees it. Or, rather, smells it. Stinky shoes and socks, dirty laundry piled high. Sandra keeps a neat house, much more so than Frances, but it reeks of boy, and Frances loves it.

"Sorry," Sandra apologizes. She picks up a damp towel from the floor and hollers, "Peter, get out here and hang this up!"

A sixteen-year-old boy with damp hair lopes out of his room, and Frances is struck by how tall he is. She can't imagine any of her boys becoming . . . this.

"My youngest," Sandra says proudly, and then

she points to pictures of Jamie, her oldest, and her middle twins, Casey and Bailey, who are in college in Vermont. There are sports trophies, sports equipment, and textbooks everywhere. It's like the big version of her home.

The front door opens again and Jamie walks in, still wearing his UPS uniform.

"Hi, Mom," Jamie says, giving Sandra a kiss on the cheek before doing the same to Hannah. He slips an arm around Hannah's waist. "I heard there was a party and thought I'd come over."

Sandra grins and Frances can tell she's delighted to have him home. She would be, too. Hannah and Jamie wander into the kitchen while Sandra and Frances settle in the living room.

"Hannah told me your family is growing," Sandra says as they sit down. "How exciting!"

"Thank you," Frances says, beaming. "There's still so much to be done, but I'm ready. We all are."

"A girl," Sandra sighs wistfully. "That used to be my dream—one boy and one girl. But two was our magic number, and then when we had the twins our entire parenting strategy changed. We switched from man-to-man to zone defense. At that point we figured, what the heck, we're already outnumbered, so then we had Peter." She laughs.

Frances wonders when she'll be able to talk about her children and parenting with the same ease as Sandra Linde. Sandra looks connected with her boys, something Frances thought she was as well.

"I guess that's why I'm here," she says. "With Mei Ling on the way, I thought I had everything under control with the boys. But my eight-year-old, Nick, has suddenly become this reticent, reluctant kid. It's harder to get him to do things with us, and he seems embarrassed by me already. He even did that eyeball roll the other day when I told him to zip up his sweater hoodie. Isn't it a little early for that?"

Sandra sighs. "Casey was like that," she remembers. "He wouldn't let me walk him into the classroom like his brothers did. He didn't want me cramping his style."

That sounds just like her son, and Frances feels stung by the comment. "But how can I cramp his style?" she asks. "Nick is only eight!"

Sandra laughs. "I don't think age has anything to do with it," she says. "It's their personalities. They come into the world wired a certain way. We can influence it, certainly, but they are who they are." She lifts her chin to point down the hallway. "Peter is my easiest kid. Agreeable, not argumentative. You can tell him to do something and he'll do it. But he also has a knack for getting into trouble. If there's something going down, Peter is never far away."

Frances thinks about the boy she met minutes ago. "Really?"

"Peter, come here!" Sandra calls. A second later Peter is there, a bag of chips in hand.

"Hey, there he is," Jamie says as he and Hannah walk back into the living room. "The conquering hero!" Jamie musses his brother's hair and Peter tries to duck out of the way.

"Quit it," Peter says, but he's grinning.

"They won another game," Sandra tells her. "Peter's on the football team. They're on a winning streak, the first time in six years. It's a big deal."

Frances nods wordlessly, still taking in these grown-up versions of her sons. She can't imagine them towering over her but she knows it's inevitable—Reed is 6'2" and the boys are already in the hundredth percentile for their height.

"Hey, no food in your room," Sandra reminds Peter, grabbing the bag of chips. "You know better."

"Aw. But Jamie gets to eat in his room."

"Jamie has his own apartment and he's an adult. As long as you're under my roof, all food stays in the kitchen." Sandra whispers to Frances. "Jamie's my neat one. Always made his bed, folded his own laundry, set the table. Very responsible."

"I'm responsible," Peter mumbles, overhearing them.

"Yeah, responsible for setting off two fire alarms in school last month," Jamie reminds him.

"But that wasn't me," his brother protests.

Sandra ignores him. "He's still grounded," she tells Frances. "I forgot to tell you about that part. This is where you hope you raised them right at the end of the day."

"I said I didn't do it," Peter says again.

"Let me guess—was it Spit Parker?" Jamie snorts. He tells Hannah and Frances, "Spit Parker is the quarterback. A legend, larger than life. He can't do wrong since he's taking the team to championships. Isn't that right, Pete?"

Peter mumbles something unintelligible. Frances catches the words, "not fair," somewhere in the mix.

"Look, Peter," Sandra says, turning her attention to her youngest son. Her voice is stern. "I know you said it wasn't you. But you knew who did it and that makes you an accomplice. I know it seems like a harmless prank, but people panic in situations like that. Someone could get hurt and I know you wouldn't want that."

Peter hangs his head.

"I know you want to be loyal to Spit, but being a good friend isn't about hiding the truth. It's about helping him make better decisions, not enabling poor ones. Do you know what I'm saying?"

A nod.

Frances wishes she could take notes, get a transcript of what's transpiring. She likes to think

449

her boys will never misbehave, will never get into trouble, but they already misbehave, already get into trouble. She may as well learn how to deal with it.

"You're a good boy, Peter, but that doesn't mean your father and I aren't going to call you on it when you do something wrong, or allow somebody else to do something wrong. I don't ever want you to look back on something and feel regret. Now go," Sandra says, waving them all away. "I want to finish enjoying my chat with Mrs. Latham before it's time to put dinner on the table."

Nobody moves. Peter is looking edgy, clearly unhappy, and Jamie has a frown on his face.

"Pete, what is it?" he asks.

"Nothing," Peter mumbles, but he also doesn't move to leave.

"I'll tackle it out of you if I have to," Jamie says. He makes a threatening move toward his brother and Peter jumps back.

"Okay, okay!" Peter's nervous now, and both Jamie and Sandra have impatient looks on their faces. Clearly this is not an uncommon occurrence. Frances would be concerned if she weren't so fascinated at the same time.

Peter takes a deep breath. "Promise me you won't get mad."

"Peter." Sandra Linde does not look happy, her mouth turning into an angry frown. "Do *not* make me call your father."

"Fine." Peter sighs, dropping onto the couch. "I have something to tell you."

This is it, the last of it. All of Isabel's boxes have finally been sorted, a large pile put aside for Ava and Max, an even larger pile for Goodwill and a few local churches. She's already sent off a box to Lillian Kidd, Bill's mother, with a long note that took her most of the night to write.

Outside of the kitchen and master bedroom, Isabel's own things occupy a small corner of the garage. She still has quite a few things but she knows what they are, has deliberately chosen what to keep and what to give away. She can't believe how light she feels, how hopeful. She no longer feels mired in all the stuff that was keeping her anchored here, all the unknown quantities that felt heavy and mysterious. Everything is in its proper place at last.

Dan and Nina are coming again this week, and Isabel is ready for them. The house is clean, the furniture comfortable and spare, every mirror and glass sparkling and clear. But it's the porch that Isabel is most excited about. Ian Braemer put the final coat on a week ago and it's perfect. The house finally looks—and feels—complete.

Isabel is about to head out the door for the scrapbooking meeting when her phone rings. She's late as it is and debates letting the machine pick it up, but decides to answer it.

"Isabel?" It's a man's voice, shaky and uncertain. "It's Buddy McGuire, Eula's husband."

"Oh, hey, Buddy," Isabel says. "What's up?"

"Eula and I are here at the hospital in Freeport. Bettie had a fall. She has a broken wrist, but she's otherwise okay."

Isabel grips the phone. "I'll be right there."

"She's about to go into surgery and then the doc says she'll be out for a while. We'll be able to bring her home later tonight, so I don't think you need to come out. I thought that maybe you could let the folks know at the scrapbooking meeting that she won't be there." He clears his throat, uncomfortable. "Eula is pretty upset. She and Bettie were having an argument and then Bettie turned to leave, and fell."

"An argument? About what?"

"Bettie was accusing Eula of poisoning her food and holding her prisoner. She grabbed Eula's car keys, and Eula tried to stop her from leaving. That's when she fell."

"Oh, Buddy." Isabel can picture how it went down. "I'm so sorry. I'm glad that Eula didn't let her get in the car, though. Dr. Richard says she can't be driving anymore."

"Isabel, I don't know if we can do this anymore. Eula and Bettie are good friends, but this isn't the Bettie we know. She forgets why she's with us half the time. We aren't able to get anything done during the day, and nights are becoming rough, too. We're not getting much sleep because she wanders and if I lock the doors, she gets upset."

Isabel doesn't know what to say but she can imagine their difficulty in wrangling with Bettie. "I'll talk to Dr. Richard, we'll figure it out," she promises.

But this doesn't seem to be enough. "Eula and I are in our mid-seventies," Buddy continues. "We love Bettie but we're out of our league here. I'm sorry to ask this, but is there someone else she can stay with?"

"I'll put it out to the group tonight," Isabel says. "And she can stay with me until we make other arrangements."

"Okay." Buddy sounds relieved, but guilty, too. Isabel can only imagine how exhausted he must be. He and Eula were the first people to step up and open their home to Bettie after the fire. No one had even given Bettie's dementia a second thought, Isabel included. It had only been about finding a safe place for Bettie to stay and to be among friends.

Isabel thanks him and says goodbye. She stares at her car keys, wondering what she should do. People were expecting to see Bettie tonight, and Isabel knows Society members have spread the word in the community about Bettie having lost everything in the fire. They're expecting a good turnout and Isabel can't cancel the meeting.

It's a short drive to the tea salon, but Isabel

takes her time, thinking. By the time she reaches Madeline's, she knows exactly what she's going to say.

The tea salon is packed with people gathering in the sitting room and standing along the walls, spilling out into the foyer. Isabel is surprised to see that there are men here, too. She recognizes Clyde Thomas, the pharmacist, sitting next to his wife as they chat with the couple next to them. There's a skinny guy that Isabel has seen on billboard signs for KAVL 94.5 FM listening avidly to an older woman who's giving a lengthy explanation about each page in her scrapbook. A few more men are hovering by the food, filling their plates and laughing. She knows they probably don't know a thing about scrapbooking but are here in support of Bettie.

Isabel sees Ava and Max, and smiles when Max waves to her. She finds Yvonne by the canapés. She'll explain about Buddy and Eula later, but now she just wants to get it over with. Isabel's never been one for mingling or drawn-out introductions, so she walks to the front of the room and tries to get everyone's attention.

"Excuse me," she says loudly, but nobody hears her. Yvonne tries to whistle but it gets drowned out in the cacophony. There are so many people in the tea salon, laughing and having their own conversations, that Isabel finally picks up the decorated wooden mallet and bangs it on the wood block. The room is instantly silenced as all heads turn to her.

"Um, hear hear, the Avalon Ladies Scrapbooking Society is now in session." Isabel clears her throat, nervous. "As you can see, I'm not Bettie."

There's a small round of laughter and Isabel sees Yvonne and Ava smile at her. "As you know, Bettie's house burned down last week. This afternoon she was taken to the hospital after she had a fall. She broke her wrist and won't be able to join us tonight."

There's a collective gasp and murmuring, heads looking around the room as if Bettie might suddenly appear.

Isabel continues. "I know there's been a lot of talk about the fire, and the real reason it started. We'll never know for sure, because Bettie doesn't remember.

"She has vascular dementia. It's the second most common form of dementia after Alzheimer's. It's caused by small strokes in the brain, sometimes called 'silent strokes' because patients don't always realize they've had them. But over time the symptoms reveal themselves—changes in memory recollection, or memory loss, confusion, a loss of cognitive functioning.

"What this means is that she'll have moments where she may be confused or won't recognize you or where she is. She may forget what day it is or suddenly get tired or frustrated in the middle of a conversation.

"Vascular dementia is different from Alzheimer's because there's no clear progression. Because of that, many of us were aware that something was going on with her, we just didn't know what. Bettie is so good at helping us with our problems—whether we want it or not—that I think we missed an opportunity to help her with hers."

Isabel looks around the room and takes a deep breath. A few women are dabbing their eyes and sniffing. Isabel feels like she might need a tissue herself. "Bettie lost everything in the fire, but I think the bigger loss she's experiencing is her sense of self. Anything that could help trigger a memory or ground her in the moment, is gone.

"I recently went through some old photo albums in my house. Even though I would have never considered Bettie a close friend, I found her in more than one photograph—she was a part of my life even when I didn't realize it. I'm sure many of you can say the same. So on the drive over I was thinking that we could all go through our own albums and see if there are any pictures of Bettie, and we can make a new album for her. If everyone can find one or two, we'll have over a hundred pictures. It'll be a good start. Thank you." Isabel sits down and then, after a second, stands back up and awkwardly bangs the gavel, signaling the official end of the meeting.

There's a long, pregnant pause. And then, a hand goes up in the air and Patsy Jones stands up.

"I know I have pictures from the year we had a quilting bee for the church," she says, her voice nervous and wobbly. "I would be happy to put some of those pictures together and write something about it. I could take pictures of the finished quilts hanging in people's homes, too." Her friend pats her on the arm, encouraging her, and Patsy smiles before sitting down.

Floyd O'Neill, a volunteer fireman and father of three, stands up next. "Hi, I'm Floyd. I'm not a lady or a scrapbooker, but I'm here because I helped put the fire out." There's a small chuckle but the mood is still somber at the mention of the fire. "I have some pictures from last Fourth of July in Avalon Park and she's in them. Every time I look at them I remember how she kept telling me how to tend to the barbecue. It was driving me nuts, but now I can laugh about it. Maybe Bettie will, too." He sits back down.

There's head nodding and one lady calls out, "The Society is open to men, too!" Floyd gives a thumbs-up and there's a small wave of laughter.

Cassandra Simon stands up. "Hermina and I have pictures of the Society for every year since its inception," she says loudly. She calls to a woman sitting across the room. "Isn't that right, Hermina?"

Hermina Hooper nods. "Bettie was *very* strict

about documenting all of our activities. We could fill two scrapbooks easily!"

"Three," Cassandra amends confidently. "At least." There are murmurs of support from several longtime Society members.

Isabel sees Madeline pass Ava a notebook and pen.

Brett Hull raises his hand. "Bettie has always been helpful to our local Boy Scout Troop. She comes every year to help with scrapbooking our annual camping trip. I'm sure I could check with past troop leaders to see what pictures they have, too."

Hope Weaver stands up. "I can try to put together some of the Society's favorite recipes," she says. "I mean, I'm not a good cook but I know there are some dishes Bettie really liked."

"My tomato salad," Sue Pendergast says proudly. "She could never figure out how to make it. That's because I have a couple of secret ingredients, you see, equal parts red wine vinegar and also a half teaspoon of dry mustard . . ."

Madeline raises her hand. "I can help. We can make the recipes and take pictures, too."

"Bettie and I both started in the handbell choir when we were in our twenties," Louella Jones chimes in. "I don't know if I still have those pictures, but I can look."

"I remember that!" someone else exclaims. It's Percy Rush, an elderly gentleman shaking his cane in the air. "It sounded like angels dancing on a xylophone! You played during the Christmas parades, I remember!"

"There might be pictures in the *Avalon Gazette*," says Edie Gallagher Johnson, Dr. Richard's wife and a reporter for the *Avalon Gazette*. She's nursing her daughter, Miranda, and some of the older Avalonians are embarrassed, making a point of looking anywhere but at Edie. "I can do a search through the archives for any pictures of Bettie. I'll look for articles, too, and make copies."

Ava is writing furiously and Yvonne is helping her get names and contact information for each promise of help.

A man stands up. His face is wrinkled from the sun, and he's wearing a vest over a long-sleeved plaid shirt. He holds a felt hat in his hands. "Excuse me. I'm Henry Tinklenberg and I want to say that I'm awfully sorry to hear about Miss Shelton," he says. "She was one of the first people my wife and I met when we moved to Avalon. And then when Abigail passed, Bettie was the first person to show up on my doorstep. Abigail had been working on a scrapbook, you see, for my grandchildren, but it wasn't finished. I didn't know the first thing about any of that. Bettie came and sat with me, helped me finish it. It took us almost a year—I wasn't as fast as you ladies with all this. But she kept coming over and helping me until we were done. I'm very grateful for her friendship, and I'm available to help in any way I can. Thank you." He sits back down.

"Me too." Ella Kline stands up. "My mother died from Alzheimer's. She loved to scrapbook, though, and Bettie would help her with small projects. It was funny, but when Mom was scrapbooking, she seemed almost like her regular self. Even toward the end, when she didn't recognize me, she still liked looking at the pictures in her scrapbook. I'm happy to help with anything, too." Ella sits down and wipes her eyes.

Madeline's Tea Salon is now thick with memories and emotions, everyone reminiscing about how Bettie has made a difference in their lives. Boxes of tissues have to be passed around, but there's laughter, too. More hands go up, and the stories start to come.

Chapter Nineteen

Connie slows the car to a stop and cuts the engine. There's a large sign over the entryway.

Doherty Farms
Cows, goats, sheep, horses,
rabbits, and chickens
Get lost in our 5-acre corn maze!
M–F, 10–3
Adults $3, Youth $1, Children under 5 are free
Ask about our special birthday packages!

There's a large red barn set on the back of the property, surrounded by fields of corn. Connie can see a white farmhouse, too, another large building, and a grain bin. A couple of wind turbines are spinning behind the farmhouse. There are a few cars parked in the dirt lot, but otherwise it seems pretty empty.

Connie unscrews the cap to her bottle of orange juice and takes a sip. She's hungry, but she all she has is a granola bar. Rayna's farm is south of Avalon, and if Connie keeps driving she'll head straight into the open prairies of Illinois. She should have packed more food before leaving Avalon, but she didn't know where she was going, and she certainly didn't expect to end up here.

It's a big place, probably sixty acres, maybe more. Connie knows she won't be able to drive in without being seen, and she's too far away to see any of the animals, much less Serena.

She closes her eyes. Connie's not foolhardy, but this is perhaps the most foolish thing she's ever done in her life. And yet she can't bring herself to drive away.

There's a rap on her window. Connie opens her eyes and sees an elderly man beaming at her, his skin tanned and wrinkled from the sun, a worn baseball hat in hand. She sees a tractor parked across the road. "You lost?" he asks.

Connie rolls down her window and tries to smooth her hair—she knows she must look like a mess. "I'm taking a break," she says. "Just passing through."

"We still got lots of pumpkins," he tells her. "You can pick your own. And we had a bumper crop of beets and parsnips so those are on special today."

Connie tries to smile. "That sounds great," she says politely.

"Terrific!" the man says. "Follow me in!"

"What? Oh no, I mean it's great that you—" but the man is already heading back across the street to his tractor. He gives Connie a wave with his hat before fitting it back on his head and climbing into the seat. "This way!" he hollers. The tractor kicks on with a rumble.

Connie doesn't know what to do. The sensible thing would be to start the car and drive away. But as she sees the man give her another friendly wave she thinks, *What have I got to lose?* She would do anything to see Serena again, if only for a moment. This might be her only chance.

The man on the tractor pulls into the parking lot, then cuts the engine and jumps down. He's a spry guy who has to be in his seventies at least, and Connie can't help but think of Madeline. She's glad that Hannah is with her and helping out at the tea salon, because the thought of Madeline alone is more than Connie can bear. She feels better knowing that Hannah and Madeline will have each other, but she hadn't counted on missing Madeline so much. She even misses Hannah, who's shown her more kindness than Connie's ever offered in return.

She looks toward the barn where there's a hand-painted sign, VISIT OUR BARNYARD! Serena must be in there.

"We sell some nice jams, too," the man is saying. "Want me to walk you in?" He nods to the large building adjacent to the barn.

"Um, I was thinking about visiting the barnyard first," Connie says. A family with small children emerges and Connie knows it must seem like a strange request. "Your sign says you have goats?"

"Sure do," the man says. "I'm headed that way myself. So where are you from?"

Connie feels a seize of panic. "Oh, all over," she says. "Like I said, I'm just passing through."

The man nods. "Here we are." They step inside the barn.

Connie blinks. There's the strong musty smell of animals and hay, of the wooden barn itself. Pens are lined up against the wall and in the center of the barn, where a handful of children are playing with rabbits or holding baby chicks. There's a horse and cow, three sheep, and a couple of goats, neither of which are Serena. Something about this feels familiar, as if she's walked into this barn before.

Connie feels faint, and for a second she wonders if maybe she did steal Serena, and didn't even know it. Could it be? It's a wild, errant thought but how else would Connie know this place?

She looks around. There's a wooden ladder leading up to a loft, a rope dangling from the ceiling. Straight ahead is the exit to the barn, a large window above the door with a stained-glass image that's casting refracted color light onto the hay.

"Is that an eight-point star?" she asks, her voice hollow in disbelief.

"How did you know?" The man is delighted. "Yep, that's our family crest. We have several quilts in our family with that same star. And flanking the star on both sides are . . ."

"Violets," she finishes for him weakly. Illinois' state flower. How she knows this, she has no idea.

"Most people think they're mini purple stars," he says, surprised. "And I can see that—they don't look like violets to me, either." He looks at Connie. "Have you been here before?"

"Yes, I mean no, I mean, I don't know." Connie feels herself beginning to sweat. "Are there more goats, sir?"

"We have a bunch in the pasture, but these LaManchas are my favorites. A good breed, very agreeable." He jerks a thumb toward the door. "Got some Pygmies outside if you want a picture. Got some Nubians, too, that will give you a run for your money."

Connie feels ill. She has to get out of here. She starts heading for the exit and feels relief when she steps into daylight.

There's a young boy standing in the clearing in between two Pygmy goats as his parents snap a picture.

Suddenly, Connie remembers.

"Did you used to have Boer goats?" she asks. "Years ago?"

The man chuckles. "We've had every kind of goat over the years," he says. He pauses to think for a moment. "But yeah, we used to have a small herd, maybe about ten or twelve years ago. Why?"

Connie looks around, feels a well of emotion.

"Because I think I came here a long time ago. With my mother. It was the first time I'd ever seen a goat up close."

The man reaches out and clasps Connie's hand. His hands are worn and calloused but Connie feels comforted by his touch.

"This is a special place," he says, and he gives her a kind smile. "It's why we're all still here."

"WHAT'S SHE DOING HERE?!"

They turn and see Rayna Doherty bearing down on them. Her hair is tied up in a red bandanna and she's wearing an apron over a flannel dress printed with daisies, garden boots on her feet.

"I'm showing this young lady around," the man says pleasantly.

"Dad, *this* is the person who stole Daffodil!" Rayna exclaims. She glares at Connie.

"I figured as much," the man says. He turns to Connie and holds out a hand. "Jay Doherty."

Connie shakes his hand. "Connie Colls. How . . . how did you know it was me?"

"Your picture was in the paper," he says. "Though you're much prettier in real life."

Connie blushes. Rayna looks incensed. *"Dad,"* she says.

"Oh, Rayna. She sent a check and a very nice note. And I don't think she did it." Mr. Doherty turns to face Connie. "Do you want to see Daffodil?"

"Oh, no, she is NOT going anywhere near

Daffodil," Rayna says, reaching into her apron and pulling out a cellphone. "I'm calling the police!"

Jay Doherty looks disappointed. "Now, Rayna," he begins.

Rayna ignores him. "Hello, Officer Daniels?" she says importantly. "It's Rayna Doherty. Yes, I have . . . what? Who?" Rayna glances at Connie then turns away, cupping the phone closer to her mouth. "They did? When? Oh. No, right. Okay . . . okay. Thank you." She presses a button on her phone and drops it back into her apron pocket. She straightens up and clears her throat.

"Rayna?" her father arches an eyebrow. "Everything all right?"

"Apparently four high school boys came forward and turned themselves in. They said they took Daffodil as part of a prank but she got loose. They didn't report it because they didn't want to get in trouble." Rayna pretends to smooth the front of her apron, her cheeks scarlet.

"Boys will be boys," Mr. Doherty says. "Foolish idiots."

"So, um, I'm sorry," Rayna mumbles to Connie, who's looking at them both in disbelief. Then Rayna looks up, annoyance still etched on her face. "Even though you should have tried to return her earlier—"

"Oh, Rayna, stop it," her father orders. "You're a grown woman and you're acting like a schoolkid. Connie here took good care of Daffodil, and I daresay she got just as attached to that damned animal as you did. Can you blame her?"

Rayna sniffs and looks away.

Jay Doherty smiles at Connie. "Well, we have your check in the house. I'll go get it so we can tear it up."

"Please don't." Connie takes a breath. "I sent you that check because I wanted to make sure Serena, I mean Daffodil, is taken care of. I still want that. It would make me feel good to know that I can contribute to her care."

"*We* can take care of her," Rayna says. "And those boys are the ones who can pay for all the property damage."

Connie looks at Mr. Doherty. "I know I have no right to ask this, but I'd appreciate it if you would let me pay for everything on their behalf. Please. I know what they did was stupid, but they're kids and they came forward even though they knew they could have gotten away with it. I'd like you not to press charges."

Rayna and her father exchange a look. "But why?" Rayna finally asks. "Why would you do that for them?"

Connie shoves her hands into the pockets of her jeans. "Because I have people who would do that for me."

"We'll figure something out," Mr. Doherty

promises. "If you agree to put that money back into your bank account. Deal?"

There's an unmistakable bleat. Connie turns and sees Serena in the pasture running toward her. Jay Doherty grins and goes to unlock the paddock.

"Have your reunion," he tells her. "And then come join us in the house for some apple pie."

"You have fifteen minutes," Chief Garza tells them.

"Okay," Isabel says. She takes Bettie by the elbow and leads her into the blackened remains of her house. Bettie doesn't resist, but looks around, incredulous.

"This is my house?" she asks. "It doesn't look like my house."

"There was a fire," Isabel reminds her. Isabel and Bettie are wearing rubber boots and Isabel runs the toe of her boot through a pile of ash. "Almost a week ago. They're letting us do a walk-through to see if there's anything we can salvage. But I don't think we're going to find much. I'm sorry."

"The walls are gone," Bettie murmurs. She looks up at a large hole through the roof that the firemen had to cut as they were putting out the fire. It's a cool but clear October day, the smell of smoke still lingering in the air. Bettie gazes up at the sky until Isabel gently tugs on her arm.

Bettie's home insurer came and walked Isabel and Bettie through what would need to be done. An inventory, first and foremost. But, he told them, it could be six to nine months before anything would be settled. They'll cover a hotel, but Bettie can't be alone. Several people have volunteered to take Bettie in but after what happened with the McGuires, Isabel is wary. Dr. Richard told her it would be stressful for Bettie to move from house to house, so Isabel is going to let Bettie stay with her until she can figure out what to do next.

Isabel feels something under her foot and bends down to pick up a rhinestone buckle buried in the ashes. "Look," she says to Bettie. She blows on it gently then rubs it with her finger. There are two rows of glittering rhinestones encircling the buckle. It's flecked with soot but otherwise in perfect condition.

"I was looking for that," Bettie says. "I haven't seen that since 1979. I used to wear it with my scarves." She holds it in her hand, then slips it into her pocket.

They find other small things—a few pieces from Bettie's silver collection, a spotted rooster porcelain pill box, a glass Pyrex measuring cup. Everything else seems to have disintegrated, only leaving a shell of a house, blackened appliances, piles of unrecognizable cinder everywhere.

"Well," Bettie says, straightening up and

looking around. "Well." Her eyes are blinking away tears.

There are bits of clothing, dishes, and furniture that were tossed onto the lawn by firemen doing what they could to save Bettie's things, but so much of it is stained by smoke and fire. Still, Isabel and Bettie's neighbors have agreed to try to save whatever they can and let Bettie decide later what to keep and what to let go.

As the fire chief escorts them out of the charred remains, Isabel sees a familiar procession. It's the children from the neighborhood pulling their red Radio Flyer wagons, accompanied by their parents. Wooden boxes are stacked in each wagon.

"We made these with some of the leftover boards from the clubhouse," the red-haired boy says, pointing. "They're sifting boxes, to help you find things. They have a mesh bottom so dirt and stuff can fall through and you can see if there's anything you want to keep. It's like panning for gold!" He gives them a toothy grin and Isabel wants to hug him.

"I'm Lauren Eammons," a woman says to Bettie, giving her a kind smile. She touches her son's shoulders. "And this is Jacob. We live down the street, Bettie, and have been your neighbors for the past six years."

Bettie stares at them for a moment and then points at Jacob accusingly. "Hey, I know you," she says. "You busted my window!"

"That was two years ago," he protests, shrinking behind his mother. "I'm better now. I even pitch for my Little League team." His chin juts out.

"Have I seen any of your games?" Bettie asks. She squints, trying to remember.

"I don't know."

"Then that makes two of us," Bettie says. She taps the side of her head comically, making Jacob grin. "I'll come to the next one," she promises him. "I gotta work on squeezing more memories into the old noodle."

As Jacob and Bettie talk baseball, Lauren Eammons turns to Isabel.

"We already have several garages filled with donated items for Bettie," she tells Isabel. "Come by anytime to see if there's anything she'd like."

"I know she'd appreciate that," Isabel says. "Thank you, Lauren."

Lauren glances over to Isabel's house, at the FOR SALE sign. "We'll sure miss you in the neighborhood, Isabel. I heard you sold your house."

Isabel looks at her in surprise. "Not officially, but it looks like it'll be going through. How did you know?"

Lauren smiles. "Bettie. She told Gennifer Kelly who told Leigh Brewer who . . ."

Isabel nods. "Yep, got it. That sounds about right."

"Well, I'd better get back to work." Lauren smiles again and gives Isabel's arm a squeeze of support, of friendship. Isabel feels a tickle in her nose, like she's about to sneeze, or cry.

Their whole neighborhood is out, dressed in jeans and boots, and for the first time Isabel feels truly sad at the thought of leaving. These same people had reached out to her when Bill died, but she'd been too closed off to pay attention, to say yes and accept any help. She hasn't bothered to participate in any of the neighborhood block parties or send over a casserole when someone was sick. Even when Bill was alive Isabel was reticent to participate.

But now as she watches the fathers and mothers coordinate their children, talking to the firemen who are raking through the debris and making sure no more smoldering embers remain, she wishes she had made more of an effort to get to know these people. There are small groups dotted across Bettie's lawn, the sifting boxes between them, paper masks covering their mouths and noses as small clouds of dust rise and fall. A man stands over one of the sifting boxes, then crouches on his knees to lift something from the ashes. He's talking to a teenager, also masked. They look familiar somehow, and when the man pulls off his mask and gives Isabel a wave, she sees it's Ian Braemer and his son, Jeremy.

After a few more minutes it's clear that there's

nothing more they can do. They carefully make their way back out of the house and meet up with Chief Garza.

"I can't even remember what I had in that house," Bettie tells them. She looks displaced, a little lost. "But I don't know if it's because of the dementia, or just me. What do you think, Abe?"

Chief Garza puts an arm around Bettie's shoulders. "I think the things that matter most will make themselves known," he assures her. "Until then, take it one day at a time."

As Bettie and Isabel cross the yard to Isabel's house, Isabel sees a car parked against the curb. As before, Dan Frazier is standing outside the house while his fiancée, Nina, is sitting in the car, looking at something on her cellphone.

Isabel wants to kick herself. She had completely forgotten that they would be coming today and realizes that she hadn't even called to tell them about the fire.

"What happened?" Dan Frazier meets her halfway as she crosses the lawn. "Was anybody hurt?"

Isabel shakes her head. "Luckily, no. This is Bettie Shelton, my neighbor . . . I mean, your future neighbor. Bettie, this is Dan Frazier." Isabel turns to stare at Bettie's house. "We don't know yet if she'll be staying, if she'll rebuild or what will happen. We're still trying to sort

474

everything out, so she's staying with me for the time being."

Bettie doesn't say anything, just gapes at Dan, looking a bit starstruck as if he were someone famous.

"I should have called you," Isabel continues apologetically, but Dan shakes his head.

"No, that's all right," he says. "You obviously have your hands full. I'm glad you're all right," he tells Bettie.

Bettie has a goofy look on her face. "Oh, Phil," she says, and giggles.

Isabel and Dan exchange a look. "Uh, I put the new porch in," Isabel says quickly. "It looks nice. And you can walk through the house again if you like . . ."

"My name is *Dan,*" Dan repeats politely, not seeing Isabel cut her eyes at him. "Dan Frazier. And that's my fiancée, Nina—"

"What?!" Bettie suddenly looks cross. "Stop it, Phil. That's not funny." She scowls in Nina's direction.

"Bettie." Isabel places her hand on Bettie's arm. "They're interested in buying my house."

Bettie turns to look at her. "You're selling my house?"

"No, not your house. *My* house." Isabel points to her house.

"You want to sell my house?" Bettie says again, louder this time. Her voice has taken on a slightly hysterical peal, and a few heads turn their way.

Nina rolls down the window and calls out to Dan. "The Internet says it's ten to twenty percent, depending on the damage." Dan shakes his head, but Nina is insistent and holds up her phone, pointing to the display. "Sometimes up to thirty," she tells him. Her lips pucker.

Dan says, "Not now, Nina."

"Is everything okay?" Isabel asks, confused.

Dan sighs. "Sorry, Isabel. But when we drove up and saw what happened, Nina started doing some research on her cellphone and apparently house values typically drop after a fire in the neighborhood. But don't worry," he quickly adds, "I'm not looking to take advantage of the situation or anything. We still like the house."

"Dan . . ." Nina calls out again. Isabel is suddenly tempted to march back to the car and roll the window up herself.

Bettie clutches the front of Dan's shirt. "We need to talk about the baby, Phil." Her voice is low, urgent.

"What?" Dan looks startled.

"I've been trying to reach you." Bettie reaches out and grabs his hand, then brings it to her cheek and starts crying.

Isabel doesn't know what to do. Chief Garza is frowning as Dan looks at Isabel, bewildered. Bettie's face is streaked with tears.

"I think we made a mistake," she tells Dan, her

eyes wild. "I can keep her by myself. You don't have to worry about anything."

"Come now, Bettie," Chief Garza is saying, trying to disentangle Dan from her grasp. "Why don't we go inside for a bit?"

"Abe, Abe, you remember, don't you?" Bettie pleads. "Phil just forgot. But you remember, right?"

Chief Garza puts an arm around Bettie and steers her into the house. Isabel gives Dan an apologetic look as she hurries after them.

Once inside, Bettie bursts into tears. "Oh Phil," she sobs. Her eyes are red and her nose is running.

"How about a nap?" Isabel suggests. "Want to lie down for a bit?"

"I don't want to lie down," Bettie says, but she lets Isabel lead her to her bedroom. "Isabel, did I make a mistake?"

Isabel takes off Bettie's boots and slips her legs under the blankets. "A mistake about what?"

Bettie gazes up at the ceiling. "I shouldn't have let Phil give her away," she says sadly.

"Shhh," Isabel says, and a second later, Bettie's asleep.

Downstairs, Chief Garza is standing in the kitchen. He starts pacing, restless. "I called Imogene, my wife. She'll be here in a bit to sit with Bettie."

Isabel falls heavily into a chair. "She must be

hallucinating," she says, not sure what this could mean. Is Bettie going crazy?

"Isabel." Chief Garza pulls out a chair as well. "Now, I don't know much. But I think you should know what I know. It happened a long time ago."

"What?" Isabel asks.

Chief Garza sighs. "Phil Frazier was a buddy of mine. No relation to this young fellow—I think the last name must have triggered something in Bettie. An old memory."

"What kind of memory?" Isabel asks.

"I knew Phil in my army days, and sometimes he'd come to Avalon for a visit. For a short time, he and Bettie had something going on."

"Really?" Isabel can't picture what Bettie must have looked like when she was younger.

"We'd double date, me and Imogene, Phil and Bettie. Phil lived in Chicago but he liked the pace of Avalon—used to say he'd move here someday. I think that was Bettie's hope—it was certainly mine, he was a good friend—but it never happened. And then Phil stopped coming to Avalon altogether. It was kind of out of the blue, but he said he was busy with work and I didn't push him on it—we were all just starting out.

"I found out a couple months later that he got married. I was annoyed that he didn't tell me until after the fact—I didn't even get an invite to his wedding. I was about to propose to Imogene, you

478

see, and I was going to ask Phil to be my best man, to stand up for me. So to not even know about his wedding was kind of a blow."

He clears his throat. "Shortly after Bettie went on a trip somewhere. Imogene told me, and I didn't think much of it. I figured she was visiting family or something. She was gone about six months."

Isabel waits for more, but it doesn't come. Chief Garza is staring at his hands. "Where did she go?" she finally asks.

"Imogene can probably give you the details, but it was some place north of here. I think . . ." He looks unhappy. "I think it was a place for unwed mothers."

"Unwed mothers." Isabel stares at him as it dawns on her. "Bettie had a child?"

"I don't know what happened. Part of me didn't want to know, I guess, and Imogene has been good at keeping Bettie's confidence. But when I put it all together, it's obvious."

"Bettie had Phil's child," Isabel says slowly. Chief Garza gives a small nod.

"Yes, that's what I think."

"But where's the baby?" Isabel asks. "Bettie never said anything. What happened to the baby?"

"I have no idea," he says.

His wife, Imogene, bursts through the front door and finds them in the kitchen. "Where is she?" Imogene demands, and Isabel points to the second bedroom down the hall.

"She's sleeping . . ." Isabel starts to say, but Imogene has already disappeared.

"I have to get back outside," Chief Garza says. He pushes himself up from the table, drained. "I guess I kind of knew all along what had happened but didn't want to think about it." He exits, still shaking his head.

Isabel slips into Bettie's room. Imogene is sitting in a chair next to the bed, watching her friend sleep, her eyes sad.

"Poor Bettie," Imogene is murmuring.

"Imogene, what happened? Was there a baby?"

"A baby girl," Imogene confirms softly. "Bettie gave her up for adoption. Has regretted it ever since."

"But why?"

"Why?" Imogene's face pinks with indignation. "He was two-timing her. Two-timing both of them, I guess. But he made his choice, and it wasn't Bettie. He told her it would be better for everyone if she gave the baby up, and Bettie didn't want to bring any unhappiness to anyone. She didn't expect it to affect her as much as it did. By the time she wanted to change her mind, it was too late."

"Why didn't she get an . . ." Isabel's voice trails off.

"We didn't do that back then," Imogene says,

giving Isabel a sharp glance. "But even if she could have, Bettie wouldn't. She wanted to give that child a chance. She just didn't count on missing it so. It was a closed adoption, meaning that she wouldn't have any way of knowing where the baby was after it was placed for adoption. That was standard, too, at the time." She pats her friend's hand and pulls up the covers, tucking her in. "We haven't talked about it for years."

"But there are ways now," Isabel tells her, her mind racing. "You can sign up for registries, get blood tests . . ."

"Oh, Isabel, you young people think everything is so easy now." Imogene's voice is an annoyed hush. "Bettie isn't about to ruin somebody's life. She made her decision, and that was that."

Bettie stirs, but doesn't wake.

"I'll stay with her," Imogene says. "And I've spoken with Abe. We'd like to have Bettie come live with us. I can have the guest room set up by this weekend."

Isabel feels her chest tighten. She hovers by the door. "Thank you, Imogene, but I'm still looking at several options for her. I'd rather not change things until we know for sure what's going to happen—"

"I took care of my mother when she had Alzheimer's, Isabel. I know what it's like to care for someone with this condition. Do you?" Imogene looks at her pointedly.

"Well, no, but . . ."

"It's a lot of work," Imogene says briskly. "I'll have to hire a caregiver to help, but we should be able to manage fine. I know she has some savings and insurance."

"Okay, but . . ."

"Isabel, you've been absolutely wonderful to Bettie these past few days. But that's all it is—a few days. Bettie needs a long-term-care plan. You're still young, you have a job, you might want to settle down again. It's very hard to do any of those things if you also have to care for someone like Bettie. Abe works but I'm retired, and frankly I could use the company. Nobody keeps me on my toes like Bettie." Imogene looks back at her friend affectionately. Bettie's snoring delicately now, the worry lines no longer creasing her forehead.

Isabel quickly ducks out of the room, not trusting herself to say anything in Imogene's company.

In the kitchen she feels herself bubbling over with indignation. Imogene doesn't know her, doesn't know what Isabel can or cannot do. Even in the short few days Bettie has been here, they've developed an easy rhythm that's not perfectly seamless, but it works. Isabel knows from her talks with Dr. Richard that this could change at any moment, but for now Bettie is comfortable here. Why would they want to change that?

Angrily, she punches in the numbers for Yvonne's cell. She's steaming. When Yvonne picks up the phone, Isabel starts talking right away, her voice low so Imogene can't hear her.

"Hold on," Yvonne says when Isabel finally pauses to catch a breath. "Isabel, hold on. Nothing's happened yet, so take it easy."

"You take it easy," Isabel retorts. Then she feels foolish, like a six-year-old. "Sorry. But she assumed I wouldn't be able to take care of Bettie, you know? She doesn't even know me! I mean, we've gotten along great these past few days. She knows this house better than her own!"

"But Isabel, how can you take care of Bettie? You're about to sell your house—you said they're paying cash so if you go through with it, your house could close within a month. And then what?"

"She could stay with us," Isabel says, her mind racing. "At your house. I'll take care of everything, Yvonne. I know what she likes, what she's familiar with . . ."

Yvonne interrupts her. "Isabel, I like Bettie, you know I do. But my house definitely isn't set up for someone with dementia. I have a lot of stairs, the hallways are narrow . . ."

"Then I'll figure something else out," Isabel insists. "Bettie *knows* me, Yvonne. I can take care of her."

"Isabel, this isn't about you," Yvonne says

gently. "It's about Bettie, about what's best for her. Everything Imogene said is true. Are you sure you want to take on that responsibility, even if you could? It's a lot for any friend to take on."

Isabel sits down at her table, looks at the whiteboard with Bettie's daily schedule, color coded and marked with different activities, people, and phone numbers. A small glass vase filled with pink colchicums from Bettie's back-yard adds a burst of color and cheer to Isabel's otherwise plain kitchen. On the counter are three containers filled with Bettie's medi-cation and vitamins.

"There's always an adrenaline rush whenever there's a crisis," Yvonne continues. "People want to help—it feels good to help. But once everything settles down, can you see yourself putting Bettie to bed every night? Helping her go to the bathroom? Bathing her? Even if you get help, those are the sorts of things you'll be doing. If not now, then someday soon."

"So you're saying I shouldn't do it." Isabel feels dejected, discouraged. She finally wants to do something for someone else, and she's shot down.

"I'm saying you should think about it carefully, that's all. A year from today, can you see yourself with Bettie watching TV in the living room? Just take a moment, Isabel. What do you see?"

Isabel closes her eyes, takes a deep breath. Fast-forward one year, carving pumpkins for the porch, readying the candy for the trick-or-treaters. She tilts her head, listening to her future. And unlike the past few years, what she sees—and hears—is far from an empty house.

Ava walks into the Avalon Grill, the sounds of forks and knives on china greeting her. Everything looks the same since the last time she was here, over five years ago. The dark mahogany tables, the slightly cracked garnet leather booths, the large oil landscape of Leaf River, the river that runs adjacent to Avalon. The waiters and waitresses are dressed in black slacks and white shirts. Ava recognizes the manager, a nice guy who used to greet Bill by name.

It's a good-sized lunch crowd. Soups, steaks, salads, French fries, onion rings. People are talking and laughing. Everything smells so wonderful it makes Ava's stomach rumble. She can't remember the last time she had a meal out, much less anything other than macaroni and cheese.

She spots Colin behind the bar, drying glasses. His face is a bit rounder, more relaxed, and he seems happy. Ava can tell that things are going well for him, and the manager, Arnold, gives him a friendly nod as he passes by. A few customers are sitting at the bar, and she watches as Colin talks with them, joking and laughing. He looks good.

What is she doing here? Maybe she'll come back some other day, when it's less crowded and she has a little more courage. She's about to walk out the door when she hears Colin call her name.

"Hey, Ava!" he says in surprise.

Busted, Ava turns around and gives a weak wave. "Hi, Colin."

"I was wondering if you'd ever stop by," he says. "I'm up to my ears in bottle caps!"

Ava nods. "I meant to come by earlier, but . . ."

"Don't go," he instructs, as if she might suddenly disappear. "I need to go to the back to grab them. Hold on?" He gives her a hopeful look and Ava nods.

He disappears behind the double doors and a moment later returns with a large burlap bag. Ava can't believe it. "Is that full of bottle caps?" she asks, amazed.

He nods. "I've been collecting them since I saw you last," he tells her. "And I asked some of my bartender friends to save theirs, too."

Ava steps forward to reach inside. There are easily thousands of bottle caps. "I'm making some money from my jewelry now," she tells him, "so I can start to pay you. Do you want to charge me per cap, or maybe by weight . . ." She suddenly frowns as she looks at the bag, wondering if she'll have enough money to pay for it.

"Ava, it's not a big deal," Colin says. "You're recycling them. They'd end up in a landfill otherwise. It's great, what you're doing."

"But I'd feel better if you let me pay for them," Ava insists. She begins to open her purse but Colin shakes his head.

"I don't want your money," he says. "And technically they're not even my bottle caps—they came from drinks that belonged to the restaurant. So you might even get me into trouble if you gave me money for them because I'd be accepting payment for something I don't technically have a right to sell." The look on his face is serious but she sees the twinkle in his eye.

Ava laughs and closes her purse, impressed. "Wow, I'm not even sure how to counter that."

"Good. Don't." There's the sound of a bell from the kitchen. "Excuse me—I'll be right back."

Ava scoops out a handful of caps, her mind filling with possibilities. She'll be able to take on more ambitious projects like belts and purses. The caps are all clean and in wonderful condition. She turns one over in her hand. It's cork-lined with "Diet Sun Drop Cola" stamped on the top. She frowns as she studies it, but she can tell right away that it's an antique. There's no way Colin or his friends removed this from a bottle of Diet Sun Drop Cola, because they don't make it anymore. She looks through the bag again. Most of the bottle caps are current but she finds another one, an old root beer cap that's in mint condition. It confirms what she's suspected all along, that Colin's been secretly adding to the collection.

Colin reemerges from the kitchen holding a steak salad. He places it on the bar and hands Ava a cloth napkin and silverware. "Here you go."

"But I didn't order this," Ava says, confused.

"I know," Colin says. "I ordered it for you. You look like you could eat a horse, Ava." A thought crosses his mind. "You're not a vegetarian, are you?"

"No." Ava can't stop staring at the salad. The steak is cooked medium rare and resting on a bed of fresh salad greens. There's fresh corn, bell peppers, and blue cheese. A small ramekin of salad dressing is tucked on the side.

"Go ahead and sit down," Colin says, filling a glass with ice and lemonade. "Lunch is on the house. Well, it's on me. They give me a generous friends-and-family discount and I don't use it as much as I should. It'd be like I wasn't supporting the place where I worked, so you're actually doing me a favor. I'd hate to offend them." He places the lemonade on the bar next to Ava's salad and grins.

She hesitates, still not sure what to do. So much is unclear in her life right now. Does she want to complicate things by inviting Colin into her life?

Colin starts to wipe down the bar even though

Ava doesn't see a crumb anywhere. "So can you stay?" he asks. "Or do you have to go?"

Ava looks into his eyes, at his kind face. The root beer cap is still in her hand and she gently rubs it between her fingers, memorizing each groove, thinking about the history in this simple item—where it's been, how it found its way to Colin, what she might make with it. For the first time she doesn't bother to look around, to see who might see her, might recognize her, might judge her. She doesn't need to think about this anymore.

"I'm staying," she says, and slides onto the stool with a smile.

Chapter Twenty

Connie pulls into Madeline's driveway, a smile on her face, so happy to see everything as if she'd been gone for months or years instead of a handful of days. She hadn't expected she'd be coming back and it feels so good to be here.

Home.

She cuts the engine and steps outside, gives a stretch. It's just past four and the street is quiet and cool. Connie pulls her jacket around her and goes to pop open the trunk of her car.

"Hey, there, missy," comes a gruff voice. Connie turns and sees Walter Lassiter crossing the yard toward her, a thick manila envelope in hand.

Connie stiffens. "Serena's no longer here, Mr. Lassiter, so you don't have to worry about her anymore."

He casts a look toward the backyard. "Yeah, no kidding. I can finally sleep nights."

Connie grits her teeth and reaches for her bags.

"So, anyway, this is for you." He thrusts the manila envelope at Connie.

Confused, Connie lifts the flap and reaches inside. She pulls out a stack of photographs and gasps.

It's pictures of Serena. Connie and Madeline are in some of them as well but Serena is clearly the focus of attention. There are close-ups, long shots, everything. There's one enlarged that shows Serena's face full of mischievous intent. "What are these?" she asks, bewildered. There are over a hundred pictures, chronicling Serena's arrival up until the day she left.

"I was taking pictures to file along with my complaint," he says. "But, seeing how your goat's gone, that won't be necessary. I was going to throw these out but with all this business with Bettie Shelton and so on . . . well, I thought you might like them instead." He clears his throat. "I put a DVD in there with the original files, in case you want to print out different sizes or something."

Connie clutches the envelope to her chest, her eyes shining with tears. Walter Lassiter's eyes grow wide in alarm.

"Oh, no," he says, backing away.

Connie laughs and springs forward to give Walter Lassiter a kiss on the cheek before he can escape. "Thank you, Mr. Lassiter, I'll treasure these forever."

He looks startled, then embarrassed. "No need to make a big deal, missy," he says, his ears red. "They're just pictures. And before I forget, you'd better tell your customers to stop parking in my driveway!" He hurries back toward his house.

"I will!" she promises, but his only response is a slam of the door.

Connie quickly gathers her things and walks through the front door, dropping her bags in the foyer. "I'm back," she calls out, when she's suddenly caught up in an embrace.

"Don't you ever leave again!" Madeline scolds as she gives Connie a tight squeeze. She steps back, her eyes wet. "That was the longest week of my life! I told myself I need to let you find your own way, but I've changed my mind. I'm going to be a selfish old lady and tell you that I need you. This is your home and you can't ever leave again, is that clear?" She looks Connie up and down, as if looking for any bruises or broken parts. "Are you all right?"

"Yes," Connie says, laughing, her own eyes still wet. "I'm more than all right."

Hannah emerges from the kitchen, wiping her hands on a dishtowel. She grins when she sees Connie. "I told you she'd come back, Madeline. Just like she promised."

"I haven't slept a wink since she's been gone, I was so worried." She grips Connie's arm as if Connie might slip away again.

"Madeline . . ." Connie begins, guilty, but Madeline waves the thought away.

"I was fine," she amends. "Just missing you terribly."

"I missed you, too," Connie says, and gives Madeline another hug. She steps forward and smiles at Hannah. "And you." She riffles through

492

one of her bags until she finds a brown paper bag and gives it to Hannah. "It's strawberry jam, some corn relish, and a cherry marmalade from Doherty Farms."

"Doherty Farms?" Madeline looks surprised as Connie hands her a bag as well.

"That's where I've been the past few days," Connie explains. "They invited me to stay with them at the farm. After they found out I didn't do it, I mean. Rayna wasn't too happy to see me at first."

"Sergeant Overby called us right away," Madeline says. "And you can imagine how upset I was that I had no way of reaching you to tell you the news." She ushers them into the dining room. "We are going to get you a cellphone, Connie Colls. I never thought much of all this technology until I realized I couldn't find you. We'll include it as part of your salary."

"That's not necessary," Connie protests, but Madeline shakes her head firmly and Connie knows better than to argue with her.

"I'm going to make us some tea. In the meantime, sit down and tell me everything. Whatever possessed you to go to the Dohertys'?"

Connie drops into a chair, happy to be back in the kitchen with all its familiar sights and smells. "I kinda ended up there. I wasn't planning on it, but I wanted to see Serena one last time. I met Mr. Doherty, and then we heard that some boys had come forward and admitted to taking Serena."

Hannah sighs. "Jamie's youngest brother Peter was part of that group of boys," she says, the disappointment clear in her voice. "They planned to unleash her in the football coach's office. She escaped before they could do anything and of course they didn't say anything because they were scared they'd get into trouble."

Madeline shakes her head. "This reminds me of what Ben, my stepson, was like when he was growing up. Steven was always quick to bail him out whenever he got into trouble, which was a lot. But in the end I don't think Ben was better for it. In fact, I know he wasn't."

"Sandra Linde and her husband feel the same way," Hannah says. "As does the school. The boys got kicked off the football team, which is huge because it's a championship year. Some of the other parents are complaining about it but the Lindes aren't going to let Peter go back on the team even if the school changes its position. They're adamant about Peter taking responsibility for this. It's not just about Serena, but about not having come forward sooner."

"To think they might have let the blame rest with Connie," Madeline sighs. "Thank goodness they had enough sense to admit the truth."

"Well, Peter, at least," Hannah says wryly.

Connie nods. "He and another boy came to the Dohertys' farm this morning," she says. "Right before I left. They volunteered to spend their weekends up at the farm until the end of the school year, helping with odd jobs around the property."

"I heard about that," Hannah says, nodding. "Peter's mom is still pretty upset, but I think she's quietly proud that Peter has stepped up, though I doubt she'll say anything for a long time. Apparently some of the other kids, like the instigator, are fighting to get back on the football team. Seeing the way Spit and his family are conducting themselves has been a real eye-opener for Peter. I think that friendship may be over, which quite honestly isn't a bad thing."

"It would have been easy to let everyone keep blaming me and go on as if nothing had happened," Connie says. "But I'm glad they came forward."

"I couldn't agree more," Madeline says with a smile.

"And I am selfishly glad you're home," Hannah tells Connie. "I don't know how you and Madeline do it, but I'm pooped. I think I'll stick to teaching music and joining you in the kitchen every now and then, but there's no way I could do this full-time. Oh, and one of the ladies from the scrapbooking society called and wants your recipe for . . ." Hannah frowns as she tries to remember. ". . . Mountain Dew Apple Dumplings. Is that right?"

Connie grins. "Yep."

"Are they easy to make?"

"Very."

Hannah nods. "Well, I want the recipe, too. On top of spending every weekend at the farm, Peter's grounded on weekdays, too. This recipe might be just the thing."

"I can help you make them for him," Connie offers.

"Oh, I'm not going to make them for him," Hannah snorts. "I'm going to have Peter make them for his family. It's going to take a lot for him to get back in their good graces. If he learns how to cook, he might be a little more helpful around the house and Sandra might be inclined to forgive him a little sooner."

The women laugh. Connie looks at the thick manila file next to her. "If it's all right, Madeline, I'd like a couple more days off. I know I've been gone, but there are still a few things I'd like to get done if I could."

"I've been thinking the same thing," Madeline says. "I've checked the calendar and we don't have any big meetings or gatherings so I say we close for the week. We both need a break."

Madeline sounds so determined and Connie wants to laugh—it's as if they've made some big decision instead of merely giving themselves some much-deserved time off.

"I want you to relax and unpack," Madeline

continues. "For good. I want you to make the room yours, Connie, for as long as you want to be here. Find furniture that you like, paint the walls, it doesn't matter to me. The only thing that matters to me is that you're happy and you feel at home."

Home. There it is, that word again. Connie runs her hand along the grain of the table, a small smile on her lips. "Thank you, Madeline," she says. "Maybe I'll do something different in the future, but for now I'm happy with how everything is. Instead I want to do something I've been putting off for way too long."

Both Hannah and Madeline look at her, curious. "What?" Hannah asks.

No more hiding her suitcase under the bed, for starters. Connie is going to unpack everything this time, including the pictures she's carried with her all this time. "My scrapbook."

It's early Monday morning and Isabel is walking the perimeter of her house, a notebook in hand, when she hears a honk from the street.

"Hey, Isabel!" Ian Braemer pulls up to the curb, then leans over and rolls down the passenger-side window. "I guess a congratulations is in order."

Isabel gives him a puzzled look. She walks over to his truck.

Oh, he looks good. Nice smile, rugged features, laughing eyes. He's wearing a barn jacket, flannel work shirt, and jeans. She shivers in her coat even though she's comfortably warm. "Hi, Ian. Congratulations for what?"

"You sold your house! Sign's gone." He nods to the empty space on her lawn. It's only been a few days but so much has happened that Isabel almost forgot the sign used to be there.

"I didn't sell the house," she tells him. "I called the buyers and told them it was off. They weren't the right people to be living here after all."

There's an expression on Ian's face that she can't quite read. "Oh," he says. "Are you going to put it back on the market?"

She shakes her head. "I've decided to keep it. I'm going to stay in Avalon."

Ian's face breaks into a grin and Isabel finds herself smiling even though she doesn't know why.

"What's so funny?" she asks.

"What? Nothing." He quickly composes himself and Isabel laughs as he dons a serious expression. "Nothing whatsoever. It's a good day, that's all."

Isabel laughs. "So what are you doing here? Are you checking up on me?" She's kidding, of course, but Ian suddenly looks embarrassed.

"No, no," he says hastily. "I have a job down the street getting Josie McGowan's exterior ready for winter."

"Josie McGowan?" This catches her off guard.

"Yeah, I met her when we were sifting through all the ash last week. Met a lot of nice folks—you have a great neighborhood here." Ian nods down the street.

Isabel's nose wrinkles as she follows his gaze down the street. Josie McGowan? Josie with her pouffy hair and short skirts, her dominatrix black leather stiletto boots? Josie McGowan is the other single woman on the street, not widowed like Isabel, but divorced. Twice. And she's a smoker, too. She doesn't seem like Ian's type at all.

Ian frowns. "Did I say something wrong?"

Isabel turns her attention back to him. "What? No, why?"

"Because you have this look on your face like you smelled something bad." He pretends to sniff his underarms. "Nope, not me. Fresh as a daisy."

Isabel laughs. "Sorry. Just . . . so, um, what kind of work will you be doing for Josie?"

"Just your basic winterizing of the house," he says. He starts ticking items off on his fingers. "Put garden hoses away, clean the gutters, blow out the sprinkler system, and so on. But Josie wants to make sure her driveway and walkways are cleaned and sealed. Most concrete and masonry surfaces have a hard time with the freeze and thaw cycles so her driveway is cracked in places. Throwing on salt and other ice-melting chemicals can make it worse."

"I never knew that," Isabel says. Then she adds quickly, "I should probably have you look over here, too."

Ian glances at her driveway. "Actually, you're in pretty good shape," he says. He leans on the steering wheel. "I noticed that before when I was working on the porch."

Isabel clears her throat. "Well, better safe than sorry," she says. "I haven't given the house much attention until now, and it's probably suffered as a result. Now that I'm staying, I should make sure everything's okay."

Ian shrugs. "Sure, but I don't think you have anything to worry about." He points to her roof. "Though you might need to get those gutters cleaned sometime soon."

Isabel had noticed that, too. "I've been meaning to get someone to work on them," she says. "Is that something you could do, too? How much would it cost for everything?"

Ian's cellphone starts to ring. He checks the number. "Oops, looks like I'm a few minutes late to Josie's house." He presses a button and lifts the phone to his ear. "Hi, Josie. Yes, I'm heading over right now. Just giving Isabel a couple of tips about her house . . . yes, of course I'll do the same for you. Okay. See you in five." He hangs up with an apologetic look on his face. "Sorry. Duty calls. Tell you what. I'm committed to Josie's during the week, but I'll swing by on Saturday and start in on those gutters. We'll play the rest by ear. Eight a.m. sound good?"

"Yes." Isabel feels giddy at the thought of seeing him again, wonders what other projects she can throw his way. "Oh, and I promise not to greet you in my pajamas."

Ian feigns disappointment. "Maybe I'll knock on your door an hour earlier then."

"Don't you dare!" she says, her cheeks flushing with pleasure. She already knows what she'll wear: jeans and a tangerine V-neck sweater that's been calling her name this past week. She'd pulled it out of her closet, her white clothes stark and bland against this unexpected burst of color. It was then that she started thinking that maybe Yvonne was right, that it was time to put away her all-white wardrobe, but not because it's way past Labor Day, but because Isabel is ready for a little more color in her life.

He grins. "Okay, okay. Eight it is. Oh, and you never did tell me how you like your coffee." His phone starts buzzing again but he presses a button to make it stop, his eyes still on Isabel.

"Black," she says. "With two sugars."

He taps the side of his head. "Black, two sugars. Got it." He gives her a wave as his phone starts buzzing once again. He ignores it. "See you on Saturday, Isabel. And if you decide to open the door in your pajamas, I won't complain."

Forever Family, Frances types into her keyboard. She looks at the computer display and, satisfied, hits ENTER.

It takes a second, and then suddenly there it is: the family photo taken last Christmas, her and Reed on the couch, the boys scrunched up around them, looking goofy for the camera. Mei Ling's picture appears in the corner with FOREVER FAMILY scrolling across the frame. Frances grins, proud.

Frances had been following the adoption blogs of other families, admiring the level of detail and information, grateful that people were so forthcoming about their adoption experiences. At first she didn't understand how people had time to write or blog about their life, much less post pictures and provide links to other resources and like-minded websites, until she realized that keeping a family blog was what kept them sane. Chronicling daily life before, during, and after the adoption seemed to help to make the hard days bearable and the good days a celebration. Frances also figures it's a great way for grandparents and friends to check in and see pictures of the kids whenever they want. Her secret hope is that over time Nick, Noah, Brady, and Mei Ling will write their own posts and journal entries, too. Maybe even Reed.

The best part is that at the end of the year she's

going to figure out a way to print everything into a book and bind it. She'll do it annually, create a Latham family yearbook of sorts, and she'll make enough copies for everyone. Frances enjoys making special scrapbooking albums but she wants to find a way to chronicle everyday life in a way that's easy to manage without stacks of photos everywhere. She especially loves the idea that the kids will have these growing up and can take them with them when they start their own families. After all, isn't that what memory keeping is all about?

In the sidebar, Frances types in the addresses to the adoption blogs that have given her the most support, especially the other families who have children with congenital disorders like Mei Ling. Right now Reed and Frances have no choice but to go by the medical report, which is insufficient in so many ways, but they won't know the full extent of Mei Ling's condition until she's here with them. Frances already has spoken with pediatric cardiologists at Rush University Medical Center in Chicago and at the University of Illinois. She even found a pediatric cardiology practice in Rockford that has worked with many adopted children with heart issues. Cincinnati's Children's Hospital also has extensive pediatric services, and it's a comfort to know these resources are so close and available to them.

The biggest challenge, Frances knows, is that

both diagnosis and treatment have been delayed for so long that issues that might have been addressed or resolved earlier are now intensified and more severe. Emboldened by their decision to go through with the adoption, they pushed for more information, for every scrap of detail. They got reports of how Mei Ling would sweat whenever she was being fed and was more tired than other children. Like many other adopted children, Mei Ling is smaller than other children her age and has that awful "failure to thrive" label. Frances tries not to get upset at the thought of Mei Ling's heart working so hard just to keep her alive.

But one look at her picture, at Mei Ling's smiling face, and Frances knows this child has a spirit that matches her own. She plans to do anything and everything in her power to give Mei Ling a shot at living a full and happy life, just as she would any of her children.

This next year will be filled with doctor's appointments as they try to assess the true nature of Mei Ling's health and medical needs. What they know (or think they know) is that Mei Ling has ventricular septal defect, or VSD. Simply put, there's a hole in the wall of her heart and she'll need open-heart surgery shortly after her arrival. Frances also knows that there may be other medical problems that weren't disclosed in the report or that may crop up later. But how is that different from anything else in life? There is no crystal ball, no money-back guarantee.

Frances decides to keep her growing to-do list on the blog as well. She's done her best to research what to bring and not to bring on their trip, and their adoption agency has been immeasurably helpful in getting them prepared. Still, Frances likes hearing from other families who've been on the ground and especially those traveling with children because she and Reed have decided that they're all going to get Mei Ling, even three-year-old Brady. As expensive as it is, it's precious and important for so many reasons. As much as they want Mei Ling to become a part of their life here in Avalon, they want to become a part of her life and heritage in China, too.

Frances plugs in her camera and uploads the pictures from the other day. She and the boys made fried rice and broccoli with oyster sauce, both of which were easier than she expected. Reed was able to join them and found a simple recipe for a cold sesame cucumber salad, which he made by himself. They ate everything in less than ten minutes. Frances knows it's a far cry from authentic Chinese cuisine, but it's a start. She decides to include the recipes alongside the photos.

Her oven timer dings, telling her that the thirty minutes she set aside for the blog is now up. Time to move on to other chores, like packing. Because as soon as they get the green light, the Lathams are going to China.

"No, no, no!"

It's a steady cry, a wail even. Ava clutches her purse and debates ringing the bell, but then Isabel's front door opens and Bettie stumbles out, still dressed in her nightgown even though it's mid-morning.

"No no no no no no no no no no," she's saying. A second later Isabel and a woman Ava doesn't recognize appear behind her. "I said no!"

"Is everything all right?" Ava asks.

"Does everything look all right?" Isabel looks exasperated. She turns to the other woman. "Imogene, I told you to let me tell her!"

Isabel tries to corral Bettie back into the house. Bettie breaks free and starts pacing the porch, distraught.

"Bettie, dear, think of the fun we'll have!" Imogene coos, her voice forced gaiety. "Abe has set up your room with a view of the backyard and we can plant flowers come spring. We'll watch all our favorite shows in the afternoon, play a little bunco with the ladies, host a few scrapbooking crops at the house. Whatever you want."

"No," Bettie moans.

Ava can tell that Isabel is agitated, but Isabel seems to rein it in as she puts a gentle arm around

Bettie's shoulder. "You'll have such a good time," she assures Bettie. "And I'll come visit whenever you want."

"But I want to stay here," Bettie pouts. "In *my* house."

Isabel leads Bettie to the porch railing and points to Bettie's lot. "Your house burned down, remember? We're trying to figure out what to do, but Imogene and Abe want you to live with them until then. She's got your room all ready. And she has lots of scrapbooking supplies, I hear."

"Oh, yes," Imogene is nodding. "Society members were quite generous, Bettie, and Abe let me convert our den into a crafting room. It's a scrapbooker's dream, you'll love it, I promise." She gives her friend's hand a pat, and it seems to calm her down.

"Well," Bettie sniffs. "All right." She turns to Ava, noticing her for the first time. She brightens, no longer distraught, and Ava wonders if Bettie even remembers the past few minutes. "Ava! Where's Matt?"

"*Max* is in preschool," Ava says gently. At the mention of her son's name, Ava notices that Isabel frowns. "Though I'm sure he'd love to be here."

"He is such a cutie pie," Bettie says. "And those glasses!" She guffaws. The Bettie of thirty seconds ago is no longer, and in its place is the Bettie Ava first met in Margot's shop two months ago.

"Come on, in you go," Isabel says, ushering Bettie back inside.

Ava has the funny feeling that she's imposing, and quickly digs into her purse and brings out a small pouch.

"I wanted to drop this off," Ava says, handing it to Isabel. "I found it in one of the boxes you gave me, but I don't know what it's for. I figured it fell in there by accident. I didn't want you to worry in case you couldn't find it."

Isabel stops to open the pouch, and a small key falls into her hand. She doesn't seem to recognize it.

"I've never seen this before," Isabel says, turning it over in her palm. She frowns, thinking.

Bettie peers around Isabel, nodding. "Hey, I have one of those," she says. "For my safe-deposit box at the bank."

"You have a safe-deposit box?" Isabel turns to look at her. "You never told me that!"

Bettie shrugs. "I forgot. Not that any of us should be surprised by that."

Isabel turns and heads to the kitchen, the other women in tow. "That's right," she says, remembering. "Yvonne and I found a key under that stone angel on your porch when we were trying to get in your house. I can call Charlotte Snyder at Avalon State Bank and see if she has any record of your box. If she does, I'm sure we'll be able to get them to open it." Isabel's suddenly excited.

"And yours, too," Ava adds. "I mean, maybe they can open your box, too, now that you have the key."

Isabel unfurls her palm and stares at the key again.

"But it's not mine," she says. "Bill and I never had a safe-deposit box. Are you sure it was in one of the boxes I gave you?"

Ava nods. "Positive. We—I—never had a safe-deposit box, either." Ava's face pales when she realizes what this could mean.

Did Bill keep secrets from Ava, too?

The key falls from Isabel's palm onto the table. Isabel glances at Ava. "No offense, but if he has another family stashed away somewhere, I might lose it. Just so you've been warned."

Ava gulps, nodding, but at the same time knows there has to be a logical explanation. There has to be. She can see Isabel building up a head of steam and doesn't want to be there when it blows. "Well, I should go," she says. "I have to pick up Max from preschool. And I also wanted to let you know that—" She stops when she sees the sudden grimace on Isabel's face. "What?" she asks.

"What what?" Isabel says, immediately changing her expression.

"You have this look on your face, like you . . . disapprove or something."

Isabel shakes her head. "Nope, just thinking

about this whole key thing." Her nose twitches like she's about to sneeze.

Ava can tell Isabel has something to say, but she's not so sure she wants to hear it. "Isabel?" she asks warily. "Say whatever it is you want to say." She'd rather know than not know, and this may be her last chance. "Tell me."

"Okay, fine." Isabel looks up at her. "I don't think that preschool is the right place for him. He doesn't seem happy there at all. I don't know how you can stand here, chatting away, while he's . . . *there*." Isabel's cheeks redden, and she looks down and starts doodling on the page again, her lips tight.

Ava feels like she's been slapped. "He likes his school," she says, but her voice wavers, giving herself away.

"I don't think so," Isabel says. It's not her words but the tone in her voice that says it all. That Ava is a bad parent. That Ava doesn't know what's best for her son. That Ava would be willing to compromise his happiness or well-being because she can't afford to do better. Ava feels herself tremble in anger, not because Isabel is wrong, but because Isabel might be right.

"You don't know," she says to Isabel, her teeth clenched. "You have no idea about me or my life, and you don't have any right to comment about Max. You are not his parent—*I* am. *Me*. And I'm doing the best I can, Isabel. Do you think I like having him there? Do you think I didn't try to have him home with me? Don't you think I wish I had more money to send him to someplace nice, where they actually care about him?"

"Plenty of places offer financial aid . . ." Isabel begins.

"Oh, right! Why didn't I think of that?" Ava pretends to knock the side of her head. She glares at Isabel. "When I said I was hoping you'd be a part of Max's life, I didn't mean I wanted you to criticize it, too."

Isabel points her pen at Ava. "So let me get this straight: you sleep with my husband, have his child, expect me to be a part of his life, put me on your emergency call list . . ." Everything Isabel says is like a stab, making Ava cringe.

"Really?" Bettie breathes. "That's gutsy." She turns to Imogene, who looks equally enthralled.

Isabel raises her voice, her eyes on Ava. ". . . and after all that, I can't make one comment about where he goes to school?"

"Yes . . . no . . . I mean . . ." Ava suddenly feels confused. She wants Max to have a connection to Isabel, but she didn't think it would be like this. She was thinking more about shared reminiscences about Bill, stories, that sort of thing.

"Why are you still here, Ava?" Isabel demands. "That's what I don't understand. What do you want from me?"

Ava can feel everyone's eyes on her. She

511

straightens up, blinking rapidly, holds on to her purse strap for support. "Nothing. I don't want anything, Isabel."

Isabel looks down at the notebook, at the key resting on the table. "Well, then, I guess you should leave."

Bettie is looking between the women, not quite sure about what's happening. Ava can see that her eyes have gone slightly vacant, the confused look returning. "You're leaving?" Bettie asks, perplexed.

"I am," she tells Bettie. She turns to Isabel, who won't look her in the eye. "I came by to give you the key, and to tell you we're moving. We were evicted from our apartment, so Max and I have to be out by the end of the week. I came to say goodbye. And thanks. For everything." When Isabel doesn't say anything, Ava gives Bettie's hand one last squeeze and leaves.

Chapter Twenty-one

Charlotte Snyder, head teller of Avalon State Bank, greets Isabel and Bettie in the lobby.

"So exciting!" she exclaims, leading them to the back of the bank. "When I got your call, I wasn't sure what to think. Lost safe-deposit keys! It's like something out of a movie."

Isabel just feels weary. She's had to take more time off from work, much to the chagrin of her kid boss who's still managing to somehow keep KP Paper & Son afloat. She'd expected that he would complain, possibly even fire her, but instead he surprised her by saying she'd been given a raise. Apparently her sales numbers have been at an all-time high, something Isabel hadn't been paying much attention to. She credits this to not really caring about her job, which makes handling rejection all the more easy. She keeps at it until she gets a yes, and then keeps at it some more.

But keeping at it is starting to take its toll on Isabel. She's been running on caffeine and adrenaline since the fire, and it's finally caught up to her. Even with Bettie now living at Abe and Imogene's, Isabel still doesn't seem to have enough time to tie up all the loose ends. There are too many to count.

And now, this. Bettie's box, not to mention the

surprise safe-deposit box that was held in Bill's name. Isabel had to get a court order to get permission to open the box, and while it wasn't all that difficult, it just makes everything feel more serious, more formal. Whatever Bill was hiding, Isabel is about to find out.

"Hey, sorry I'm late." Yvonne comes up behind them and gives Isabel's arm a squeeze. "Have you opened the boxes yet?"

Isabel shakes her head. "I'm thinking maybe we should leave Bill's alone. There must have been a reason I didn't know about it, right? And I'm not so sure I want to find out what's inside."

"I sure hope I stashed some goodies away," Bettie tells Mrs. Snyder. "I could go for a nice surprise. Say, are you still serving free pastries?"

"Every day before ten," Mrs. Snyder titters. "Though we've replaced the doughnuts with Amish Friendship Bread. So delicious!"

Bettie turns to Isabel, eager. "What time is it?"

Isabel looks at Yvonne. She doesn't have the energy to even lift her wrist to look at her watch.

"It's ten," Yvonne confirms.

Bettie lets out a whoop. "Charlotte, I tell you, there is nothing sweeter than free Amish Friendship Bread."

"I couldn't agree more," Mrs. Snyder says, nodding her head fervently. "Today was my baking day, so I brought in chocolate-dipped

Amish Friendship Bread biscotti—it has a touch of coconut. Perfect with your morning coffee!"

"I can't stand Amish Friendship Bread," Isabel mutters, "but coffee?" Her tired eyes perk up.

"Try water," Yvonne says. "You could fuel a rocket with the amount of caffeine in your system." She turns to Mrs. Snyder. "So, what now?"

"Well, we have Bettie's box ready. And if you have your key"—she nods in Isabel's direction— "we can have yours brought out right after. Since you got that court order, the box is all yours. It's a shame you didn't know about it earlier."

"I don't think I could have handled it earlier," Isabel says. She turns to Yvonne. "I'm not even sure I can handle it now. Bill probably meant to give someone else power of attorney after the divorce was final. Ava, maybe. She should be here, not me."

"It doesn't matter," Yvonne tells her. "At this point you need to see what's inside. It could even be empty, Isabel, and all your worrying will be for nothing."

Empty? Isabel's not sure what's worse. Finding something she didn't know about or wondering what Bill had been planning to put inside.

"Enough chatter," Bettie declares excitedly. "I want to see what's in my box—I have no idea what's in there!"

Mrs. Snyder's face is washed in pity. "Because

of your . . . condition?" She whispers the last word like it's a secret.

Bettie gives her an exasperated look. "No, Charlotte. Short of having it deducted from my checking account once a year, I haven't bothered to touch it in almost fifteen years. I forgot I even had it."

Mrs. Snyder nods. "It's funny how people tend to forget what they have. Okay, have a seat and I'll be right back!"

Bettie and Yvonne sit down, but Isabel is pacing. Bettie is considering the possibilities, running through each one with Yvonne.

"What about gold bars? Wouldn't that be something? Or a wad of cash!"

"Diamonds," Yvonne adds. "Rubies from Madagascar."

Isabel gives her friend a look. This is definitely not helping. "Bettie, whatever is in your box is something that *you* put in. Did you have gold bars or a wad of cash?"

"No," Bettie says, her face falling for a moment. "But you never know, right? If my brain's no longer reliable, who knows what I might have done over the years?" She turns to Yvonne, her face bright once again. "Stock certificates! Lottery tickets!"

Isabel resumes her pacing. Regardless of whatever is in Bill's safe-deposit box, what's troubling Isabel the most is that she can no longer trust *what* she knows. She's starting to doubt her own memories about her life with Bill, because there is clearly so much that she didn't know about.

Ava, obviously. She hadn't seen that one coming but once it happened, she could see it for what it was—a series of chance and missteps, a fork in the road, his ultimate decision to choose one path over another. She knew her marriage had issues, and while she hadn't expected he would ever leave her, she knows why he did.

But this is different. It's deliberate, intentional, premeditated. Bill came to the bank, signed his name to the form, put money down for a box that neither she nor Ava knows anything about. He came here with the express intention of putting something into that box that he didn't want to keep at home.

So what is it?

Mrs. Snyder reappears with a long metal box. She slides it onto the table. "Here you go, Bettie. Buzz me when you're finished and then I can take you back to the vault, Isabel."

Isabel and Yvonne flank Bettie as she stares at the box. "It's bigger than I remember," Bettie says, fingering the numbered plate on the front. She takes a deep breath and pushes back the metal lid.

It's full of plastic bags, old magazines. Bettie pulls out a few Ziploc bags filled with documents folded in half. Isabel reaches for them, opens the first bag. The original deed to the house, the pink slip for her car, insurance papers, Bettie's birth certificate, social security card, medical records. Isabel's relieved to see them, because it makes a lot of things easier. She'll make copies as soon as she can.

"Wow," Yvonne breathes, and Isabel looks up to see her holding up a bundle of cash, mostly twenty- and hundred-dollar bills, also in a sealed Ziploc bag. "So you do have a wad of cash in there after all. It looks like there's a few thousand here, Bettie. Is this yours?"

"Yes," Bettie says, her voice hollow. She glances at it, uninterested. "Twenty thousand, I remember now. Proceeds from the first five years of my scrapbooking business."

"Why didn't you deposit it?" Isabel asks. She knows Bettie has both a savings and checking account at the bank, as well as an IRA.

"I did deposit some," Bettie says absently. "I was saving the rest for . . ." Her voice trails off as she pulls out a Ziploc from beneath the magazines. Inside is something soft and rectangular wrapped in white tissue. Fabric? A sweater? Bettie's face suddenly crumples.

Isabel slides into the chair next to her. Bettie's hands are shaking. "Do you want me to help open it?" she asks.

Bettie's eyes are wet. She shakes her head. "No.

I'll take it home with me." She clutches it to her chest. "I want to go now."

Isabel nods. She puts everything else into a bag and closes the lid of the empty safe-deposit box. They all stand up.

"Wait," Yvonne says. "What about Bill's box?"

Bettie's face is drawn and pale, and Isabel wants to get her back to Imogene's. "I'll do it later," she says, but Yvonne shakes her head.

"Do it now," she says firmly. "I'll take Bettie to the Garzas'. Call me later." Yvonne puts an arm around Bettie's shoulders and leads her out.

Isabel watches them leave, tempted to run after them. She'd been counting on having some company when she opened the box and hates that she has to do it by herself.

"How are we doing?" Mrs. Snyder enters the room and looks around in confusion. "Oh, did Bettie leave already?"

"She wanted to go home." Isabel holds out Bill's key. "So do I give this to you?"

"Oh, no, dear. You hold on to that. Follow me."

They walk into a small room filled from floor to ceiling with three walls of safe-deposit boxes. Mrs. Snyder lifts a ring of keys as she scans the wall. "Two-one-five, two-one-five . . . here it is." She motions for Isabel to step forward. "You put your key in there. I'll put the master here . . . and turn."

Isabel does as she's told and the small door

swings open. Mrs. Snyder briskly removes the long metal box inside and hands it to Isabel. They walk back to the small table outside.

"Usually when a safe-deposit box is dormant we turn it over to the state treasurer's office," Mrs. Snyder tells her. "But Mr. Kidd paid for it in advance, twenty-five years! You still have nine years to go, isn't that nice?"

Isabel counts back the years. That would have been right around the time they got married.

"Let me know when you're finished," Mrs. Snyder says, pointing to the small button on the wall. "Don't you run off on me, too!" She gives Isabel a wink and disappears.

Isabel slides into the chair and stares at the box. It's gunmetal gray, just like Bettie's, but smaller. She looks for a clue as to what might be inside, but there's nothing. It's a standard-issue safe-deposit box.

Isabel puts her hand on the cover and hesitates. The last person to open this box would have been Bill, his fingers in the same spot as hers. She wonders what he was thinking, if he knew that someday she would be the next person to touch this box. She suddenly feels anxious, unsure if she should look inside. After all, there must have been a reason that he didn't tell her about it.

She flips open the lid before she can give it a second thought.

At first she stares at the contents, blinking.

Yvonne was right—it's practically empty. There's a thin manila envelope and a small white envelope with Isabel's name written in Bill's unmistakable style.

She slowly reaches for the envelope, her mind spinning. An apology, maybe, or a belated confession? *Isabel, I want to explain what happened.* Or maybe a favor from the grave? *Isabel, I know you must be angry with me but there's something I need you to do.* Isabel turns over the possibilities in her mind, none of them quite convincing enough.

She finally turns the envelope over and breaks the seal. It's a card. Isabel pulls it out, stares at the simple drawing of two red intertwined hearts. Below it are the words, MY BELOVED WIFE.

This can't be right. Isabel feels almost light-headed as she opens the card. It's dated March 17, the year after they got married. Their first anniversary.

Dear Isabel,

Today is our first anniversary. Hard to believe that a year ago we exchanged rings and a promise to be together forever. I am so happy to be sharing my life with you, and I look forward to all the years to come.

So much has happened lately—our first home, the dental practice, the news of our first child on its way. I don't think there's anyone happier than me in this moment. I don't want to ever forget it. I'll admit the idea is not my own—I borrowed it from an article in *Reader's Digest*, about writing down the details of our first year together and putting it in a safe-deposit box to open on our 25th anniversary. It seems like a fitting way to make sure the small memories of the beginning of our life together don't escape us.

So here it is. I can't wait to see what the future holds. I love you.

Always,
Bill

Inside the manila envelope she finds a handful of pictures—waiting in line at the Ferris wheel at the county fair, large plates of spaghetti from the questionable Italian restaurant near Bill's dental college, the night he proposed, their wedding, their disastrous honeymoon in the Bahamas where they both got food poisoning. Standing in front of the house the day they bought it, Bill's hand resting proudly on the mailbox as Isabel stands next to him, laughing, tucked under his arm. A notarized copy of Bill and Randall's partnership papers, his first business card. A long list written by hand of what was happening in that year, the beat-up Honda they were driving, places they visited, their favorite foods and movies. A bar napkin with a short list of baby names they'd come up with when they found out Isabel was pregnant, two weeks prior to their anniversary. The miscarriage would happen five weeks later.

Isabel looks at the evidence of her early life with Bill, spread out in front of her like a show-and-tell project. She feels her eyes sting with tears and, at the same time, is shaking her head with a wry smile. Because this is exactly the kind of thing Bill would have done. A romantic gesture that would have been lost on Isabel because Isabel is the least romantic person in the world, but it would be just like Bill to do it anyway.

It's been so long since she's thought of him in this way. Her chest hurts, like the ache that comes with holding your breath for too long. To be able to think of him with fondness, with a smile on her face, to remember the good moments. When was the last time she could do this?

The pain catches her off guard, a sudden sting, a punch in the gut.

Bill, she thinks. He can hear her, she's sure of it. She glances around, then settles back in her chair.

"Bill," she says aloud. "If you're up there somewhere, watching me look through all this, well, I can't help but wonder if you forgot about this box. We were so young . . . I'm sure you didn't think it'd end up like this. I sure didn't."

She hesitates, then takes a deep breath. "So things are going okay for me. I've been fixing up the house, as you probably know. Bettie's house burned down, though, but she's okay. We've become friends, actually. I know, I know. To think she used to drive me crazy all these years. Turns out she's all right. More than all right. She's kind of become like family to me. I'm glad you helped her out as much as you did when you were alive.

"You know how you were always telling me to go out and meet new people? Well, I have a new friend, Yvonne. She's a plumber here in town. Really nice, very pretty, great teeth, gums to die for." Isabel smiles. It was a standing joke between her and Bill—while most men judged women by their bodies, Isabel would tease him that the first thing he looked at was their teeth. "Work is going okay, too. I keep thinking I'm going to leave, but I just heard from my boss that I'm going to get a raise. Did you know I haven't used a single vacation day since you died? I guess I should have taken one earlier—I seem to make more money that way." She shakes her head, gives a small smile.

"So I guess if you hadn't died you'd probably be married to Ava by now, maybe even have another kid." Isabel is silent for a while. "Max is cute, Bill. He looks like you. I gave him some things of yours that I found in the attic. Well, gave them to Ava. She's been hanging around a lot, but you probably knew that, too. It looks like they'll be moving. It's probably a good thing—the place they lived in was a dump, and Randall was a jerk to her so she can't get another job as a dental assistant. She does these bottle-cap things—necklaces and rings—they're pretty good but it's not enough. When you died all our money was tied up with the dental practice, and you know how that went. Randall bought out your share of the business, but it was such a paltry sum based on your partnership agreement. The lawyer explained it to me like you tried to a million times. Wish I'd listened better but I was too mad at the time.

"Ava's all right. Not that you're asking me for my approval or anything. I mean, I suppose if you're going to leave me for someone, you could have done worse than her. Lately it seems like I'm the one who's married to her. Did you see what she did when she put my name on her emergency call list? I had to go pick up Max from school! We had a fun time, though. I do wish he was at a better place. Ava and I kind of got into a fight about it. Not that it's any of my business."

Isabel picks up one of the pictures. Their first Thanksgiving as a married couple, gathered round the large oak dining table at Bill's parents' house. Everything was too big—the table, the turkey, the amount of food. Edward and Lillian had teased them, saying that they were waiting for grandchildren to fill the table.

"Anyway . . ." She gestures to the things on the table. "I'm not sure what I'll do with it, but it's nice to have it. I threw out a lot of things when you left, I was pretty angry. But I'm not angry anymore, and I'm glad to have them. So thanks." She glances up at the ceiling, unsure if she should say anything else. "And um, take care."

Isabel is gathering everything together when Mrs. Snyder pokes her head in. "Everything all right?" she asks, eyebrows knit in confusion. Her eyes look around the room. "I thought I heard you talking to someone in here."

"It's just me," Isabel says. She stands up. "I'm finished here. Thanks for all of your help." Her arms are full but she suddenly feels lighter.

"That's what we're here for," Mrs. Snyder says, still looking around the room. She gives Isabel one more perplexed look. "Are you sure there wasn't anyone here with you?"

Isabel pauses for a moment, feels a shimmer of electricity that tickles her arm. "No," she says honestly, but before Mrs. Snyder can ask any more questions Isabel steers them out the door. "You know, I think I'll take some of that Amish Friendship Bread after all."

"Connie, there's someone here to see you!" Madeline calls from the bottom of the stairs. A

526

familiar bleat fills the tea salon followed by the sound of running footsteps. "Serena, goodness, give that back!"

Serena? Connie quickly finishes trimming a photo with her new paper cutter and hurries to the door. She throws it open and runs down the stairs, her face bursting into joy when she sees Serena run past, a dishtowel in her mouth, her nails skittering on the hardwood floor. Connie lets out a whistle and Serena skids to a stop, the dishtowel falling out of her mouth as she does an about face and trots toward Connie.

Connie already has her arms around Serena's neck when Madeline appears behind her, slightly out of breath.

"I swear, that goat knows this house better than me," Madeline says. "She had us going every which way."

"Us?" Connie says. She looks up and sees Eli Ballard hurry into the room, a relieved look on his face. She almost doesn't recognize him without his white lab coat.

"What are you doing here?" Connie asks, not sure if she's referring to Eli or Serena.

"Supervised visitation," Eli says with a wink. "Jay Doherty came into town to run some errands and brought her with him. Asked if I could babysit Serena for a couple of hours so I thought I'd bring her by."

At the mention of Jay Doherty's name, Connie

smiles. Connie's grandparents had all died when she was young, and Connie thinks that was one reason why her father's death was so hard on her mother. Connie doesn't have a memory of them at all, but if it were up to her, she'd have a grandfather like Jay Doherty.

"Don't you have patients to attend to?" Connie asks, straightening up. Serena leans hard against her legs, happy, and Connie scratches her under her chin.

"This is technically my lunch hour and I am allowed to eat," he says. "But why is the CLOSED sign up?"

Madeline smiles. "It's just for the week," she says. "We're closed for inventory." She exchanges a smile with Connie. They've both been working on their scrapbooks, getting some much needed rest, and enjoying their quiet days together. It's also given them a chance to talk about the tea salon, about setting some new goals for the next year. Connie still wants Madeline to think about selling her tea blends online. Another stream of revenue might mean that they won't have to feel as much pressure about the tea salon doing well all the time. This time off is giving them a chance to talk about all that, and they both agree that closing the salon more often is a good idea. The tea salon is Madeline's labor of love, but it's no fun if they're laboring all of the time.

Eli looks disappointed. "Just my luck. The one

day I choose not to bring in a sandwich . . ."

"We still have to eat," Connie says quickly. "And I've got to feed this girl, too, don't I, Serena? I got a nice green salad waiting for you!" Connie sits down on the bottom step and wraps her arms around Serena, giving her a big hug.

"Okay, then," Eli says. "Then I'll have what she's having." He turns beet red when both Connie and Madeline turn to look at him with their eyebrows raised. "I meant the salad."

"Oh dear, I think that's the phone," Madeline says suddenly, disappearing even though Connie didn't hear the phone ring.

"Thanks for bringing her over," Connie says. With Madeline out of sight, she lets go of the leash and lets Serena sniff and wander.

"Boy, it's like you're asking for trouble," Eli says. He goes to pull the two side parlor doors closed. "This place is like one big playground for her. Goats like to get into everything."

"Serena's a good girl," Connie says loyally. "She listens to me."

Eli nods but continues to grunt as he works the heavy pocket doors. "Someone needs to add oil to these rollers," he says.

"That someone has heard you and will add that to her list," Connie says with a grin.

"It's just the two of you?" Eli asks. He manages to get the doors closed and satisfied that Serena won't be running amuck, flops onto an over-stuffed Victorian parlor armchair.

Serena looks up the stairs, curious, and Connie shakes her head. "Don't even think about it," she tells the goat. She turns back to Eli. "Yes, but we have a lot of friends around." Connie likes how that sounds.

"I mean, is there a boyfriend, fiancé, husband? Anyone available to help you out? For, um, either one of you?"

Connie hides a smile and decides to be direct. "Eli, are you interested in asking me out, or Madeline?"

Serena wanders over to Eli and gives him a sniff.

"You," he says, his ears turning red.

"I'd love to," she says honestly. "But are you sure you want to go out with a girl who hangs with goats?"

"Connie," he says, arching an eyebrow. "You seem to be forgetting that I'm a vet."

"Good point." She rescues the new supply of business cards from Serena's mouth and Eli takes them from her, replacing them onto the table. They grin at each other, and Connie feels butter-flies in her stomach, suddenly self-conscious. "So I guess we're on then."

"I hope so."

Serena is looking restless so Connie stands up. "I know that look. I'd better get her outside before I end up having to scrub out the rug."

Eli stands up, too. "I'll go with you." He reaches the door before Connie and holds it open, and Serena is the first to exit. If Connie didn't know better, she was sure she saw Serena wink at her as she passed by.

Frances sorts through the remaining squares on Mei Ling's One Hundred Good Wishes quilt. She'd love to have it done before they go, but if not, it won't be the end of the world. After watching the pandemonium that erupted after Peter Linde admitted to the goat-napping, Frances realized that all she wants is for her family to be together, to learn how to help each other out.

She'd watched as Sandra stared at Peter in disbelief, and then anger. His brother Jamie was livid; Hannah was horrified, since Connie was a friend. Frances had held her breath, scared for Peter while wanting to shake him at the same time.

Then Sandra got on the phone with her husband and they agreed to go to the police station. As Frances watched them pile into the car, grim but together, she realized that she didn't care about all of the things she'd bought for Mei Ling or whether or not Nick was going to let her sew him a Halloween costume. She didn't care about the size of their house or whether or not they had enough money for a family vacation. As long as they're together, be it through good times or bad, is all that matters to Frances.

She went home with a renewed sense of clarity. Some clever rearranging of furniture, a purging of things they no longer needed, and suddenly there was enough room for everyone.

Now she lays a few squares next to each other, thinking, when the doorbell rings. When she answers, she's surprised to see it's Bettie Shelton.

"Bettie!" she exclaims.

"I only have a few minutes," Bettie announces. "Got my babysitter waiting in the car outside." She turns and gives Isabel Kidd a wave.

"Would you like to come in?" Frances asks.

Bettie shakes her head. "I'm paying a visit to all Society members, to let them know that I'm okay. Of course, things get spotty for me sometimes but I'm still me and I'm available to help you with any of your projects, at least while I can."

"Thank you," Frances says gratefully. "I think I'm hooked for life. I've already made several albums for my boys and I just mailed another small album to Mei Ling in China. I want her memories of us to start now—she's already a big part of our life, and she's not even here yet. It's a huge comfort to me to know that she has these pictures of us, these images of our family and our home in Avalon. *Her* family, *her* home."

"Yes," Bettie says. "She's a lucky girl."

"We're the lucky ones," Frances says, and she means it.

Bettie stands on the porch for a moment longer, lingering. "October is one of my favorite months," she tells Frances. "I love the smells, you know? The end of autumn, the onset of winter. Leaves, crackling fires. Of course, I hadn't expected I'd be getting a lungful of smoke with the fire at my house. I meant the kind that's contained in a fireplace, but what can you do."

"I was so sorry to hear about your house," Frances says gently.

"Everything is gone," Bettie says with a look of amazement on her face, as if she were recounting someone else's bad news. "My life went up in smoke, literally. Except for a few things in a safe-deposit box at the bank. I'd completely forgotten about it. We got the manager to drill the box open, and it turns out I was smarter than I realized. Had copies of all my important documents and a few other important things in there." Her eyes seem to be misting and she blinks rapidly.

Frances nods, making a note to talk to Reed. They don't have a safe-deposit box but she definitely wants to get one now.

Bettie pulls a small square of pink felted wool from her pocket. "I wanted to give you my square for your quilt," she says quietly. "It's from a baby blanket I've had for a long time. It's very special to me and it makes me feel good knowing that it'll be with a baby girl who'll be in a family who loves her."

Frances takes the square from her. It's soft and thick, and she presses it against her cheek. "It's lovely, Bettie. Thank you."

Bettie doesn't answer right away, suddenly squinting as if the sun's too bright. "Well, I should go," she finally says. "I'm working my way through the membership list and I want to finish up before dinner."

Frances nods. "Of course." She waves as Bettie makes her way down the walk and climbs into the waiting car.

She closes the door, pressing the square against her chest, can picture Mei Ling running her fingers along the different textures of her quilt, lingering on this simple, pale piece. Frances imagines Mei Ling tucked in with the quilt at night, a reminder of all the people who love her and who waited for her arrival.

"Mom." Brady suddenly appears at her side, clutching a toy pilot in one hand and a toy stewardess in the other. "Play with me."

"Not now, Brady," Frances says, wanting to get back to Mei Ling's quilt.

"*Now,*" Brady intones, a hint of whining in his voice. It's a new thing still, the two of them in the house during the day, though in a month that'll all change again. Frances reluctantly puts the new quilt square on top of the others and lets Brady drag her into the hallway. "Look!"

He's pointing to the dollhouse in Mei Ling's room. Frances sees that he's brought in all his cars and trucks, his trains and mini people, the wooden trees and animals. In fact, it seems as if he's dumped his entire toy box onto the floor.

"Brady!" Frances scolds, dropping to one knee so she can start picking things up. "This is Mei Ling's room—you can play in your room."

"Play here," Brady insists, patting the play carpet. He puts the airplane pilot into the living room of the doll house. The stewardess follows. Within minutes the house is crammed with little toy people and animals.

"No, Brady," Frances begins, about to pluck everything out, when she realizes that Brady is playing with the doll house. Not just playing, but creating scenes—people watching pretend television, their faces pointed to the screen. People gathered around the dining room table, eating a meal. Three ponies are hanging out in the attic. A fireman is lying in the master bed, an astronaut is standing in front of the bathroom mirror. Lego people are playing outside with a small rubber ball between them and a giraffe is standing next to a girl holding a balloon. "Oh, Brady, this is wonderful!"

Brady stops for a moment to beam. "I know! Thanks, Mom!"

Frances sweeps the stray pieces aside and settles down on the carpet. In the small nursery a stewardess stands over a crib with a panda bear inside.

Her breath catches. "Brady," she says gently. "Did you know that pandas are from China? See your panda in the crib? It reminds me of Mei Ling."

Brady stops for a moment to study the panda in the crib. He frowns. "No, Mom," he says with a shake of the head.

"No, what?"

"Mei Ling isn't a panda. She's a girl!" he crows.

Frances smiles. "You're right about that, Brady."

Nick and Noah appear in the doorway. "We're home," Nick announces, dropping his backpack on the floor. "Can we get a snack? Hey, what're you doing?"

Frances beams. "Brady's playing with the dollhouse."

Brady is lining up cars in a row in front of the house. "Look, car wash!" he says.

Noah sits down next to him and reaches for a handful of airplanes. "Gotta wash these, too," he says.

"Yeah!"

Nick peers into the house. "That's cool, Brady."

Brady nods to the nursery. "That's a panda," he says. "From Chiner. Like Mei Ling. Except she's not a panda. She's a girl."

"And our sister," Nick adds. He picks up a few stray items that have fallen to the wayside and sets them up in the house, then begins to rearrange the fake trees and hedges.

"Sister," Noah agrees as he brings a helicopter in for a landing.

"Sister," Brady repeats, then pretends to wash the vehicles. "Pssshaw!"

Frances leans back against a dresser, watches her three boys playing together, a smile on her lips. It's a small thing, this new word that will soon become a part of their everyday vocabulary, and for all the months it's taken her to get her family to this point, it suddenly feels moot. Brady's acknowledgment of a sister, of whether or not they'll be able to handle the challenges ahead, or even if they're challenges at all. Being in her mind these past few months hasn't done her much good, just created more anxiety and doubt if anything. But being in her heart is something else altogether.

Frances feels the same heightened awareness as she did when she was expecting each of her boys, the rush of adrenaline that comes as the "delivery date" grows nearer. It's the difference between thinking something and knowing it. And right now she knows it's all perfect—her, sitting on the floor of Mei Ling's room, and her children talking and playing around her. She doesn't have to think about it—she knows it feels good. It *is* good. If she stops the chatter in her mind and lets herself feel, this is exactly where she wants to be. Period.

She knows this is a moment like any other, one that can change in a second if Nick gets a phone call from a friend or if Brady has to go to the bathroom. It's a snapshot in time, just one of many, and Frances knows there are still many more to come.

Frances gets that she doesn't have to have it all figured out. That she doesn't need to try and predict the future, which is impossible anyway. She needs to be here, present and observing, participating if she wants to but above all, appreciating what she has.

Chapter Twenty-two

Ava's short hair is tucked into a tie-dyed bandanna as she drags a box full of junk to the landing from their apartment. She's accumulated several boxes and trash bags already, feeling lighter each time she dumps a new load by the railing. Ava can see her neighbors peeking out from behind their ragged curtains, ready to pick through her discards once she turns her back. Well, more power to them.

The good thing about not owning a lot is that it makes packing and moving all the easier. A few of Max's favorite things, that's all they'll need. Wherever they end up they'll be able to get more, but for now everything has to fit into the Jeep.

The interim plan for all intents and purposes was the plan of last resort. Ava had finally broken down and called her parents, who didn't seem surprised to hear from her but didn't exactly sound excited, either. It was a humbling call, one Ava had hoped never to make, but she's trying to tell herself that it's not all that bad. It'll be good for Max to see her parents, to get to know her family though she's praying they treat him with kindness. Praying because she knows it would be just like them to make a jab at Ava or even Bill, to cut her down in front of her own son in a misguided attempt to make them face the "realities" of life. But maybe things are different now. Maybe enough time has passed that they'll be different, too.

Ava notices Max's Shrinky Dinks mobile hanging by the doorway and carefully begins to take it down. The string is tangled and dirty, the bright colors having faded to a bland monotone. She tries to untangle it but everything is knotted and worn, the mobile having taken a beating outdoors. She finally gives up and yanks the whole thing down before tossing it into the trash. There'll be other Shrinky Dinks in their life, she tries to console herself, but even she's not so sure she believes it anymore.

Who is Ava kidding? As much as she'd like to think otherwise, people don't really change. Her parents, Dr. Strombauer, Isabel Kidd. Maybe that's been Ava's problem all along—she's been holding out for the impossible, for things to be different, for people to be different. Was she being hopeful or just naïve? Neither, she decides. She was just plain stupid.

"Mama," Max calls from inside the apartment. He appears in the kitchen holding a plastic pumpkin as if ready to go trick-or-treating. "Look what I did." He holds up the pumpkin proudly.

Ava sees that he's taken a few of her bottle caps and taped them onto the pumpkin. Two for the eyes, one for a nose, five for a mouth. The mouth is crooked so the pumpkin looks like he's grimacing rather than smiling. The tape peels back from the plastic and one of the eyes slips off.

On any other day Max's effort would bring a smile to her face, but instead she feels more like crying. Ava kneels down and quickly gathers him in her arms so he can't see the tears filling her eyes, threatening to spill over. Ava knows that if she lets that happen, it's all over.

"Hey," comes a voice from behind her.

Max is the first to react. He squirms out of Ava's arms. "Auntie Isabel!"

Ava stiffens, quickly wiping her eyes with the back of her hand. She doesn't bother to stand up right away.

"Hey, kiddo," she hears Isabel say. There's the sound of Max's laughter and suddenly Ava finds herself more irritated than upset.

"Max, go inside," she says when she turns around.

"But I don't want to," he protests. He edges closer to Isabel, which irritates Ava even more.

Ava picks up the plastic jack-o'-lantern and the stray bottle caps that have fallen off, drops them inside the jack-o'-lantern, and then jams the whole thing into the large trash bag. Max doesn't even notice; he's too busy gazing up at Isabel like she's some kind of superstar. Ava looks at the plastic pumpkin rolling around among the trash, is tempted to pluck it out for a moment, but doesn't. It won't be much of a Halloween this year anyway. Ava's parents have never been big on Halloween, and she doubts they'll let Max do much trick-or-treating if at all.

"Max," Isabel says, her voice more animated than Ava's ever heard. "I need to talk to your mom about some grown-up stuff. Can you run inside for a sec?"

"Are you going to see my room after?" he asks.

"Maybe," Isabel says, not looking at Ava. "Go on, okay?"

Max nods his head and shuffles into the house, looking at them forlornly.

"Go on," Ava says. "I'll be in soon." She closes the front door softly, then turns to look at Isabel, arms crossed. "What?"

"Okay, take it easy," Isabel says. "I didn't come here to fight."

"It doesn't matter why you're here," Ava says. "You won. I'm gone. You'll never be bothered by me again. Problem solved."

"Come on, Ava. Don't get all third grade on me. I know I was out of line with what I said about Max's preschool, and I'm sorry."

Ava studies her, unsure of Isabel's sincerity. When she sees that Isabel means it, she gives a reluctant nod. "You were totally out of line," she says.

"I just said I was," Isabel says. She leans against the railing and then jumps back when it wobbles precariously, sees the bolts loose in the cement.

"Before you say anything, yes, I know the railing isn't safe and yes, I know my landlord should fix it. In fact, he's right over there in unit A-5 if you want to take it up with him." Ava turns around and knots the top of the garbage bag.

"Very funny," Isabel says. "I thought I was about to fall to my death for a second there. That would be ironic, wouldn't it?"

Despite herself, Ava feels a smile tugging at the corners of her mouth. "Yes," she says. "It sure would be."

"And before you get any ideas about pushing me off yourself—which, okay, I might deserve—I'm here because I have a proposition for you and Max."

"A proposition?" Ava looks at her warily.

"A proposition," Isabel repeats. "I don't know if you know, but I took my house off the market. I won't be selling, and I won't be leaving Avalon after all. The truth is I thought that maybe Bettie would want to stay with me, but Abe and Imogene want her to move in with them and Dr. Richard thinks it's worth a try." Isabel's nose is wrinkling in a funny way, like she's about to sneeze. "Anyway, I suddenly have a house that's way too big for me. So I'm looking for renters. Housemates."

Ava stares at her. Is she serious? "You want me

to rent from you? Live with you?" Her voice rises to a squeaky pitch. "In Bill's old house?"

Isabel suddenly looks nervous. "Um, yes. Though I hadn't really thought of it like that, but yes."

Now Ava has to sit down. She opens the front door and walks inside, then remembers she sold all of their furniture. She leans against a wall and lets herself slide down until she's sitting on the box of Max's toys. "Is this a joke?"

"I know it's weird," Isabel says, coming in after her. "I know we don't even get along . . . yet. But here's the thing. I think Bill would like Max to be in that house. And you, too."

"What about you?"

"Well, yeah, me, too. It is my house, after all." Isabel looks snippy now but blows out her breath. "So it'll be the three of us. There's plenty of room and we won't get in each other's way. Max could even have his own room."

Ava lets out a wry laugh. "Us, living together," she snorts.

"It isn't the craziest thing in the world," Isabel says, a little offended.

"It's definitely the craziest thing in the world," Ava tells her, her voice taking on a slightly hysterical peal. "What would people think?"

Isabel looks at her. "Why do you even care?" she asks. "I personally don't think I give a damn anymore. I think the only people still thinking about it are you and me. And Bill, if you count him, but he's dead, so he doesn't really get a full vote."

Ava gives a sad shake of her head. "How do you do that?" she asks, her voice suddenly quiet. "How do you not miss him?"

Isabel stuffs her hands in her jacket. "I tell bad jokes to get through it," she says. "I stay mad and look for people to blame."

Ava looks away. "I miss him," she says. "But lately it's been feeling different, I don't know why." She looks back at Isabel, her face stricken. "I'm afraid I'm going to forget about him. And then Max won't know anything about his father at all."

"So move into the house." Isabel comes to stand next to her, then crouches down. "Let Max live where Bill lived. I can't shake the feeling that I'm supposed to stay in the house a little while longer, but not by myself. I thought it was about Bettie, but I see now it's you. And you are the one who said you wanted Max to get to know me," Isabel reminds her.

"Oh," Ava says, sniffing. "Great, blame me."

"It was your idea," Isabel points out, and there's a smile on her face. "Look Ava, it doesn't have to be a forever thing. Just a now thing. When you're ready to move on, move on. Unless you have someplace else you'd rather be."

Ava shakes her head. "I was going to stay with

my parents back in Montana," she says. "But to be honest, that's the last place I want to be."

"So it's settled," Isabel says. "I'm going to call Yvonne and have her come help us move." She pulls out her cellphone but Ava grasps her arm.

"Isabel," she says. "I can't pay you any rent. I don't have any money, I don't have a job . . ."

Isabel snaps her phone shut. "Oh, that," she says. "I ran into Oma Frank at the Pick and Save yesterday. She's Dr. Tindell's receptionist. Apparently Dr. Tindell's dental assistant is about to quit her job to go work for Dr. Marks over in Barrett. He's offering a generous compensation package that Dr. Tindell can't match, so she's leaving."

Ava's breath catches in her throat. She remembers Dr. Tindell, about how Bill wished he'd partnered with him instead of Randall.

"It's a small practice, as you know, and he's been keeping more of a part-time schedule. Both he and Oma will probably retire in the next five to ten years. So anyone coming on board should know that."

Ava nods her head, afraid to say anything in case it all disappears.

"It also means that whoever works for him would have some flexibility, which would let them, I don't know, spend more time with their son." Isabel can't help grinning. "And work on their bottle-cappy thingy."

A cloud comes over Ava's face. "But Dr. Strombauer . . . he won't give me a job recommendation. Dr. Tindell will be expecting one, don't you think?"

"Probably," Isabel concedes. "Which is why I'll be writing it for you."

Ava looks at her, not comprehending. "You?"

"Well, technically Bill's share of the dental practice was his and mine, at least on paper. I never had much interest, as you know, and that was probably part of the problem. So I'll write about my relationship to the practice and what I observed through Bill. Professionally, that is. Dr. Tindell knows what happened between you and Bill. But he also knows you were a good dental assistant. My guess is that if I, of all people, can vouch for you, you'll probably have a fair shot at being considered. Would you be interested if that were the case?"

Ava nods quickly, her eyes bright with tears. Happy ones.

Isabel's looking a bit weepy herself, but she straightens up and clears her throat. "So to recap, you and Max leave this"—she looks around distastefully—"place and move in with me. Check?" Isabel waits, then says impatiently, "This is where you say check back."

"Oh!" Ava wipes her eyes. "Yes! Check!"

"Next, you apply for that job with Dr. Tindell with a recommendation from me. Check?"

"Check!"

"And finally, you get Max enrolled in the Montessori preschool in Avalon, at least on the days when you're working. I'll help cover tuition until you're back on your feet—consider it part of the Bill Kidd Scholarship Fund. We can argue about this later. Check?"

"Check!" Ava stands up. "Isabel, I don't know how to thank you." She takes a step forward and is about to give Isabel a hug when she can see that Isabel's already embarrassed enough. "Okay, I'll save the hug for another time."

"We can work up to it," Isabel mumbles in agreement.

"I can't wait to tell Max," Ava begins, then stops. She turns to look back at Isabel. "Isabel, do you know why I wanted Max to know you? Why I felt it was important?"

Isabel shakes her head. "Aside from thinking you were a bit crazy, no, I have no idea."

"Because I knew that someday I would have to explain this all to him. Why his father and I weren't married when he was conceived, the circumstances under which we met. And if Max couldn't have Bill, I wanted—hoped—he could have or be a part of the things his father loved. Like you."

Isabel looks stunned. Her mouth opens and then closes.

For the first time since she and Isabel have met,

Ava is pleased to see that she's rendered Isabel speechless. "Yes, I'm talking about you."

Isabel's cheeks pink but she's quick to recover. "So I'm the next best thing?" she says, pretending to look offended, but she's grinning, too.

Ava laughs, feeling her spirits rise so high she wouldn't be surprised if she took flight. "Most definitely."

Yvonne picks up the phone, listens to the dial tone, then puts it down again. She does this two or three more times before finally punching in the number on the scrap of paper in her hand.

If anyone else was doing what Yvonne was about to do, Yvonne would have been a good friend and told them to let it go, to hang up the phone, to move on. That's why she didn't tell Isabel what she was doing. Yvonne doesn't want to be persuaded to let this go. She needs to know.

She holds her breath when the phone on the other end starts to ring. It takes several rings before someone finally picks up.

"Hello? Wait, hold on." The woman answering the phone sounds young. A baby is crying in the background and Yvonne hears the phone being muffled as the woman shouts, "Annabelle, can you check on your brother for me? Thanks."

Yvonne sinks down into the plush armchair. She should hang up. This is such a bad idea and she knows she's going to regret it later, but she can't bring herself to put the receiver back in the cradle. She's never let herself think about what his life might be like, never even considered other women. It's a little more reality than Yvonne is ready for, but still she can't hang up.

"Sorry," the woman says. "Hello?"

Yvonne clears her throat. "I'm calling for Sam Kenney. Is he available?"

"No, sorry. Would you like to leave a message?" There's a loud pop and Yvonne realizes the woman is chewing gum.

"That's all right," Yvonne says quickly. "When do you expect him back?"

"In about three hours. He and Mrs. Kenney went out for dinner. Hold on . . . Annabelle, did you check on Harry? Well, why not?"

It dawns on her that she's talking to the babysitter. Yvonne wants to laugh with relief, but at the same time, it's a small triumph. It's finally confirmed. There is definitely a Mrs. Kenney, and she's with him right now. And there are children.

"Who's calling?" the babysitter asks.

"Um, Census Bureau," Yvonne lies. "I'll try him later, thank you." She quickly hangs up, cheeks flaming.

What was she thinking, almost interrupting Sam's life like that? Yvonne shakes her head, then stares at the piece of paper with his number on it. Finding out that he lived in Bangor, Maine, was easy enough—Yvonne suspects he's the only

Samuel Anami Kenney out there in the world. His middle name was the result of a hospital clerical error—when his parents couldn't agree on a middle name, they told the hospital administration to write "NMI"—No Middle Name—on the form so they could be discharged. The clerk thought it was his name and wrote Anami, and they never bothered to change it.

"It could have been worse," Sam had joked. "She could have written Enema."

Yvonne smiles at the memory, and it's enough. She takes one last look at the piece of paper, then tears it up into small pieces. She goes to the bathroom and tosses the scraps into the toilet, and flushes.

As she watches the water swirl and carry the papers away, the phone rings. Yvonne's answering machine picks up and a second later she hears Isabel's voice wafting through the room, telling her the good news that Ava and Max have both said yes and could she please bring her truck? Like now?

Yvonne was quick to grab her keys, happy for the distraction.

"This is weird, isn't it?" Ava kept saying, more to herself than anyone as they lugged her things into Yvonne's truck and then later into Isabel's house.

"It gets weirder every time you say it's weird," Isabel had retorted. "So stop it."

That was pretty much when Yvonne knew they'd be all right.

When the bulk of the moving was done, Isabel, Ava, and Max headed back to Ava's apartment to give it a thorough scrub-down so Ava could get her security deposit back. Yvonne just wanted to take a hot shower and crawl into bed.

Her answering machine light is blinking when she walks in. Yvonne glances at it as she walks by, intent on getting into her pj's, when she sees the number of messages. 15. It's not for work, because all of those calls go to her cellphone, but people can find her just as easily in the book. She's about to hit the PLAY button when her phone suddenly rings, making her jump back. She reaches for the receiver.

"Hello?"

"Yvonne?"

At the sound of his voice, everything seems to stop. "Sam?"

"It is you," he says, and she feels a leap of joy. His voice is warm and reassuring, carrying a hint of amusement. "Yvonne Tate. So you work for the Census Bureau now?"

Oh God. There's no use in pretending. "I know, I'm sorry. I didn't want to . . . well, never mind. How did you know it was me?" she asks.

"Caller ID. I almost had a heart attack when I saw your name. I figured it couldn't be right, but it was. Is. I can't believe it's you, E."

E, her nickname. Yvonne closes her eyes, doesn't know if she can pretend that this conversation is like any other, that the person on the other end of the phone isn't someone she's loved, and lost. "Sam," she finally manages. "I didn't mean to call out of the blue—"

"But you did," he tells her. "Why?"

"I don't know."

"You don't know? You've disrupted me on the eve of middle life and you don't even know why? Am I supposed to pretend you never called?" He sounds upset.

"I'm sorry!" she bursts out. "I . . . I needed to . . ."

"Yvonne, take it easy," Sam says quickly with a laugh. "I was kidding. I'm just nervous and you know I mess around when I'm nervous. Some things never change, I guess." He sighs, then says, "It's great to hear from you. You sound exactly the same." His voice is softer now.

Her chest feels like it might cave in. She knows she should end it now, that she's gotten what she wanted. A chance to hear him say her name.

But she can't hang up, knowing that he's standing there, heart beating, on the other end of the line. It's almost more than she can bear. She wishes she could reach out and touch him, make sure it's really him, that this is really happening. "So how are you?" she asks. "What do you do?"

"My job, you mean?" Sam chuckles. "Nothing as glamorous as what you're doing, I'm sure. I'm a ranger with the National Park Service, stationed over at Acadia National Park."

"A man in uniform," Yvonne says, and smiles.

"That's me. I offer hikes, walks, boat cruises, talks, show the kids the peregrine falcons and raptors. I take my job very seriously." Even though it's been ten years, Yvonne can almost picture him leaning back, the phone tucked under his chin, arms crossed.

"You're a long way from the bogs," she says.

He laughs. "Six hours away," he says. "I didn't exactly put a whole lot of distance between us."

"It was enough," Yvonne says. There's a long, awkward pause.

"Can I see you?" Sam says. "If that's all right with you? I can come to wherever you are—is this area code Illinois?"

"Yes, but I don't know if that's a good idea," Yvonne says carefully. "I just wanted to know that you're okay."

"I'm okay. More than okay, actually."

"And you have Annabelle and Harry now," Yvonne says.

"Last time I looked. They're around here somewhere though it's nearing bedtime."

"Harry," Yvonne says, finally putting it together. Sam's father.

"Yeah, he's named after Dad. He passed a

couple years back. It's been rough on my mom—she still misses him."

Yvonne feels a longing for Sam's family. At times she felt closer to them than her own parents. "I'm so sorry, Sam."

"Thanks, E." They're both silent.

"So," she says, wanting to get to the heart of it. "And your wife? How's she?"

"My wife?" Sam sounds puzzled.

"Your wife," Yvonne repeats, hating the words and at the same time wanting to know. "What's she like?"

There's a long, stunned silence. "I'm not married, E."

Not married? It takes Yvonne a moment to process this. "But the kids . . ."

". . . are my niece and nephew. Rachel's kids. They're here visiting with mom so Rachel can get a little down time."

"Rachel." Sam's older sister. Mrs. Kenney, Sam's mother. "But I heard you were married," she says.

"Me?" There's a wry chuckle. "No. Under the circumstances, I don't think I'm marriage material. As I'm sure you'd agree."

"But I don't understand," Yvonne says, her thoughts all jumbled. "Claire told me you were married. A few years back . . ."

"To my job, maybe." His voice is scornful. "Claire. And you believed her?"

"Well, I . . ." Yvonne suddenly feels weak and has to sit down. "Oh my God." Her sister lied to her. Why is Yvonne so surprised? Her sisters are classic Tates, clones of her parents. Yvonne is the odd Tate out.

Sam's voice catches in his throat. "E, I wish things had been different for us. I wouldn't have left the way I did, except it seemed like the only option at the time."

"You don't have to apologize, Sam," she tells him. "I know why you did it, and I don't blame you."

There's a long pause. "You don't blame me for what?"

"For taking the money. Your family . . . your dad . . . I know it was a chance for your family to get out of Wareham, for Lizzie to go to college . . ." She clears her throat. "I want to say that I understand. It was a hard decision, but you chose right. Your family needed you."

"Yvonne . . ." Sam's voice is strained. "I'm sorry, but what in the hell are you talking about?"

Yvonne frowns, confused. "Sam, I know my parents offered you two hundred fifty thousand dollars to call off the wedding," she says. "I know they took advantage of the situation, that they knew your dad had cancer and you were all so worried about Rachel with that guy she was running around with. And Lizzie, she was so smart, and your poor mom . . ." Her voice trails off, uncertain. "I mean, how could you say no. Right?"

Even though she can't see him, Yvonne can tell he's simmering, that something is about to erupt.

"Uh, right that Dad had cancer, and right that Rachel was running around with that loser, Tony." Sam's voice is tight, controlled. "Totally right that Lizzie had her whole future ahead of her, and she still does. She just got her masters in social work from BU. And right that my mom was stressed, definitely stressed, and scared. You're right about all that, E. The only thing you're wrong about is the money. Your parents didn't offer me anything, and I wouldn't have taken it if they had." His voice is hard. "Is that what you thought it was?"

"But . . ." Yvonne grips the phone. "Your note, Sam. The one you wrote. *I'm sorry, E. I have to do what I have to do. Be happy . . .*"

"Yeah, as in, *I'm sorry, E, that you are still in love with that jerk Nathan, and that I can't go through this, knowing that I might be standing in the way of your happiness.* That's all I ever wanted for you, E. For you to be happy."

There's a long pause, their mutual disbelief hanging in the air.

"Wait, are you saying that you're not with him anymore?" asks Sam as Yvonne says, "There was never any money?"

"I'll go first," Sam says. "There was never any

money. No talk of it, no offer. Never. But what about Nathan? Are you still together?"

"Nathan who?" Yvonne is perplexed until she suddenly remembers. "Nathan Cameron? Why would I be with him? And what does this have to do with him anyway?"

"E, in all the years I'd known you, he's the only guy you dated for more than a week. He was at Harvard, you were at Smith . . ." Sam sighs.

Yvonne wishes he were there so she could shake him. He was always jealous about Nathan even though she told him—repeatedly—that they had never been serious. "We dated for two months, Sam. And most of that was over fall finals—I was too busy to break up with him sooner. You know that."

"I know that's what you said, E, but there was always a part of me that wondered. You proposed only a few days after you broke up with him. I didn't think much about it at the time, you know? It seemed right, marrying my best friend.

"But seeing him that night at the rehearsal dinner, mooning over you—it was making me see red. He would give me these haughty looks, like he knew something I didn't know."

Yvonne sighs. "He always looked at people like that," she says. It was one of the many reasons Yvonne never really cared for him. He'd been invited to the wedding along with his parents because they were close friends of the family.

"When your mother asked me to come over, I thought maybe it was a peace offering, that your parents wanted to bury the hatchet before the wedding. There was part of me that knew I was walking into an ambush, but I was overconfident. I mean, it was the night before our wedding. What could go wrong?"

Yvonne feels her skin grow clammy. "What did they do, Sam?"

"They didn't do anything. They didn't have to. Your father sat there drinking a Scotch and looking bored while your mother told me that the only reason you'd proposed to me was because Nathan had broken your heart back when you were together. That you had proposed to me on a whim—which we both knew you did—in an attempt to forget about Nathan. I'll admit it was an easy snow job, and for a second I thought it was entirely possible that I had fallen in love with you and you only loved me because of our history together, and that maybe she was right, that he'd hurt you and you were trying to forget about him by marrying me.

"But what really got me was this: Your mother said that she'd heard you crying, pleading with Nathan, at the rehearsal dinner. That you wanted out and didn't know how, that he was devastated about losing you, that your chance for happiness was going to be lost. I didn't want that, E. I was always happy to be your fallback guy, but I didn't want to be the reason that you couldn't find happiness."

"Sam, you were never my fallback guy. You were my guy."

"And you were my girl. Which is why I didn't want you to give up a chance at true love if that was what was at stake. That's when your mother pushed the notepaper toward me, told me I had a chance to make it right. She told me that as long as I stayed in Wareham, it would be too hard on you so she offered me a choice—go through with the wedding, or leave. She knew I'd choose the latter. I wrote the note, and I left. I couldn't even tell my parents what happened, just said that I had to go, that the wedding was off."

Yvonne closes her eyes, tries to breathe. She can see it unfolding exactly as Sam describes, Sam confused and conflicted but wanting Yvonne's happiness, and Yvonne, readying for bed without a clue that her own heart was about to be wounded, that the following morning her mother would deliver another deception that catapulted Yvonne into another direction, another life.

Sam sounds miserable. "I left Wareham that night, went to Boston to stay with a friend, tried to figure out what to do next. I heard from my folks that you had left, too, and it made me think that your parents had been right, that you were just there for me. I figured that you went off to live your big life somewhere with Nathan. I never looked back. It was too hard."

Yvonne knows this is unexpected for both of them, and even she's not sure what's coming next. "I did leave that day," she says. "I couldn't bear it."

"I tried to look for you once," he admits. "It was right after my dad died. I thought for sure I'd find you in New York or San Francisco. Finding Nathan was easy enough—head of a bank, on his second wife, but there was no mention of you. It was like you disappeared off the face of the earth. My mom hadn't seen you back in Wareham and your family wasn't talking about you at all. The only Yvonne Tate that I could find was a plumber in Wichita, Kansas."

She smiles. "That was me, Sam. I *am* a plumber, except I live in Avalon now."

There's a long pause, and then Sam starts to chuckle. "So I did have the right girl after all. And I let her slip away again. What kind of idiot does that?"

They both laugh, but Sam is the first to grow quiet again. "So I have to know, E. Are you married?"

"I'm not married," she says, her breath catching. "Fiancé?"

"No."

"Boyfriend? Or boyfriends?"

"No. No one, Sam. Though I did date a schmuck last month. Does that count?"

"Is it over?"

"Did you hear the word schmuck?" Yvonne smiles.

"I did," he says. "I just wanted to make sure. So what's the closest airport to . . ." Sam is tapping into a keyboard. "Avalon?"

"Rockford, but you may have better luck flying into O'Hare. More flights."

"Nope, that won't be necessary . . . Rockford's closer and I can fly in tomorrow morning. I can be in Avalon by noon."

"Tomorrow?" Yvonne says in disbelief. "Noon?"

Sam hesitates. "I'm sorry. I got carried away . . . is it too soon? Do you want to do the phone thing for a while or . . ."

"No!" Yvonne is laughing and crying. "No, definitely not. I want to see you, too, Sam. But you need to know something first. I broke up with Nathan because I realized I wanted to be with you. My parents had given me an ultimatum, telling me that we couldn't be friends, and I realized that I didn't want to be friends. I wanted more, I wanted us to be together. When I proposed it was on a whim, but I also knew it was right. Marrying my best friend."

"I love you, E. I always have and always will. It's settled—I'm coming tomorrow."

Sam. *Her* Sam. It may end up completely weird and awkward in person, or maybe they'll end up staying friends, but at least they'll be able to finally figure it out. "Give me your flight details and I'll pick you up," she says, grabbing a pen and paper. "Which airline?"

"No airline. I'll be flying in myself—I have to file the flight plan, but it looks like I'll be arriving around eleven a.m. at Emery Air FBO. You should see signs when you turn into Chicago Rockford International Airport. You'll have to go to where the private jets are—I have fractional ownership of a Cessna Five-Ten Mustang with four other rangers."

Yvonne grins. "You have a private jet?"

"Again, fractional ownership. I won it in a poker game, if you really want to know. I'm a government employee, E. I'm comfortable, but I'm not exactly rolling in the big bucks."

"And in case you missed it earlier, I'm a plumber. Also comfortable, but not planning to jet off to Europe anytime soon."

"Tomorrow, E. I can't believe it. I'll be the guy flying the plane anxious to get to you."

Yvonne smiles, pulls the phone closer to her. "And I'll be the girl on the ground waiting for you to get here."

Chapter Twenty-three

"Knock, knock!" It's 7:45 a.m. on Saturday morning. Isabel checks her hair and hurries to the front door, her robe wrapped tight around her body. Max collides with her in the hallway.

"Someone's knocking," he reports, still in his pajamas. His hair is tousled and his glasses are askew. He looks absolutely adorable.

"I know, Max. I'll get it—you can go back to sleep."

"Back to sleep?" Ava steps out of the bedroom. "I wish. We've been up since six. Max is an early riser."

"No kidding." Isabel stops. "I've been up since six, too. I didn't want to wake you guys so I stayed in my room."

Ava stifles a laugh. "Oh no. Us, too. Not that we're complaining—I think this is the best sleep we've had in weeks. It's so peaceful here. Thank you so much, Isabel. I don't know how to express my—"

Isabel holds up a hand. "Ava, we have to set some ground rules if this is going to work. First, you can only say thank you once in a twenty-four-hour period, and it's preferable if you not say it at all. Second: No more tiptoeing around. For either of us. Go help yourself to whatever's in the fridge, make breakfast, bang pots or pans."

She looks at Max. "Wait, I take that back. No pot banging, at least not before eight. Deal?"

Max grins and nods his head.

The doorbell begins to ring. Incessantly.

"Hold your horses," Isabel says. Ian's persistent, she'll give him that. Ava and Max slip into the kitchen.

By the time she reaches the door, there's knocking *and* ringing. Okay, so this is a bit over the top. Isabel clears her throat, then cracks the door demurely, opening it as far as she can before the security door chain stops her.

"Isabel? Let me in!" A skinny hand snakes into the door crack and grapples for her. "It's Bettie!"

"Bettie?" Isabel pushes Bettie's hand back outside, then carefully closes the door, quickly sliding the chain off the track. She swings the door open.

Bettie is standing on Isabel's porch dressed in her bathrobe. Her purse is hanging primly from her arm. Bettie gawks at Isabel, then herself. "Look, we're twins!"

Isabel pulls her robe tight around her body and gives a shiver. She looks out onto the street. She doesn't see Abe's or Imogene's car anywhere. "How did you get here, Bettie? Where's Imogene?"

Bettie ignores her, stepping into the house. Isabel sees that the soles of Bettie's slippers are worn and dirty. "Mmm, is that breakfast I smell? Sausages!"

Isabel's about to follow her into the kitchen when she hears a truck rumble up to the curb. Ian Braemer waves from the cab, then cuts the engine. Jeremy is in the front seat, listening to his headphones. Ian steps out of the truck, two steaming cups of coffee in hand.

"Morning!" he calls, coming up to the door. He hands a tall paper cup to Isabel and grins. "Looks like I caught you in your pj's after all."

Isabel loosens the tie around her robe until it falls open, revealing jeans and the V-neck sweater she'd been planning on wearing. "You weren't here early enough, sorry. I'm getting ready to paint the living room, actually." She grins.

"Oh, you're one of those women," Ian says with a wounded look. He takes a sip of his coffee. "Whoops, still hot. Be careful, I just burned my tongue."

One of those women? Isabel has never been one of those women. She blows on her coffee and smiles, tries the idea on for size. Isabel, a tease. She pictures herself in playful lingerie, revealing necklines, flirty makeup.

Nah. "So can I get you anything?"

"We're fine. Just going to set up the ladders and take a closer look, see what will need to be done. I'll get started today but in case I can't finish, I'm happy to come back tomorrow. Is that all right? I wouldn't want you to get sick of me."

Not a chance, Isabel thinks, but instead she says, "No, that's great."

Ian gives her a wave as he heads back to the truck, whistles for Jeremy to get out and join him.

Isabel goes back inside the house, follows the sound of laughter. When she steps into the kitchen, she sees Bettie is already seated, a plate of food in front of her. Max is eating scrambled eggs with ketchup. They all look up when she walks in.

"Hungry?" Ava asks. Isabel shakes her head, lowers herself into the chair next to Bettie, Ian's coffee warm in her hands.

Bettie's hair is messy, her cheeks rosy. When Isabel touches her hand, it's ice cold. "Bettie, did you walk here?"

Bettie shakes her hand free and picks up her fork. "Sorry, don't remember."

"Nice try, but that won't work on me. How did you get here?" The phone rings and Isabel already knows who it is. She gives Bettie another look. "Last chance."

"Fine, I walked," Bettie grumbles. "Abe and Imogene are married. I feel like a third wheel. They're getting ready to retire, go into their golden years. They don't need an old lady like me around." She eats a forkful of eggs. "Oh, this is good, Ava."

"Here," Max says, squirting some ketchup on Bettie's plate.

"More," she demands, then grins when her plate has more ketchup than eggs.

"Would you like a spoon with that?" Isabel shakes her head as she goes to answer the phone. "Hi, Imogene."

"Oh, please tell me she's there," Imogene pants, her voice strained. "I've looked everywhere. Abe is on his way over."

"She's here." Isabel turns away and lowers her voice. "I thought you had locks on the doors."

"I do, but she went out the bathroom window. It's so narrow I didn't bother safe-proofing it but I'll get on it this afternoon. Is she all right?"

Isabel turns to see Bettie chatting with Ava. Bettie dips her finger and scoops up some ketchup, and laughs when Max does the same. Other than being disheveled and underdressed, Bettie is her usual animated self. "She's fine. I'll send her back with Abe. Bye, Imogene."

"No, sir," Bettie says as soon as Isabel hangs up. "I'm not going back. Put me into one of those homes if you will, but I'm not going to impose on them any longer. It's weird."

"Weird is the new normal," Ava says. She glances at Isabel. "At least that's what Isabel tells me. Isabel invited us to live here, to be house-mates. Max and I moved in yesterday."

"What?" Bettie puts down her fork, amazed.

568

"No kidding." She looks approvingly at Isabel. "Got your big-girl pants on, now don't you? Good for you!"

"That's enough from you," Isabel says, but she flushes in pleasure at the compliment. "Those homes cost money, Bettie. I don't think you should go in until you absolutely need to."

"I have long-term-care insurance," Bettie reminds her. "And some money saved up."

"Not enough," Isabel says. "Remember? We went through all the numbers with an accountant. Depending on how your condition progresses, if you can stay with friends for the next five to ten years, then we can look into a facility."

"The next five to ten years? How long you think I'm gonna last? I'm already seventy-seven, for goodness' sake!" She turns to Ava. "I'm not scared of death. A lot of people are, but not me. I even have my plot picked out at the Avalon Cemetery. Number two-four-one, lot B, block eight. It's right on a little knoll, has a view and everything."

Isabel hates it when Bettie starts talking like this. "Can you at least stay with Abe and Imogene until we come up with some kind of plan? They went through so much trouble to make their place nice for you."

"I know," Bettie says. "And that's what I hate about it. I don't like to be indebted, Isabel. I appreciate everyone wanting to do something, but . . ." She sighs. "This is all too much fuss. I want things to be normal again."

"By normal do you mean weird?" Ava asks, confused. "Since weird is the new normal?"

"Well, I don't know," Bettie says, perplexed now. "Do I want weird or normal?" She and Ava turn to Isabel, a questioning look on their faces.

Isabel takes a long sip of her coffee. "I think I'll have some of those eggs now," she says.

As Ava scoops some eggs onto a plate, Bettie temples her fingers. "You know, Isabel, I was thinking that if it's all right with you, I'd like to host a scrapbooking crop here at the end of the year. That's when we scrapbook all day. We'll be using Madeline's Tea Salon for meetings, but the crops usually run all day and I'd like the women to be able to spread out. Since we already know how to utilize your space . . ."

"Fine," Isabel says. "Whatever. But the bedrooms are off-limits." She looks at Ava. "Sorry, I forgot to ask you. What do you think?"

"I think that sounds like fun," Ava says. "So we scrapbook all day?"

"All day and all night," Bettie says.

There's a rap on the back door and the women turn to see Abe standing awkwardly on the back porch. "Looks like your ride is here," Isabel says. She leans in and whispers, *"Be nice."*

Bettie sighs and pushes herself into a standing position. She smooths her hair and gives Isabel,

Ava, and Max a dignified nod. "Well, I'll be going. Thanks for breakfast." She marches to the backdoor, unlocks it, and leaves with Abe, who gives a polite wave to everyone.

"Poor Bettie," Ava murmurs as she clears the plates. "It must be hard to feel so displaced. What's happening with her house?"

"She's not going to rebuild," Isabel says. "Her house was insured for the appraised value, not replacement value—it's not enough to put the same size house on it. And it was probably more house than she needed anyway. She might sell the lot but for now, she doesn't want to rush it."

"I'm going to go to the library to work on my résumé today," Ava says. "And then I'll get it to Dr. Tindell right away."

"Can Max stay here?" Isabel asks. "I mean, if he wants to? I have to do a little painting—I'm getting tired of the white walls."

"Yes!" Max exclaims, pumping his little fist. His glasses slip off his nose and he pushes them back on. Ava laughs.

"If it wouldn't be too much trouble," she says. "I'll actually be able to get more done."

"Me too," Isabel says. "I could use a helping hand. Finish your breakfast, Max, and then we'll go get our paint brushes."

Yvonne stands in the passenger terminal, rubbing the grooves of her car keys, the embossed silver

571

name tag at the end of her keychain. It's just past eleven and she's standing by the window watching the small planes come and go, her heart clenching each time she sees a plane approach.

How is it that less than twenty-four hours ago, she had no idea where Sam was, and now she's standing here about to see him face-to-face? That's all it took. One day for your life to turn upside down, one day for it to right itself again. Ten years ago she woke up ready to slip into a wedding dress, to walk down the aisle. Less than twelve hours later, she was sitting in the passenger seat of Harold Stroup's plumbing van, driving away from the only life she'd ever known.

Yvonne hadn't been able to sleep last night, and she's sure it shows. She tossed and turned, adrenaline coursing through her veins, her heart beating so hard she thought it might burst. Her body was clammy and damp, tears streamed down her face until her pillow was drenched. Every hurt, every heartache, found its place in Yvonne's bed last night. It felt as if morning would never come.

This is why she never let herself think about Sam—it's too hard on her mind, her heart, her body. It threatens to rip apart the fragile threads of her life, to mire her in the pain of the loss, to hold her back from moving on. The devastation of lost love—no one warns you about it because it's impossible to describe. There's nothing you can do about it, you either get through it or let it pull you into the black hole. An abyss.

Yvonne eventually got up, pulled back the curtains. She wrapped herself in a blanket and watched the sun rise. When the first pale ray of light began to warm the horizon, she gave herself permission to do something she hadn't since that day.

She let herself hope.

There's a bustle of people around her as a private charter is ushered toward the tarmac. Yvonne closes her eyes, touches the glass in front of her. Somewhere out there, Sam is flying toward her.

"Eleven-oh-six, that's your boy," a dispatcher tells her, pointing to the sky. Yvonne doesn't see it at first, and then the Cessna comes into view. She watches it descend, sees a flash of him as the plane touches down, the same mussed russet-brown hair, the rugged outline of his face, a look of steady concentration. At that second he turns to look at her, the unmistakable recognition that was there the first day they met.

When the smile breaks across his face, Yvonne chokes a cry, her hand covering her mouth as the tears start. Then she's moving, pushing open the door and hurrying toward the plane. A second later she's running.

By the time she reaches him, the plane has

slowed to a stop and eased into a tie-down. The door opens, and then he's there. A second later, she's in his arms.

"E," he breathes, and he holds her, tight.

"Don't let me go," she whispers, her cheek pressed against the cool leather of his jacket. He smells exactly the same and she breathes him in. His arms tighten around her, his lips brushing the top of her head.

"I won't. Ever."

Ava drops a quarter into the machine, presses the START button. There's a hum, a roll of light. A few seconds later, a copy of her résumé emerges from the copy machine. It's followed by a copy of her cover letter, signed and ready to be dropped off at Dr. Tindell's office.

Ava pulls the originals from the document feeder, folds them carefully, and then slides them into a matching envelope. This is it. Even though it's Saturday she'll drive by his office and slip it into the mail slot. Isabel told her that Dr. Tindell was expecting to hear from her, and even though Ava knows there's no guarantee, she wants to be the first in line.

She looks around to see if she's left anything behind when she hears someone call her name. She turns and sees Colin standing by the checkout desk, his arms full of books.

"What are you doing here?" he asks, surprised.

She holds up the envelope. "Résumé," she says. "I'm hoping to get a job in town."

"Here? In Avalon?"

Ava nods.

A grin breaks across his face as he puts down the stack of books. "That's great. Good luck, Ava—they'd be lucky to have you."

"Thanks." She gives him a shy smile. "So what are you doing here?"

"Research." He pats the stack of books. "I've been working on a book. A novel. Turns out my main character is an astronomer but unfortunately I'm not. Hence the need to do a little research."

"You're writing a book?" Ava cocks her head to skim the titles. *Great Astronomers. Practical Statistics for Astronomers. Astronomy Hacks: Tips and Tools for Observing the Night Sky. The Backyard Astronomer's Guide.* It goes on and on, and Ava is amazed. There're at least twenty books in all.

"Well, I'm trying to. It started as a short story and kind of bloomed into this. I may be in over my head but I'm having fun."

"I think it's amazing that you're an author," Ava says, trying to think of the last book she had time to read. That's one thing she's missed since motherhood, but now, with their new living situation, she might even have time to pick up a book. Maybe she'll browse the shelves and pick one up today. "You're an author," she says again.

Colin blushes, the first time Ava's ever seen him self-conscious. "I don't know about that," he says. "I mean, I'm not published and I don't have an agent or anything. I just like to write and when this idea for a story came in I couldn't ignore it." He looks at her in surprise. "I got it the day you came into the Avalon Grill."

"Really?"

"Yeah." He studies Ava for a moment. "I hope I don't embarrass you by saying this, but I think you're my muse."

Ava laughs. "Your what?"

"No, seriously. My best writing days are always after I see you—I get inspired and end up writing stuff I like. Unlike the other twenty-nine days of the month." He grins.

"Just so long as you remember me when you're rich and famous," Ava says. "And don't forget to give me a signed copy of your book." She's joking, but suddenly she pictures him sitting at a table in a bookstore, a tall pile of books next to him as people stand in line, waiting to meet him. The scene is so real in her mind that she believes it'll happen for him someday. It's not so far-fetched at all.

"You're on," Colin says. "Though I have to finish the book first. And at the rate I'm going, that might be a while." He frowns. "Unless . . ."

A mischievous grin spreads across his face.

"Unless I get to see you more often. This would be for purely literary purposes, of course."

"Oh, of course." Ava says, and she's smiling, she can't help it. She likes the idea of seeing Colin more often. "I mean, I wouldn't want to be responsible for you not finishing your novel. Your fans would never forgive me."

"From your lips to God's ears," Colin intones, a smile breaking across his face. "Wouldn't that be great?" He looks wistful.

"I can see it, Colin," she tells him. "All of it."

He looks at her, surprised. "You can?"

She nods.

"You see, you *are* my muse. And the least this poor starving writer can do is offer his muse lunch."

"I can pay for myself," she says, even though she doesn't have much money on her. She'll order water or something light—she doesn't care about the food. She simply wants to sit with him, hear him talk, laugh.

Colin shakes his head, adamant. "No way—it's the least I can do, what with you being my own personal muse. Besides, I was only kidding about the poor part—tips were great this week. But I am definitely starving."

"Give me a minute," she says. "I need to check in with Max and Isabel." It's funny saying Isabel's name, but Ava likes it, too, likes that it's some-thing that she can now say without repercussion or fear (though Isabel still scares her a little bit). "We just moved to Avalon," she explains. "And we're staying with . . ." Her voice trails off.

Okay, so she's going to have to work on this one. She's going to have to figure out what to tell people, explain her relationship with Isabel, how they know each other. Colin is waiting politely as Ava searches for the right word.

"We're staying with family," she finally says, and smiles.

Chapter Twenty-four

Halloween in Avalon. It's dusk, the sky is filled with pinks and blues as the sun makes its way down the horizon. The younger children are out, bubbling with excitement as they walk with their parents door-to-door, arms outstretched as generous handfuls of candy are dropped into plastic pumpkins and cotton pillowcases.

Generous handfuls of candy, that is, except at the home of Isabel Kidd & Co.

Max and Bettie are stationed at the door, a bowl of candy between them. Max will go out later with Ava, but right now he wants to be there when the first trick-or-treaters arrive. He's dressed as Batman while Bettie is dressed as . . . well, Isabel's not too sure what Bettie is dressed as. Imogene had called to warn her that Bettie was heading out the door toward Isabel's even though Imogene had planned a little Halloween party with some friends of theirs.

"No thank you," Bettie had said when Isabel met her halfway down the block. "I have no intention of sitting around eating canapés with a bunch of grown women dressed like fools." She marched on toward Isabel's, wearing something that made her look like a cross between a fairy princess and school crossing guard. She managed to sneak Abe's fire chief hat to boot. She saw

Isabel taking in her costume with amusement and snapped, "Before you say anything, Isabel Kidd, I am the exception. I always am."

Isabel couldn't argue with that.

So Max and Bettie are on door duty while Isabel and Ava figure out dinner. Isabel knows they don't both need to be in the kitchen at the same time, but it's fun cooking with another person. As odd as it is, what started as a simple spaghetti dinner has turned into spaghetti alla chitarra, one of Bill's favorite dishes. There's dough and flour everywhere as Isabel tries to remember how to put the pasta maker together. Yvonne is going to join them, and has said she has big news. Isabel tried to press her for deals, but Yvonne wouldn't say.

Max appears in the doorway, looking sad. "No one's coming to the house anymore," he tells them. His glasses shine beneath his mask.

"What? Why?" Isabel gives the pasta maker a crank and grins when it seems to work.

"The candy . . ." Max starts to say, when they all hear a screech from the front door.

"GIVE THAT BACK!"

Ava and Isabel wipe their hands on their aprons as they hurry to the door. Bettie is engaged in a tug-of-war over a plastic trick-or-treat bag with a boy dressed as Superman.

"What's going on?" Ava asks, bewildered.

"She's taking my candy!" the boy says, giving

one final jerk as the bag breaks free from Bettie's grasp. He stares at her. "What are you supposed to be, anyway?"

"It's obvious," Bettie sniffs. "But if you don't know, I'm not going to tell you." She's about to reach for his bag again but he puts it behind his back, looking to Isabel for help.

Isabel turns to give him some candy when she sees their bowl is overflowing. In fact, there's much more candy in there than Isabel had originally bought.

"Here you go," Isabel says, scooping up a handful and dropping it into his bag. "Don't forget to brush your teeth!" She ushers the boy out the door and closes it quickly. "Um, Bettie?"

Bettie puts her hands on her hips. "What?"

"Is everything all right?"

"Of course. Why wouldn't it be?" There's a knock on the door and Bettie's face brightens. "Duty calls! Max, come on!"

Isabel and Ava watch as Bettie throws open the door. "Happy Halloween!" she sings.

Well, that's not so bad. A little dramatic, maybe, but not anything that seems problematic. Isabel's about to turn away when she hears Bettie add, "Now what do we have here? Ooh, Tootsie Rolls! My favorite!" Bettie reaches into the little girl's pumpkin and comes up with a fistful of candy, which she promptly adds to the candy bowl before closing the front door. She turns to look at them. "This is one of my favorite holidays," she tells them.

"You're not doing it right," Max says, taking the words right out of Isabel's mouth.

"He's right," Isabel says. Ava is giggling, no help at all. "You're supposed to *give* the kids candy, not take it."

Bettie looks at them blankly. "But it's Halloween," she says. "You always get candy on Halloween!"

"Only if you're the trick-or-treater . . ." Isabel gives Ava a helpless look. "You want to try?"

"I can take them trick-or-treating," Ava suggests. "If you want to man the door. They say exercise is good for dementia, and that way we can get candy, too. We can finish up the pasta when we get back."

"Don't talk about me like I'm a child," Bettie says, looking hurt for a moment. "I haven't completely taken leave of my senses." But she looks a little confused.

"I'm sorry," Isabel says. "But Ava's right—a walk is a good idea."

"I'll wash my hands and grab my jacket," Ava says.

Bettie sniffs. "Well, hurry up then. The good stuff's going to be gone if we don't go soon." She asks Max, "Do you want gum or chocolate? If you had to choose?"

"Gum," Max says instantly.

"Good, because I want chocolate. We can trade later. Promise?"

Max nods solemnly.

Yvonne comes up the walk, a bottle of wine tucked under her arm. She looks more radiant than usual, and she's beaming.

"Nice gutters," she says with admiration. "So what do you have him working on now?"

"That's enough from you," Isabel says with a roll of her eyes, but then she grudgingly adds, "He's going to ramp the steps leading into the house. And I have a few other projects . . ."

Yvonne grins as Ava, Max, and Bettie step out onto the porch. Ava has Max so bundled up that it's hard to see what he is save the Batman mask and cape. Bettie is wearing one of Isabel's white fleece jackets and has Abe's fire chief hat on her head.

"We're off," Ava says. "Hi, Yvonne!"

"Hi, Ava. All settled in?" Yvonne smiles.

Ava nods. "It's wonderful," she begins, then glances surreptitiously at Isabel before quickly ushering Max and Bettie down the steps.

"Hey Yvonne!" Bettie calls over her shoulder. "I ordered some new 3-D stickers just for you. It's the 'Home Improvement' line—you can even lift the lid on the toilet! Will you be at the next scrapbooking meeting?"

"I wouldn't miss it." Yvonne gives them a wave as they merge onto the crowded sidewalk.

"What was that?" she asks as she follows Isabel inside. She puts the bottle of wine on the side table. "That look that Ava gave you just now?"

"She's trying to keep it under wraps because she knows it makes me nuts when she gets all emotional and Pollyanna about everything," Isabel complains. "I threatened to lock my bedroom door and never come out if she says thank you one more time."

Yvonne laughs as the doorbell rings.

Isabel opens the door and a throng of children are on the porch, their pumpkins and treat bags thrust at Isabel. They're all talking at once and Yvonne has to whistle to get their attention.

"Is she gone?" one kid asks breathlessly. It's a boy, and he's dressed like a Dr. Seuss character, a tall red and white striped hat leaning precariously to one side. "I heard she emptied out Stewie Lane's entire stash!"

"And she yelled at Bernadine Preston," a girl says snootily. She's wearing an angel costume but hardly looks angelic.

"That's because Bernadine made fun of her costume," another boy says loudly. Isabel would recognize that shock of red hair anywhere. Jacob Eammons is dressed like Tom Sawyer, which is as perfect a costume for this kid as any. "Bernadine's mean; she deserved it."

"You kids should consider yourselves lucky," Isabel tells them. "My ex-husband was a dentist and he used to make you brush, spit, *and* floss before leaving the porch."

There's a shocked hush as the kids just stare at her.

"Nice way to kill the crowd," Yvonne whispers as she grabs handfuls of candy and starts dropping them into outstretched bags. "Happy Halloween!"

"It was a joke," Isabel mutters. "I stink at this kid stuff."

"You'll do better next year," Yvonne assures her as the kids walk away. "Max will make sure of that."

"It's so different having a kid in the house," Isabel says. "And not just any kid, but Max. He wants to know everything—the questions are never ending. And I don't have the answers. My favorite was, how big is the sun? I couldn't tell him to go look it up since he can't even read yet."

"You don't have to have the answers," Yvonne says. "But you can help him figure them out. It takes a village, remember?"

Isabel makes a face but then the two burst out laughing. Isabel's sure there hasn't been a village quite like hers before.

"I'm glad things are working out for you, Isabel," Yvonne says, giving her a hug. "I know you're disappointed that Bettie didn't move in, but this ended up happening instead. You might have gone through with the sale of your house otherwise."

"I know," Isabel says. There's knocking on the door as little voices call out "trick or treat!" They go to answer it and start passing out candy. "And the funny thing is that Bettie is here anyway. Ava and Max still sleep in the same room because he's not used to the house yet, so the other room is basically a guest room for Bettie to take naps or whatever. She sneaks over all the time, which drives Imogene and Abe crazy, but I think it's great for them, too, because it gives them a break. During the day Ava and I will both be working, so Bettie's better off with Imogene during that time. So far we don't have to hire anyone else to help with her, it seems to be working between our two houses." Isabel looks guilty. "Though I guess it's lonely for you, since we were going to be housemates for a while there."

Yvonne gives her a big goofy grin. "Oh, I don't know about that. I think it might work out well for me, too."

"Oh?" Another wave of children heads up the walk. "Are you going to tell me what's going on?" Their candy supply is depleting quickly, and Isabel's wondering if maybe Bettie had the right idea after all.

"I'll tell you later," Yvonne says, smiling at a little girl dressed as a mermaid. "When it's a good time."

Isabel turns to face her friend. "Yvonne Tate, it's never a good time," she reminds her. "This is life, remember? Tell me now!"

"Okay, okay." Yvonne clutches the candy bowl in her arm and waits until the last child has disappeared from the porch. "I saw Sam the other day. He came to Avalon."

"Sam?" Isabel is confused at first, and then recognition crosses her face. "But how? Where?"

Yvonne's eyes are shining. "He's living in Bangor, Maine. He's a forest ranger. After this whole thing with Hugh and watching you with Ava . . . I wanted to know, you know? If he was all right, if things had turned out okay for him. I didn't want any unfinished business between us."

"That was pretty unfinished," Isabel agrees. Then she looks at her friend, eyebrows raised. "But now?"

Yvonne doesn't say anything, just gives a small nod, her face bursting with happiness. "It's good. We're good. Sam's not married. He thought I was married and living in New York, a socialite, two-point-five kids in private school." Her face clouds for a moment. "My parents and sisters— they didn't tell me the truth about Sam. And they didn't tell Sam the truth about me. You'd think after all these years I'd know not to trust them, but for some reason it was all so awful and all so possible that all I could think was that it had to be true. All this time, lost." She looks into the waning night, lit up with lights and laughter.

"I'm sorry, Yvonne," Isabel says, sensing her friend's sadness.

Yvonne quickly looks back, wipes her eyes. "No, it's okay, Isabel. Sam and I talked about it and we both feel the same way—we weren't old enough to know better, and getting married might not have worked out anyway, because I was still listening to my family. My family is all about control, financial and emotional. If we had gone through with it, they would have found a way to sabotage or break up our marriage, I'm sure of it. But now . . ." She smiles. "It's just us. And I don't care what they have to say about Sam or my life anymore."

Isabel's mind is spinning. "If you weren't standing here in front of me, telling me all this, I wouldn't believe it."

"I know. I'm waiting for the eyeball roll," Yvonne says, poking her friend.

Isabel shakes her head. "Not this time. I like the idea that two people can find love. It's nice to know that anything is possible."

"Well, you're living proof of that."

Isabel grins. "I guess so." She looks at Yvonne. "So what now? If he's living in Maine and you're in Avalon . . ." A thought crosses Isabel's mind and she clutches Yvonne's arm. "You can't move!"

"I'm not planning on it . . . yet. He was only here for a day, Isabel, but we've been talking and emailing and we're going to set our schedules so we can see each other every week. He's flying here again next weekend and you'll get to meet him then. He'll also be talking to his boss at work—Illinois has over sixty state parks so he wants to see if there are any opportunities nearby."

"Wow," Isabel says. Things are moving so fast for Yvonne and while Isabel is happy for her, she doesn't want her to get hurt, either.

"I know it seems fast," Yvonne says, reading her mind. "And while we both agree that we need to spend more time together to get to know each other again, we both also know that this is it. We've been waiting for this moment, Isabel, and we aren't going to sit around asking each other about our favorite movies or our idea for the perfect vacation. We're past all that. We just want to be together."

"Don't get angry," Isabel says. "But what if it doesn't work out? If you move or he moves, what if you do all this and it still doesn't work out?"

"Then we'll know. I'm not scared to try, Isabel. I'm more scared *not* to try." Yvonne continues handing out candy to the kids.

Isabel thinks about this. "Better to have loved and lost than not to have loved at all?" she quips.

"Or . . ." Yvonne takes her friend's hands in her own, gives them a reassuring squeeze. "Maybe it's better to have loved and lost and then found love again." Yvonne gives her a knowing look and Isabel knows Yvonne's not talking about herself, but Isabel, too.

"Sheesh, get a room already," comes a call from the walkway. They turn and see Bettie marching toward them, hand in hand with Max, their plastic jack-o'-lanterns already overflowing.

"That was quick," Isabel says, giving Yvonne's hands a final squeeze before turning to face them.

Ava looks a little dazed. "Bettie knows everyone," she says. "People were *very* generous with her and Max. I think someone even gave her a ham."

"The Jaffertys. Horace and Aurora owe me big-time for the time I helped them find Chuckles, their pet iguana. It was the day before the state competition. Chuckles ended up with a blue ribbon, he did." Bettie nods, satisfied. "I told them we'd pick it up in the morning. It's frozen, so we can save it for Thanksgiving."

Isabel is staggered by the thought. Thanksgiving already? They haven't even gotten through Halloween!

And then, of course, the holiday rush won't end. Christmas, New Year's, Valentine's Day, Easter. Max's birthday, Ava's birthday. Isabel's birthday. Bettie's birthday. Yvonne's birthday.

April Fool's Day, St. Patrick's Day. The list goes on and on.

Isabel looks at the people around her, talking and laughing all at once. This is it, she realizes with a smile.

This is my life.

"Trick or treat!" The kids line up outside Frances's house, clamoring for the apples dipped in caramel and wrapped in an envelope of wax paper.

"I still cannot believe that you did this," Reed says in amazement, looking at the trays and trays of apples. He had to work late at the office and has just arrived home, his tie pulled loose around his shirt collar. "How many did you make?"

"One hundred and fifty," Frances says. "But I took a couple of shortcuts. I used those mini Braeburns and the microwave to melt the caramel." She hands the apples out, making sure each one has a tag with their name on it. She doesn't want the neighbors worrying about the apples or where they came from, so she included their name and phone number just in case.

Reed looks around. "I think kids from Barrett and Laquin are here," he says. "Word spreads fast."

Frances smiles. "I have extra candy in case we run out."

"Where are the boys?"

"Nick took them out with a couple of his friends. They have a parent with them, so don't worry."

"I'm not worried," Reed says. There's a chorus of delighted screams from across the street. "What the . . ."

"Oh, that's just Ida Church," Frances explains. "She decided to dress up as an alien this year and scare all the kids. She has a fake spaceship in the driveway but that's a decoy. When you walk over to it, she jumps out from behind a tree. The big kids love it, of course, but I told Brady and Noah they can't go over. I don't want them having nightmares." There's another chorus of screams and Frances shakes her head, a smile on her face.

"You're doing too much," Reed tells her as he watches her unwrap another tray of caramel apples.

"No, this is good," she insists. "I'm glad to be busy. I can't bear the waiting anymore." She hears all sorts of stories from the adoption boards about last-minute crises or glitches. No matter how close they seem, Frances isn't going to be able to relax until Mei Ling is home with them.

"Come inside for a second," Reed tells her gently, and Frances hears something in his voice that makes her freeze.

If it's bad news, she won't be able to take it. If that's what this is, another delay or unforeseen problem, a complication with Mei Ling's condition, Frances will be a mess. Okay, a bigger mess. As it is she can hardly sleep at night.

The look on Reed's face—impassive, giving nothing away—makes Frances pull back. She's not ready for whatever it is he has to tell her.

"It's trick-or-treat rush hour," she tries to joke, but Reed shakes his head.

"Come on, Frances," he says, and pulls her into the house.

"What is it?" she asks. She's shaking, and the doorbell is ringing with more trick-or-treaters. Her nerves are shot and she's going to throttle her husband in a second if he doesn't stop pacing and answer her. *Now.* "Reed, tell me!"

He turns to her and pulls an envelope out of his suit pocket. "It's here, Frances. Our official approval to travel to China. We can get Mei Ling in three weeks. Three weeks!" He sweeps Frances up in a hug and swings her around. "She'll be home with us for Thanksgiving!"

"Oh my God, oh my God, oh my God!" Frances can't believe it. "Oh my God!" She's laughing and crying, the dam of emotions finally let loose. "Where are the boys? The boys! We have to find the boys!"

"Frances, slow down . . ." Reed says, but he's laughing, too, his eyes shiny as well. "Let them enjoy themselves, and we'll tell them when they come home on their sugar high." He pauses for a moment and then catches her in his arms again, tight, and kisses her. "She's coming home," he says to his wife, and it starts to sink in.

Mei Ling is coming home.

And then the excitement takes over again.

"I have to book flights," she says, her mind racing. "The hotel. Finish packing. Oh, we have to call your mom, my parents! And her room! I have to wash the sheets, and an advent calendar! I want her to have an advent calendar so she can open a door every day until Christmas! And I have to let the school know when the boys will be gone . . . My God, Reed, it's happening. It's really happening!" Frances is literally jumping up and down, tears streaming down her face as she runs around the house, not quite sure of what she's doing or looking for, but knowing no other way to contain her joy. Sometimes it's just best to let it all out.

Across the street there's another round of screams from Ida Church's driveway, but it can't compete with the screams of joy coming from the Latham household.

Chapter Twenty-five

Connie looks over the spread of baked goods, checks the carafes for hot water.

"We're all set," she declares, turning to look at Madeline and Hannah. "We're ready for members of the Avalon Ladies Scrapbooking Society to descend upon us."

"Good," Madeline says, nodding. "We're expecting a full house tonight." She glances at the clock.

Hannah peeks out the window. "Here they come!"

And here they come indeed. It's many of the same people from the last meeting and they've brought food along with scrapbook albums of different shapes and sizes. They place them on a table up front. Isabel is already there, talking earnestly with Ava and Yvonne.

Frances Latham walks through the door, comes over to Hannah and gives her a quick hug. "I'm so sorry I can't stay," she says. "We leave this weekend for China. I'm so excited I think I might faint." She hands Connie a platter. "*Cōng yóubǐng*—scallion pancakes. I think I'm getting pretty good at them now—my boys are addicted."

"I'm addicted," Hannah tells everyone, sniffing appreciatively. "Frances makes the best *cōng yóubǐng*. You'll love them. I'll bring the dish back for you, Frances."

"Thank you," Frances says, smiling at her friend. She dabs at her eyes. "Gosh, I'm a mess! I can't believe that we'll be home with Mei Ling the day before Thanksgiving. I can't wait for her to meet all of you."

"And we can't wait to meet her," Madeline tells her. "We also know it may take some time for you to settle in as a family of six, so we're going to make sure you and your family are well fed in the meantime. When you get home, we're going to have a food tree waiting for you, just like we would for any new mother. And if you'd like to join us for Thanksgiving dinner, we'd love to have you, but I completely understand if you want some peace and quiet."

"Or sleep!" Hannah adds.

"Thank you so much," Frances says. "I don't know what to expect—we're going to play everything by ear. We'll follow her lead."

"Take lots of pictures when you're in China," Connie says. "It's on my list of places to visit one day."

"I will," Frances promises. "And I'm going to be putting everything on my blog, too. I'll try to post something every day while we're there. Pictures, observations, everything. When I come home I'll put it all together in a memory book." She looks at her watch. "Oh, I have to go! Reed and the boys are waiting for me."

"Go home and finish packing," Hannah says.

"Here," Frances says, holding out a small booklet to Madeline. "I don't have a lot of pictures of Bettie, but she was kind enough to contribute to Mei Ling's quilt. I took a picture of her square, and then of the entire quilt. I also included Mei Ling's picture in there. I wrote a short explanation under each picture. I was going to wait until I could get a picture of Mei Ling with the blanket, but I can add that later. I want Bettie to have something for tonight."

"It's lovely," Madeline says when she sees it. "I'll take it over and add it to the table. Travel safe, Frances, and we'll see you when you return."

Frances waves goodbye, and Hannah grabs a couple of tissues from a nearby tissue box.

"She's making me think of adopting someday," Hannah says, dabbing her eyes. "I never thought about it much, but it seems like a beautiful way to grow a family, you know?"

Connie puts an arm around Hannah's shoulders. "You're going to make a great parent someday," she tells her. Hannah smiles and gives her a hug.

Connie sees Imogene and Bettie coming up the walk. "Hurry, everyone! Here she comes!"

There's a commotion as people rearrange themselves in the tea salon. Isabel throws a sheet over the table filled with albums.

"It's too quiet!" Connie whispers, and then says

in a louder voice. "Act normal! Start talking! About anything!"

There's a burst of animated conversation as Bettie and Imogene walk through the door.

"Huh," Bettie says, her brows knit in confusion as she looks around. "I didn't think so many people would be interested in using ink mists and chipboard accents."

Connie and Madeline refrain from giggling as Isabel hurries forward.

"I have a quick announcement to make first," Isabel says. "Come on, Bettie, keep me company." She leads Bettie up to the podium.

"Oh, I think I'm going to need that box of tissues," Madeline says, already sniffling. Connie grabs a couple of tissues as the box passes by. She doesn't consider herself an overly emotional person but she wants to be prepared, just in case.

At the front of the room, Isabel stands behind the podium. Bettie is seated behind her. "Excuse me, everyone? If I could have your attention for a moment, please?"

The crowd quiets as everyone finds their seats. Others line the walls and spill into the hallways.

"I want to thank everyone for joining us tonight," Isabel begins. "As you know, Bettie's home burned down a couple of weeks ago. She lost almost everything in that fire, including her scrapbooking business. Her personal effects were gone or destroyed."

Isabel turns to her. "Bettie, for years you've been the keeper of our memories. Now, we want you to know that we'll become the keeper of yours." She walks over to the table and pulls back the sheet. There's a burst of applause as Bettie gapes at the pile of albums wrapped and stacked on the table. Isabel motions for her to come over.

"What in the world . . . ?" Bettie murmurs, a flushed look on her face. "Holy Jumpin' Jehoshaphat. Are all these for me?" She picks one up.

"Everyone here went through their own albums and contributed pictures that you were in," Isabel explains. "We didn't want you to lose all your wonderful memories."

Bettie is flipping through an album, already commenting on each and every picture.

"Oh, I remember that day!" Bettie is saying. "And that day!" She giggles. "Boy, stripes really didn't do me any favors, did they? Look, Isabel. Oh, goodness, is that Seymour March picking his nose in the background?"

There's a ripple of laughter through the crowd.

"The parade!" Bettie exclaims. "1979. Oh, what a day that was! Who did this album? I love all the stamping on this page. And the gridded patterned paper is lovely!"

"Thank you, Bettie!" comes a cry from the crowd.

Bettie picks up another album covered in leather,

this one filled with photographs, articles, small letters and notes. "The Society biography!" she exclaims. "Christopher Barlowe, where are you?"

A man raises his hand and gives a shy wave.

Isabel passes her a small pink album. Bettie chuckles before she even opens it up. "Margot West, are these pages scented?"

"Guilty!" comes Margot's delighted reply.

Isabel passes album after album to Bettie, who takes a look before passing it down into the crowd. Everyone is laughing and pointing at pictures while Society members make observations about the different layouts and choices of paper stock and embellishments.

Madeline comes over and loops her arm through Connie's. "My own album is coming along nicely," she says. "I think I'll be able to give it to Maggie for Christmas. What about you?"

"I'm almost done," Connie says. "And when I am, I want to show it to you."

"Sweetheart, I'd be honored," Madeline says.

Connie's going to show it to Eli, too, because she wants him to know where she came from. He already knows her family history, but she's taken the time to add more written memories and pictures printed from the Internet. Serena's in there, too, as is Madeline. In short the album is full of the things Connie loves best, of memories most precious to her, and she wants to share it with him.

Everyone around them is talking and laughing, and some women have tears in their eyes. The albums are still being passed around when Bettie suddenly stands and picks up her sequined mallet.

"Excuse me," she says, and there's an immediate hush. "Thank you, everyone, for all of this. I'd like to thank you all in person, too, but with the way my brain's been acting these days, I'd be just as likely to thank the same person three times and forget someone else altogether. So thank you, everyone." There's a round of applause and Bettie turns to look at Isabel. "Is there anything else?" she asks.

Isabel smiles, shakes her head.

Bettie brings down the sequined gavel onto the podium with a bang. "Then the November meeting of the Avalon Ladies Scrapbooking Society is officially in session. Let's begin."

"That was a good meeting," Bettie says as Isabel drives her home. Imogene is in the car ahead of them, her passenger seats filled with albums and gifts.

"It was," Isabel agrees. "Are you tired?"

Bettie shakes her head. "I feel awake. Really awake. Like everything's been muddy but now it's clear." She looks at Isabel hopefully. "Maybe I'm getting better. My mind, I mean."

Isabel manages a smile. "Maybe," she says, but she doubts it. From what she's been reading, dementia is like this. Good one day, lousy the next. Clarity, then confusion. It can go on like this for a long time.

Bettie shifts in her seat, pulls her scarf tighter around her neck. "It's going to be a cold winter," she says. "It'll probably be harder for me to walk over, what with the snow and all."

"Don't even think about it," Isabel says sternly. "If you want to come over, I'll come and get you. Anytime, okay?"

Bettie gives her a hopeful look. "Really?"

"Really." Isabel looks at her and smiles. "And if you want, we can talk about having you stay over a couple of nights whenever you want. I know Max would love it. Me, too."

Bettie is nodding. "I'd like that," she says. "It'll give Abe and Imogene a chance to get a little cootchie-cootchie in. One night I was looking for my catalogs when I saw them—"

"I'll work out a schedule with Imogene," Isabel says quickly, not wanting to hear any details about the Garzas' love life. "That reminds me. We have that scrapbooking crop at the house next month. You can stay over then, too. We'll rent a movie and pop popcorn. Anything with Jennifer Lopez, right?"

"She's so good in *Maid in Manhattan*," Bettie says with sudden fervor. "And that Ralph Fiennes. I could watch it a million times over."

"*Maid in Manhattan* it is, then."

There's a pause and then Bettie says in a small voice, "Isabel?"

"Yes?"

Bettie reaches out to touch Isabel's hand on the steering wheel, but doesn't say anything else. They drive like this all the way to Abe and Imogene's house.

At Imogene's house, Isabel helps Bettie out of the car and walks her up the walkway to the front door. Imogene carefully eases her car into the garage and they watch as the garage door closes behind her, until the last bit of light disappears.

"Well, good night, Bettie," Isabel says. She leans forward and gives Bettie a hug. Bettie feels small and fragile in her arms.

"Thank you for being so good to me, Isabel," Bettie says. She's about to turn away when she hesitates. "I think if I ever had a daughter, I'd be lucky if she were like you. Good night." Bettie opens the door and steps inside, closing it quickly behind her.

On the drive home, Isabel keeps touching her cheek and smiling. When she turns the corner for her street, she sees a familiar truck parked to the side, her porch light on.

Isabel parks in the driveway, then walks up to the porch. Ian Braemer is there, two steaming cups of coffee in hand, waiting for her on a brand-new porch swing.

"Surprise," he says, and holds out one of the cups of coffee. "Care to join me? It's decaf."

"You did this while I was at my meeting?" Isabel asks, even though the answer is obvious. She takes the cup of coffee and it instantly warms her hands.

"I did. I ran to the coffee shop and got us two tall decafs."

She gives him a playful punch in the arm. "I meant the porch swing, Ian."

"Oh, this," he says, as if noticing it for the first time. He grins. "I hope it's all right. I was going to ask you but I didn't want to spoil it. I figured I could always take it back down if you hated it. This space always seemed as if it was waiting for a porch swing."

"Yes," Isabel says. "It was." She sits next to him and he gives the swing a little push with his feet. "And don't you dare take it down, I love it. Thank you, Ian."

"You're welcome. Oh, and if you don't like the color, we can always paint it something else."

The swing is white, of course. Isabel laughs. "It's fine," she says. "Though I think I'm over my white phase once and for all. I've been colorless long enough." She runs her hand along the chain of the porch swing. "Maybe we'll paint it yellow in the spring."

"Whatever the lady wants," Ian says. They swing for a moment in silence, watching the stars.

The sky is full of them tonight, twinkling and winking at them from afar. "Though I hope you don't mind me correcting you on one little point."

Isabel takes a sip of her coffee, holds it against her cold cheek. "What's that?"

"Black is the absence of color," he says. "But white is the blending of all colors. It's like sunlight. Sunlight is white light that's made up of all the colors in the spectrum. So while you may have thought you didn't have any color in your life, in truth it was filled with every color of the rainbow."

Isabel thinks about this, then looks at him. "You're kind of a know-it-all, aren't you?"

"Only when I know it all," he says. "Which isn't often. It's just that color is one of those things you know about when you do what I do for a living. Besides, something tells me I may have met my match."

Isabel tilts her head, gazes at Ian Braemer. He's handsome in a simple, rugged way, and she likes that he knows who he is. "I don't know how to thank you for everything you've done for me, for the house."

He smiles. "It was my pleasure, Isabel."

"And you know you never sent me an invoice," she says. "We should probably settle that before you move on to the next job."

Ian plants both feet on the ground, stopping the swing. "Isabel," he says, and his voice is full of amusement. "You don't owe me anything. I told you, it was my pleasure."

Isabel had figured as much, but she didn't want Ian to think she was taking advantage. "Can I cover the cost of materials at least?"

He shakes his head. "I'm glad I could help a friend."

A friend? When he says this, Isabel feels her temperature drop. "Oh," she says, standing up. "Well, thanks. *Friend.*" She rubs her nose, like she's about to sneeze.

He watches her. "Uh-oh, you're mad at me."

"What? No, I'm not," she lies. "It's getting late, I should probably go inside." She stands up but Ian reaches for her hand.

"Isabel, stay out here a little longer," he says. He pulls her gently back toward the swing, but she resists.

Her feelings are hurt. Does he see her only as a friend? "Why?"

Ian stands up, still holding her hand. "So I can kiss you." He pulls her toward him and gives her a tender kiss on the lips.

Ohhh. Isabel feels her body tingle at the touch of his lips, smiles at her own foolishness. They kiss again. "I think I could get used to this friend-ship," she says when they finally break away.

"Or," Ian says. "We could try for something a little more. A proper date, maybe?"

Isabel nods, breathless.

"Still want to go back inside?"

She shakes her head.

They sit on the swing, hand in hand, and drink their coffee while they look out onto Isabel's sleepy street, at the families moving about in their homes, the occasional car hurrying to reach its destination. They sit like this together, quiet and comfortable, but above all, happy.

Epilogue

The table is set, the napkins folded and tucked into silver napkin rings, acorns and leaves serving as place cards. The tables of the tea salon have been lined up to create a long, generous space for everyone to sit together with room for last-minute guests to pull up a chair. Heirloom pumpkins provide a simple centerpiece as do sprays of spider mums and dried craspedia in crisp yellows and oranges. Loaves of fresh bread are stacked in baskets, the cranberry sauce already on the table. The turkey is in the oven. Bettie's ham is honeyed and glazed and resting on the cutting board.

It's a guest list that couldn't have existed a year ago because many of the names are new, at least to each other. There's Madeline and Connie, of course, with Connie's guest, Eli. Hannah has brought Jamie. Isabel, Ava, Max, and Bettie; Ian and his son arrived in their own car. Yvonne and Sam will have to leave before dessert to spend the rest of the evening with Sam's mother and sisters in Maine. Madeline's stepson, Ben, will be coming up from Ohio with his wife and daughter. The Lassiters are here, seated next to the Dohertys.

The tea salon is officially closed but that doesn't discourage people from stopping in.

Throughout the day people come and go, friends and neighbors wanting a cup of tea or to drop off a plate of cookies. The items on the dessert buffet seem to grow exponentially. Guests linger in the sitting rooms, the hallways, the kitchen. Max helps toss a platter of roasted vegetables with a pomegranate vinaigrette, Madeline's own recipe. Rayna Doherty has brought an apple tart. Ian's son, Jeremy, is mashing the potatoes.

No one takes notice when the brass bell above the door tinkles, heralding another guest. Hannah is the first to see her beneath the bundle of coats and scarves, mittens and woolen hats.

"You're back!" she cries, rushing forward. There's a hush as everyone turns toward the latest visitor who turns out to be not one, but two people.

Frances Latham and her daughter, Mei Ling. Both of their noses are red from the cold, their eyes bright and shining. Mei Ling, twenty months old, doesn't pull back but instead looks around, cautious yet curious.

"We got back yesterday," Frances says as she begins to unravel them. "Reed and the boys are right behind me, parking the car. Thank you so much for having us, Madeline. We're tired, but not as tired as if we'd had to figure out Thanksgiving dinner on our own. I hope it's all right that we're showing up like this."

"Of course it's all right," Madeline assures her.

"It's easy enough to find extra chairs, and we have plenty of food. And you're welcome just to put your feet up and rest, too. If it gets to be too much, we can pack up your food to go."

"Oh no," Frances says with a shake of her head. "We've all been looking forward to this. The trip was so exhausting and emotional, we passed out once we boarded the plane to come home. But now we're wanting to be with friends. This is a special homecoming for us—we have so much to be grateful for." She brushes the top of Mei Ling's head, her hair thick and dark, then gives it a kiss. Mei Ling squirms, then looks up at Frances before resting her face against Frances's chest.

There's a murmur and someone gives a sniffle. Isabel offers Bettie a tissue but Bettie bats it away.

"I'm not crying," Bettie informs her curtly, blinking as though something is in her eye. "I'm not." Her eyes look suspiciously damp, there are a few wet eyes in the room. Isabel smiles and puts an arm around Bettie's shoulders.

Reed, Nick, Noah, and Brady appear behind Frances. There's a heartfelt round of congratulations and hugs, introductions. They move to the sitting room where Frances gets down on the floor with her daughter. Mei Ling is unmoving, watchful, her small hand clinging to the hem of Frances's sweater.

"She knows you," Hannah says with a smile.

Frances smiles back. "Yes," she says. "I don't know if she knows what's going on or that we're her family now, but she knows who I am. She knows who all of us are." She gestures to Reed and the boys.

"She likes me best," Noah says.

"She likes all of us," Nick says, giving his younger brother a playful shove.

"Yes, but she likes me best," Noah insists.

"Me too!" Brady chimes in. Everyone laughs.

"It was those scrapbooks," Reed tells everyone. "Frances kept sending them over and the foster family would show them to Mei Ling."

"I think the foster family enjoyed looking at the scrapbooks as much as I enjoyed making them," Frances tells them. "So they showed them to her all the time. We were lucky with that. She recognized us when we arrived—she couldn't place us right away, but we weren't total strangers to her."

There's the sound of the kitchen timer going off. "Time to take the turkey out," Madeline says. "And I believe we'll be ready to eat soon. Reed, may I impose upon you to slice the turkey for us?"

Reed smiles. "I'd be honored."

"Oh, I wish I'd brought my camera," Frances says. "I think I left it on the dresser at home with our passports and everything else."

"I have my camera," Walter Lassiter says. "I'll make sure to get some nice pictures for you."

"He takes wonderful photographs," Connie says, patting his arm before following Madeline into the kitchen.

Walter turns scarlet, but there's a pleased look on his face.

Mei Ling tugs on Frances's sweater and Frances immediately seems to know what this means. She digs through her purse and produces a small baggie of Cheerios and opens it. Mei Ling dips her hand inside and grabs a handful.

"I know she's still grieving," Frances says in a lower voice. "But she's a spirited child, generally happy and very curious. And she's a regular little chatterbox, mostly to herself and of course in Chinese, but that's okay. We're not in any sort of rush and I know we'll get there, won't we, sweetheart?" She picks up a wayward Cheerio and places it in the center of her palm. Mei Ling reaches for it, a small smile breaking across her face.

"She likes the dollhouse Mom got her," Nick reports. "She almost threw a fit when we had to come over; she didn't want to stop playing."

"I'm going to get her a portable one," Reed says. "So she can take it with her wherever we go. I've seen some that have handles on the roof so they're easy to carry."

Frances beams, touches her husband's arm. "I'd

tease you about this if I wasn't so totally in love with you at this moment."

"I thought it would help for the long car rides to the medical center," Reed says. "And for those long doctor appointments we have coming up. She'll always be able to have it with her all the time. Like us."

"Crap, now I'm going to cry," Bettie says, fanning her eyes. "What did you do with those tissues, Isabel?"

"I used them," Isabel says, showing her the damp wad in her palm. Her own eyes are shining, but she's smiling.

"I've got some right here," Ava says, sniffling, handing some to Bettie. She beckons for Max to join her and pulls her son in close, kisses him. Yvonne and Sam are sitting on the couch, content, Sam's arms wrapped around her. Yvonne leans back and sighs, happy.

They all watch as Mei Ling finishes the Cheerios and then brings her fingers to her lips.

"She's thirsty," Noah says. Frances smiles and nods.

"Dinner!" Madeline calls.

Smiles are exchanged as people help one another up, the men clapping each other on the back, the women leaning into one another, grateful for this day, this time, these people. It's not quite the end of the year but it's a new beginning for all of them. On this day their hearts are filled with gratitude, each detail leaving a gentle imprint in their minds, their hearts. It's a day of sharing and togetherness, of family and friends, of memories being made and not easily forgotten.

A Taste of Avalon
Scrapbooking Recipes and Tips

In Avalon, Illinois, food is what brings family and friends together. It's how neighbors show their appreciation and support for each other, how one community comforts another in times of difficulty or loss. In particular, Amish Friendship Bread has made its way into the homes of many an Avalonian, which means that new recipes and variations based on this simple sugar-cinnamon bread are always being featured at church or school potlucks, left on doorsteps, or—of course—brought to meetings of the Avalon Ladies Scrapbooking Society. Because these recipes are at the heart of this small town, some favorites are included here, along with ideas for hosting a scrapbooking crop of your own.

The Amish Friendship Bread recipes use one cup of Amish Friendship Bread starter. Detailed instructions about the starter, FAQs, and over two hundred fifty Amish Friendship Bread recipes can be found at www.friendshipbreadkitchen.com, home of the first Avalon novel, *Friendship Bread.*

Amish Friendship Bread Starter

Amish Friendship Bread starter is passed from one friend or neighbor to another, usually in a gallon-sized Ziploc bag or ceramic container. It's an actual sourdough starter, meaning that if you continue to feed it over time, it will become more flavorful and distinct. You can use the starter for loaves, muffins, brownies, even pancakes. If you haven't received a bag of Amish Friendship Bread starter but would like to experiment, here is the recipe for creating a starter. It will take ten days before you are able to bake with it.

Ingredients
  1 package (¼ ounce) active dry yeast
  ¼ cup warm water (110° F)
  1 cup all-purpose flour
  1 cup white sugar
  1 cup room temperature milk

Directions
  1. In a small bowl, dissolve the yeast in the water. Let stand ten minutes.
  2. In a nonmetal container, combine flour and sugar. Mix thoroughly.
  3. Slowly add in milk and dissolved yeast mixture. Cover loosely and let stand at room temperature until bubbly. This is Day One of

the ten-day cycle. You can leave it in the container or transfer to a Ziploc bag.

4. On Days Two through Five, mash the bag daily (if your starter is in a container, give it a good stir with a wooden spoon). If the bag gets puffy with air, let the air out.

5. On Day Six, add 1 cup flour, 1 cup sugar, 1 cup milk. Mash the bag.

6. On Days Seven through Nine, mash the bag daily.

7. On Day Ten, pour entire contents into a nonmetal bowl.

8. Add 1½ cups flour, 1½ cups sugar, 1½ cups milk. Mix well.

9. Measure out four separate batters into four one-gallon Ziploc bags.

10. Keep one of the bags for yourself and give the other bags to three friends along with the recipe for Amish Friendship Bread (a printable copy can be found at www.friend shipbreadkitchen.com).

Lorna's Hazelnut Cappuccino Amish Friendship Bread Cake

MAKES 1 4-LAYER CAKE

Ingredients
1 cup Amish Friendship Bread Starter
3 eggs
1 cup oil
½ cup milk
1 cup brown sugar
1 teaspoon vanilla
1½ teaspoons baking powder
½ teaspoon salt
½ teaspoon baking soda
2 cups flour
2 small boxes chocolate instant pudding
5 tablespoons International Café Toasted Hazelnut Cappuccino

Topping
Nutella Buttercream Frosting (recipe follows)
½ cup mini chocolate chips
Chocolate syrup
½ cup hazelnuts or pecans, finely chopped

Directions
1. Preheat oven to 325° F (165° C).
2. In a large mixing bowl, add ingredients as listed.

3. Grease two round cake pans and dust with flour.
4. Pour the batter evenly into the cake pans.
5. Bake for 40 to 45 minutes, or until a toothpick inserted in the center comes out clean.
6. When cake is completely cool, carefully slice each cake into two layers with a very sharp knife.
7. Frost each layer with the Nutella Buttercream Frosting. On top of each layer, before adding on the next cake layer, lightly sprinkle 2 teaspoons each of mini chocolate chips, chocolate syrup, and nuts. You can prepare this cake one day in advance.
8. ENJOY!

Nutella Buttercream Frosting

Ingredients
¼ cup butter plus 1 tablespoon, room temperature
½ cup Nutella hazelnut spread
1 teaspoon vanilla
3 cups powdered sugar
¼ cup milk
1 teaspoon International Café Toasted Hazelnut Cappuccino Mix

Directions
1. In a large bowl, mix butter and Nutella with electric mixer. Add in vanilla.
2. Gradually add the powdered sugar, one cup at a time, beating on medium speed.
3. Scrape sides and bottom of bowl often.
4. Add milk and beat at medium speed until light and fluffy.
5. Right before using the frosting, stir in, by hand, the International Café Toasted Hazelnut Cappuccino Mix.
6. This will yield enough frosting to frost each layer of the Hazelnut Cappuccino Amish Friendship Bread Cake. If you'd like to frost the sides, double the recipe.

Charlotte Snyder's Amish Friendship Bread Coconut-Walnut Biscotti

MAKES 24

Ingredients
1 cup Amish Friendship Bread Starter
⅔ cup granulated sugar
½ cup butter, softened
1 teaspoon vanilla
1 egg
3 cups flour
1 teaspoon baking powder
½ teaspoon salt
½ cup flaked coconut
1 cup walnuts, chopped
Dipping Chocolate (recipe follows)

Directions
1. Preheat oven to 350° F (175° C).
2. In medium bowl, cream together starter, sugar, and butter. Stir in vanilla and egg.
3. In another bowl combine flour, baking powder, and salt. Stir into creamed mixture. Fold in coconut and walnuts.
4. Divide dough into 2 pieces. Roll each piece out into a log about 10 inches long. Place them on ungreased cookie sheet and flatten until they are about 3 inches wide.

5. Bake for 30 to 35 minutes, until firm. Cool on baking sheet for 10 to 15 minutes.
6. Slice logs crosswise into ½-inch-wide slices. Place slices cut side down on baking sheet.
7. Return to oven for an additional 15 minutes, until crisp and light brown. Cool and store in airtight container.
8. ENJOY!

Dipping Chocolate

Ingredients
1 cup (6 ounces) chopped semisweet or bittersweet chocolate or chocolate chips
½ cup (4 ounces) heavy cream

Directions
1. In a double boiler, melt the chocolate in the cream, stirring occasionally until smooth.
2. If you prefer to use a microwave, combine the chocolate chips and cream in a large microwave-safe bowl. Microwave on medium power, stirring after every minute, until the chocolate is melted.
3. Dip cooled biscotti into chocolate and let cool.

Lemon Rosemary Olive Oil Amish Friendship Bread

MAKES 2 LOAVES

Ingredients
    1 cup Amish Friendship Bread Starter
    3 eggs
    1 cup extra virgin olive oil
    ½ cup milk
    1 cup sugar
    ¼ teaspoon lemon extract
    ½ teaspoon vanilla extract
    ¼ cup fresh lemon juice
    2 teaspoons grated lemon rind
    1½ teaspoons baking powder
    ½ teaspoon salt
    ½ teaspoon baking soda
    2 cups flour
    2 tablespoons chopped fresh rosemary
    1 small box lemon instant pudding
    1 tablespoon flax meal (optional)
    Easy Lemon Glaze (recipe follows)
    Sprig of rosemary (optional)
    Lemon rind (optional)

Directions
    1. Preheat oven to 325°F (165°C).
    2. In a large mixing bowl, add ingredients as listed, and mix until smooth.

3. Grease two large loaf pans.
4. Dust the greased pans with flour, coating the pans evenly on all sides.
5. Divide the batter evenly into loaf pans.
6. Bake for one hour or until the bread loosens evenly from the sides and a toothpick inserted in the center of the bread comes out clean. Remove from oven and let cool on a wire rack.
7. Drizzle with the Easy Lemon Glaze (recipe follows) and garnish with a sprig of rosemary or lemon rind.
8. ENJOY!

Easy Lemon Glaze

Ingredients
Juice of 1 lemon
2 cups confectioner's sugar
Dash of lemon extract

Directions
1. Mix lemon juice and powdered sugar and stir until desired consistency is reached.
2. Add dash of lemon extract and mix in thoroughly.
3. Drizzle glaze over cake before serving.

Wally Miller's
Spanish Pork Chops

MAKES 4

Ingredients
   4 pork chops
   2 tablespoons flour, or as needed
   Salt and black pepper to taste
   2 tablespoons vegetable oil (to coat the bottom of the skillet)
   1 onion, sliced
   1 red bell pepper, seeded and sliced in rings
   4 tablespoons uncooked rice
   1 16-ounce can chopped tomatoes with juice
   1 tablespoon Worcestershire sauce

Directions
   1. Preheat oven to 400°F (200°C).
   2. Dust the pork chops with a mixture of flour, salt, and pepper.
   3. Add the vegetable oil to a skillet, and brown pork chops on medium-high heat.
   4. Place pork chops in a casserole dish.
   5. Place a slice of onion, a ring of red bell pepper, and a tablespoon of uncooked rice inside the red pepper ring on the pork chops.
   6. Pour the can of tomatoes evenly over the pork chops.

7. Add the Worcestershire sauce, salt, and pepper.
8. Bake for about 45 minutes. Serve with a salad and hot rolls.

Connie's Mountain Dew Apple Dumplings

MAKES 16

Ingredients
- 2 large Granny Smith apples, peeled and cored
- 2 8-ounce cans of crescent roll dough
- 2 sticks butter
- 1½ cups sugar
- ½ teaspoon vanilla
- 1 teaspoon cinnamon plus cinnamon to taste
- 1 12-ounce can Mountain Dew soda

Directions
1. Preheat the oven to 350° F (175° C).
2. Butter a 9 × 13-inch baking dish.
3. Cut each apple into 8 slices. Roll each apple slice in a crescent roll. Pinch to seal and place in baking dish.
4. In a small saucepan over medium heat, melt the butter, then add the sugar, vanilla, and cinnamon.
5. Pour the mixture and then the Mountain Dew over the apple dumplings. Sprinkle with cinnamon and bake until golden brown, about 30–45 minutes.

Bill's Spaghetti Alla Chitarra

SERVES 4

Ingredients
  2 ounces extra virgin olive oil
  2 cloves garlic, finely minced
  1 shallot, finely minced
  ¼ teaspoon pepperoncini
  2 cups plum tomatoes (San Marzano if possible), seeded and crushed
  4 ounces fresh spaghetti
  2 tablespoons Parmigiano-Reggiano cheese, freshly grated
  Salt and pepper to taste
  2 tablespoons fresh basil leaves, torn into small pieces

Directions
  1. Heat and salt a large pot of water. Bring to a boil.
  2. Add 1 ounce of the olive oil to a medium-sized pan, and sauté the garlic, shallot, and pepperoncini. Add tomatoes and sauté on high heat for about 2 minutes.
  3. Drop fresh pasta into water and cook for about 30 seconds. Add to mixture in sauté pan.
  4. Add 2 ounces of pasta water to sauté pan and turn the heat down to low.

5. Toss the pasta until cooked to desired doneness. Add additional pasta water as necessary.
6. Remove from heat. Toss with cheese, extra virgin olive oil, salt and pepper. Garnish with basil leaves and serve immediately.

Frances's Scallion Pancakes
(Cōng Yóubǐng)
MAKES 8

Ingredients
   2 cups all-purpose flour, with extra for
      dusting and as needed
   1½ cups boiling water
   5 tablespoons sesame oil
   ½ teaspoon salt
   ¼ teaspoon white or black pepper
   ½ cup chopped scallions, white and green
      parts
   1 cup vegetable oil, as needed

Directions
   1. In a large mixing bowl, combine the flour
      and boiling water, stirring with a wooden
      spoon until a soft dough ball is formed.
   2. Once the dough is cool enough to handle,
      continue to knead with your hands. Divide
      the dough into 8 portions. Leave in bowl and
      set aside.
   3. In a small bowl, mix the sesame oil, salt, and
      pepper.
   4. On a floured surface, roll one portion of the
      dough until thin.
   5. Drizzle a layer of the sesame oil mixture over

the dough, using your hand or pastry brush to coat the surface evenly.

6. Sprinkle scallions over the dough.
7. Starting from one edge, roll up the dough (scallions included) to form a log.
8. Coil the log into a circle.
9. Use the palm of your hand to press the circle flat. Use a rolling pin to roll into a pancake, about ¼ inch thick. Continue to make pancakes until all the dough has been used.
10. Heat the vegetable oil in a skillet over medium heat.
11. Place one pancake in the skillet pan, cooking until the edges and center are a crisp golden brown. Flip pancake and brown other side. Drain on paper towels.

Basic Scrapbooking Tips

Scrapbooking is a fun way to preserve memories from a particular event or moment in time. It can be as simple or elaborate as you want.

You can also scrapbook as a gift—the material objects of our life come and go, but what's often the most precious in people's possessions are the pictures and memories of their life. Add some journaling and other ephemera (ticket stubs, programs, restaurant napkins) to give your pages personality and depth. And, most important, have fun with it!

How to start:

~ Choose the photos you'd like to scrap. Cluster them by theme, people, or place in chrono-logical order. You can also choose an event or special occasion (holiday, birthday, trip or vacation, new baby, etc.). Place them in a Ziploc bag or paper envelope until ready to use, labeled with the theme of the album.
~ Choose your album size. You can buy pre-made albums or create your own.
~ Choose your papers and embellishments. Craft stores carry a wide selection of materials, the only limitation being your creativity (and possibly your budget!).

~ Begin laying out your page, which means putting everything down on the page. Don't glue anything yet. Have fun, move things around, experiment with different looks. If you're not sure where to begin or what looks good, flip through some magazines to get layout ideas. Think about adding a title to your page that captures the theme and photographs.

~ Journal each photo or page. Write down details, memories, key words. Think of it as a caption or diary entry. Don't forget to include dates. You can write directly on the page or use pre-made journal cards. You can also type it up on your computer and then trim to fit the page.

~ When you're ready and everything is positioned as you'd like, glue everything to the page.

~ Insert finished pages into page protector sleeves or into your album directly. You can also scan the page and create a digital image so you can share your album virtually with friends and family.

How to Host a Book Club Meeting and Crop

Why host a book club meeting when you can host a book club meeting and crop, Bettie Shelton–style? Make the most of your book club discussion by stepping into an Avalon Ladies Scrapbooking Society meeting. Here are some suggestions:

~ Choose and agree upon a theme. Some ideas are family, friendship, holidays, birthdays, trips, school, sports, pets. Why not scrapbook about your book club meetings and members?

~ Tell members to bring 4–6 photos that fit with the theme, sharp scissors, glue, and any other ephemera they'd like to include.

~ Provide 12 x 12 scrapbooking paper (solids and patterns), fun embellishments (brads, eyelets, buttons, ribbon, stickers, alpha letters, chipboard shapes, rub-on transfers), extra glue and scissors. A paper cutter, paper punches, rubber stamps (and ink pads) are also great to have on hand.

~ Provide and/or have people bring Amish Friendship Bread cakes, cookies, or muffins. Over 250 Amish Friendship Bread recipes are available on the website. Or try any of the recipes in the book, such as Connie's Mountain Dew Apple Dumplings or Frances's Chinese scallion pancakes.

~ Download discussion guide questions from the website.

~ Share your layout or a photo of your book club with Darien by posting it on the book's page at Amazon.com or on the Friendship Bread Kitchen Facebook wall.

For More Information

The Alzheimer's Association focuses on dementia and Alzheimer care and support. To find a chapter near you or to learn more about dementia, visit www.alz.org.

There are so many wonderful organizations that support domestic and international adoption, as well as fostering adoptions of special needs children. There are also many parent-advocate groups on Yahoo that try to get the story out about children in need. Because they are too numerous to list here, I am sharing a resource for those of you who are interested in learning more about China adoption. **Half the Sky** is an organization dedicated to ensuring that Chinese orphans have nutrition, love, and support, regardless of whether or not they find their forever family. Learn more about what they do at www.halfthesky.org.

For more than 250 Amish Friendship Bread recipes or to join our online friendship bread community, visit us at the **Friendship Bread Kitchen** (www.friendshipbreadkitchen.com), or find us on Facebook (www.facebook.com /fbkitchen) or Twitter (www.twitter.com/fb kitchen).

About the Author

DARIEN GEE lives in Hawaii with her husband and their three children. She is also the author of *Friendship Bread*.

Center Point Large Print
600 Brooks Road / PO Box 1
Thorndike ME 04986-0001 USA

(207) 568-3717

US & Canada:
1 800 929-9108
www.centerpointlargeprint.com